AR

OMNIBUS ONE

BOOK ONE
FORTRESS BRITAIN

BOOK TWO
MOGADISHU OF THE DEAD

BOOK THREE
THREE PARTS DEAD

GLYNN JAMES

MICHAEL STEPHEN FUCHS

First published 2014 by Glynn James & Michael Stephen Fuchs - London, UK

This is a work of fiction. Names, characters, places, and incidents either are the product of the authors' imaginations or are used fictitiously. Any resemblance to actual persons, living or dead, events, or locales is entirely coincidental.

ISBN-13: 978-1500239930

ISBN-10: 1500239933

Readers are calling the ARISEN series:

"a non stop thrill ride" ... "unputdownable" ... "the most original and well-written zombie novels I have ever read" ... "riveting as hell - I cannot recommend this series enough" ... "Knock Down Drag Out FANTASTIC!!!!!!" ... "Wow. Just wow." ... "the action starts hot and heavy and does NOT let up" ... "astonishingly well-researched and highly plausible" ... "non-stop speed rush! All action, all the time" ... "left me with my mouth hanging open" ... "May be the best in its genre."

A world fallen - under a plague of seven billion walking dead

A tiny island nation - the last refuge of the living

One team - of the world's most elite special operators

The dead, these heroes, humanity's last hope, all have..

ARISEN

NOTES FROM THE AUTHORS

GLYNN

When I had the original idea for the ARISEN series (a name Michael came up with), I was planning on writing something involving much less combat and military, and not special forces, but then it occurred to me that all of the zombie fiction that I'd read lacked something – really fast-paced fight scenes. So the idea developed, and I was getting more and more enthusiastic about it, but I also became convinced that I would need expert help. This was too big for me. Fortunately I had a good friend and an excellent writer to turn to.

It was a huge and crazy experiment. Neither of us had tried co-writing before and the two genres we write in are very far apart in terms of style, so it was unexpected when we found ourselves half-way through the second book and unable to stop. I'm so glad we tried it and I want to thank Michael for both taking the leap and for making a good idea become an awesome reality. One that I couldn't have achieved alone. We had no idea that this was going to turn into something we were both very proud of and I certainly am.

NOTES FROM THE AUTHORS

MICHAEL

First and foremostly, thanks to my writing partner Glynn for suggesting this project, for coming up with such a great concept, for making it happen, and for being so fabulous to work with. Very, very many thanks also to Mark George Pitely, Alex Heublein, SNaFu, Michael & Jayne Barnard, and Jacqui Lewis – Lady Editrice(.co.uk) non pareil.

To those readers of this book who may have very kindly read one or more of my D-Boys books (D-BOYS, COUNTER-ASSAULT, and whatever I'm calling the third one ;^), you might have noticed in ARISEN a very slightly more cavalier attitude toward details of tactics, tech, weapons, and other SOF minutiae. Basically, I figured since we were writing a series of Zombie Apocalypse novels, I could probably rely on a bit more suspension of disbelief as well as push things further. But you may trust that the high standards of military realism to which you have been accustomed in the D-BOYS books will be right where we left them. Thanks so much for reading (both series).

“Only the dead have seen the end of war.”
– George Santayana

“And he doeth great wonders, so that he maketh fire come down from Heaven on the Earth in the sight of men.”
– Revelation 13:13

BOOK ONE

FORTRESS BRITAIN

NO EXITS

Its face appeared through the mist, the mouth torn and the left side of its skull shattered. Ragged and bloodstained shreds of clothing, hanging from the gaunt frame, grew visible as it advanced. Congealed black fluid leaked out of sores that burned red with infection, and its bones cracked in defiance with every movement as it staggered into sight.

And there was no hiding from it. Poor visibility meant nothing to the wretched creature that now lumbered forward, slowly closing the gap between them. Handon raised his rifle and sighted in, quietly waiting and hoping that he wouldn't have to take the shot. The noise of gunfire was all that was needed to bring the whole neighborhood down on them.

"Contact, my twelve," he whispered into the chin mic curling around from his lightweight tactical helmet. Even as he spoke he could see more dark shadows stirring behind the first. There was no mistaking their direction – straight toward his team – but they were yet to latch on, to spot them *en masse*, and the wave of moaning had yet to begin. But Handon knew that it would soon. And then every poor dead bastard within a mile would be shambling mindlessly in their direction. And that was if they were lucky, and it was only shamblers out there, and not the fast ones. *Come on*, he thought. Just a little more time was all they needed.

It didn't matter how many of these creatures

Handon had seen, each one still made his heart lurch. And every time he fired and one of them fell, he wondered who that person had once been. Unlike the men and women on his team, he had not developed the ability to switch off, to put the dead and the living in firewalled mental boxes. He had yet to accept that the creatures had no souls. Medical science was divided on how much was actually going on in there, whether there was even anyone home. It was known that the creatures lived for just one purpose – to devour the living – but little else was understood as to what drove them, what motivated something that should be rotting away quietly under six feet of soil to haul its ass up from the ground and seek out the nearest anything with a pulse.

He had questioned every theory he'd heard in the last two years, but Command Sergeant Major Handon's doubts on the subject didn't really matter, and he sure as hell didn't voice them openly. It was best if his guys had only need-to-know access to what was going on in his head. He could shelve his own doubts, put them to the back of his mind, for now. But for those who depended on him, well, his resolve had to be unquestionable.

"*Unfriendlies, nine o'clock,*" came the call on the team's radio. "*Multiple Zulus.*" This time it was Predator, their enormous and seemingly unkillable assaulter and combat medic – everyone did double duty these days – who would now be standing fifty meters to Handon's right, holding the north side of their landing zone at the edge of the target structure. Handon didn't need to glance in that direction to know this, and even if he had he wouldn't be able to see the man, or most of his team for that matter. The mist that had descended in the last hour was so thick you could almost drink it.

"*Yeah, ditto on our three.*" This was Pope, a seasoned paramilitary with what used to be the Central Intelligence Agency's Special Activities Division. That was in what used to be the United States. African American, soft-spoken, keen on knives, he was also rumored to have killed more people than smallpox, back in America's counter-terror wars. That was before virtually everyone was dead already.

And now the dead were surrounding them. Again.

On the other hand, they were always surrounded, even at the best of times, holed up as they were in Fortress Britain. But right now, the four of them, Handon's detached half of Alpha team – and for all he knew a significant fraction of the Tier-One special operators still left alive anywhere in the world – simply needed to hold this one building entrance. The large plain lettering on the front of the warehouse-like structure read "Merck KGaA." The top of the letter M had fallen off and the final A was cracked and barely legible. Handon wondered how in just two years everything could go so quickly and completely to shit.

His team was raiding the research labs of what used to be Germany's largest pharmaceutical company – from back when there were things like companies, and Germany. This also meant they were *way* too deep into fallen Europe for anybody's safety or comfort – so deep that one screw-up could mean disaster for the whole team. But there was nothing for it. It was, if anything, an understatement to say that any hope of survival humanity still had hinged on operations like this one, even if the remaining population would never know about it. Most of the time it was best that way.

Handon blinked, but maintained target lock as he heard Pope switch smoothly to the command net. "*Hotel X, this is Alpha-Two, requesting ETA on extraction. We're pretty much ready to hit the road here.*" Speaking of understatement, the first thing about Tier-One operators is that they are not prone to panic. Even when panic was fully justified – especially then. Unconsciously, Handon cocked his head into his earpiece, willing the channel to perk up. But it stayed silent as the grave. Maybe they were in a radio skip zone, in addition to being neck deep in zombie soup. A dead zone.

Fifteen seconds passed, several lifetimes in a combat situation. All around the team, the mist shifted with movement. And with that, and no other preamble, the lead creature, the one with only half a head, was upon him. Handon placed the red target reticule of his EOTech holographic sight on the zombie's chin point. Directly behind that would be the brainstem. He applied a quarter-pound of pressure to the trigger, then hesitated. The creature, almost instantly driven to frenzy by the scent of living flesh, wheezed out a guttural roar, accelerated to its top speed of about 7mph, and lunged forwards.

Handon let his rifle – a heavily customized HK416, one of the last in the universe and thus nearly priceless – swing down on its single-point tactical sling, and switched in a blur to his secondary weapon. In this new, fallen, deeply strange world, that was no longer his .45 autoloading handgun. It was a wakizashi, a samurai short sword, worn in side-draw configuration above his duty belt in the small of his back.

In the same motion as the draw he whirled the razor-sharp blade around in a tight arc – the curved blade was designed precisely for drawing and striking at once – and separated what was left of the creature's head from what was left of its body. The fragile, torn abomination lost its animation and fell forward at Handon's assault boots, its knees cracking as the weak bones splintered with the impact of the hard pavement. The body fell sideways, hitting the pavement with a rich, wet sound. Decapitation wouldn't actually kill the head – only destruction of the brainstem could do that – but it would stop it getting to him. It would be a few weeks or so before the head dried up and whatever constituted the zombie inside it finally died. Until then it would lie in the same spot, gnashing its jaw at the open air.

And then he heard it, just a split second before it came thrumming into view – the indistinct electric whir of suppressed rotor blades cutting through the muffling mists. It was the unit's Stealth Black Hawk, inbound on short final. You didn't hear these things until they were practically on top of you. And, especially in poor visibility, you couldn't locate the origin of the sound with any accuracy. All of which was intentional. Sound drew zombies. Any sound. In a world shut down by the dead, almost anything audible was the sound of a survivor.

Handon's thoughts of their dead world suddenly became less abstract, as the Stealth Hawk flared, nearly instantly blowing away the mist for a hundred meters in every direction. And in every direction, Handon could now see the soulless... hundreds upon hundreds of them, back up to the tree line, oozing forward like a mass of maggots, searching for healthy flesh. He had no idea where this many had come from that damned quickly. Aerial recon hadn't given any indication of this kind of density. Blame the thick mist. Plus, in the Zulu Alpha, sometimes you just got swarmed out of a blue sky. *Pretty damned often, actually*, Handon thought with resignation. Surveying the incoming horde, he saw there were too many for his sword, and many more than he had rounds for his rifle or pistols. The team's priority now had to be to exfil, RFN – "right fucking now."

The helo rocked on its four wheels as it touched down dead center in the diamond described by the three operators and the building entrance. As Handon got a boot on the lip of the open side door and heaved his heavily loaded frame inside, he heard the first suppressed shots being fired by Pope and Predator. If they were shooting, things weren't good. The ammo situation had gone from tight to catastrophic in the last few months. But the helo had landed facing south, which meant Handon could still cover his sector, the east, from inside the cabin. The other two would have to hold their positions, until their entry team, and their haul from the target site, got out and got onboard.

Handon spared a look over his shoulder and saw their PO ("Procurement Officer," a fancy term for a scavenger with heavy IT skills and biotech experience) and his security escort emerge from the front door in a hurry. The "escort" was the fourth member of their detachment, Juice – a large, puffy, heavily bearded man in a ballcap, and former operator with what was sometimes called The Intelligence Support Activity. (AKA the Field Operations Group, Gray Fox, Sentra Spike, and a host of other opaque names – but usually just referred to as "The Activity.") Juice now served as the team's comms operator and all-round tech badass. Also a completely lethal commando, he was the perfect choice to keep the PO alive. And as an IT genius, he was also uniquely suited to help him do his job.

Which it looked like he had done – the fifth man, more lightly armed and armored, had a full rucksack, sagging with weight, slung over one shoulder. He held one hand in front of his face against the swirling dust and rotor wash. The pair emerged from the entryway and pivoted left and right, the PO with a handgun, Juice with his SIG SG 553 assault rifle at his shoulder. Handon could see their mouths going wide in response to the Zulu Dusk that had risen up on all sides of them. The mouth shapes for "*FUCK me*" were familiar enough at this point.

Ordinarily they'd be doing this extraction up on a nice safe rooftop. Zulus – what the military had designated the regular, slow moving zombies that were the early stage victims of the disease – climbed poorly when they climbed at all, and rooftops were the preferred ways in and out of buildings. However, drone footage had indicated this building had likely taken fire and looting damage in the weeks after the fall. A couple of winters of heavy snow on the rooftop, with no maintenance, hadn't helped the world's structures any either. It was too unstable to be trusted. This intel flashed through Handon's memory as he now watched the front of the building collapse – disastrously, and without warning.

It was either the heavy rotor wash, or the press of dead bodies surging around the corners, that kicked it off. Maybe a bit of both. Either way, it happened in one second of shuddering crash, a whole lot of dust, and the shouts of the men in the doorway. By sheer luck it didn't extend to the helo, which was parked nuts-to-butts with the building for security. Juice was knocked clear, but lay prone and still. The PO was face down on the pavement, the lower half of his body crushed by hundreds of pounds of concrete and rebar.

Handon didn't spare the time to curse fate. Turning to face out to the east again, he spun up the door-mounted GAU-17 minigun and burnt through hundreds of irreplaceable rounds of linked 7.62mm, the weapon whining and buzzing and spilling piles of casings as it spat 4,000 rounds per minute. On any other mission, with any other team, the rounds might actually be worth more than the men. But not on this one. Firing in an arc from extreme left to extreme right, a bit below neck height, Handon watched the first dozen ranks of amassed undead collapse into a rancid meat pile. Many of them were effectively turned off, with nerve connections severed between their bodies and the unholy infections raging in their brainstems. Others simply got too dismembered to locomote. With this precious breathing room, Pope and Pred could hold the flanks for the few seconds Handon needed here.

As he hurled himself back out of the door facing the building, he drew his sword with his right hand and his custom Kimber .45 with his left. By the time he hit the ground, a handful of leakers had already slipped through the perimeter and were rampaging in their rear, going straight for the incapacitated men on the ground. Wheeling and flashing, Handon took off two heads and sent single .45 ACP slugs whumping into three other brainstems. Back in the world, he had been trained always to fire doubletaps. Now they were a luxury.

He came to rest and kneeled at the side of their PO. The man was obviously in unendurable agony. But everyone here already knew that this pain was almost certainly the best thing he had left to look forward to. Just to try it on, Handon threw his weight into the largest piece of rebar pinning the man on the ground. It didn't budge.

"*Falling back by sectors.*" That was Pope, speaking levelly in Handon's earpiece. "*Hate to rush you, man…*" And that was Pred. "*But just about all out of room to back up here. Ten seconds tops.*" Handon looked down into the agonized eyes of the half-crushed man, whose earpiece was tuned to the same squad net. And, anyway, the man could see perfectly well what was happening around them. They were being overrun.

With his ebbing strength, he wiggled out of the ruck and pushed it across the dust and debris. He tried to speak, but couldn't draw enough breath. Handon laid his palm across the man's forehead. Another soul winking out. But at least this one would never rise up. Nor would his last experience be that of becoming a one-man live banquet. Handon used the .45. This man was worth the bullet. He'd only been posted to Handon's team for a few weeks – POs tended to have a short half-life – but he was obviously a brave man.

Straightening up, Handon stuck his sword in the face of a zombie breaking through on his left. Its skull burst in two, spewing the blackened contents of its head backwards in an arcing spray. Before the body had even hit the floor he had scooped up the ruck with his right hand, and with a powerful motion tossed it into the helo. Firing spaced single shots with his left hand, dead bodies falling deader around him, he pulled Juice up and into a fireman's carry, yanked his sword free from the dead face on the ground, then heaved himself forward and into the collapsing pinhole of their escape.

As he lurched into the cabin, throwing the unconscious operator ahead of him, he could see Pred backing in the opposite door, alternately firing and jabbing the barrel of his assault rifle *through* the heads of those that were nearly on top of him. Pope appeared from nowhere, proceeding to do basically the same routine behind him at the other door. Gore was splashing close and thick all around, but they all wore their face shields, as well as bite-proof assault suits. The powerful twin engines of the heavily modified UH-60 Black Hawk whined and surged and the bird rocked off the ground, climbing and accelerating. Pope and Pred hacked off a few clinging arms on the door edge and the fixed landing gear, while Handon stuck his head into the flight deck to confer with the pilots.

In less than a minute, they would be flaring in over their secondary target site – where the other half of Alpha team was heavily engaged on the rooftop.

* * *

Captain Connor Ainsley, formerly of the SAS's ultra-elite Increment unit, burst onto the building's flat roof, with his left hand on his PO's shoulder. They'd got the goods, and they'd gotten out alive. Now – where the bloody hell was their air? The SOF pilots that flew these Black Hawks were American, and Ainsley couldn't shake the feeling they flew just that bit faster to extract other Americans.

Dusk was still an hour away, but an oppressive overcast sky blotted out the low sun, and of course there was all that damned mist, lying low and thick on the ground. Any cursed thing could be out there. He hailed the American sniper chick, emplaced out on the edge of the roof for surveillance and security. But he spotted her before she answered so he just trotted over.

"Sitrep."

"Unchanged," she said, not taking her eye from her scope. "Romeos in ones and twos. Manageable." Romeo was the designation for the other ones – the runners, the ones who moved fast. Her scope sat on an enormous rifle, an Accuracy International Arctic Warfare in .338 Lapua Magnum. It would take the head off anything with a head, out to over 1,000 yards. It was also fitted with an internal suppressor and subsonic ammunition to keep the noise down when necessary – very necessary in bandit country – though that dinged her range.

As Ainsley nodded and turned, she took a shot on a runner, at about 350 yards, as it broke from the tree line. This one, like the others, had been drawn by the noise of the original helo insertion. The Delta sniper, Aaliyah, or Ali, had been keeping them off the building for the last twenty-two minutes. The Romeos were a hell of a lot more dangerous than the bog-standard Zulus – not least because they could open doors. It wasn't through a form of developed coordination that they managed it, just blind, fast fury. Where a slow zombie would bang the door down over time, a fast one would usually open it by accident much quicker.

And with that thought, the other two members of their four-man detachment, Homer and Henno, burst onto the rooftop. Both brandished short swords and handguns, their assault rifles hanging on their slings. This meant they'd been in close contact. They also glistened with gore.

"Henno, talk to me," Ainsley said into his throat mic.

"*No drama, boss,*" he said, backing away from the stairwell entrance, while Homer produced a hammer and nailed three eight-inch spikes diagonally into the door frame, sealing it. Henno trotted up to the captain, flipping up his face mask. "Heaving Romeos down there now, and this building's right Swiss cheese at this point. Danger Girl there can only shoot in so many directions."

As Homer pounded the last nail home, a tumult, including a variety of gurgling roars, erupted from the opposite side of the rooftop. Ainsley belatedly noted a large maintenance structure – and also quickly deduced it must have additional stairwell access – around which Romeos in platoon strength were pouring. The ghouls put their shoulders down and sprinted.

The three operators and the PO hunkered down in all-around defense and started putting out rounds. Ainsley had the presence of mind to think of the girl. Swiveling his head and sparing a look, he saw that she was tightly wired and switched on as usual – flipped on her back, firing her sidearm through her raised knees. Ainsley breathed evenly and made his shots count. Romeos were dangerous, but the team knew their capabilities, and they had enough open space to work with here.

And, thank God, that's when the Stealth Hawk roared in low and fast and from out of nowhere. The men onboard the bird also started putting out rounds, and the rooftop started to clear as a SPIE rope (Special Patrol Insertion/Extraction), with D-rings at three-meter intervals, dropped out the side. The team on the roof executed the drill, covering, withdrawing and clipping in. The captain went last, and the bird began to climb instantly, pulling the men off the ground in sequence.

And that's when it appeared.

From out of fucking nowhere.

Ainsley actually froze – not good. He'd never

seen *anything*, never mind anything dead, move that fast. For a second he thought it was coming right at his face, but it wasn't. With an ungodly shriek and an inhuman leap it launched itself into the air, over Ainsley's head, and straight at Homer in the number four position on the rope. The eyes of the utterly unflappable former Team Six SEAL went wide, and he pulled the only evasive maneuver open to him: he unclipped in a blur and slid down the rope right onto Ainsley's head.

Everyone had trouble following exactly what happened from there, but piecing it together later, they couldn't avoid the conclusion that the ghoul had *grabbed onto the rope* – and then scampered up far enough to maul the PO, who was in the three position. And the attack was the strangest thing of all: instead of going for the man's flesh, either a bite or a ripped-out handful, as they'd all seen happen too many times, it instead raked its splintered nails across the man's face, leaving deep furrows amid a smear of mixed blood and viscera.

It then leapt away, disappearing into the gloom and mists on the ground as the helo buzzed away. Somebody thought they saw it running flat out, away from them, like it was fleeing.

And it did that after a twenty-meter fall that should have broken half of the weakened, rotten and infested bones in its body.

Unseen hands above pulled the stunned and bleeding PO into the cabin. Ainsley simply clung to the rope where he was, twisting gently in the aircraft's slipstream. A voice came over his earpiece, from the air mission net. "*Raptor One-Zero to Alpha Actual. Uh… what the fuck was that, over.*"

Ainsley blinked once, heavily, before remembering that he was being pulled up, and needed to get a leg over and into the cabin.

Whatever the hell it was, he wasn't hallucinating.

The pilot had seen it, too.

This was something new.

EVEN ZULUS LONG FOR HOME

The PO's breathing was shallow and fluttery, but his pulse steady and strong. He wasn't going to die of his wounds. And he wouldn't die from the infection, assuming he'd been infected, for many minutes, or maybe even hours. After hauling him aboard, Homer carried him to the back of the cabin, and Predator did some of his battlefield medicine magic. This was more in basic decency, than any kind of hope. The PO's face was a bloody mess. The poor man had flipped his face shield up when he hit the rope. Homer thought placidly: *it's always the one from the direction you're not looking that gets you.*

He shook his head and tried to reconcile himself to it. *No one can out-think the mind of God.*

He looked out the cabin doors, where the very last light was all singed orange as the sun set on the west. The wind whipping through the airframe was cool and without sin. Homer breathed deeply and let the wind gently take the beading sweat off his face.

Looking back inside, he saw Predator working on Juice, who was coming around now. That was good. Shifting his gaze down again, he removed his glove and placed his palm over the trembling PO's forehead – sure enough, the skin was ratcheting up to stovetop temperature. If there were any hope of him escaping infection, after deep scratches like that, the fever sunk it. Homer shook his head at Pred to let him know. He kept his hand on the man's simmering head and started reciting Psalm 23.

"The Lord is my shepherd; I have everything I need. He lets me rest in green meadows…"

"Hey, Homer, mate." Homer looked up without reacting. It was Henno, the other SAS soldier, and Captain Ainsley's man. "Why don't you ask the bloke if he *wants* last rites before just charging in?" Homer smiled at him, in as much honest kindness as he could manage. No point in explaining that there's no basis in Scripture for last rites, which are a man-made (and Papist) invention. Anyway, the wounded man was too doped up on morphine to consent to anything. And the terrified look in his eyes told Homer he wasn't going to turn down consolation – of any denomination, or none.

"He leads me by peaceful streams. He renews my strength, he guides me along right paths…"

"Let him alone," said Predator to Henno. "If nothing else, the pious shit makes Homer feel better. And when Homer feels better, I feel better." Pred swiveled in his squatting position toward Handon, changing the subject. "Okay, boss, I'll bite. What the fuck *was* that?"

Homer looked up and watched their top sergeant, Handon, maintain his poker face; it hardly ever deserted him. Homer'd always personally thought the sergeant major was a dead ringer for the Punisher. That heavy, lined brow. The wavy black hair. And the shadowed, ice-blue, deeply sad eyes. Weight of the world. The world that was.

"Runner?" Handon said, though even as the word spilled out Handon knew he wasn't convincing anyone that it was merely that. He knew, and more importantly he knew that everyone else there knew, that this was something different. They'd all taken down runners before.

Predator laughed rumblingly. "Yeah, the zombie of Michael fucking Jordan, maybe. With a forty-eight-inch vertical leap."

Handon in turn looked to Captain Ainsley. The British spec-ops officer, and team commander, shook his head, looking just as confused as Handon was. "Never seen the like." His expression changed fractionally as he scanned the cabin. "Say – where's *your* PO?"

Handon shook his head. *No.*

"Both of them. Christ." The last word was almost a curse. "Secure the data?"

Handon patted the big ruck full of pharma research drives.

But Ainsley shook his head again. "Fuck sake, Handon. We can ill afford to lose more tech guys. You've got to be more cautious. What in the hell happened out there?"

"Bad luck." He nodded toward the dying man in the back of the cabin. "How about yours?"

Ainsley held his gaze. (Staring contests in the spec-ops world can be epic. Backing down is really not the done thing.) "You saw it as well as I did." Handon didn't respond to that. But it was a poorly concealed secret that he thought Ainsley, who commanded Alpha team, had been showing unexceptional tactical judgement lately.

And no one needed wonder about Ainsley's feelings for Handon, the American senior NCO, whom he believed to be systematically undermining his authority with the mostly American team. Homer figured one day there was going to be a reckoning between those two. And God save them all then – from tearing themselves apart from the inside, when the whole Rapture was tearing at what was left of them from every other side. Would they destroy themselves from within, in the end?

The English Channel appeared now on the horizon, the setting sun flashing on the white tips of wind-driven surf. Another change from the old days, Homer thought – daylight ops. SOF, Special Operations Forces, used to own the night. Now even they feared it. *There are things more dangerous than us out there now*, Homer thought. Predator saw the sweat pouring off the PO, and gave Homer a pointed look. *Five minutes*, Homer mouthed. They didn't have to do it until just before they cleared the Channel. And something made Homer want to give this man the blessing of a last few minutes alive. Amongst the living. Amongst his brothers.

He unwrapped the *shemagh*, the black-and-white checked scarf he'd picked up in Libya, and worn habitually ever since. He used it to mop the man's sweat-drenched brow.

* * *

“I think I caught it on my shoulder cam,” Juice said a little weakly, pausing to spit tobacco juice out into the slipstream. “Whatever it was.” Handon nodded at him. Combat video feeds could be seen as a luxury, for a military unit, a whole species, on the brink. But even more than in the high-tech terror wars, all data was precious. They captured everything, so it could be analyzed and exploited after they returned to base. *If we return to base*, Homer mentally amended. But knowledge was definitely life.

They were flashing toward the cliffs of Dover now, and Homer spotted the cruciform shape way out. It was a landmark for them. The lacerated, worm-gnawed figure nailed to it didn’t resolve until a few seconds later. But it was still there. In the early days of the quarantine, English country people, farmers mostly, had gone around nailing the soulless up on crosses, all along the coast, at mile or two intervals. Homer figured it was nice that Christian symbols retained some of their talismanic, or protective, power.

Unfortunately, many of the ones they nailed up never did get properly destroyed. Homer didn’t know whether it was through carelessness, or cruelty, or as some kind of warning to the others. But many of them were wiggling up there to this day. Some of course rotted right off, or pulled free of their own limbs, tumbled down, and wandered off to kill and infect more. Which was a reminder that you didn’t want faith getting in the way of tactical considerations. But, at a certain point, faith, however groundless, however forlorn, can be all you've got left.

The helo continued its unrelenting flight, landfall coming up on them faster and faster. The PO's remaining seconds in this world ticked down.

And then Homer saw the other one – the buddy. He recognized this one, he'd swear he did. You see millions of the soulless, you kill thousands, they blur. But this one he knew. Usually it just walked or stood on the cliffs, a hundred meters or so from the edge, all alone, shoulders slumped, looking lost and profoundly forlorn. The Lord alone knew how it'd survived, what with the regular shoreline patrols, the recons in force going out to tamp down outbreaks, the combat air patrols over the Channel… but somehow this one poor creature was almost always there, when they flew back in this air corridor. It looked like it was searching for someone, or had lost something. Like nothing mattered enough – or it all mattered too much.

The Existential Zombie.

As noted, it was usually alone. But sometimes, like today, it would stand at the foot of that crucifix, its last shreds of clothing flapping in the wind, head bent down toward the ground, standing almost perfectly still like it was on some kind of vigil. Like that was its brother up there. This vision was deeply affecting to Homer, and also, of course, extremely creepy. Homer wondered how long it would be until they would fly over this way and see the clifftop devoid of that figure. Would it eventually give up its post and wander off, or maybe find peace at the bottom of the cliffs? Everyone had put a bead on the thing at one time or another, but for some unfathomable reason no one ever pulled the trigger. Maybe one day it would look up and see what it had lost. Or maybe it would be there forever.

Homer pulled his eyes from the scene outside and looked down into the pale blue eyes of the fevered, dying, frightened man before him. His pupils were already growing paler and more translucent, dark flecks and lines already forming in that spiderweb pattern as the blood vessels died, even as Homer watched. It was a sign of the turning. But then his expression softened. Homer thought he'd maybe somehow passed through the fear, and found some kind of peace. Waving Predator off when he tried to help, he cradled the man under his arms and eased him over to the open cabin door. They held each other's eyes as Homer put the single round through his brainstem. The deformed bullet left him and sped off out into the lonely Kingdom of Heaven, way out above this fallen world.

As they approached the tall, noble clifftops, Homer's mind's eye flashed back to the cliffs of La Jolla, near San Diego, back when he was stationed with the West Coast SEALs at Coronado. His wife, his son, and his daughter, he could see them with such beautiful clarity, the four of them together amid so much peace and joy, their bellies and hearts so full, basking in the warmth of that world's California sunlight, the ocean named for peace stretching out past God and man's horizon. Knowing nothing of what was to come.

The dead man's own weight took him right over the edge, and as he fell he picked up speed, tumbling peacefully toward the last stretch of the darkening water.

"Your rod and your staff protect and comfort me. You prepare a feast for me in the presence of my enemies..."

SHADOWS IN THE MIST

Andrew Wesley, Corporal with the UK Security Services, and officer in charge on the night watch at the entrance to the Channel Tunnel in Folkestone, England, shifted uncomfortably in his chair. He pulled a precious cigarette out of the crushed packet on the desk in front of him and lit up. He looked up at the clock and was relieved to see there was only an hour and a half of his shift to go. It had been another long and boring night. Addison and Chambers, his two subordinates, were likable enough, but boy did those kids talk a load of rubbish, and he had to put up with it night after night. If it wasn't aliens then it was superheroes. If it wasn't superheroes, then it was Bible conspiracies. He was tired of it.

"They never bother with zombies anymore," he muttered under his breath, guessing that subject was now far too real to allow for many "what ifs," even with the mystery of the creatures' origin still intact.

It had been half an hour since he had sent the pair of young recruits out into the dark to walk the perimeter. They had to do it every hour, on the hour, and even though they complained about it, Wesley had to admit that they always just got on with it – even though the Channel Tunnel terminal was probably one of the dullest security duties going. The soulless still walked up onto beaches, straight out of the Irish Sea or the North Sea, well into year two of the ZA. But the Channel Tunnel was sealed up tight. It had been for a long time.

As usual, the two young men had complained a bit before trudging out into the cold. Tonight was particularly miserable as far as the weather – the mist that had descended at around 2am was biting cold. Wesley normally smoked outside of the building, even though no one bothered with the smoking laws anymore – or any of the other old health and safety laws, for that matter. Tonight he had gone out for just one smoke outside the door, and he hadn't been out since.

He took a deep drag on the cigarette and watched the smoke swirl around the room as he exhaled. He wondered how long his two apprentices would stay at the tunnel. They were very young and far too enthusiastic, he thought, to be stuck in a post this dull.

How many zombies had been spotted in this sector? Maybe ten in the whole year that he had been in charge, and they had been putrefied enough that they were barely mobile. And none had come out in the last six months, which meant the Conspiracy Twins – as Wesley liked to think of them – had quite likely never even seen one. Why Central Command, CentCom, had even bothered to send him two additional people was puzzling. He could understand them replacing Jones; the old man was just too frail to be traipsing around at night, and the old guy had been suffering with his knee joints for the whole time Wesley had been there. But two young and untrained guards? Wesley would have traded them back in for Jones any time, even with the arthritis.

He stubbed his cigarette out and looked up at the clock again. Where the hell were they? Twenty minutes, tops, was all it took to walk the perimeter and check the tunnels. They didn't even need to check them, really. Both entrances were sealed off, and the maintenance tunnel was locked up tight. He hadn't been there when the teams of soldiers had blocked the entrances off completely in just a couple of days, with debris from abandoned buildings; that had been done before he arrived, but old man Jones had told him all about it. They had filled the tunnels with the rubble from demolished buildings, and there were plenty of those around Folkestone. No one wanted to live near the tunnel anymore, at least not after the early days when the dead making a break out of it represented a constant threat, even after the military had flooded some of the sections to get rid of the problem.

Wesley picked up the radio from the desk.

"Addison, come in," he said, and coughed. He needed a drink. A beer would be nice. His throat was dry.

"Addison, come in," he repeated.

All that came back was a static hiss.

"Addison, come in, you little git. Where are you two?"

Nothing. Just dead air.

"For crying out loud," he cursed, heaving himself off his chair and grabbing his coat from a row of hooks near the door. He stepped out into the cold, pushing the radio into its holster and pulling his torch and short-handled axe from his belt. He glanced back at the cabinet on the wall of the office, wondering whether he should take the shotgun with him, but then decided that getting it out and loading it was more hassle than it was worth. He knew exactly where the two young guards would be and why they were late.

The gravel underneath his feet crunched as he started along the track toward the fence, carelessly leaving the door open behind him. The cold mist that had settled over the entire area seemed even colder now. It was the kind that clung to you and bit your throat with every damp breath. Wesley hadn't realized quite how thick it had become while sitting there in the warm office. It also meant that visibility was reduced to a few dozen yards, the white blanket of it seeming to just hang there, casting an oppressive pall over the landscape. Wesley always found it creepy in the yard when the mist settled, which seemed to be more and more often these days. He had never lived this far south before taking this posting, but he was sure that Folkestone was supposed to have had reasonably clear weather most of the year. He had no clue where that idea had come from.

He went the opposite way round the perimeter, trudging up the long gravel track that wound around the fence, and eventually descended back toward the train tracks themselves. Years ago the area had always been clear, but that was back when the trains ran with a startling regularity through the tunnels to France, and before the military had taken over Folkestone. Where there had once been open ground, with only the tracks running toward the tunnel, there were now row upon row of containers and derailed train carriages, all used for storage. He had never asked what the military stored in them, but it was important enough to warrant daily visits, enough for the dirt trail from the gate to the storage area to have compacted and formed a road of sorts. They never spoke to him, the soldiers who came and went each morning, they merely showed him their badges and went about their business. And Wesley had been given strict instructions to stay in his office when they were onsite. Dodgy as hell, he thought. But he also knew it was in his best interests to ignore it. Ignorance was sometimes best.

Tonight, the outer fence was quiet. *Too quiet*, he thought. The only sound was the crunch of his own boots on the gravel path, and he was relieved when he finally rounded the fenced edge and started down the slope back into the yard. He presumed Addison and Chambers would be sitting there, on one of the containers, chattering as usual. He had lost count of the number of times he'd had to tell them to get their circuit done on schedule. It wasn't as if he was that bothered, but over at CentCom they liked their regular calls to confirm that all was still clear. One more box to be ticked. This didn't seem to have registered with the pair of new recruits, but at least they had taken note of his complaints about their endless nattering and scheming, and taken their conversation elsewhere. No doubt they were arguing about what secrets were held in the yard right now, instead of seeing to their own jobs.

Wesley had been a security guard for most of his forty-five years, including in a number of very well paid jobs back before the zombies turned up and changed everything. He had actually been working over in France when the outbreaks began, and he vividly remembered standing at the bar in his favorite drinking hole in the Latin Quarter and staring up at the TV screen, dumbstruck, as report after live report from around the world played out. He couldn't remember the exact night it had happened, but he could remember how haunting it had been when the first live news team went down under a zombie swarm attack.

The whole world had been shocked by that scene, and until then most people had talked about the trouble as though it was a foreign thing, and something that would never affect them. Then the footage had been shown of the reporter and the camera crew being pulled to the ground and literally torn to shreds by the marauding dead. Even though the camera had fallen on its side, it clearly captured one of the horrendous creatures gorging on the neck of a reporter. Within an hour of that news event, which seemed to replay on nearly every channel over and again, Wesley had received the call from his boss, instructing him to get his ass on the next train home.

It was hard to think back to those days. They seemed so far in the past, even though only two years had gone by. All the folks he had worked with during his time in Paris, all of the other security personnel, the airport workers, the shipping office clerks, the girls in the main office – all gone now. He often wondered what had happened to Amarie. Had she managed to escape? Had she fled back to the south of France to be with her parents? Wesley felt a twinge of regret at failing to find her in her flat when he had paused in his frantic flight from the city to look for her. He had only known her a month. Yet it pained him deeply to know that he would almost certainly never see her again.

His thoughts drifted to the streets of Paris back then – people rushing in all directions, the first looting in the shops, police sirens rising and falling. That was before the virus was even close to the city, and before the first real outbreak – the one in Villiers-le-Bel that people initially thought was just a riot. He could clearly remember the feeling of shock and revulsion as he watched a group of young men ransacking a shop across from his apartment. They hadn't even waited for the cover of night, or for the shop to close.

"You need to get the next train back," his boss had said on the phone, just after the first reports of rioting in the city had hit the headlines. "Everyone is heading home as soon as possible, before the docks are closed. Rumour is they are closing the border completely."

It wasn't good news. Civilian air traffic into the UK had been brought to a halt for three days already, meaning that anyone who wanted to get back had to use the tunnel or go by ferry. There had been all sorts of stories coming back about the difficulty of getting into the country, even for those who held British passports.

But Amarie's phone rang through every time he called, and she hadn't been at home when he went there. Wesley had rushed around the apartment building, asking the neighbours if they had seen her, but no one knew anything. Finally, he had sat in the kitchen of his own apartment, counting the hours and watching the news, before he finally grabbed his bag and headed for the station.

The throng of people trying desperately to get onto the trains was mind-boggling. Thousands struggled even to get into the station, let alone the terminal itself. Wesley was too jaded to be surprised at the outbreaks of violence amongst the crowds, and it was evident that the police had little control over events. What few officers hadn't been called up for riot control in the streets were too few to control the mob of people pushing and shoving to buy tickets.

Wesley felt a pang of sadness to remember that the train he caught was the last one ever to travel the Channel Tunnel. The chaos in France had exploded out of control after that, and by the time Wesley arrived at his old flat in Peckham and switched on the TV, most of Paris was in flames. The riots had spread so quickly in the City of Light that a state of complete anarchy existed within hours. The police and emergency services collapsed shortly after. Most of the police and ambulance staff had abandoned their posts and run for their homes and family.

What about the Scottish family that he had become friends with over the last week before the end? They had stayed in the hotel opposite and had taken to dining in the cafe on the street below Wesley's apartment. Had they managed to get out? He hadn't seen them for the whole day before he left. Wesley sighed, and hoped to

God that they got their two little kids out. He shook his head, trying to push the memory from his mind, but it was difficult.

Maybe that family had been lucky. So many hadn't been as the virus spread with alarming speed. The progression of the infection varied from person to person, but rarely took more than ten or twenty minutes to render the victim unconscious. Wesley had even seen it claim a person merely seconds after she stopped bleeding. As soon as a victim was no longer in control of his or her body – either out cold or else done bleeding to death – they were at its mercy.

He remembered the old woman outside the pharmacy, as he made his way hurriedly to the Metro. She had been the fastest turning that he had ever seen, and she had been one of the first that he had witnessed. The woman had been trying to leave a shop when an infected man had stumbled out of the alleyway next door. Before Wesley even clocked him he had bitten the woman on the neck, tearing out a chunk of flesh and ripping open her jugular vein. Wesley remembered the alien feeling of battering the man to the ground. He had been in mortal conflicts before – it sometimes couldn't be avoided if you worked for a major international security firm – but this had been different. The man hadn't even tried to defend himself. He was too busy trying to grab hold of and devour the woman. Less than a minute later, as Wesley staggered away from the man's body, the woman had grabbed him by the leg from her prone position on the ground and bitten him. Fortunately, she bit into his boot, or else Wesley's survival of the apocalypse would have been very short lived.

Now he snapped out of his reverie, and realized that he had stopped walking, and was standing at the foot of the slope and the beginning of the storage yard. He was just staring at the ground and had been completely lost in his own thoughts.

He looked around, and then grabbed his radio again. This was where he had expected to find Addison and Chambers, and if they weren't here then they hadn't even gotten a quarter of the way round their circuit.

"Addison, come in," he said. "Chambers, come in. Anyone? Where the hell are you two?"

He peered through the mist and began walking across the yard between the huge containers stacked high on each side. The place seemed so peaceful now in comparison with the chaos of the last two years. Was it like the calm of the Phony War at the beginning of WW2? After the invasion of Poland, but before the Battle of France? No. Only if Hitler had overrun the whole world, and those he killed risen up again. This was more like the silence of the grave.

A noise snapped him out of his thoughts. It was distant, but he was sure that it was a cry.

He dismissed it, thinking that it was probably just a bird or a fox.

No. There it was again. Not a cry. That was someone screaming.

WHISKEY TANGO FOXTROT

Herefordshire was dead and black by the time Alpha team zoomed low over its hills and flared into the former SAS compound at Hereford – now home to the Unified Special Operations Command (USOC). This was where the last few hundred of the world's very best military superheroes operated from, deployed in defense of the world's very last fifty million or so human beings.

The perimeter of the dirt helipad was bathed with red combat lights – the UK countryside was relatively cleared and safe, but white light was still just too damned irresistible to the dead – and Handon's boot hit sod before the bird had settled onto its four fat tires. He lit the remnant of a cigar with one hand and with the other smacked the two rucksacks full of hard drives into the chest of Juice, who had followed him off the bird.

"Check these in," Handon said, blowing smoke off into the fragrant night. "Report the loss of the POs. With our respects." Juice nodded, sliding his ballcap back over his matted mane. Through his trademark beard – thick, dark and red – he said flatly, "And the other thing?"

"Yeah, that too. Put in an intel spot report." Handon hesitated. "How's your head?"

Juice nodded. "All squared away, Sarge." The building collapse had basically just knocked him cold for thirty seconds. The two men turned and strode off in opposite directions as the rest of the team unassed the helo and began hauling down their kit and the remains of their combat load-out. Ainsley had already stalked off wordlessly for the BOQ (Bachelor Officers Quarters).

Juice spat again in the red-tinged darkness, hitched up the two rucks on his shoulder, and began to thread the rows of uniform wooden structures until he found the Head Shed. Opening the door and pulling back the blackout curtain, he entered and hailed the officer of the watch. The guy was expecting them, had heard their inbound radio chatter on the air net. Had already heard about the casualties.

"Mission outcome?" he asked, taking the rucks as Juice handed them over.

"Successful," Juice said, still squinting through animal eyes into the brighter light of the Ops Center. "Both target sites taken, both exploited. It's all there in the bags." The officer gave him a long, vacant look. Both of the dead POs were his men. Juice got it. "Sorry, man. We did everything we could."

A pause. "Shit happens in the Zulu Alpha," the officer said, shrugging. "We'll go down the list and try to get you new attachments."

"Thanks." Juice paused, reining in the impulse to spit on their floor. "There's something else." The officer arched his eyebrows. "We lost the Second Detachment PO to a Romeo." Another pause. "But not one like we've seen before."

"Like what, then?"

"It was fast."

The officer just gave him a *No, shit?* look. That was sort of the whole point of runners.

"Faster. A lot faster. Plus it could jump – like a meth-head on Wile E. Coyote springs. I've never seen anything like it. It took a leap at your guy on the SPIE rope. It scored him across the face, hit the ground – and then *ran away*."

The officer didn't react for a couple of seconds. "You got any video?"

Juice unslotted a flash memory chip from his shoulder rig – he'd earned the call sign "Juice" because every single thing he carried ran on batteries, which constantly needed charging – and handed it to the officer, who jammed it in a machine. Juice took the mouse and fast-forwarded through the video. Expressionless, the officer watched from Juice's POV, looking out of the helo and down, helping reel the others in. A gray shape came out of the bottom of the frame and flashed by. It latched onto the rope and there was some kind of scuffle. And then it was gone. Juice froze the frame, unwittingly on the mauled face of the PO. He looked up at the officer, then killed the window.

The other man's expression turned a few degrees more grim – more even than everyone in this unit looked all the time. "We've been getting scattered and broken reports of Romeos like that. On over-the-water raids. One border patrol. They think it might be some kind of mutation. A new kind."

"What kind?"

"The kind that doesn't feed."

Juice worked his wodge of tobacco. "What kind of

zombie doesn't feed?"

"They just seem to infect people and move on – *fast.* The guys in the Med Shack think maybe it's a new adaptation of the virus. Now that the dead outnumber the living by such a high multiple, they've given up on trying to feed. They're now just out to spread the virus. Or, rather, the virus has hijacked them to spread itself." The officer ran the fingers of his right hand across his regulation buzzcut. "Into the last corners of the living."

Juice shifted his weight. He was still wearing eighty pounds of combat load. "Got a designation for it?"

"Not an official one. But, colloquially, they've been calling them Foxtrot Novembers." Juice held his gaze. "The Fucking Nightmare."

Juice nodded his goodbye – SOF guys didn't salute very much, in the old world or this one – then turned and exited. *Great,* he thought, angling for the Alpha complex, with their ready room, briefing areas, and billets. *As if this world wasn't nightmarish enough already.*

As he banged through the door toward his gear locker, Juice realized this month would be the second anniversary – two freaking years since the quarantine, and the fall that came almost immediately after. Now into year three of the ZA.

And welcome to it, he thought, the exhaustion hitting him, stumbling through camp like the walking dead himself.

HELL HATH LESS FURY

"Oh my fucking God!" screamed the voice that echoed across the yard.

Wesley took off at a run, his boots crunching heavily on damp ground. He crossed most of the distance in just a few seconds, but then slowed to a halt as he rounded the last train carriage. Ten yards away he spotted Chambers leaning over the struggling form of Addison. There was blood flowing heavily from the latter's arm. Wesley felt a wave of fear as he ran forward, drawing his axe and pulling it back, ready to strike.

But he didn't have to. Chambers turned round as he approached.

"Oh thank fuck. Help. We've been attacked," he yelled. Wesley slowly lowered his axe.

The look on Chambers' face changed as he realized what had nearly just happened. He was holding tightly onto Addison's arm, and Wesley could clearly see blood trickling from between his fingers.

"I'm not infected!" he yelled. "It didn't bite me. It didn't bite either of us."

"It?" Wesley hissed.

"It came out of nowhere," said Addison.

"Keep your voice down," said Wesley, spinning

around and peering into the mist. Nothing moved around them, no wavering shadows or sounds. His mind raced. Where had it come from? It couldn't be the tunnel, which was flooded, and had been for well over a year, the entrance filled with rubble. Nothing could physically get through.

"It came from nowhere," repeated Addison, obviously on the verge of tears. "It was so fast. I didn't even see it. All I knew was the pain in my arm. Oh God, it's not a bite is it?"

"No," said Chambers, shaking his head. "It's just a cut. Same as what it did to me. it just cut you deeper. It's okay. No bites."

Wesley turned back to the young trainees, thinking how naive they were and wishing that he could be so innocent. But he knew. A bite was a guaranteed infection. A scratch? It was still high risk. If the creature had blood or gore on its hands then the two young officers were as good as dead. He needed to get the gun.

"We need to get you back to the office. Get up. Quickly."

Chambers struggled to his feet, then helped Addison up, and they both followed Wesley as quickly as they could.

"Where did it go after it attacked you?" Wesley asked, without looking back, hoping that the injured junior officers were close behind him. He didn't have the luxury of keeping track of them; he was too busy scanning the dark corners of the yard and the gaps between the storage units, searching for signs of movement or a distant noise.

"I don't know," stuttered Chambers from a few yards away. "I was in shock. I didn't see it run off. I thought we were going to die."

"Okay. Right. I need the gun. I'm going to run for it. Get in the office as fast as you can and shut the door behind you."

The search for the two youths had taken Wesley along nearly the entire circuit of the fence, and this end of the yard was only a few hundred feet from the office. He hurried through the gap between two huge train carriages and by the time he hit the foot of the grass slope he was already running.

"Three Acres, come in," he wheezed as he tried to climb the slope and use the radio at the same time. He wasn't feckless like the young guys, but he wasn't young like them, either, not anymore. Dirt and grass churned underneath his feet and he had to stop for a moment to regain his footing. "Three Acres, come in."

What the hell was it with people not answering their radios? Three Acres was the centre of communications in Folkestone, and had once been part of a retail park. Now there were armed forces from six different countries occupying the warehouses, and this included the security monitoring office that should be answering his call very quickly. They had people in that office 24/7 to organize every coastal patrol from Margate to Eastbourne. On a clear night, Wesley would have been able to look out of his office window, across the M20 motorway just a few hundred yards away, and see the lights of the Comms Centre. But tonight the mist obscured everything further than fifty feet away.

"Three Acres come in… Come on, God damn you, answer me," Wesley spat as he contemplated contacting CentCom in London directly. But that would mean a military reaction, and a single zombie escaping into the countryside wasn't something that CentCom wanted to be contacted for.

He glanced back down the slope. The two injured men were halfway up now and still climbing. His gaze drifted across the yard. So much of it was obscured by the fog and darkness that the creature could be anywhere. It would be there somewhere, stumbling in the darkness in search of more prey, Wesley thought, as he ran up the remaining forty yards of slope and through the open doorway to the office. He didn't stop, but made a dash straight for the cabinet.

"The keys… the keys. Where the fuck are the keys?"

The shelf above the kettle, where a spare set of office keys always lay, the set with the gun cabinet key on it, was empty. Had he moved them? Wesley glanced over to the wooden cabinet in the corner. The door was still shut. He looked on top of the cabinet, but there was nothing, just a layer of thick dust. He rushed around the office, pulling open drawers and scattering the contents, frantically searching. How could they be gone? No one had been in the office and the keys were always on the shelf. Always. Had he moved them and forgotten? He stood in front of the cabinet looking at the lock, and then reached to his waist, pulling the axe from its loop.

A noise behind him made his nerves tingle. He

spun round to see the first shadow pass the office window. The office door creaked open, mist obscuring his view out. Chambers or Addison.

"Have you seen the..."

The words died in his throat. Addison lumbered into the doorway and stood glaring at him – except this wasn't the young, foolish trainee that Wesley knew. Addison had changed. His face was drained of all colour, his skin an alien, pale gray, with darkening lines that had once been veins visible beneath. Zombie Addison's eyes now burned inside blackened sockets, with what Wesley could only feel was hatred. Hatred of him. Those eyes almost bored into his mind. From Addison's mouth there hung something bloody and dripping; something that Wesley couldn't identify. The blood had soaked into a spreading patch on the dead officer's shirt.

Addison hissed and bared his teeth, dropping the lump of flesh to the floor. He stumbled forward and tripped over the chair next to the door. He fell sprawling, his hands reaching out, but not to stop his fall. Those hands reached out for Wesley.

Another shadow loomed in the doorway behind the undead officer. Chambers staggered into view, and hit his head on the glass panel in the door, smashing it in his desperation to get inside. As Wesley backed up toward the far end of the room, he saw that the left side of Chambers' neck had been torn out. The dead trainee's head swayed unsteadily as he moved, his neck no longer able to hold the weight. There was blood soaking his jacket, but no blood flowed from the wound now. Chambers had bled out already.

That was what Addison had been eating. He'd eaten his own friend.

A survival instinct that Wesley didn't even know he had snapped him out of his panic. He was no longer frozen to the spot as the two creatures struggled to negotiate their way through the office and around the furniture, toward him. The mess that Wesley had created during his rush to find the keys now slowed them down. Chairs that had been moved out of the way, tables that had been pushed and drawers that were still open; all of these meant precious seconds as the dead clambered across the room to get at him.

He turned to the cabinet and smashed the door with his axe, grabbed the shotgun and turned over the box of shells, snatching the nearest.

Addison was barely three feet away when the single chamber snapped shut and Wesley raised it to the dead man's face and pulled the trigger. Addison's head vanished in the blast, replaced by a cloud of blood and gore that splattered across the office. The noise was terrific, echoing in Wesley's head for seconds afterwards. He had forgotten how loud shotguns were, especially in enclosed spaces. He sidestepped the body, slipped a new shell into the chamber, snapped it shut and aimed over the desk at Chambers.

The one thing that had always unnerved Wesley about the undead was their sheer lack of fear, and their complete ignorance of any form of danger. He aimed the shotgun at Chambers' head, and the zombie just kept coming. It was only a few feet away when Wesley pulled the trigger, and right up until that moment the creature hadn't even acknowledged the weapon, hadn't considered the danger that it was rushing toward. Not until it was too late, and its unthinking brain splattered across the brick wall at the back of the office.

Wesley jumped over the nearest desk, slammed the shotgun down and grabbed the radio from the wall.

"Three Acres come in! Come in!"

A minute later, Wesley's boots were thudding against the tarmac road as he jogged toward the car park. He unlocked his car with his key fob and jumped into the driver's seat, throwing his radio and axe onto the passenger seat. He carefully placed the reloaded shotgun into the passenger footwell, double-checked his pocket for the remaining shells, and then rammed his keys into the ignition. The car skidded out of the gravel drive and tore up the ground as he raced toward the roundabout that would take him over the M20 and toward the Security Centre. He put his foot down, speeding up the slope toward the main road, but something caught his eye, something in his peripheral vision.

He skidded to a halt and wound the window down. There, down in the yard, right near the blocked-up entrance to one of the tunnels. There was movement, and lots of it. For just a moment the wind must have blown the mist away, because his view of the tunnel entrance cleared, and in the darkness amongst the rows of storage units, Wesley saw dozens of figures moving about. He saw clearly that a small section of the blocked-in tunnel had now been opened up.

There was a hole.

Wesley slammed his foot on the accelerator so hard that his knee popped. The car shuddered once in defiance before it lurched into motion and screeched up the road toward the bridge. Wesley knew what was happening now, and he realized the urgency.

He changed channels on his radio with one hand, then pressed the transmit button. "CentCom come in," he shouted into the pickup, but cursed as he saw the battery indicator go dead. He tossed the radio aside and grabbed the steering wheel so tightly that his knuckles turned white.

He had to get to Three Acres and warn them.

Fortress Britain was breached.

LOVE SPREADS

Predator and Juice sat in silence in the Alpha ready room, squaring away their weapons and gear. In this world as in the old one, it was the personal responsibility of every Tier-1 operator to ensure the perfect functioning and reliability of his own kit. After a mission, but before secondary matters like sleep and food, weapons got cleaned and lubed, magazines and grenade pouches refilled, radio batteries recharged – and everything carefully stowed away where it could be got at on a second's notice.

One difference between this world and the old, though, was that if you failed to take care of your shit, there might not be any replacement weapons, parts, or repair services. You only appreciated industrial society, and international trade, once they were gone. Predator in particular mourned for Delta's master gunsmiths and armorers, all of whom were presumed to have died when Ft. Bragg, in North Carolina, went down.

He sat at a bench, carefully stroking a wire brush on a brass rod down the barrel of his beloved 7.62mm SCAR (SOF Combat Assault Rifle). He'd been carrying this weapon since 2nd Iraq and had no plans to break up with it now. Predator originally got his call sign for seeming to be seven feet tall, unkillable, and unstoppable; for being expert at a wide variety of extremely deadly weapons; and, in particular, for moving awfully close to silently and invisibly for a guy the size of a truck.

Juice, hairier and cuddlier, stood nearby, pulling batteries out of his devices and plugging them into a wall multi-charger. Neither man spoke, both working in the cordial silence and placid concentration of a ladies' sewing circle.

Other members of the team would be doing the same, but elsewhere, so they weren't all on top of one another. (In a depopulated world, space was strangely at a premium.) Ali and Pope were next door, in the quad billet they shared with Pred and Juice. While the latter two were still stripping off dirty assault suits, they caught sight of Aaliyah slipping out of the room, pressing the door closed, and padding off into the blacked-out moonscape of the base.

"There she goes again," said Juice, checking the soles of his assault boots for gore.

Pred grunted in response, sniffing at a pair of thick socks. "Yeah, it's funny. I've worked with Ali for a decade. Ordinarily, she'd sooner chew her own head off than get involved with anybody she's serving with."

Juice nodded, grabbing a towel and a pair of shower shoes and shutting his locker. "Ordinarily, the dead wouldn't be walking the Earth."

"True. True."

Pausing at the door, Juice looked thoughtful. "She hook up with someone in headquarters company, maybe?"

"Maybe. But somehow I don't quite see her hooking up with a REMF, either." Tier-1 guys were so far removed from "Rear Echelon Motherfuckers" that they generally couldn't be bothered to look down on them, as the regular infantry grunts did.

Suddenly, the sound of shouting floated in through the propped-open door – then crescendoed and multiplied with frightening speed. The two big men exchanged looks with each other, then looked back at their shut weapons lockers.

* * *

His kit and weapons squared away, but the grime of the mission still on him, Captain Connor Ainsley took a few breaths sitting on the rack in his private quarters in the BOQ. He then speed-dialled his wife. The sat phone he'd previously depended on to reach her from around the world was now just a particularly heavy and useless brick – ever since the telecom sats started falling out of their orbits. And the civilian mobile network was dodgy at best. But military packets at least had priority.

She picked up after a few rings – probably the degraded and patchy network of towers trying to locate her. "Hello?" She'd never learned to keep the fear out of her voice, even just answering the phone.

"Hello, darling. It's me. Everything alright?"

"You're okay?" Neither wanted to take the time to answer, before the other did.

"Fine, just fine."

"Us, too. The boys are okay."

"How's the city?" Ainsley's wife and two boys lived in central London – in theory one of the safest places in Britain, and thus in what was left of the world. They used to own a house in Surrey, but moved in after the quarantine, and a bit before the fall. And with military comms and scuttlebutt being as unreliable as they were, he often got better intel straight from her than from briefings in his own chain of command.

He could hear her pause and swallow before answering. "It's okay. The regular military units are still like the bloody Gestapo – every time I get stopped on the street, I want to tell them my husband is a *real* soldier, an elite one, out fighting the real war."

"We've all got our roles to play, sweetheart."

"I know… The streets seem safe. There have been no outbreaks that I've heard of. Just the odd one wandering in from the countryside. They don't get far or last long. So far."

"You're all staying indoors after dark, though, right?"

"Yes. But it's hard. The rationing bites a little worse every month. The boys are on the verge of boycotting potatoes, no matter how I cook them… I feel like they're not growing as quickly as they should do…"

"It's fine. They'll be fine."

"What about your leave, Connor? What did they say?"

Ainsley sighed quietly, not wanting to upset her any more than necessary.

"It's still no. For the time being."

His door knocked, then cracked open. It was Handon.

"I've got to go. I'll call again in a few days. *Inside after dark*. Okay? Bye."

Ainsley rung off and gave Handon a weakly expectant look.

Handon's expression started out as its usual granite surface. "The Colonel wants us. A briefing." But then it unexpectedly softened. Ainsley looked like he was in physical pain.

"You okay?"

Ainsley looked away, then back into Handon's steely blue eyes. "It's my family. I've been trying to get leave to go look after them for a little while. Fortify the house better. Try to lay in more provisions…"

But with that, Handon's expression froze back into rock. Instantly, Ainsley realized he'd misstepped. He knew as well as anyone, and better than most, that few of the Americans fighting here had the least idea whether their families back home were alive or dead.

Or that other thing.

Handon didn't respond, but Ainsley got the point perfectly. He changed the subject.

"Who's in this briefing? When?"

"Just us. Right now."

Unexpectedly, shouting erupted from outside – the same noises that caused Juice and Pred to freeze in the ready room. Handon turned and put his palm on the butt of his sidearm. The shouting grew louder quickly.

And then the two of them rushed outside and across the menacing darkness of the compound.

* * *

During the run-up to the fall, the militaries were the last to go down. Military installations – walled, guarded, heavily armed, and generally designed to withstand attack – at first seemed the perfect anti-zombie bastions. But what finally brought them down was camaraderie. *Esprit de corps*. The military brotherhood.

Not a single American or British military base was overrun from the outside. They all fell from within. When soldiers were wounded, their brother warriors erred – far, far too much – on the side of bringing them back inside the wire. Either not believing they'd been infected… or thinking they could be treated, or at least controlled… or just credulously taking their word for it that they weren't bitten or scratched… they walked or carried their own doom right inside the walls with them.

Now, tonight, long after the world outside Britain had been overrun… whatever was going on, whatever the cause of the tumult at Hereford, it was near the NCO's mess. Just outside the entrance, a mass of bodies was grappling in the bad light, grunting and swearing, elbows pistoning for punches. One figure lay on the ground at the foot of others, literally getting the shit kicked out of it. It was violent, shadowy chaos.

Handon kept ten meters between himself and the melee, his .45 in one hand and Surefire LED flashlight in the other, the two crossed at the wrist. Ainsley moved out, spreading the flank on the left. There were no shots yet. Before Handon could work out the tactical situation, or acquire a target, a new, large figure charged in – and immediately started *tossing* bodies out.

"*Cut it out, you goddamned sons of bitches…!*"

It was the Colonel.

Somebody went flying and rolled up at Handon's feet, coughing.

Scanning to either side – constant, total situational awareness is pretty much rule number one in spec-ops, and the first ten rules in zombie fighting – Handon saw a couple of corporals spill out of the mess and swing wide around the perimeter of the fighting. Handon grabbed one of them by the collar.

"Sitrep."

"It's just a soldier fight, Sarge." Handon didn't let him go. "One of the staff clerks from H&S company thought one of the operators from Echo Team looked dodgy. They were just back inside the wire, and the clerk thought he was twitchy and told him to get tested. Guy's team told him to get fucked. It went south from there."

With that, Juice and Predator skidded up to a halt, holding their assault rifles forward at the low ready position, night vision goggles protruding from their faces like African tribal masks. Juice wore only a towel wrapped around his waist, and flip-flops. Predator was ass-naked.

"What went south?" Pred growled, pivoting and aiming.

Handon couldn't help but crack a smile. "Master Sergeant, get that cannon out of my face." He didn't mean Pred's SCAR. "And stand down. It's just a fist fight."

Ainsley stepped up again and lowered the hammer on his .45 with his thumb, his expression darkening at the two huge and undressed men. Turning away, he muttered, "I could have gone my whole life without seeing that…"

By now the Colonel had gotten to the bottom of the dust-up, and was letting the perpetrators have it with both barrels. "The next time you dubious motherfuckers want to have a fight that doesn't involve Zulus, you fucking well do it outside the wire, where you can't scare anybody. Except the dead. Got it?"

Several dusty and bleeding soldiers, variously standing, sitting, or lying, nodded or *Yes, sir*'d in response. The Colonel scanned and pointed at a big and grizzled operator from Echo – presumably Patient Zero of this outburst. "You, First Sergeant. I don't give a shit how many decades of operational time you have in, or how many thousands of Tangos and Zulus you've slotted. You follow the goddamned fucking rules. I don't give a shit if it's the soup lady who doesn't like the look of you. You drop your shit where you stand and get your ass tested."

"Roger that, sir."

"Now!"

The operator pulled himself up and stomped off toward the Med Shack.

There were quiet mutters of approval from some of the scrawnier, bloodier guys.

"And *you* rear echelon motherfuckers. Next time you've got concerns about somebody's health, you goddamn well take it up through channels. You're no use to me or humanity with your heads torn off and shoved up your asses."

The four Alpha men, grinning or shaking their heads, were now turning to leave. Juice tapped Pred on the shoulder and pointed off behind them. They could just make out a figure climbing down from the tallest structure in that part of camp, a three-story warehouse. It was slim and lithe, with long hair, black and curly, and a rifle across her back.

"Looks like someone got her rendezvous interrupted." Juice whistled. "She moves fast."

"You have no idea, man," Predator said. "At least we weren't the only dumbasses who thought the shit was coming down in camp..."

With a toss of his head, the Colonel rounded up the two senior Alpha men and began fast marching them back toward his command post. The Colonel did everything fast. He knew they were all running out of time.

RUNNING BLIND

Aleister leaned back against the laundry trolley and took a long drag on his cigarette. It was a cold night, and he hadn't seen mist come off the sea like this in years. He exhaled slowly, feeling the nicotine working its magic on his nerves. It wasn't very often that he got a few moments to himself these days, not with so many soldiers coming and going, and at every hour.

He had worked at the Premier Inn even before the world fell apart. But back then he'd worked the rooms, as cleaning staff. That meant a whole lot of piling up sheets onto trolleys and emptying bins. People had stopped coming to stay after the tunnel breakouts and even though the building was left open, there was barely any staff. The manager had left to head north in a hurry, and most of the other staff didn't turn up for work. Eventually Aleister was left there on his own. Unlike the others, he had nowhere else to go.

When the military took over Folkestone after the town was abandoned by civilians, he had stayed on. Overnight, the hotel went from being an empty shell to a catering center for the mass of troops now being housed in the multitude of empty houses. Major Grews, the old-school, gray-haired officer in charge of what was now called "Camp Folkestone" had turned up with a group of heavily armed soldiers and informed Aleister that the hotel was being commandeered for military use. When asked who was in charge, Aleister couldn't think of anyone to name, being the sole occupant and effectively a squatter. So he told them that he was the manager.

That had been over a year ago, and now none of the military personnel who lived in the rooms of the inn, not even Mess Chef Lanslow, questioned him being there. Oddly, it was presumed that he was now drafted and in charge of the cleaning staff.

Tonight had been the busiest night in the hotel since he could remember, with every room full of soldiers on their way to somewhere. Aleister wasn't privy to the comings and goings, but on occasion he would overhear something, and this was one of those occasions. Two of the squaddies had stood at the bar for an hour later than most of the others, drinking cans of cheap lager and talking a little too loudly. Something big was happening, something that involved a lot of people travelling a long distance. The second soldier, the more vocal of the two, complained about suffering from seasickness.

Aleister stood up, dropped his cigarette on the concrete behind the bin and stubbed it out. He was about to go back into the building – back to the unpleasant job of filling up the washers for the night – when something caught his eye. There was movement over on the other side of the motorway. Someone running fast, and whoever it was obviously in a great hurry to get across the bridge. Six months ago there had been a copse of trees obscuring the view, but the Army had chopped them down for fuel, and now – even with the mist as thick as it was – he could see across the main road. The roundabouts on either side of the bridge were clearly visible.

The figure continued to sprint, and was nearly halfway across the bridge when a white van sped out into the road and rushed toward it.

Oh shit, he thought. They didn't even see the person running.

"Stop!" he shouted, but the van was too far away, and all Aleister could do was cringe as the vehicle ploughed into the running pedestrian at nearly forty miles per hour. The body bounced off the wing of the van, tumbled along the road and came to a halt next to the pavement. The van screeched to a halt.

ACROSS THE BRIDGE

The car shuddered in protest as Wesley swerved the vehicle, nearly taking the roundabout head on. It was a clapped-out old thing, and certainly not used to this kind of treatment. He eased off the accelerator and the juddering stopped.

He squinted, focusing on the road ahead, and further across the bridge. Something was blocking the way, but he couldn't make out what until it was thirty feet away. A white van had stopped in the middle of the road, three quarters of the way across. Wesley hit the brake, slowing the car, and crawled it forward in the near darkness.

The door on the driver's side was open, yet there was no sign of the driver. In the passenger seat a man struggled with his seat belt, a double-barreled shotgun lying across his lap. But the blood on his hands was causing him to fumble. Wesley yanked hard on the hand brake, grabbed his own shotgun, swung his door open and rushed around the car to the other side of the van – where he nearly tripped over a headless body lying in the road. He slowed, stepped carefully over the splayed limbs of the corpse, and pulled the van door open.

"Fuck, he bit me," blurted the passenger, his face pale and his voice cracking. "Alex bit me. I had no choice. I had to shoot him."

"It's okay. I can help," said Wesley, not sure how much he could help.

"That thing. It came out from nowhere. We didn't see it. I spotted it just before we hit it, but I didn't shout quick enough. I thought it was a man, but then it got up and rushed at us. No man could get up like that after being run down. It smashed the window and bit Alex's neck. Oh crap. He was bleeding everywhere. I tried to stop it, but too late. He changed so quickly."

"What about that thing? The zombie?"

"The what?"

This was delirium setting in. The man was obviously infected, and badly. Wesley's stomach churned at the thought that he would have to deal with him very soon.

"The zombie. The one you hit. Where did it go?"

"Oh. It ran off. Fucking ran. They aren't supposed to run like that are they? Not like that. Not that fast. Even the fast ones aren't that fast. Oh, God, I'm gonna be one of them."

The man was shaking, his hands still fumbling at his seat belt, but Wesley could tell that he was already losing control of his extremities.

Wesley leaned forward and gently picked up the shotgun from the man's lap, popped the remaining live shell out of the chamber, pocketed it, then moved the weapon away from the door. He glanced at the scattered shotgun shells littered across the footwell of the van, but decided that the risk of leaning in – even though the man was yet to turn – was not worth it. In a few minutes he could get those in relative safety.

"Do you have a radio?" He immediately felt cold and heartless as he ignored the man's fear. But it was no use. There was nothing else he could do.

"Yes. In the back. We're telecom engineers. Alex was my boss. Oh, God, I shot him in the face. I didn't know the shotgun would take his head off. I've never fired it before. Not *at* someone."

Wesley nearly wrenched the back door of the van off its hinges pulling it open. He had expected more resistance. Inside the van, piles of equipment lay strewn across the floor. One of the shelves that had held dozens of boxes of screws and nails and small clips in a million shapes and sizes had collapsed, spilling its contents everywhere. Fortunately, he didn't have to clamber over any of it. The radio was attached to the left side panel, just inside the door. Wesley grabbed the receiver, twirled the channel selector, and pushed the button so hard he felt his thumb pop.

"CentCom, come in. CentCom, come in," he said weakly.

A moment of silence passed.

"*CentCom receiving, over. What is your designation, please?*" The voice was female, and cold – emotionless and following protocol.

"Corporal Andrew Wesley, Security Services, Channel Tunnel. We have an emergency."

"Oh fuck it," cursed the injured man in the front of the van. Wesley barely heard him as struggled. "Fuck it. Fuck it. Fuck it."

"*What is the nature of the emergency?*"

"Zombie incursion out of the tunnel. They're out here and people are dying."

"Hold one moment... what did you say? An incursion?" The voice had changed, the simple mechanical tone in the girl's speech now wavering. *"They got out? Where are you now?"*

"I'm on the bridge between the Channel Tunnel terminal and the Premier Inn. There was a van in the middle of the road. I think the zombie came this way, because the driver is dead and the passenger infected."

"What zombie? Where did it come from?"

"Look, this is bad," snapped Wesley. "A runner got out of the tunnel somehow. It's into Folkestone. I've already lost two guards here and found another one dead on the..."

BANG!!

The sound hammered through Wesley's head, making his eyes involuntarily shut tight. His ears rang, and he fell to the floor, stopping his fall with both hands, but not stopping his head from colliding with the van door as it swung back toward him. The radio receiver bounced off the aluminum wall of the van with a thud. Wesley could vaguely hear the woman's voice, but it was too quiet and his hearing overloaded.

A trickle of blood ran into his eyes and he raised his hand to the top of his head, where a long thin cut had appeared. He glared up at the van door, at the two-inch hole – the one the bullet had made as it whizzed past his head at a distance of barely two inches, travelling at 1,200 feet per second. The bullet that had just a microsecond before blown the passenger's brain all over the cab partition.

"Hello? Hello?" chattered the radio. *"Acknowledge!*

Acknowledge?"

But Wesley was too stunned to acknowledge anything but the arrival of another death.

He staggered to his feet, leaning against the side of the van to steady himself as his head spun. Unsteadily, he walked around the front of the van and peered into the open window.

The engineer had decided that he didn't want to become a zombie. On his lap, still clenched in his pale fingers, was a handgun. His head was at an awkward angle, leaning off to one side, but his comfort was the very least of Wesley's concerns right now. The gaping hole in the back of his head, and the spray of blood, bone, and brains across the interior of the cab said that this was no longer going to be an issue.

Wesley grabbed the handgun, careful to not get any of the blood on him or make contact of any kind with the dead man. Even a minute or two after a zombie had expired, the virus was still active enough to spread and infect.

The handgun must have been in the glove compartment directly in front of the dead man. It lay open, contents spewed across the floor – papers, empty cigarette packets, pens, all manner of junk. But more importantly, a small black pouch containing two more magazines for the handgun – which was already fully loaded except for the one round expended.

Wesley ran round the back of the van and grabbed the radio. The woman's voice could still be clearly heard.

"*Hello? Hello? Are you still there?*"

"Yes. I'm still here."

"*What happened? What was the noise? It sounded like gunfire.*"

"Yes, it was. The remaining occupant of the van just blew his own brains out."

"*Ah.*"

"Look. Is Three Acres still safe? Are there people there?"

"*Yes. I have alerted them and the other checkpoints, as well as the military barracks. You should proceed to Three Acres immediately for debriefing. Let the military take care of fighting the outbreak.*"

"What about civilians? There are people still in the town. The thing headed that way."

"*Please proceed to Three Acres immediately. The Army are on their way. You should move out of the infected area as soon as possible.*"

"Okay, thanks," he said, placing the radio back into its holder. He shuddered as he glanced at the hole in the back door that had been barely inches from his head.

Wesley looked toward the town. Lights were on in various places, signs of the few people that had remained. The zombie would be death to them. He had to do something.

And then every window of the Premier Inn exploded outward.

FOLKESTONE IN CHAOS

Wesley hit the ground hard, diving behind the van as debris from the explosion in the hotel flew in all directions. Needle-sharp slivers of glass and bits of mortar and brick scattered across the road with a loud hiss. He stayed still for a moment, bundled up with his legs tucked in as tight as he could pull them, feeling the hot caress of debris hitting his back. After a few moments, the downpour ceased and the noise of clattering across the tarmac road petered out, so he peered out from around the side of the van. He was shocked. A sea of glass, brick, plasterboard, and not just a few small lumps of something red and wet had almost completely covered the road.

Wesley looked in the direction of the explosion. Every window in the outside of the large building was gone, and even at two hundred feet the debris was carpet-thick on the ground.

Something moved amidst the smoke and dust that now billowed from every hole in the building. As Wesley watched, dumbfounded, a figure jumped from the upper floor, landed hard on the ground and began running in the direction of the road, a noticeable limp in his gait. More movement, then, but in pursuit. Several shadowed figures staggered from the gaping holes that had been the ground floor doors only a few seconds ago, and ran after the lone survivor.

As the man drew closer to the road, Wesley could see that he was dressed in army fatigues and carrying an assault rifle – the standard British Army SA80. The soldier spun on his heels, fired half a dozen rounds into his pursuers, and then carried on running across the rough ground toward the road. The soldier took a minute to clock Wesley, but instantly dropped to one knee and took aim when they unexpectedly made eye contact.

"Don't fire!" shouted Wesley, holding the handgun out to his side. The soldier nodded, spun round again and planted four more shots into two of the figures still chasing him across the grass verge. He stopped firing then, and began frantically changing his magazine. Wesley ran toward him, stopping at the curb, raised the handgun and aimed at the nearest dark figure lumbering through the fog. He wasn't as accurate a shot as the soldier obviously was, and steadied himself, taking a deep breath and releasing half before squeezing the trigger.

Just as he fired, the mist around the nearest figure cleared, and Wesley's stomach churned as he saw what was chasing the soldier. The creature may once have been one of the soldier's own teammates. Its attire, what was left of it, was almost identical. One arm dangled from a few shreds of torn flesh, but the other was missing completely. A stump only a few inches long jutted out from the dead thing's shoulder while pale bone smeared with blood jutted out of the wound. The creature's face was barely recognizable as human. Its eyes were gone, as was its lower jaw. Black gunge now oozed out of the hole that would once have been a nose.

Wesley's first shot hit it in the chest, knocking it backwards. It stumbled and rose up again, staggering forward, but no longer in the direction of the soldier. It had a new target now, and so did the three other zombies, their torn and twisted forms lumbering across the barren ground. They all turned, almost as one, and began to move frighteningly quickly toward Wesley.

"Oh, fuck."

He fired again at the same zombie, this time hitting it in the shoulder.

Why the hell didn't I do more firearms practice?

His third shot ended the creature's afterlife, striking it through the raw open wound that had been its mouth, tearing a hole the size of a fist in the back of its neck. It fell over and hit the grass silently, even as the spray of its blood splattered the zombie behind it.

Wesley kneeled down and tried to steady his hand, panning around to take aim on the second undead pursuer, now only twenty feet away. The recoil jarred his arm, then the round caught the creature in the neck. But it was a glancing shot, and not centered enough to drop the thing. It continued to advance, even as its head flopped to one side.

Automatic gunfire assaulted Wesley's ears as the soldier finished his reload and opened up again. Relieved, Wesley stopped firing, but kept his sights on the zombies as each of them fell in turn. The sheer firepower of the assault rifle ripped their broken forms apart.

Finally – silence, though not for very long. A scream erupted from the hotel, and gunshots echoed from the street beyond.

"Come on," shouted Wesley. "We need to get to Three Acres."

The soldier shook his head, breathing heavily.

"I won't make it that far. Knackered ankle. I think I ripped some tendons."

"But you just…"

"Yes, I know. Had to. Can't do much more, though."

"I've got a car." Wesley indicated behind him.

"Okay, but we have to help. They're everywhere. We can't just leave these people."

"I was told to go to Three Acres."

"There are civilians in the town. Repopulation and Scavs. Two hundred moved into the center of town last week. They've got families with kids down there."

Wesley hesitated, then moved to help the soldier, pulling his arm over his shoulder to take some of the weight. Together they stumbled across to where Wesley had abandoned his clapped-out rust-bucket of a car.

"Okay. Look, we can drive through the streets. Maybe we can get down there and warn folks before the zombies get there."

"Sounds good," replied the soldier, pulling himself into the passenger seat. "I'll ride shotgun and keep the window down. Maybe I can take a few out as we go."

"A few?" asked Wesley as he ran around the car

and jumped into the driver's seat.

"The hotel had dozens in it. One of the fucking things must have got in somehow."

Wesley turned the ignition and cursed as the vehicle shuddered.

"They normally keep the place locked up," the soldier continued. "I was asleep. And suddenly there's the fucking cleaning boy bursting through the door and biting my mate's face off. Shit, we even flipped coins for nearest bed to the window. Guess I won more than the best bed tonight."

The car finally coughed and hummed. Wesley put his foot down and they tore off toward the roundabout. The road led around the hotel, and he hoped that they might just catch any zombies making their way to the town. They took the roundabout at fifty miles per hour, skidding around the corner and only just avoiding the curb.

"There must be fifty of the things by now," coughed the soldier, as though he sensed Wesley's thoughts. "I reckon I took out maybe half of them in the hotel with that blast – but a lot had already busted out and headed toward the town. I need to radio the base at Risborough and find out what the hell is keeping them."

"They already know. I spoke to CentCom."

"CentCom? Shit! Now we're fucked. Should have left it to Grews. He'll be pissed if he finds out it went out of his hands before he could deal with it."

"CentCom alerted the barracks. Grews already knows," said Wesley.

"Hell. Grews knew minutes ago. I radioed before I started chucking grenades."

The car sped toward the town. Ahead, in the fog, Wesley could see figures moving. Some ran, some staggered, but all moved with intent.

"CentCom will be calling out the dogs now. We'll be blockaded in this town in an hour. Guaranteed. How the hell did one of those things get up here? It can't have washed in on the tide."

"It got through the tunnel."

The soldier frowned, looking at Wesley as he would a squashed bug. "Don't be ridiculous. That thing's been flooded and blocked up for over a year."

"Yes, I know. I work security detail down there. It got out and chewed up some of the other security guys. There are more coming through as well. I saw them."

"What? You mean they are coming out of the tunnel still?"

The soldier reached to his waist and pulled out a radio that Wesley hadn't noticed.

"Kilo Four to Risborough. Come in Risborough, over."

Only silence came from the radio as the car barreled down the hill toward the dead, shuddering through the fog.

"*Risborough here, Kilo Four. Go ahead, over.*"

"Update on the Premier Lodge outbreak. We have estimated fifty Zulus on the streets of Folkestone and we have a fix on the origin. The Channel Tunnel is breached. Repeat. The Channel Tunnel entrance is breached."

"*Roger that, Kilo Four, all received. Will re-route a team to the tunnel entrance. Confirm your location, over.*"

"We're following the Zulus. Will attempt to intercept, over."

"*Copy that, Kilo Four. Proceed to intercept. Be aware that the Harbour barracks division is mobile and currently sweeping toward the town from their base. Expect friendly crossfire and watch for blue-on-blues. Proceed with caution. Your main objective is to secure the repopulation area and await their arrival.*"

"Roger that, Risborough. One last thing."

"*Go ahead, Kilo Four.*"

"CentCom has been alerted."

"*Understood, Kilo Four. We are aware. We have thirty minutes to contain.*"

"Then what?"

"*Hammer down, Kilo Four. The plane is already on its way.*"

"Understood. Kilo Four out."

"*Be careful out there, Martin. Out.*"

"Always," muttered the soldier to himself, as Wesley rammed the first of the walking dead, breaking its spine instantly and sending it tumbling under the wheels. Nearly every bone in its body shattered as the vehicle ploughed over it. The soldier clipped the radio back onto his belt and flipped the safety up on his weapon.

"One down!" he shouted, opening up on two other zombies trying to break down a door across the street.

MEMORY, THAT TRICKSTER

"Everyone's getting wound too tight."

The Colonel spoke quietly now, across the open air above his spare desk. Handon and Ainsley sat stiff-backed on chairs opposite. The Colonel only shouted when he needed to. Or when he was pissed off. Otherwise, his authority came across well enough at low volume.

"I don't suppose it needs saying that we can't afford to be tearing ourselves apart. There are few enough left of the living. And eating us alive is the job of the dead."

"Yes, sir," Ainsley said. Handon just nodded.

The Colonel paused a beat, then his tone softened. "What happened out there?" He was referring not to the fight, but to the mission just ended. Where the team lost both their POs in the course of half an hour.

Ainsley and Handon looked at each other. Ainsley screwed himself up and said, "No excuses, sir."

"Just bad luck?" the Colonel asked.

Ainsley nodded. "You could call it that."

Handon leaned forward in his chair. "But bad luck is also cumulative, Colonel," he said. "These missions deeper and deeper into Europe. They're getting close to the bone. Keep it up and we're going to lose a team.

Maybe two, when a second goes over to bail them out."

"That's why you sons of bitches get paid the big bucks," the Colonel said. "And, anyway, always has it been thus. If hardcases like you don't take the impossible missions, then who will? You don't like it, go be a farmer, or a coal miner. God knows we need more of them. And, anyway, your missions are deep because that's where the remaining labs are."

It was true that the diciest and most critical jobs had always been reserved for the Tier-1 special operators – Delta Force, SAS Increment, Seal Team Six, and the USAF 24th Special Tactics Squadron. Now, unsurprisingly, the job of saving humanity had mostly fallen to them. The coalition government in the UK knew that every big pharmaceutical company and biotech lab in the world had been frantically working on a vaccine, or a cure, or both, at the time of the fall. But then the lights had gone out.

The Internet had started to blink out within minutes of the world's power grids going down. Phone networks shortly after that. Now, whatever the state of research amongst the world's top virologists and biomedical researchers, their findings were walled up with them, entombed. The researchers were assumed dead (or undead). But their data, still buried in there with them, remained of critical interest to the living.

Now the job of the surviving Tier-1 operators was to go there in person and try to get it. At the very tip of the spear for this work was Alpha team at Hereford. There were also a half-dozen other teams of highly skilled SOF guys doing similar kinds of high-value jobs.

But Alpha was unique – made up of representatives of all the very top commando and SOF units in the world. They were mixed in together because they'd been teamed up for a nearly impossible job just before the fall. And they were still together now because they knew and trusted one another; and because most of their home units no longer existed; and because they wanted it that way.

Across the UK, most of the specialized military units did less dramatic but still critical things like scavenging Europe for electronics, food, medicine, seeds, and other supplies. And the regular military, well, they were now basically a home guard – fighting outbreaks in the cities, hunting the scattered soulless in the countryside, and holding the borders.

But at the very top of the whole military heap, well, Alpha was called Alpha for a reason.

They had been hitting European labs so far because that's what they could get to. It was as far as their capabilities for force projection stretched.

"And it's either that," the Colonel added, referring to the missions to scour the labs, "or hang out on this island waiting for the walls to come down. And the last lights to go out."

Neither Handon nor Ainsley spoke back. They already knew the score.

"Your latest haul has been shot up to Edinburgh." The high-tech ecosystem around Edinburgh University had been the UK's center of biomedical research before the fall. And so it remained now. Everything the operators and their POs dug up was immediately sent up there for exploitation – usually by ghosting the drives and sending them over the wire, which was fastest. Time was not on their side.

"With luck, you'll get a new target package out of that last intel." One of the first things the geeks in Scotland looked at was actually email. All the world's labs, scientists, and university researchers had been collaborating and sharing findings. These email trails often revealed which labs had made the biggest strides – and thus which ones the survivors should hit next. "You men rearm, refit and stay on one-hour alert."

"Sir," said Ainsley. He started to rise.

Handon stayed seated. "What's this about some new type of Romeo?"

The Colonel shuffled a paper. "You tell me. Heard you saw one." He paused, looking up and holding Handon's eye. Finally, he looked down again and spoke, more quietly. "There's been an outbreak down in Folkestone. Bad. Happened fast. Police and regular military say they have it contained." All three men let that hang for a second. "Contained" had often been a euphemism for "catastrophe." But if this outbreak and the new Romeos were connected, the Colonel wasn't going to elaborate.

"You're dismissed," he said.

* * *

Handon went straight from the briefing to the base gym, where he dressed out and hit the free weights. It was also the personal responsibility of every Tier-1 operator to maintain a razor edge of physical fitness. The job had always been like being a professional athlete, but with no off-season – and death or dismemberment if you lost a game. Now, as an added bonus, if the game clock ran down to zero, everybody in the stadium died with you.

With his earbuds in, sinking into the music of a world that used to be, warming up by bench-pressing 180 pounds without a spotter, he let his mind wander back.

He remembered the madness after the quarantine, but before the final fall. Chaos engulfing Europe, government control failing in state after state, waves of refugees streaming west and north from the Mediterranean and the Levant... Britain simply keeping the borders closed after the 11/11 attacks... and then the waves of the desperate, crossing the Channel on everything from cabin cruisers to container ships to inflatable two-man rafts.

For a while, they were simply turned away *en masse*, from Dover, from Folkestone, from Hastings. But, finally, the RAF had resorted to strafing the Channel with Tornado and Typhoon fighter-bombers, setting alight the oil slicks from crippled and listing seacraft. In addition to tens of thousands of floating dead, Britain got something like a moat. It had become necessary for national survival. The UK simply had no way to accommodate 500 million refugees – never mind to test them all for infection. To let them in would have been to doom their island home. The dead would have swarmed from Land's End to John O'Groats in days.

So the kinder, gentler modern Britain of EU membership and international human rights accords had reverted to its Churchillian spine of steel quickly enough when it had to. The RAF fought a second Battle of Britain. That it was largely against civilians made it no less a struggle for survival.

Handon remembered getting back to Hereford after the aborted North Korea mission, and getting on the horn with Bragg for a sitrep – and for a new tasking, given all the chaos.

"*Yeah, you guys hang tight where you are for now...*" There had been shouting and gunfire in the background. "*The 101st Airborne is being mobilized to try and secure the borders north and south here. National Guard units are being called out to lock down the cities...*"

As usual, the Big Green Army had moved too slowly. It was too enormous a bureaucracy to turn on a dime, let alone to try and keep up with a virus spreading and mutating like wildfire through a population that was about as ready for it as the Native Americans had been for smallpox. Also as usual, the elite Joint Special Operations Command, and its constituent SOF units such as Delta, had considered themselves above this kind of ponderousness and panic. And certainly no one could say they ever lost their cool.

But when the American south started to go down, as the unsecured southern border with Mexico became a raging and unmanageable vector for the virus... and as the military bases became beleaguered outposts in a rising sea of the dead... and then when well-meaning combat medics poked a hole in the dike by bringing infected men inside…

Well, the elite operators were too few to make any difference then.

And this next war was one that no part of the military, even its elite, had been prepared to fight. Finally, the only survivors were scattered small units of SOF in remote locations overseas – and particularly those training for an ultra-secret joint mission on a certain hardy island nation in the stormy North Atlantic…

* * *

Sergeant Major Handon realized, almost too late, that he'd somehow lifted all the way to the point of muscle failure – even with the low, warm-up weight. *How many freaking reps was that…?* The transporting music, and the transfixing vision of his memory and mind's eye, had caused him to lose track completely.

With a last pulse of strength, he heaved the bending and trembling bar up to the lower pegs on the rack above and behind him, and rolled out from under it. Sitting up, he regarded his hands in the low light, while the music still rolled over him, and his breathing slowly came back down to normal.

It took 100,000 years to build up all of human civilization, he thought to himself, almost amused. *And it took the virus, a strand of RNA barely 100 nanometers long, less than 100 days to bring it all down…*

KEN TAI I-CHI ("ATTACK AND DEFENSE ARE THE SAME")

"*Onegai shimasu*," Ali said to Pope, bowing deeply, her wooden sword, or *boken*, held straight before her in both hands. Pope bowed in mirror image. The two stood facing each other on the padded floor of the "dojo" that they had cobbled together in the basement of the Hereford gym.

Pope was Alpha's guy from the elite paramilitary arm of the CIA, the Special Activities Division (SAD). A child of immigrants from the Caribbean, he had served as a Marine officer through a half-dozen tours in Afghanistan and the Horn of Africa, before being recruited by the Agency. Guarding spooks and rescuing hostages in some of the world's very dodgiest corners had been his idea of a relaxing retirement activity. Thin, dark, and extremely soft-spoken, Pope was also the prototypical "gray man." You didn't notice him until he killed you.

Coming out of his bow, he hauled back and launched a powerful diagonal strike at Ali's neck, which she countered with a loud snap, while pivoting around him like a big cat.

Despite the wooden swords, the bamboo armor,

and the pleasantries in Japanese, Kendo (literally, "Way of the Sword") was not practiced at Hereford in any form that pre-apocalyptic devotees of the sport would have recognized. As Neal Stephenson once noted, "Kendo is to real samurai sword fighting what fencing is to real swashbuckling: an attempt to take a highly disorganized, chaotic, violent, and brutal conflict and turn it into a cute game." Needless to point out, the men and one woman of Alpha had no time for games in the ZA.

Pope and Ali traded a half dozen more high strikes, spinning and grunting, before Pope tried for a decapitation strike. Ali dropped out from underneath it, and took Pope's legs out with a mighty side swing. Now they half lay facing each other.

Just-in-time learning and training, for specialized missions and environments, was old hat for special operators. But, who, really, would ever have guessed that Japanese sword fighting would become the new rage, after the fall? At various times, the fashion had been for Brazilian ju jitsu, Krav Maga, the Close Quarters Defense system… and always the incessant pistol, assault rifle, submachine gun, and sniper rifle work. But it turned out the medieval Samurai had the best line on close-quarters, silent combat in varied terrain against multiple, swarming opponents.

The pair of duelers banged swords four times at close range on the ground, neither able to generate any power while prone, before Ali closed to grapple. But Pope was already rolling away and back onto his feet.

Virtually everyone operational at Hereford now

carried a wakizashi, the samurai short sword, as a secondary weapon. Some also went out with the long sword, the katana, for certain kinds of specialty work – for instance, in heaving strongholds of the dead, where silence was non-negotiable. And where backup wasn't coming – ever.

Inevitably, of course, it was now the fondest dream of some of these badasses to get to the point where they could fight with the long sword in the right hand, the short in the left, whirling and flashing, and holding off unlimited zombies, with no support. ("My left hand is my fire support," as the saying went.) Alas, fighting with two swords was a lot like shooting two pistols simultaneously: looks very cool in Hollywood (or Hong Kong) movies, but takes an insane level of specialized skill, plus a very particular scenario with multiple moving opponents, for it to be worthwhile. It was virtually always better to just focus on one weapon and using it masterfully.

Both coming to their feet again, sucking for air, swinging and slashing close-hauled and with zero room for error, the two dancers whirled around the room.

For Ali, the swordfighting was like an intense meditation. Every motion was instinct and improvisation, and her mind was set free, for reverie, for recollection… for revolving again around to her memories of how they got there, the bizarre gravity well of the fall…

* * *

She remembered a much earlier moment of looking at

Pope's handsome and serene face, unmasked and unarmored then, as they sat in the back of a humming Royal Air Force BAE 146, a small military passenger jet. They were finally on their way to the staging area for the North Korea op. Six months of intensive planning, training, logistics, and rehearsals – all to infiltrate their hybrid team into the world's last Stalinist police state.

North Korea had already gone nuclear while the world stood and stared. They had even been involved in nuclear proliferation, supplying Pakistan and Iran with technology and materials. But now they had been found to be manufacturing Plutonium-239, in one of their existing fission reactors. HEU, highly enriched uranium, had been one thing. It was the primary ingredient in the atomic bombs of which the North Koreans already had several.

But plutonium was something else entirely – it would allow them to produce hydrogen bombs, orders of magnitude more destructive than what they already had.

The U.S. and UK had decided that could not be allowed to happen.

By this point in time, the strange pandemic, the one that made its victims dazed and violent, that had them turning on and attacking medical personnel, friends, loved ones… had begun to filter through the news. It had just started to get the attention of the world's medical authorities, not to mention cause paranoia amongst travelers. The ever-present white face masks of the bird flu and swine flu days made a major comeback.

But no one yet knew what they were really dealing

with.

So Alpha team's mission had proceeded on schedule. There would always be pandemics. But loose H-bombs could spell the end of civilization as humanity knew it.

The RAF plane was a small one, with only thirty seats, so when it turned on a dime, everyone on board could feel the lurch. Ali and Pope exchanged looks across the tiny table. Captain Ainsley came in from the forward compartment.

The seven other operators, and the dozen support personnel, turned to face him.

"We're standing down," he said. Everyone at this level was far too professional to grouse. They just took it in. Ali's first thought was that it must be something to do with the pandemic. But she was wrong. The captain visibly swallowed a lump in his throat.

"Two BA triple-sevens have just gone down on approach to Heathrow. One crashed into a populated area just outside of London, in Slough. The other ditched in the Channel."

There was a small reaction to this, an intake of breath, a ripple of shock throughout the cabin. The age of terror was back – it had actually never left. But it seemed like too many threats at once now. Too much to take in, never mind to take on.

"All incoming flights to the UK have been diverted, all those scheduled going out canceled. As a military transport, we're just getting in under the ban. Our plan is to RTB and regroup there. I don't know what the status of our mission is now. We may be re-tasked."

It turned out that the terror plot had actually been against a half-dozen civilian aircraft, with multiple terrorist cells that needed to be taken down. The total air ban in the UK stretched out to over a week. The tightened security also slowed train and ferry traffic to a trickle.

What no one at the time could have known was that these terrorist attacks of 11/11, coming too late in the day ever to be really infamous, ultimately saved Britain. By cutting off all long-haul air travel and immigration into the country, just at the most critical time, and by sheer luck, they also cut off the most rapid method by which the virus spread.

In the few days that followed, the plague reached a global tipping point – much more rapidly than anyone could have predicted. The majority of victims went down before they even had any idea what was going on. By the time the horrible truth started to get out, the dead outnumbered the living. And the downfall of mankind was more or less a foregone conclusion by then.

The ban on air travel, and the reduced ground travel, didn't prevent the virus getting into Britain. It just gave them an indispensable few extra days to work out what the hell was going down – and to hunker down against it.

Many infected came in on trains and ferries. But by that time, most Britons were locked up in their homes, wearing thick clothing and carrying weapons when they went out. Thus the virus never reached that tipping point in the British Isles. The military was able to squash the biggest outbreaks, impose martial law in the cities, and hunt the small packs of zombies that roamed the countryside.

And when the final fall started to come, when the panic drove the waves of refugees toward Britain, both the healthy and the infected, with the millions of dead pushing behind them… the UK just kept the steel shutters locked down. And reinforced the hell out of them.

Ali for one knew that people will take to the streets and riot after three days without food – which meant we were all nine meals away from anarchy. But now she, and the whole world, had seen it play out in real time. Since then, Ali hadn't swapped two words with any child in the ZA without recalling that chilling exchange from the film *Aliens*: "My mommy always said there were no monsters – no real ones… Why do they tell little kids that?" "Most of the time it's true."

What a crapsack world we've inherited… she thought bitterly.

* * *

Without quite realizing how she got there, Ali found she had the edge of her sword pressed up against Pope's throat – and the man himself pressed into the corner of the dojo, bleeding from some kind of light head wound, which dripped from under his helmet and face guard.

"Your point," he said, breathing smoothly but deeply. "Nice one."

Tier-1 guys tended not to cry foul. And they definitely didn't complain.

Ali withdrew her sword with a start, and gave her brother operator a hand up.

She made a mental note to reserve her angst and rage for the dead.

NEVER WATCH THE NEWS

The problem with an armed camp, Homer thought to himself, is not the enemy outside the gates. It's the people inside – and never being able to get away from them. Of course, on those occasions when he had been posted to an ocean-going vessel, he had got used to being crammed in belowdecks. But there was still always somewhere to escape to – a deserted stretch of gangway abeam… the forecastle on the night watch…

And better yet, back on land in Coronado, a headland or spit of sand at ebb tide could be its own private vault of Heaven.

But here… well, the nearby Malvern Hills of Herefordshire called to him, from so very close outside the fortified walls. But there was no going out there. Not for a nice evening stroll, anyway. But Homer was sure he could feel God's presence out there. Even amidst all this death.

He was actually alone now, but not the right kind of alone. He decided to take a turn around the base. Just twenty minutes for himself. Then he'd start making himself useful again. There was always so much that needed doing. Idle time was a luxury lost to this world. As was luxury itself, when he thought about it.

"*…through all the fleeting life which God has given you in this world, for this is what you are meant to get out of your life of* *toil under the sun.*" The writer of Ecclesiastes wouldn't have been surprised by any of this, he figured.

No sooner had Homer slipped the flap of his billet than he was spotted and hailed. "Hey, Homer, mate, all right?" The British were lovely people, and stalwart as hell. But where's all this "I keep myself to myself" ethos Homer had heard about? Not in the military, that's for sure.

He threw a friendly wave and veered off. His new route took him past the Intel Shack, where he remembered getting his very first briefings – within minutes of hitting the ground, actually. Meeting the other Tier-1 guys, from units scattered across the English-speaking world. He'd known right away that it was going to be one hell of a team – like nothing that had ever operated before. No one but the supremely elite could make that mission happen. And that was when they all thought nothing could be more dangerous or urgent than North Korean nukes. Those ideas they used to have about Armageddon, the way the End of Days would come…

Before long, Homer found himself at the closest thing this place had to a forecastle – underneath the guard tower at the far northwest corner, where the two fortified walls met. He huddled up in the dark beneath it, about as alone as he was going to get. At his back, the dead world spread out into the gloom. And before him he could now make out much of the little kingdom that the survivors had carved out for themselves. He let his mind wander back.

* * *

It was a couple of months after those first onsite briefings, when they were well into their rehearsals, that they started getting the very first reports – first via intel, then on the news. Some new virus out of the interior of Africa. The reports were conflicting. Some victims it was said to kill. Others it made crazy. Stories of the sick getting delirious, and then violent – attacking medical personnel, or loved ones. Like some weird strain of rabies – which had always ticked over in the dark corners of the saddest continent, Africa. Homer remembered being curious, and quizzing one of the medical officers – a surgeon, and a colonel.

"Is it like Ebola? Marburg? Should we be worried?"

"I don't think it's like Ebola."

"Some other kind of hemorrhagic fever?"

The medical officer paused heavily, not looking like he was enjoying this. "It might be related – people have been coming in bleeding out." He paused again. "But mostly from their mouths."

But Homer knew how it was with the nightly news – always happening somewhere else. And happening to the less fortunate. This world, this Middle Kingdom, this stopping over place, was always producing new horrors. The operators still had their work. And Homer had his family.

"*Come, eat your food with joy and drink your wine with a glad heart… enjoy life with the woman you love, through all the fleeting life which God has given you in this world…*"

* * *

Something loomed out of the shadows and into Homer's reverie. Before he was even aware of it, he'd drawn his SIG 226, thumbed the hammer back, and sighted in. Behind and just above his three-dot tritium night sights there was now a face – a living one, and familiar.

"Exactly the same twitchy motherfucker I remember. Stand down, brother."

"Mikey? Good Lord."

"Yeah, Homer – at your service. They told me you might be out here. In the shadows."

The newcomer stepped into the deeper shadow under the guard tower and pulled Homer into a hug that was equally heartfelt and lung-crushing. Homer and Mikey had served together for two years with SEAL Team 3 – in Coronado, and also off in much more dangerous places. Homer knew the man, and damn well respected him. They had parted company when Homer left for Team Six (or DEVGRU, as they were known, the Naval Special Warfare Development Group) – which can be a bit of a black hole, swallowing an operator and his whole former life, and immersing his every waking moment in the job.

Homer pushed Mikey back out to arm's length and looked into his soulful brown eyes. "Not only alive and still in this world. But in the UK! At Hereford! How?"

Mikey let out a long, slow breath. "A few months before it all came down. I was posted to a surface vessel – the *Arleigh Burke* herself. With a half-platoon, eight

SEALs." The Arleigh Burke was the lead ship for the whole Arleigh-Burke class of Aegis guided missile destroyers, some of the meanest warships in human history.

"We were doing counterproliferation and interdiction work, right at the seam of the Pacific and Indian Oceans. VBSS, that kind of thing." Visiting, boarding, searching, and seizing ships suspected of carrying contraband was a classic SEAL mission, one for which they were supremely qualified. Any frogman would be happy doing it. Particularly after the mountains and deserts, and the bloody losses, of Afghanistan and Iraq.

"And after the fall?" Homer asked.

"Man. We were like the goddamned Ancient Mariner." He winced slightly, remembering Homer's faith, which had never been a secret, but he'd had to be pretty easygoing about it – most sailors swear like, well, sailors. "Sorry, man. Pardon my blasphemy. Anyway, we were roaming the oceans, trying port after overseas port. Just making a living as far as fuel and supplies went. Some places we could dock, some we couldn't. Some were abandoned by the living – but we could fight our way into."

"And your orders?"

"At first, it was just 'Hold station' or 'Continue patrol' or 'Stand by'. Then, nothing, of course. Finally we got news that overseas American military personnel, every branch, by every conceivable conveyance, were making their way to England. That there were living people there. Something like civilization left. And it's true."

It was true. Something north of 30,000 American servicemen and women had fought their way to safety there. Now they fought for everyone.

"Why'd it take you so long?"

He shook his head. "We had a few adventures along the way. Anyway, it wasn't quite that long. We've been docked at Southampton these last three months. Been going out on milk runs, moving supplies from one place to another. Plus the odd search and salvage. But it was only last week that somebody with stars on his shoulders figured out our old boat had a fully-kitted SEAL team onboard. They put two and two together – or, rather, put us eight and however many badasses you've got here together. Doing whatever kinds of jobs you're doing."

Homer smiled. "They won't have told you much yet, I guess."

"We're getting briefed in the morning. And going out in the afternoon. No time wasted."

Homer squinted slightly at his old friend, concerned. "Got a sense of what you're going to be getting into out there?"

Mikey chuckled. "That's the whole point of the years of ballbreaking SEAL training, right? So we'll be ready even for the things we aren't ready for. Especially them."

"Good enough."

Mikey sensed Homer's unease, though, and shifted slightly. "What's your thinking, brother?"

Homer pivoted, a little evasively, regarding the blackness outside the wire. He let out a long breath. "Honestly?"

"You know how to be anything else?"

Homer laughed once, not very mirthfully. He put his hands on his hips. There was an orange glow out in the hills. He didn't know where it came from. He turned again and locked steady gazes with his old friend.

"You know, when it all started I honestly thought the Rapture was here – not some freakshow zombie apocalypse. And all I could think of, for the longest time, was, Why am I still here? Why do I have to get my gun in the fight, in the last battle between Heaven and Hell, while everyone else is sitting pretty in Heaven? I've done my service for God and man. Don't I get to go to Heaven?"

Mikey reached out and put his hand on Homer's shoulder.

"But you know what worries me the most? It isn't who will win. It isn't what's going to happen to me, or to any of us. It isn't even whether any of this will ever be over." Homer looked back in his friend's kind face. "It's, which side am I fighting for? Am I fighting for God? Am I fighting for the good of all? Or am I one of the bad guys? Did you ever consider that we might just be the evil ones? And those things out there are God's cleaners?"

He hadn't been able to tell anyone else this, all this time.

And Mikey knew just what he was talking about. He hardly had to say it.

The SEAL Brotherhood – stronger than death, stronger than the end of the world.

THE STREETS HAVE NO NAME

Wesley swerved the car sharply to the right, missing the girl by just a few inches. She fell backwards, buffeted by the strong breeze and reeling from the surprise of it. She had appeared from nowhere in the mist – and, from her perspective, so had the car. It now barreled across the road and smashed into an abandoned vehicle, which sat across from the house that the girl and her parents had been given when they arrived two weeks earlier.

She saw the man in the passenger seat burst through the front window and roll across the pavement. The man in the driver's seat stayed put. The noise had been overpowering, like nothing she had ever heard – first the screeching of brakes that pierced her eardrums, and then the loud crash as the car collided with the other. Windows exploded outwards and metal crumpled as the front end of the moving vehicle compacted to two thirds of its original length.

"Oh, God!" It was her father's voice, from behind her. He had seen the whole incident while trying to open the driver's door on the other side of their own car. The girl, Alison, leapt to her feet and ran to him. He held her tightly.

"Mary, get out here!" he yelled. "There's been an accident."

"I'm sorry, Daddy," Alison sobbed, her whole body

shaking with fear. "I didn't see it."

"It's not your fault." His heart was beating double-time as the dread thought of what could have just happened dawned on him. He had sent his daughter out to get into the car. They had been told to evacuate ASAP to the harbor zone.

Mary rushed out of the house with their other daughter – two-year-old Madison – in one arm, and a backpack filled with a few possessions that she couldn't leave behind slung over her shoulder. "What happened?" she stammered as she saw the wreck and devastation on the other side of the road.

"No time," barked her husband, Ruben, as he threw the carryall full of supplies onto the back seat. "Get the kids in the car. I'll see if I can help them. Ali, get in the car, sweetheart." The eight-year-old sobbed as she jumped into the back seat, closed the door, and buckled up. Ruben knew that she would be distraught after this, but he also knew that she was a tough one, and the two passengers in the crashed car might need his help urgently.

He rushed over the road, and around the car to the driver's side, hoping not to see some gory mess that had once been human. He kept his hand on the gun at his waist just in case he needed to stop them from turning. But the driver was still conscious and rubbing his head.

"Are you okay, mate?" he asked.

"I think so," said Wesley. His head was swimming, and he shook it, trying to regather his thoughts. Then he remembered the last few moments. The girl's eyes bright in the headlights. The swerving and the crash. "Is she okay? I didn't hit her, did I?"

"She's fine. Are you injured?"

Wesley sighed with relief and then moved his legs, pushing open the now bent car door and stumbling onto the pavement. He steadied himself against the side of the vehicle as his brain tried to catch up with all the chaos. Then his instincts clicked and he reached in and grabbed the shotgun from the floor and checked that the handgun was still in his belt.

"Yeah. I'm okay. Look, you need to get the hell out of here, and fast. The dead are on the way. You have maybe a few minutes. Crap. Where did the soldier go?" He spun around, noticing the broken front window for the first time. "Fuck."

"I'm good," called a voice from a few yards away. "Well, nearly."

Wesley spun around again, to see the man lifting himself up using the side of the parked vehicle they had destroyed, a red convertible.

"Shoulder hurts pretty bad and my ankle is even more screwed. But I won't need to be put down just yet."

Ruben's jaw dropped.

"You flew out of the car. How the hell did…?"

The soldier leaned down, picked up his helmet and showed them the dent in the top.

"It probably saved my life," he said, dropping it to the ground. "And the body armor helps."

"Rube, we need to go," called Mary from the car.

Wesley looked up the road. Dark figures were now

stumbling through the shadows, and deep guttural moaning echoed down the street. Ruben was also staring at them.

"Is that what I think it is?"

"Yes. Now go," said Wesley. "Get the hell out and don't stop 'til you've gone through a line of squaddies. They're on their way."

Gunfire erupted from a few feet away. The soldier was already back to work. The nearest shadow in the mist fell backwards and didn't get back up.

"Are there many other people near here?" Wesley called to Ruben as the man ran to his car.

"Yes," he yelled, trying to shout over an automatic weapon that was now lighting up the whole street. "Lots on this street and the junction down the road. They would all have got the call."

"The call?"

"CentCom called and told us to evacuate immediately."

Even as Ruben finished speaking, the doors of houses were opening, spilling out the families that had lived in them for only a few weeks. Most of them rushed straight to cars and started bundling children and possessions inside, jumping in, and firing up engines. Wesley realized that these people lived their lives this way – frontier families used to working in the border towns near places that were quarantined. They were civilian scavengers, people who the government used to retrieve supplies from abandoned towns across the country or reclaim an urban location that those in charge deemed useful. They were ready to move out at any moment.

A man ran out of the building next door and stopped dead, backing away from the soldier as he fired round after round into the zombies that now appeared in greater numbers. Wesley had also taken up a position across the road, behind another rusted car. This one already had broken windows and looked as though it had been sitting there since the apocalypse began.

"My car," the man mumbled. "It's trashed."

The soldier stopped firing for a moment. No more soulless in view.

"You seriously chose an open-top car?" he asked.

"It was what was there and no one needed it. Shit, I have to get out of here." The man took off at a run down the street away from them, pushing and shoving his way past the families that thronged the road, and not appearing to give a damn who was in his way.

"Selfish fucking idiot," cursed the soldier. He glanced over at Wesley, who was swapping out his handgun magazine.

"How many rounds you got left?"

"About thirty, I think," replied Wesley, his voice barely audible over the noise of people and cars rushing away from them.

"Take these," he said, and pulled two magazines from his belt. Even from ten meters, he recognized the same model as his own sidearm, a SIG P226, standard British Army issue. He dashed across the road and dropped the mags on the bonnet of the car before Wesley.

"Cheers."

"No problem, mate. Heads up. Here they come again. Better make those count. What is your name, anyway? If I'm going to die standing next to you I'd like to know."

"Wesley. Andrew Wesley."

The soldier nodded. "Martin. Captain James Martin. Pleased to meet you."

They stood next to each other, staring into the mist as the next wave of walking dead appeared. There were not merely fifty as he had suspected, and when they surged into view even Captain Martin's heart skipped a beat. There must have been one hell of a breakout through the tunnel, for now the whole street heaved with them. Hundreds of the creatures pushed and shoved each other as they shambled through the streets. The howls and moans intensified as the ones at the front spotted the soldier and the security guard standing waiting for them.

Wesley glanced behind him. Cars were pulling away nearby, but they weren't moving fast enough. Most of the civilians were making a good escape but they were queued up. The terrified eyes of a small child stared back at him from the rear screen of the nearest car.

"We have to hold them," shouted Martin as he opened fire.

Wesley spun back to see the mass of zombies clawing their way down the street, lifted his pistol and took careful aim at the nearest. "Absolutely," he said. He knew that the two of them would never be able to stop all of the creatures. There were just too many. They didn't have enough bullets and the dead were coming too fast and too thick, but he was going to make damn sure those frightened eyes that stared back at him from the window of the rearmost car wouldn't close forever.

The two guns echoed down the street, and for the first time in his life Wesley felt a surge of hope. Not for himself, but for the possibility of redeeming himself for his failure to find Amarie. He thought of her now as the mass of raging limbs and bloodshot eyes surged down the street toward them. He thought of her long hair and her smile. How they had laughed until they nearly cried that first evening that he had met her in the bar in Paris.

I expect I'll be with you soon, he thought. He had never been a religious man. But right then, just when he knew that his end was rapidly rushing toward him, he felt something stir. A calmness that he had never felt before flooded his body. Those fearful eyes of the child in the car flashed in front of him. *This is what I was meant to do*, he thought.

"Pray, let me hold," he muttered under his breath and squeezed the trigger again.

Someone somewhere answered.

One moment there were but two guns blasting their noise into the night sky, and the next moment they were answered by many. Wesley almost felt the air move around him and tried not to take his eyes off his task as other figures appeared in his peripheral vision and more guns blazed at the horde. First one, then two, then dozens.

The British Army was here.

And the dead began to fall.

FORLORN HOPE

"Sarge. Wake up, man."

Handon came awake instantly. Sleepyheads didn't make it into Delta. And the drowsy were all dead now anyway. He followed Pope out of his billet into the dark – it was still a good two hours before dawn – and the two threaded the alleys of Hereford to the Tactical Operations Center (TOC). There, they found a full house: commo guys, aviation desk, tactical, ops, medical, everyone. Back in the days of the world, the TOC would hum all night – night missions were all their missions. Now, usually, people slept. No one went out at night.

"What's up?" Handon approached Captain Ainsley, who was hunched over a console with the Colonel, as well a couple of ops desk guys.

"The new SEAL Team," Ainsley said, not looking up. "They've got into a spot of trouble."

Handon knew about the new SEALS. Homer had briefed him.

"Who are they out with?"

Ainsley paused a beat. "Just the eight of them. A Stealth Hawk crew inserted them."

The TOC speakers were even now playing the radio traffic from the mission command net. Handon and Pope could hear the TOC-side mission commander going back and forth with the SEAL team on the ground.

"Mud Snake Six, interrogative: can you update me on your casualty status, over."

The channel squelched as someone on the ground team keyed his mic. "*Hotel X, Mud Snake, wait one.*" Behind the SEAL's voice came the sound of rapid firing, one or more people spitting out curses – and the now totally unmistakable moaning of frenzied dead. Ones that were riled up, hungry, and attacking *en masse.*

Pope and Handon shared a look. It said, *This ain't good.*

"Where?" Handon asked.

"Calais," Ainsley said, still not looking up from a digital multi-map display.

"Mission objective?"

Ainsley looked over at the Colonel, who frowned, paused, then finally answered himself. "They're checking the fortifications at the Frog end of the Channel Tunnel."

"At *night*?"

"It was priority highest. And their skipper volunteered them. All of them volunteered."

"Of course they volunteered," Handon said. "They're fucking SEALs. There are no words for 'negative' in their vocabulary. But they've been in theater for about five minutes."

Ainsley sighed. "They've been fighting the dead for two years, just like the rest of us."

The Colonel removed a headset and laid it on the console. "Or so they said."

The radio traffic was going from bad to worse. From the chatter around the TOC, Handon worked out that the SEALs had been in a running urban battle for the worst part of an hour – and hadn't yet been able to fight their way to an extraction point. And that they'd also taken casualties – dead or bit, or both.

Handon straightened up. "Let me get this straight – you sent a bunch of FNGs out on a mission over the water, *at night*, and *by themselves*. And now they're getting eaten and everybody's all surprised?"

The men at the desk suddenly realized that someone was standing behind them. It was Homer. And he was completely kitted out and tooled up – weapons, assault suit, mags, the works. The Colonel turned to face him. "Appreciate your initiative, Master Chief. But stand down. Alpha's not going out into that. Not now, anyway." He didn't elaborate. It probably meant Alpha had already been tasked for a new save-the-world mission. They generally were.

With Handon, Ainsley, Pope, and the Colonel watching, Homer didn't speak. He just gave them that look. Pretty much everyone knew it meant he was going to Calais if he had to backstroke it. He turned on his heel and marched out.

"Just four men," Ainsley said to the Colonel. In his heart, he honestly didn't know how he was going to stop Homer either. All he could do was go with him. "We'll be careful."

"Jesus H. Tapdancing Christ," the Colonel said, putting his palm to his face. *Why had command become such a fluid concept since the world ended?* He waved his hand tiredly. "Go."

The three Alpha men jogged out. In eight minutes they were on a rotors-turning helo with their weapons and go-bags. They'd suit up in the air.

* * *

This time their ride wasn't a Stealth Hawk, but a Sikorsky S-97 Raider. With twin coaxial main rotors, two vertical stabilizers, and a pusher propeller, it had a theoretical top speed of 299mph – making the Raider the fastest military or civilian helicopter in the history of the world. (And, most likely, its future, too.) It was also a prototype, and the only one flying.

Ainsley, Handon, Pope, and Homer sat in the near-black cabin pulling on their assault suits, face shields, load-bearing vests, radios, pouches, grenades, and other combat load. The sky was still dark purple, with a little orange on the horizon in the east. Finally, the four charged their weapons, monitored radio traffic – and waited, as the bird blasted low through the sky.

Well, Handon thought to himself, *if we get killed or turned, it's only half the team, anyway*. They used to say that death walked with SOF guys every day. Now that was so literal it was beyond parody. The real difference was that dying was no longer merely accepted as a price that might have to be paid. Sometimes it was relished as a possible escape. The world was fucked, and didn't look like getting particularly better anytime soon. Santayana had said, "That life is worth living is the most necessary of assumptions and, were it not assumed, the most impossible of conclusions." But it was getting harder to assume all the time.

Oh, well, Handon thought to himself. He'd do what he'd always done – Ranger on. Maybe the world would take care of itself. Though he doubted it.

He looked over to Homer. The man looked untroubled as always. A little more determined perhaps. Handon watched him unconsciously rub the gold crucifix that always hung around his neck. The guy's faith really was a sword and a shield. Handon truly envied him that. After the undead, the greatest danger to survival in the ZA was doubt, loss of faith. When hope is all you've got, doubt is a lethal and implacable foe – always surging, never going down for good.

Handon moved over and hunkered down beside Ainsley, who pulled out a ruggedized tablet device. The two of them reviewed maps and drone video of the target area. They had an insertion to plan. Ideally, they'd plan it in some way that wouldn't get them as jammed up as the SEALs were. Or maybe at least not as quickly. You can't help anyone when you're dead.

And you're a positive menace when you're undead.

* * *

By the time they got the five-minute warning in the air, the TOC had lost comms with the SEALs completely. Everyone knew what this probably meant. But everyone also knew enough not to jump to conclusions. Loss of radio contact wasn't the same as death, or infection. Radio comms are fiddly, and they get wedged for all kinds of reasons. Wedged comms are more often the *cause* of getting killed, than the result.

Anyway, the rescue force had come too far to turn back now.

The red combat lights flashed twice – two minutes.

The helo flared down into a flat area in the dark and shadowed western ruins of Calais, near the Channel Tunnel entrance. Scattered debris was the only obstruction to their insertion. This bird was a hell of a lot louder than their normal ride, though, so the only tactic to play here was to come in low and fast, kiss the ground just long enough for the four operators to pile out and take off, and then for the bird and the soldiers to part ways fast.

By the time the Raider was zooming out to its stand-off marker offshore, the four-man team, back and shoulder muscles hunched up, rifles held expertly at the shoulder, moving fluidly and as a single organism, had slithered out of the open landing area and into the maze of abandoned buildings and the ruins and detritus of fallen Europe.

Correction: the buildings were abandoned only by the living. The dead still lived there. A mass of them were already making their way to the LZ, drawn by the fading noise of the helo. But by then the operators had gone.

As long as they kept quiet and moved with speed and perfect economy, they could, with a little luck, stay out of contact. At the very least, they'd avoid a firefight, and getting jammed up in a nexus of hungry dead bastards. The odd one or two, sometimes even the faster Romeos, stumbled upon and surprised, were never a problem. They could easily be dispatched with melee weapons.

Homer took point, moving like a man on a mission. Out front, not even slowing, he quietly topped three undead in the first minute of their movement – just wrong place, wrong time dead guys. Unusually amongst the operators, Homer eschewed the Samurai swords, carrying instead a boarding axe – an old pirate standby, like a long-handled tomahawk. Its bladed edge could cleave or remove heads; and the spike tip opposite it, when deployed expertly, could puncture a brainstem right through an eye socket.

A handful of dead went down without ever quite waking up.

They had just got between Homer and his brother SEALs.

* * *

The moving map GPS on Ainsley's heads-up display told them they were 200 meters from the location of the SEAL team's radio transponder. The captain touched Homer's shoulder, and communicated the distance. Almost everything was touch and hand signals on live ops. Chatter cost lives.

The team, which had fanned out somewhat, slithered back into a tight line, and slipped into the dark entrance of the ruined building next door. All four paused to pull down their NVGs (night vision goggles) from their helmet mounts. By now, there was a little thin light outside. But the interior of this building would be much darker – and they wouldn't dare turn on the lights even if they worked.

The four now executed their room-clearing drills as they made their way to the northwestern edge of the structure. As they hoped, sections of wall there had crumbled or been torn down. They paused at the edge of the adjacent structure for a full thirty seconds, to tune in to the new building. They didn't hear anything as they passed through the vestibule – but did soon after that, freezing in place while they tried to make it out.

Whatever it was, it was in the next room over. This was also pretty close to the location of the SEALs' transponder. (In the GPS-degraded era, with fewer satellites working less reliably, geo-location was a thornier problem.) The noise they heard could possibly have been whispering, or rustling. It could also have been shuffling, or feeding. This wasn't necessarily the death of hope – the transponder could have shaken loose. Also, the rescuers already knew the SEALs had casualties. They could still have survivors.

Homer dictated the hard entry parameters with hand signs, and the other three stacked up behind him. On the count, they spilled into the room, splashing it with the IR lights mounted on their weapons – and making the room bright as day through their NVGs.

A SEAL in full assault kit knelt in the corner, over the prone form of another. Homer's heart leapt with hope – that stupid, intransigent hope – thinking it was a medic working on a wounded SEAL. The "medic" turned around instantly.

And then issued a deep, hissing groan from between blue lips.

"Mikey," Homer said flatly, flipping his NVGs up onto his head and staggering back.

The others saw that what used to be Mikey had two handfuls of his brother SEAL, which he resumed stuffing into his mouth. Handon grabbed Homer by the arm and hauled him back into the other room. Pope and Ainsley stayed inside to do what was necessary.

Later, Handon would say that he saw Homer's faith flicker out in that moment.

Whether there was still a smoldering ember, something that could be fanned back into a cleansing flame, would be determined in the next few days.

SECUNDA MORTEM

The reunited Alpha team, all eight operators, sat now in two ranks of chairs, in one of the USOC briefing rooms at Hereford. Ainsley, Handon, Homer, and Ali in the front; and Pope, Predator, Juice, and Henno jostling for space in the rear. Absent from this room, but also very present, were the eight SEAL team members who would never be coming back from their one trip outside the wire.

Standing at the front, before a large digital whiteboard, the Colonel shared a brief look with Handon. Neither repeated Handon's "keep this up and we're going to lose a team" line from the day before. But each knew the other was thinking it. Captain Ainsley, seated beside Handon, looked away.

The Colonel wasn't prone to big presentations or theatrics. So his opening line got the men's attention: "They're calling this one Operation Secunda Mortem." His emotionless ice-blue eyes scanned the faces in the room. "And they think it might be the big one."

The Colonel picked up a folder of papers and put his narrow ass on the desk in its place. "The pointy heads in Edinburgh have gone through the data you pulled out of Merck in Germany. The bad news is, it doesn't look like Merck had shit. No breakthroughs, nothing promising in either therapeutics or vaccine research. As you already know, this bug is a double-stranded RNA virus, and a complete cocksucker. It took down humanity before we even made a dent in it."

He flipped open the sheaf of papers to the first page. "So, Merck didn't have shit themselves – but they did have some email that makes for a helluva read. As you'll also know, all the labs and biotechs were collaborating like crazy sons of bitches, before the lights went out. IP protection went out the window when everyone's ass was on the line. So a couple of scientists at Merck had some incoming mail – from an outfit that wasn't even on our radar before today…"

He paused to pull a rectangular pair of reading glasses out of his shirt pocket, and refocused on the page. "NeuraDyne Neurosciences was, and I quote, 'a specialty biopharmaceutical company focused on the development, manufacturing, sales, and marketing of bespoke biopharmalogics, as well as game-changing neuroscientific research.'" He looked back up to room. "Big on brain drugs. Breakthrough, fourth-gen antidepressants. Alzheimers. Behavioral genetics and molecular and cellular neuroscience."

Juice raised one of his ham-sized hands. "How come we hadn't heard of 'em before now?"

"Biggest names got attention first. And this one is definitely a boutique outfit. Like fifteen guys in a white room."

Ainsley started to look impatient. "What does the email say?"

The Colonel held his gaze for a bit, then looked back to his papers. "Says the team there had worked out a method of dsRNA interference – one that suppresses a critical gene in the virus. And as a result selectively induces apoptosis in any cells containing the viral dsRNA."

"Apoptosis," echoed Juice. "Cell suicide."

"An ice cream cone for the big bearded man," the Colonel said, tapping his pen. "They also claimed it rapidly kills infected cells without harming healthy, uninfected cells."

"We've heard this kind of big talk before," said Juice. "Does their shit work?"

"They claim it had demonstrated effect in multi-celled bacteria, mice – and chimps."

This earned a couple of respectful whistles. Chimps share 98% of DNA with humans.

"So then we're looking at a cure," Captain Ainsley said.

The Colonel shook his head. "Only for those the virus hasn't killed yet. More of an antidote – if you administer it quickly enough. But useless on the reanimated. Too late after it's killed you."

"As J.B. Watson said," Ali intoned, "'When you're dead, you're all dead.'"

Juice snorted. "J.B. Watson's out there walking around somewhere."

"*Touché.*"

"But more fucking importantly," said the Colonel, looking impatient, as he often did with his precocious polymath commandos, "they claim their dsRNA-i technique can also be used in vaccine development. And that they were in the ballpark of making it work."

A few beats of silence filled the room. An antidote

would mean hope for the recently infected. But a working vaccine would be a way back for humanity. Salvation.

"Well let's go get it, then," said Handon. "Where?"

The Colonel cleared his throat and shuffled his papers again.

* * *

"Fugly Chi-town," said Pope in a goofy voice.

"Da Bears," said Juice, in another, looking off into a dark corner.

The six non-command Alpha team members had been ejected from the briefing room, and were now piled into one of their quad billets.

"Fucking Chicago? Seriously?" Predator asked rhetorically.

"As in Chicago, Illinois, USA?" asked Henno. He'd obviously heard of it. He just didn't believe it.

Despite their joking, no one in Alpha was really finding any of this funny. It was nervous tension, gallows humor. Though Pope looked dead-level and composed as always. "A U.S. mission would be an incredible stretch of our capabilities and logistics."

"Bloody suicide mission, more like," said Henno.

"You lose it out there," added Pred, "you're in a world of hurt."

No one had heard a peep out of North America for over a year. It was assumed to be wall-to-wall corpses, from sea to shining sea. Even worse than fallen Europe. An enormous frontier country of the dead.

"Ain't no Quick Reaction Force on *that* continent," said Juice. "Ain't no humans."

"We don't know that," said Ali in measured tones. "There could still be isolated pockets of survivors."

Juice gave her a look. "What's the last new episode of *Mad Men* you've seen broadcast?"

"Point taken." Ali looked down sadly. "And it's not just in the middle of the continent. It's also inside a city of three million people. Three million dead people."

All of the Alpha operators knew the score. Each of them had fought numerous urban battles, both before and after the end of civilization. From engagements going back to Mogadishu, to Beirut, and even before, they knew that urban areas were bad fucking news. Time, personnel, resources – such as ammo, radio batteries, and water – cities had a way of burning through them all – usually *much* more quickly than expected.

Before the fall, major cities had been the scenes of epic set-piece battles between the living and the dead – and also amongst the living, as survivors battled one another for dwindling resources, access to which meant continued survival. So a city also presented the additional danger of friendly fire from any remnants of the living. If they'd survived this long, they hadn't done so by asking questions first and shooting later.

Cities were also the perfect setting for industrial accidents, raging fires, toxic spills, navigational snafus (anyone remember "the lost convoy" from *Black Hawk Down*?)… and that was aside from the simple goddamned population density. That alone virtually assured any visitors of a full-tilt rollicking Zombie Festival immediately upon arrival.

If you lost your mobility or initiative in a city, if you got in trouble or bogged down, you'd generally find yourself holed up in some large structure, barricaded in. And the thing about zombies is that once they are onto you, they just *will not go away*. You're now in a siege, one of unlimited duration. And in a siege, the moans of the besiegers will bring more besiegers. And the newcomers never leave either. So you could theoretically trigger some kind of zombie singularity – and find yourself at the center of a mass of *all the zombies on that entire continent.*

And no matter how high your walls, or how many levels above the street you've barricaded… given enough Zulus, they will eventually climb on top of one another until they've surmounted whatever it is you've constructed.

And even if that didn't happen, and even if you had supplies for a long siege… you could still be hunkered down in your fortress, feeling nice and safe – and then a fire breaks out. Enjoy your fire drill. Your rendezvous and evacuation point is down there, on the corner of Dead Guy Ave and You're Fucked Street.

A somewhat stunned silence had now descended over the team.

"And what's up with the op designation?" Predator said, finally. "Secunda Mortem? I opted out of Latin at Ranger School, but I'm pretty sure mortem means death."

Homer looked up. He hadn't spoken until now.

"Secunda mortem – second death." He looked back down to where he held his crucifix before him, pressed between his palms. "It's a Biblical reference, Christian resurrection theology. 'Blessed and holy is he who has part in the first resurrection. Over such, the second death has no power, but they will be priests of God and of Christ, and will reign with him a thousand years.'" He looked up into the room again. "Revelations, verse twenty, chapter six."

Predator snorted and stood. "I've gotta take a shit."

"Sounds like a plan," said Juice, rising and following him out.

* * *

Ainsley, Handon, and the Colonel now sat in the latter's office in the dim light. They were going over the high-level tactical options that had been produced by the planning staff so far.

"…Yeah, we could insert by air direct from here," the Colonel said, leaning back in his chair. "We could just about pull off the logistics of the flight and the refueling. The problem is support."

"Sir?" Ainsley said.

"Once you arrive in theater, you haven't fucking got any. Not a sweet rat's. Totally on your own. Now I know you Tier-1 guys have got a collective death wish. But being air-dropped, eight guys alone, into the middle of Zombie City U.S.A. might be too much for even you dubious sons of bitches."

"Okay, so then it's a sea voyage," said Handon.

"On what? Frigate? Destroyer?"

The Colonel didn't answer. Handon tried, "Catamaran?" He didn't know if the *Waterworld* reference would be lost on the others.

The Colonel tapped his pen. "Carrier."

"There are no carriers," Handon said.

The Colonel tapped his pen once. "Carrier strike group."

"Come on."

"Carrier Strike Group Six. The USS *John F. Kennedy*."

Handon squinted unbelievingly at the Colonel. "The *Kennedy*'s still floating. Seriously?"

"Seriously. But it's been need-to-know until now." The Colonel spared a look at the mission status board mounted on his wall, cables snaking to the floor. "Basically, some people thought that it might become Noah's freaking Ark – the last bastion of the living on Earth. Hasn't come to that yet. But she'll make a hell of a transatlantic cruise liner. Not to mention a hell of a forward operating base for your mission. About half her support ships are still floating, too."

"Jesus," said Ainsley.

"Just so," said the Colonel. "This whole goat rodeo may prove to be an impossible job. Not one of you hardcases may be coming back. But if there's any possibility of a cure, we've got no choice but to do it. Unless you've been sitting on a vaccine we don't know about."

Ainsley was thinking that it didn't matter very

much whether any of them came back. As long as they were able, somehow, to transmit back the secret to ending the plague.

The Colonel tilted his chair forward again, and spun around a map pack on the desk. "Okay, from the Atlantic coast to Chicago is too long a stretch for a helo insert, and we don't need you going in there all noisy and waking the dead, anyway." There was evidence that the dead went dormant when all prey in their region had been devoured. That when the last survivors went down, the undead world went quiet.

"So we're thinking if you do a HAHO jump, the aircraft won't even need to overfly the city... You parachute in on the prevailing winds off of Lake Michigan and land right about here..." The Colonel stubbed a spindly finger on the map. "This is just a very early, high-level concept. I'm gonna get us all in a room with joint mission planning staff before the sun goes down tonight."

The three men leaned in, and tried to imagine a way in.

And maybe a way out.

For everyone.

SEEING GHOSTS

Major Grews paced the floor, glancing at the radio operator every few seconds, his irritation growing by the minute.

"Hail him again," he said. "Get him on conference."

The comms officer tapped intently at his keyboard, his hands twitching nervously, but he kept it together. The major was always like this when things were tense. He could become insufferable if left waiting for too long.

Grews hated being stuck in an office, commanding from a chair. It just wasn't his style. Despite the fact that he'd been ordered to stand back and cease leading from the front, he still yearned to be out there. This was the first real outbreak he'd had the opportunity to handle, even if you counted the defensive year when Zulus walking out of the water regularly threatened the coasts. Since then, there had been small outbreaks across the country, but this was different. He glanced at the clock on the wall. Eight minutes. Eight minutes and that damn plane would level half of the town, along with everything he had worked to rebuild. And CentCom wouldn't give a damn if it meant losing a hundred infantry with it.

"I've got him, Major," said the radio operator. There was a pop and a high-pitched buzz as the microphone picked up the speakers and fed them back.

"Bordell?" asked the major.

"*Speaking, sir,*" answered a voice. The signal was weak and dulled by static.

"Status."

The was a cough from the other end. "*Situation is stable, sir,*" answered Bordell. "*There are a few still wandering around, but the main concentration has been destroyed.*"

Grews sighed heavily, feeling the flood of relief soothe his tattered nerves.

"Wait one, Bordell." Grews turned to the second network operator sitting across the room, waiting.

"Tell them to stand down."

"Yes, sir." The operator nodded and flicked up his headset microphone.

"Three Acres Actual orders stand down on the air mission."

The major turned back to his microphone.

"Bordell. You still there?"

"*Yes, sir. Still here.*"

"Good work, soldier. Many casualties?"

"*Only five of ours, sir. Civilian casualties total eight. But, unfortunately we lost everyone in the outgoing team that were in the hotel. Well, all but one.*"

"Christ. That many?"

"*Afraid so, sir. We have one survivor, a Captain Martin. Oh, and we also have one of the security detail from the tunnel.*"

The major closed his eyes, once more feeling the pressure building between them.

"Clean up, Bordell. Tell everyone good job."

"*Yes, sir.*"

"Bordell?"

"*Sir?*"

"Send me this captain and the security bloke. If they check out, of course. I still have to send out my quota tomorrow."

"*Sir.*"

"And get back here as soon as you can. We need to decide which squad is going instead. I have no choice on this. You know that, don't you?"

There was a pause at the other end.

"*Yes, sir.*"

"Grews out."

The line went dead. The major sat back in his chair and sighed. "Great. I have twenty-four hours to get another crew together or my arse is going to be in a sling."

"Sir?" called the second operator.

"Yes?"

"CentCom confirms stand down on the air mission."

"Good. Excellent."

"But sir…"

"What now?"

"They said to inform you to prepare for a full-scale sweep of the area and also for an excavation team on the tunnel."

"They what?"

"They are going to open the tunnel up, sir."

"Why? What the hell was their reason?"

"They didn't say, sir."

"Get me CentCom and ask for Colonel Mayes."

* * *

"*Andrew, I have no choice. I'm under orders just like you are.*"

"Bob. You know that opening the tunnel up is just crazy. We always knew it was a weak point."

"*Yes. I know that. But we didn't deal with it as we should have done. You also know that. We have to get it right this time. It also means that we can clear up what was left behind. Don't you want to do that?*"

Grews exhaled heavily. The refugees. He had tried to put them to the back of his mind over the last two years, but the video surveillance from the tunnel still haunted him. They had expected some kind of riot at the French end of the tunnel when the gates were closed. But a full-scale assault by civilians, one that completely overpowered the already dwindling French security forces, was much worse than they had anticipated.

Their civil affairs advisor had told them that most French refugees would spill out into the streets and the harbors. And that the south of England should be reinforced on the coast to stop a wave of unauthorized entries by boat. But it didn't happen that way – it happened much, much faster. The disease was already amongst those in the queues, in cars and vehicles backed up for miles.

So Grews had watched as the tunnel was overrun. He had watched as the mass of bodies pushed its way to the trains; trains that wouldn't be running regardless of what anyone did. No fuel. No power. No train. The last one out had already left. In some ways, Grews thought the terminal being overrun had been inevitable, even though he hadn't voiced the thought at the time.

Instead he had sat there, staring at the screens that showed views from the cameras dotted all over the complex. He had sat there watching, awestruck and, deep down, somewhat proud of those people who dared go into the tunnels themselves. He would never forget their determination and bravery, even when he had been forced to stop them. They couldn't get across the Channel by train, so they were damn well going to walk the whole way.

Or so it had seemed.

"They won't live more than a few weeks, even if they manage to stay in there and keep the dead from following them," the security operator had said. The man was bald and fat and was sweating profusely as he sat there flipping through the camera points as Grews had ordered him to.

"What?" asked Grews, his attention not really shifting from the screen.

"No food, unless they have some with them," continued the man, who looked like he could probably last a few months without food himself. "No water."

"Indeed," Grews had said, inwardly wishing the sweaty security guard would shut up, and damn sure he would swap him in an instant for any one of those poor folks running into the tunnel. If there was one thing Grews couldn't abide, it was overindulgence, and this guy was off the scale.

"Oh, hang on," the operator had said, and stopped switching cameras, shifting his hands to another terminal. He started flicking through lists on the screen, bright coloured lines flashing by, his eyes squinting above a deep frown.

Grews had leaned over, impolitely shunting the man's chair so that he could reach the controls. Twenty minutes of watching and he'd already figured out how to flip through the cameras. *Click. Click. Click.* There they were, right down the tunnel by at least two miles. What the hell were they doing? Were they smashing a door down? Some kind of access route? There were at least thirty of them that had made it this far. He couldn't tell the ages or genders. They were just shadowed figures in the dark, and some of them were small.

"Oh, God. They could."

Grews snapped his head from the screen.

"Could what?"

"When we cut the power and closed the gates. There was a train outbound. They left it on the tracks because there was no time to get it to the French terminal and turn it around."

"People? Are there people on it?"

"No. No, they would have evacuated. It's freight."

"What kind of freight? Why didn't they just drive it backwards?"

"Hundreds of tons of canned goods, heading for Belgium by the looks of it, and they couldn't reverse the engine. It's an old one, and no rear engine – and the front-engine type, to the best of my knowledge, wouldn't be able to push that many carriages."

"They just left the damn train on the lines, full of *food supplies*?"

"We were told to evacuate immediately."

Grews had watched on those cameras over the days that followed, even after the security guard had not turned up for work a few days later, and then not again after that. Grews made it personal somehow.

Further back down the tunnel, a long way behind those few outliers who were far more resourceful, thousands of living and dead were pouring into the tunnel. The living, mostly already infected, running from the dead that followed them. Grews had asked if they could send troops down before closing the tunnel, retrieve the few who had made it nearly all the way along the tunnel, had found the supply train, breached the maintenance corridors and disappeared from camera view… but the answer from on high had been no.

Close that tunnel, Grews had been told.

And then when they'd realized that the tunnel was filling with the dead, word came that it had been hit from the air. RAF bombers undid in just a few seconds what had taken decades of planning and construction. They tried to close the halfway gate, the one that had been put there for this very purpose, but the mechanism failed. The midway failsafe was closing, but it was closing at such a slow speed that it would take hours to shut, and by then the tunnel would be overrun.

The bomber hit the tunnel just three miles from Calais and the evacuation call had gone out to clear the area around the entrance. They had expected the floodwater to come spewing out at such a rate that hectares of countryside might become a marshland. Entire divisions were mobilised and sent to the area to prepare for a massive clean-up of thousands of dead and infected.

Grews had sat in front of those screens and watched, unable to do a single thing, as one by one the cameras blinked out from power loss. He watched as the water flooded different sections, and saw the mass of dead, and the undead, carried forward by the flood.

Thank God we collapsed the tunnel at this end. Or we would have just flushed half of the undead of France onto British soil.

It had been his idea. And it had been done in a hurry. A dozen charges just fifty feet inside had collapsed the tunnel. It might stop the water, he'd thought, and then maybe they could check the maintenance tunnel for those survivors. But orders from above came that the maintenance entrance was to be collapsed, too. No one was to come out.

But something had happened, and he had never found out what. Somehow the half of the tunnel on the English side hadn't flooded completely.

That had been nearly two years ago.

"*Andrew? You still there?*"

Grews snapped back to the present. "Yes, I'm here."

"Are you with me on this? You know that tunnel needs clearing out."

"Yes. I know."

"I'd get someone else on it, but you know how things are now. We're short of officers and men both, with this damn call-up mystery that no one is telling us about."

"I know. And I need to do this. You know that."

Bob did know. He had been Grews' direct superior then, even as he was now, and he'd been the one to decide that those refugees weren't getting out. What Bob didn't know was that Grews had seen occasional movements in the unflooded sections of tunnel at the English end even after many months, even after nearly a year, movements that were not always the lumbering and slow trudge of the dead. Sometimes there were even flickers of light down in the darkness. But Grews had never caught any clear view of who they were. But he knew. They were his refugees. The heroic and trapped survivors of the tunnel.

But they had vanished again after the first year, and Grews had presumed they had starved, or succumbed to the undead floating in the water.

He wondered at what point he had become this very different man, when it had happened? He had spent so many years commanding peacekeeping forces and relief missions that his instinct had always been to help where he could. Those instincts had even garnered him a reputation as a soft touch, a weak commander, but back then he had been proud of that. This new Grews had managed to become, somewhere along the way, a man more interested in hiding what he had seen than in facing it.

Why? He knew why. It had been the moment they bombed the tunnel and turned down the chance to help just a few more people get out. That had been the moment he had changed. There had been ample time to send a crew in. He could have saved them.

And then the inexplicably fast zombie that had now emerged from the tunnel. Was it some mystical super-zombie, a claim that had been making the rounds of the rumor mill? Grews for one didn't believe it for a second, even after the chaos of the night before. But whether or not that was real, all of this meant something new, and stunning. It meant that the refugees who had for a while managed to survive down there were now lost. But maybe now he would get the chance to at least put them to rest.

"*So you'll get this done?*" said the voice on the radio again.

Grews blinked. His concentration was fading.

"Yes, of course. I'll get it done."

"*And you'll clean up, as well? No damn heroics. They're all dead things now and you know it. We can't risk bringing anything or anyone else out of that tunnel.*"

"Of course."

Time to face the ghosts, Grews thought.

BIG JOHN

It came out of the mists, making a low hissing sound as it pushed both air and water before it. Gray and indistinct, its hulking shape slowly resolved through the fog.

"Big son of a bitch," breathed Predator, standing shoulder to shoulder with the other Alpha operators.

"Only the second of her class," said Homer, the sole sailor in the team. "And the last."

"Never say never," said Predator.

The eight commandos stood in a single rank on an ancient pier, at the border between two worlds – the land and the sea. Britain had come to rule the largest empire the world had ever seen mainly by being a very hardy, and very clever, seafaring nation.

But they ruled the sea no longer.

The supercarrier USS *John F. Kennedy* (CVN-79) hove into view, dominating the entire horizon like an ocean-going ice shelf, like the God of a hundred thousand sperm whales, and began the elaborate process of docking and tying up.

"Grab your gear," growled Handon. "Let's move."

He knew the *Kennedy* wasn't going to risk staying tied up for long. In the ZA, you had to watch your mooring lines, and your anchor lines, like a hawk. One submersible Zulu crawling up them and onto your deck could turn your floating sanctuary into a self-consuming, flesh-rending charnel house. An outbreak belowdecks isn't pretty.

* * *

The *Kennedy* was only the second in the new Gerald R. Ford class of nuclear supercarriers to be floated out of Newport News Drydock in Virginia. She was launched nearly a year ahead of schedule – and so just slightly ahead of the collapse of civilization that halted shipbuilding, and virtually all other kinds of building, for the duration. The Ford class was designed to replace the aging Nimitz-class carriers that went into service in 1975. The *John F. Kennedy* was the second carrier to bear that name – the original being the first of the Nimitz-class carriers, now long retired.

A nuclear-powered supercarrier with an 85-plane air wing and a full complement of nearly 5,000 crew, the new *Kennedy* stretched the length of the Empire State Building laid on its side, with five acres of flight deck and a control tower (called "the island") looming five stories over it all. She was fully electric, with twin A1B nuclear reactors that could power the whole operation for *15-20 years* at sea. She also had her own giant, onboard desalination plant, capable of turning 600,000 gallons of salt water into drinkable fresh water every day. She was a nearly totally self-sufficient floating city. And thus did she survive two years afloat after the fall of civilization.

Before the fall, it was truly said that a carrier strike group could single-handedly win a war against any nation on Earth. Unfortunately, aside from Britain, there were no longer any nations on Earth. And unfortunately for those serving in it, this carrier strike group originally also consisted of a bunch of ships not nearly as self-sufficient as the supercarrier – two Aegis guided missile cruisers, four destroyers, a nuclear-powered submarine, and an ammunition, oiler and supply ship. Half of them had not been as lucky as the *Kennedy*, going down to infection after port calls, or being abandoned and scuttled for lack of fuel and supplies.

Nonetheless, the miniature fleet that was the *Kennedy* strike group was an awesome display when she powered into what was left of the Royal Navy Command Headquarters at Portsmouth. She retained awesome capabilities for ocean-going force projection – and now represented humankind's last, best hope for salvation from the Hell it had blundered into. She breathed hope into the breasts of everyone who laid eyes on her.

Surely any race that could build such a wonder couldn't be destroyed by a virus? Surely any life force behind this was too strong to be dragged down by death.

* * *

The eight-man operational Alpha team crossed over 50 meters of gangway – then still had a half-mile walk across and down into the bowels of the gargantuan warship. All around them, exterior bulkheads rose to the sky, yawning hatches descended out of sight into blackness, and enormous, ancient, building-sized stacks of machinery groaned, steamed, and clattered. It was like being welcomed aboard some floating city of the gods.

And throughout all this, the operators carried, or pushed before them on rolling pallets, about three times their mass in weapons, ammo, and other mission-critical kit. By the time they were shown their bunks, they were ready to hit them. Their area consisted of a suite of four-man sleeping berths, a briefing room, a staging area – and even a live-fire range, where they were invited to zero their weapons. Like every place on Earth, the *JFK* was a little depopulated.

"The XO's on his way down," said the Marine master gunnery sergeant, head of the four-man security detail that brought Alpha aboard. Handon clocked his insignia as that of the Marine Special Operations Regiment. This caused him to raise an eyebrow, but he kept his comments to himself. Ainsley thanked the man, and the Marine team cleared out smartly.

Handon picked out a bunk in a room with Ainsley, Predator, and Juice, tossing his personal gear on a bottom rack, before Ainsley scored it. (In both the British and American militaries, it had long been not so much "rank hath its privileges" but rather "first in gets dibs.") When Handon turned toward the hatch again, there was a smart-looking naval officer filling it.

"I'm Commander Drake, ship's XO."

Ainsley took his hand. "Captain Ainsley, USOC. This is CSM Handon, my first sergeant."

Drake, late thirties, angular features, immaculately turned out and squared away in tan service uniform and

#1 haircut, squinted at this, and his eyes glinted. "I suppose that's the advantage of a slimmed down service structure. A lot of guys in jobs they're overqualified for."

Handon almost smiled himself. He liked this guy immediately. "What was with the MARSOC security detail?" he asked, referring to the Marine Special Operations Command. "I thought Navy MPs, or at least maybe SEALs, would provide shipboard security."

Drake nodded. "When the shit started coming down, we had recently disembarked two fifteen-man Marine spec-ops teams – Teams 1 and 2, A Company, 2nd Marine Special Operations Battalion. They radioed for pickup, fought their way to the coastline – then *swam* out to the boat. After a two-week quarantine, we pretty much put them in charge of all security and combat operations throughout the strike group."

Handon didn't have to ask why. MARSOC Marines were drawn from the Marine Corps Force Reconnaissance community – the very best of what's already a smart, deadly, elite outfit. They were notoriously bad hombres, as cunning as they were lethal. When you had fighters like that, you let them do your fighting.

"You guys might have cause to particularly appreciate that they're here. They're the B team for your mission – and also your QRF if you get in trouble." Handon made a mental note not to piss them off, in any inter-service drinking contests that erupted. "But that's getting into material for your first briefing. Which I'm going to give you whenever you get yourselves squared away. You squared away yet?"

Ainsley and Handon shrugged, ducked their heads at the hatch, and followed him to the briefing room. No time like the present.

JUST DON'T USE THE Z WORD

Predator and Juice watched their commanders go, then took advantage of their absence to more advantageously arrange the compartment. Juice took a brass spittoon out of his ruck and placed it carefully in the near corner.

"You brought *that*?" asked Predator.

"It's gonna be a long passage. And swabbies get pissy if you spit on their freshly-swabbed decks. It's either that or sleep up top." Just as he tossed his head toward the hatch, a shadowy figure glided by. Juice stuck his head out into the passageway. "It's your girl again. Wait a minute…"

"What?"

"Whoever she's fooling around with is back at Hereford. Right?"

"Maybe she met a nice naval aviator. Iceman or some shit."

"In five minutes?" Juice looked disbelieving.

"You said it yourself – she moves fast."

"Or maybe she's shtupping anything that lives."

Pred gave him a very unamused look, then touched his toe to the deck between them. "That's the line right there, buddy." Alpha was very much an in-group – as was humanity itself at this point. However, when the shit really came down, loyalty would always be to service and to unit. Predator and Ali were Army – and both Delta. You didn't fuck with that.

"Sorry, man," Juice said, taking half a step back. "I'll change that to 'killing everything that's dead' and I think I've got it about right."

"Much better," said Predator, punching Juice in the shoulder – a blow that would have knocked most normal men down.

* * *

Pope and Henno were still squaring away kit in their berth, while Homer was, as so often when off duty, God only knew where. Ali had simply evanesced, also as usual, disappearing and reappearing in different places, never seeming to move through the solid 3D world, but just ghosting her way around the aether. This ability was half the reason for her status as last best sniper in the world. The other half was that she virtually never missed, out to ranges of 2,000 yards and beyond.

"Looks like we're in for some heavy weather," said Pope, stuffing clothing in his footlocker.

"What's that?" asked Henno. "The ocean crossing?"

"No. When we get there. Chicago. Three million walking corpses, in a high wind."

"Don't mind the wind. And the corpses we can handle." Henno stuck his face into his open ruck, before adding, "As long as your boss doesn't mind slotting 'em before it's too late…"

Pope almost let this pass entirely. But he took a

chance that he could smooth something over, rather than stirring it up. "How do you mean, brother?"

Henno came out with a double handful of his stuff, then sighed. "Sometimes I get the impression Handon is a little slow on the trigger. Something more than ammo conservation and noise discipline. You know what I mean?"

Pope did, actually. He just nodded, letting Henno go on.

"Made some remark the other week. Sumint that sounded like he thinks there are people still alive inside the dead bastards."

Pope propped his rifle in the corner and took a deep breath. He lowered himself down onto the lower bunk, steepled his fingers, and pinned Henno's eye. "You want the backstory?"

"Aye," Henno said. "I always want to know about aught that might get me killed."

Pope paused before going on. "I served on one of the Task Forces with Handon, in Iraq."

"TF135."

"Or whatever it was designated that week." A mixed special mission unit (SMU) of Tier-1 and other special operators, plus a support, intel, and aviation apparatus, the Task Force, and another like it in Iraq, had been charged with hunting HVTs – high-value targets. This meant the worst of the worst of al-Qaeda, the Taliban, al-Qaeda in Mesopotamia, the Mahdi militia – tangos galore. Tango being the military slang term for terrorists. Pope went on.

"At that point, we were doing this incredible tempo of ops – out every night on kill-or-captures, bringing intel back, crunching it for the next target, then going out again. Sometimes several times a night."

"Yeah, you were the ones kicking down all the doors – and killing all those civilians."

"A few, unfortunately." Pope knew how the Brits viewed the American ethos – which valued aggression more than caution, or public relations. "We went out one night to take down a safehouse. Hardcore AQ types, the intel said. Handon pointed out that this village had never been anything but helpful to us, no reason to think they were harboring AQ. Intel disagreed. We went out, it turned into a big firefight, we ended up killing everyone in the building."

Henno didn't look surprised by any of this.

"Next morning," Pope said. "A bunch of the villagers came out to the patrol base, carrying the bodies of young men we had killed. Handon wasn't supposed to talk to them, but he did. A couple of grandmothers, tear-stained and half-crazed with grief, convinced him their grandsons were good kids who'd just gotten in with the wrong crowd. But now they were dead."

"Yeah," Henno said, "that's the kind of shit you find out when you actually talk to people before shooting them. So Handon got religion or something because of this?"

Pope paused before answering. "Handon spent most of his career hardening himself against all the killing he had to do. Came to think of terrorists as non-human. Operating with the Task Force, night after night, you almost had to. It was the only way to keep functioning. But these grandmothers, and these dead boys… well, they made him doubt his whole methodology. He found he was no longer able to just write Tangos off into some non-human category."

"And now he feels the same about Zulus?"

Pope shrugged. "Who amongst us can prove him wrong?"

Henno had no answer to this.

* * *

Predator and Juice now emerged out on the flight deck, dressed out in physical training gear. They wanted to find the permitted running routes around this floating airport. They also wanted to announce themselves with a big *Fuck you* to the thousands of sailors onboard – their PT uniforms consisted of black shorts and gray T-shirts with "ARMY" in big letters across the front. (Juice had been an 18X Intelligence Sergeant with the Army's Fifth Special Forces Group before being headhunted by the Activity.) With Predator bulging out of his T-shirt and shorts, and Juice displaying way too much curly body hair around his, they both looked like Bruce Banner halfway into becoming the Hulk.

As soon as they hit open air, they seated their ballistic Oakley wraps (Juice also wore his permanent reversed ballcap) and took off at a fast jog. The open air and sea breeze felt fantastic, even with the sky gray and overcast. They could also see that even now the *JFK* was putting back to sea. The gangway was in, the mooring lines cast off, and they could sense what felt like the Earth moving beneath them – a nuclear-powered supercarrier getting underway.

Predator also noted that only one of the other ships in the strike group was pulling out with them – one of the Arleigh-Burke class guided missile destroyers. That seemed strange – a carrier generally needed its support ships around it to survive. But Pred queued this factoid to investigate later. Anyone in the military, at any level, is used to not being told all kinds of things.

The pair of them settled into a good eight-minute-mile pace around the edge of the flight deck – figuring someone would tell them if they ran somewhere that might get them killed. While they ran, they also talked around their deep breathing. Pred and Juice, though they hadn't known each other before being put together on the North Korea mission, were getting a bit like an old married couple now. Most of their conversation consisted of retreads of stories they'd heard a thousand times, or observations on the deep silliness of life under both the military and the ZA.

"Hey, man," Juice said. "Remember all those zombie movies, back in the day, where no one had ever heard of zombies? Like they lived in some universe where George Romero had never existed? What a load of bullshit."

Predator laughed and shook his head. "Yeah, now that you mention it… nobody ever knew what they were dealing with – the dead would rise up and try to eat them, and they'd all be like – 'What the fuck!' Whereas anyone not totally cut off from pop culture would be like, 'Zombies! Shoot 'em in the head!' Oh yeah, and they always had some other name for them – like 'walkers' or 'infected'…"

Juice turned to look at him sideways. "…or 'Zulus'?"

Pred chewed on that for a second. "Good point."

"I don't know." Juice turned to spit off into the ocean. He chewed tobacco even when running. Amazingly, it appeared to make it all the way over the deck, and nearly a hundred feet down into the North Atlantic. "We probably should have predicted this. Between brain parasites… neurotoxins… mad cow disease and brain prions… neurogenic stem cells… we should have seen it coming. And with all the zombie fiction, it's not like we can say it never occurred to anyone."

"Maybe all the movies and TV shows and books were our way of getting ready."

"Well, if it was, it worked out about as well as a dick sandwich."

"True," said Pred. "If there'd been just a few hundred guys on the ball, handier with axes and shotguns, at critical times and places, maybe all this could have been fucking headed off."

That made Juice sad to think of it. All these months and years of horror, all the people gone, virtually all that humanity had built up laid low – that it might all have been unnecessary.

So he just ran, and enjoyed the feeling of still being alive.

AFTERTHOUGHTS

Wesley sat in silence, and spent the time monitoring the ashen faces opposite and on either side of him. The hum of the truck's engine offered a little comfort, but his thoughts were scrambled.

Twenty-four hours ago he had been sitting in his tiny office expecting just another quiet day, and now here he was drafted and on his way south to God knows where. They hadn't even told him that much. He had been informed that their experience on the streets of Folkestone during last night's outbreak would be invaluable to the people they were travelling to meet, but not much else.

Wesley looked across at Martin, who was also very deep in thought. The man looked like the shock of the previous night might be catching up with him. These military types, Wesley figured, are not all hard and stoic. They're just people able to put a grim face on and do what is necessary. Nothing that most folks wouldn't be able to, given the right conditions. Wesley supposed that the main difference lay in the training. He didn't think that the training could prepare anyone for losing his entire platoon, though.

Of course, Martin wasn't the only one to lose his whole team.

The other faces that stared back at him from the seats around him were not much different – quiet, contemplative, all deep in their own troubles.

The truck had come from London, so these were probably men and women leaving their families behind to go, well, wherever they were going. How long would they be away? From what Martin had said during their brief, pre-sleep conversation at the barracks, these postings could be for a few months, years – or forever.

"I was posted in the Outer Hebrides, for over a year, before this. That's out in the middle of nowhere north of Scotland, if you didn't know," Martin had said.

Wesley nodded. He knew the place.

"After Europe fell, the islands became home to any random naval ship that stumbled into port. They have new docks all over the islands now. I'd been there once before when I was a boy, on holiday with my parents. It was so quiet and remote back then. Not so now."

He'd seemed to pause for a moment, and Wesley could almost see the man's thoughts drifting back to happier times.

"Two months of fixing APCs out of Hereford before that. And some shore duty up near Yarmouth for six months. No permanent post yet. I guess they need engineers wherever they need them."

Wesley had thought his job at the tunnel was going to be permanent. But then everything had changed overnight.

"That area is restricted now," he'd been told that morning by the pimple-faced clerk perhaps half his age. The boy had probably never seen action. Wesley had repeatedly asked if he would be guarding the entrance again, once the Harbour barracks division had cleared the way. Asking anyone he could find.

"Your orders are for a change of station."

"Orders? I'm not military. I work for the UK Security Services."

"CentCom, and UKSS, have both already approved this."

"They can't do that."

"Yes, they can."

"I'm not military," he had repeated.

"Basically, you've been drafted. My instructions are to give you your next assignment, which is to report to the barracks down in the harbor."

"This is a joke, right?"

"No, sir. Your previous position is null and void. Security at your old station will be performed by military personnel as of this morning. Of course, if you wish to catch a transport to London and go and work in the coalfields, that's always an option."

Wesley visibly wilted.

"Your rank in the Security Services will be carried over into your position in the military… corporal."

Wesley was fuming. At least that had been his initial reaction, but he'd had the chance to stew over it all in the last few hours, just sitting in the back of the truck, staring blankly at the other distant faces.

Maybe this wasn't so bad, he thought. But then he shook his head. This was bad, and he knew it full well. He wasn't going to be sitting behind the lines guarding some quiet post that the military thought was dealt with already. He wasn't going to spend quiet evenings just watching the night sky, sitting with a cup of coffee and listening to his two young charges babble away about all the weird stuff that the universe might throw at the world.

No. He would never hear their voices again. Not now that their brains were almost certainly washed away into the dirt, and their remains burned, probably only a few yards from the place where they had spent all those nights mulling over the state of the world.

Wesley was going to miss those two boys now. As much as he had groused and been irritated by their constant yabber, he had somehow found it comforting to listen to at the same time. It had reminded him of a world where there were no zombies, except in the movies and comics; a world where you could buy a four-pack of beer on a Friday night and chill out in your living room watching terrible repeat programs. Those programs wouldn't be repeated again now that the TV stations were all but gone.

The last things Chambers and Addison had talked about were aliens and alien invasions. Wesley shook his head and even laughed a little when he considered the futility of aliens arriving on our planet now. *They would get a hell of a surprise*, he thought. Maybe some little alien guy on the mothership would get sacked for not researching the planet enough.

His laughter stopped when he heard Addison's distinctive laugh, and that of Chambers, ring out in his mind. He thought of how alive they had been an hour before the attack, and how they had then changed so quickly. The burning glare in their eyes, the pale skin, the already blackened teeth and bloodshot eyes. How was it that those changes happened so quickly? Was that even humanly possible?

Now it seemed he was in the Army. And he would be going out to face those things, probably every day. Until last night, he had never witnessed the creatures *en masse*, but only heard tales from soldiers who passed through Folkestone. So many stories that had made his blood chill and his skin feel like something had crawled over him while he slept. Paris was overrun. The Americas were overrun. The tales of massive swarms of the dead all trudging along some insane and unfathomable path. Millions, no, billions of them now.

He'd been so sheltered in Fortress Britain. But the horrible reality outside was going to be part of everyday life for him now.

The truck shuddered and came to a stop, snapping Wesley's mind back into the now. Voices outside called to the driver and were answered quickly, and then they were moving again, gates clanging shut behind them and the sound of gravel crunching under the tires. A sound just like that from under his feet when he made the circuit around the tunnel yards. The truck swung slowly around a winding road for a few minutes and they passed other trucks, groups of soldiers hurrying about. Finally they came to a stop and the back door fell open.

"Out you get, fellas," barked the soldier, a man with a bright red beard and piercing green eyes. There was nothing pretty about the man, his face was scarred and weather worn, his insignia suggested… Wesley couldn't think of it. He'd seen so many, but… wait. Sergeant. He was a staff sergeant and outranked him.

"Get a move on."

Everyone filed out of the truck and fell into line along the side of the road. Wesley was in awe of what he saw. Everywhere around him was a buzzing mass of movement. Thousands of troops and vehicles came and went while he stood and stared.

"Okay," said the sergeant with the red beard. "I need Corporal Wesley and Captain Martin. Step forward."

Didn't Martin outrank the sergeant? He stepped forward.

"I'm here, Sergeant."

"Ah, good. Sorry about the hurry and informalities, sir. I was told to collect yourself and the corporal and get you to the helipad as soon as you arrived."

"We're going flying?" asked Martin, puzzled.

"Yes, sir. I'm sorry, but I have no further details. Only your immediate priority to get into the air."

Martin nodded. "Understood."

And he did, thought Wesley. Martin understood something that Wesley had not been able to figure out yet.

Martin flashed him a look that said, *Odd*. But he didn't question the sergeant further. Wesley wished that he had. He didn't much like all this foreboding secrecy.

Twenty minutes later and Wesley was soaring through the air, feeling quite sick, the bone-trembling roar of the blades and engines gripping him, as he tried to calm his nerves and keep his stomach straight. He watched the coastline of the British Isles disappear into the distance, and then there was nothing below them but miles upon miles of endless Atlantic sea.

"Where are we going?" he finally asked, looking at Martin.

Martin glanced back, taking his gaze away from the ocean.

"Oh, you don't look so good. Not used to flying?"

"Not in a helicopter," replied Wesley, shaking his head.

Martin looked back out to sea.

"We're going nowhere at the moment," he said, frowning.

"What do you mean?"

"There's nothing this way, not for thousands of miles, unless…" Martin's frown deepened.

"Unless what?" snapped Wesley, unable to suppress the irritation in his voice. Martin turned back, and looked like he was going to snap back in return, but then his eyes softened.

"There must be some sort of sea platform out here. Maybe a rig. Or a ship."

Wesley absorbed that in silence. He couldn't decide whether this fact made things better for him, or worse.

CLOSE! STAND CLOSE TO ME, STARBUCK

Homer found it all too easy.

Basically, he just made as if he were having a nice evening stroll around the outer edge of the carrier flight deck. Most of that wasn't a total no-go area, unless flight operations were actually going on right then. And with the aviation fuel situation, flight ops now happened only as often as needed, and not much more. He carried with him only a modest-sized duty bag. Then it was just a question of waiting until a couple of the flight deck crew in their brightly colored shirts passed by, shielding him for two seconds from sight of the control tower, or "island."

That was all it took to tie off on the railing, hurl the rope bag over, clip onto his own D-ring, and leap overboard. A single bound, and he had rappelled himself down to the center of nowhere. The sweet spot for solitude on a Ford-class supercarrier turns out to be a little side-deck, two levels below the top, facing out to the sea, and nestled between the Sparrow missile launchers and the Phalanx Close-In Weapons System (an electric Gatling gun and radar array used mainly to shoot down anti-ship missiles). Basically, unless there were maintenance issues with one of those two weapons bays, this deck was virtually guaranteed to be empty. It also sat out of view of *everyone else onboard.*

The only problem was, of course, that the ship's ID keycard they gave the Alpha men – for access into their team's suite, the mess hall, a few common areas, and up top via direct ladders – didn't allow Homer access to it. But never try to keep a SEAL out of someplace he wants to go on a boat – or under the water, or across a desert, or up a mountain, for that matter… Pretty much their whole job is gaining access to places they aren't supposed to be. And it's by popping up where they're not remotely expected that they are able to wreak such havoc with such small numbers.

But Homer found it all really funny. No sooner had he been sitting around Hereford reminiscing about the solitary joys of shipboard life than here he was, in the blink of an eye, aboard the largest warship ever built by man – and almost certainly the most formidable. With literally about a billion individual parts, it was also probably the most complex machine ever built – or, on current trends, ever would be. But it seemed that anything could happen to you in this world, even in the ZA.

Ma'shallah, Homer thought, and as he knew his Muslim brothers to say. *What wonders God hath wrought…*

* * *

As he sat watching the light fail over the North Atlantic, listening to the wind and the rush of water against the hull, he thought about all the changes that he'd seen in the last two years. Many mornings he'd still wake up and say his wife's name – assuming it had all been a horrible, displacing dream. Then the reality would come back to him in a sickening rush.

Homer supposed, in many ways, the ZA was a lot easier for warriors than for civilians. And he didn't just mean their weapons and training and much greater ability to survive. To a great extent, the zombies were the least interesting thing about a zombie apocalypse. What was really gripping, and wrenching, and awful, was what it did to the survivors – what men do to each other, and to themselves, when the structure all around them, and upon which they've relied all their lives, catastrophically fails.

But military personnel, especially SOF, had been operating in catastrophic vacuums of order and structure for most of their careers. Think Somalia, Bosnia, Afghanistan, and Iraq during its civil war. Being able to be effective in such wretched, menacing places was much of what it meant to be a special operator. Homer supposed the end of civilization really just supercharged what had always been the main human problem – working together to survive. The civilians had been shielded from that for a long time.

But Homer and his brethren hadn't.

After the virus reached the tipping point, most people went down before they even knew what to be afraid of. It raged out of control that quickly. By the time the dead outnumbered the living, it only helped marginally to know what the hell was going on. It was too late then. And when the delicate latticework of civilization failed – the daily food deliveries to grocery store shelves, the constantly pulsing power grids, the free-flowing clean water, police and ambulances that came when you called – well, at that point, the other survivors started to become as dangerous as the dead. Survival became as much a matter of competing with the living for resources, as about battling zombies. And that's where things got really tricky.

That was the whole "working together" part.

And that's where Homer and others like him really had the advantage. The military brotherhood is well known, going back at least to Henry V's St. Crispin's Day speech. But special operators – they were a breed apart. They operated in such severe and austere conditions, and against such appalling odds, that the only way to prevail was through the perfection of their training *as a team*. It was said that the average officer in the special operations community had more formal education than the average university professor. And so it should be. The training was unending, and relentless, and exacting, because it had to be for them to succeed at the job. Even to survive it.

So the brotherhood of special operators was definitely a family. And one thing that hadn't changed, Homer figured, was that family was still the most important thing. The whole world had changed, but they hadn't – not really. And having your brothers around you was how you knew you weren't a zombie – that you were still one of God's children, and still made in his image.

Because the first thing you notice about zombies is… that they don't notice each other. A dead guy could be surrounded by 5,000 others, and wouldn't pay them any mind. Well, with the possible exception of that one on the cliffs, with his buddy on the cross… Homer thought maybe he'd call him Job from now on. Maybe God was testing him.

Homer figured perhaps these thoughts about family had been prompted by this mission – by sailing, then flying, so close to where his wife and children were last known to be alive. He expected the ship was going to anchor only a few hundred miles, if that, from his home in Virginia Beach, where they'd moved after he joined Team Six. And that was a whole ocean closer than Homer thought he would ever again get to them. Some part of him always believed they were still alive. Some part of him thought he would see them again in this world.

But he did know he would see them in the next.

Also, a big part of him wrestled daily with his duty as a warrior. Every day he got up and thought of reasons why he shouldn't leave, that second, just take off, to go look for them. What kind of father was he? What kind of husband? His children might be crying out for him now, lost, in pain, afraid. And even if they weren't, even if Homer died in a futile search for the already departed… well, that would just hasten that day they would all be together again.

Some of the other guys said it was only by sheer, dumb luck that they had all been deployed overseas when it happened. That they were in the one island nation that, also through sheer dumb luck, escaped the implacable armies of the walking dead. But was it luck? Handon would say that it's an operational principle that Delta makes its own luck. But Homer knew that what looks to us like luck, and what looks to be skill, are all the same thing.

God's plan for every one of us.

* * *

And this plan had showed itself even today – in Homer's recon of the ship areas leading to this isolated half-deck. Posted up in a common hallway was a bright yellow flyer for a daily shipboard chapel service. It didn't mention the denomination, but he didn't suppose it mattered all that much at this point. The timing was perfect. A half-hour for himself up there, another half-hour for the meeting whose name he dare not speak, then a half-hour for the sermon. And then back to work.

It was always good to meet other believers. It was a shame that those the ZA didn't kill outright – eaten by the dead, infected and turned, killed by the desperate living, or just starved out by the fall – had a strong tendency to lose their faith over the matter. So the faithful were pretty few and far between these days. But, as the man has said:

Faith isn't faith until it's all you're holding onto.

BEST LAID PLANS

Commander Drake sat across from Handon and Ainsley in the small briefing room. He said, "I've asked the MARSOC team leader to join us for this one. You're going to want to be on good terms with this guy. As I mentioned, it's him and his men who are going to be on standby to pull your bacon out of the fire when and as necessary."

"Or, more likely," said Ainsley, a little dryly, "it's his men who are going to inherit our mission if and when my team goes down."

"That, too. CentCom has made it very clear to me this one's in the too-big-to-fail category."

"So you must have a C team lined up?" said Handon.

Drake just nodded.

Need to know, Handon figured. Since he wasn't going to elaborate on that, and since they had a second here, Handon tried on a question that had been vexing him.

"I understand your reactors can provide power for decades."

"That's affirmative. Though, when we do need to refuel, that can take a couple of years. You might have seen we have only one support ship sailing with us, to save on fuel. But it's a hell of a backup – one of the Arleigh-Burke destroyers, and the latest. The *Michael*

Murphy."

Handon nodded. "And on top of unlimited power, you've got all the fresh water you can drink from your desalination plant… but last time I was on a supercarrier, I was told it could only store about 70 days worth of food. How has that worked?"

Drake nodded. "Well, for starters, and as you'll have already noticed, ship's complement is massively under strength. We sailed with 4,660. As of today, we're at 2,132."

"Killed or infected?" Ainsley asked. "Outbreaks?"

Drake nodded. "We've lost people on land. But there have been zero outbreaks on the *JFK*. Every shore party is quarantined for a week on the *Rainier*, our oiler, ammo, and supply ship."

"But max incubation period is only 72 hours."

"Yeah, but we didn't know that in the early days. And we couldn't afford even a single incident shipboard. So we've stuck with the policy."

Ainsley and Handon nodded and waited for him to continue.

"No, our losses were different. Desertions were big, particularly in the first few months. A lot of people jumping ship, some of them too far out to realistically swim to land. They were trying to get home to their families. God preserve them." Drake took a look off to the corner of the cabin. "And then there were the suicides. It's a fact of life in any military outfit. But ours have ticked up over time."

"How do you sail the ship with so few?" Ainsley

asked.

"Well, we just picked up a few in Britain – donated by your own CentCom. Filled a few critical roles. But it's a lesser known fact that most of the crew on a supercarrier is actually in support of the air wing. And we haven't been flying much. So little fuel, so little point. More on which in a second. Anyway, obviously it wasn't just air wing people we lost. So we've had to do retraining. But, hell, this ship is so automated, in many ways it sails itself. To a great extent, the people are here to look after the other people, and the aircraft."

Drake seemed now to come out of his dark reverie. "Anyway, half the mouths to feed solved half the food problem. But for much of the first year, we spent most of our time raiding ports and coastlines for supplies. We'd hope to find someplace quiet and abandoned. More often it was a matter of fighting our way in, then holding a perimeter while food was onloaded. The MARSOC guys were invaluable there. Fight like bulldogs on meth."

Handon well knew. Also, he'd known and worked with enough Marines to know that they're not just ferocious – but they actually tended to be disconcertingly smart and cagey, as well. *God knows how the myth of the knuckle-dragging, Neanderthal jarhead hangs on*, he thought to himself. *Hmm – maybe it's because they want it to. Now THAT's smart…*

Drake went on. "Anyway, the shore parties were our biggest risk of infection, of course, and some of our junior officers were already looking ahead. A few months in, we planted huge potato and wheat beds, under sunlamps, down in the hangar. Three levels of them, actually. We're now about 50% self-sufficient on food, at least as far as calories goes. Since then, shore parties focus on canned fruits and vegetables, spices, and yeast to make bread. That and multivitamins. Meat's pretty few and far – the frozen stuff went when the power failed, and the fresh stuff you have to hunt and slaughter, all of which burns time on shore. And dairy's a memory, aside from tinned milk and powdered eggs, when we get lucky." Drake laughed mirthlessly to himself. "Something I never thought I'd see – a bunch of vegans on a U.S. Navy warship..."

He laughed again, easier. "Anyway, we've been a bit like the *Battlestar Galactica* – guarding our dwindling fleet, wandering the galaxy looking for a new home. Instead of being hounded by the Cylons, it was the dead."

"And so what did you do with the air wing?" Handon asked. The flight deck couldn't hold more than a couple dozen aircraft at a time – ordinarily, most of them lived belowdecks in the cavernous – three-story high, 700 feet long – hangar bay.

"We pushed quite a few of them into the ocean."

"That's a bit of a shame," Ainsley said.

"Starving to death's a shame." Drake, Ainsley, and Handon turned to see that this was spoken by a newcomer, who'd slipped into the doorway without anyone noticing. He wore a khaki utility uniform, boots, and a sidearm. Two deep furrows of scar tissue ran down the left side of his face. "And in zombie warfare, air superiority is about as useful as nuts on a nun."

"Captain Ainsley, Sergeant Major Handon," Drake said, "this is Master Gunnery Sergeant Fick, who commands the MARSOC team, since their LT went down." It was the same guy who had escorted them onboard.

"We met," said Handon.

Fick nodded. "Wanted to check out the new hotshots myself. Find your comfy racks okay? Pillows nice and fluffed for you?"

Ainsley looked disconcerted, in that British way of abhorring a scene. Handon just smiled. *God love the Marines… Hell,* he thought, *they're probably loving life in the ZA.*

Another thing about the Marines: used to very austere living conditions.

* * *

Gunnery Sergeant Fick took a seat and put his thick arms on the table.

Commander Drake said, "Truth is, we do have several dozen security personnel, Navy MPs and shore patrolmen. But Fick asked to bring you onboard himself."

The stocky Marine nodded. "Being as the fate of the world evidently rests in your no-doubt capable hands." Left unsaid, but pretty obvious to Ainsley and Handon, was that Fick figured his own guys were more than up to the job.

Both Ainsley and Handon felt for the guy. But, then again, neither of them gave that much of a shit. If they went around giving away missions to every SOF or elite force that fancied themselves the best men for the job… well, SOF guys aren't given to backing down or shrugging with humility. And, in the end, everyone went where they were damn well ordered, and damn well did the jobs assigned to them. Especially in Handon's Delta, where professionalism was job one.

Ainsley said to Drake, "I gather you've gotten the high-level concept from our OC."

Drake and Fick looked at each other.

"Officer Commanding," said Handon. "A little Brit-speak for you."

"Ah, right," said Fick. "Everything bass-ackwards."

Ainsley almost smiled. "No, that's the Frogs, actually – *les bâtards morts*." Like many English of his class, Ainsley spoke good French. (Unlike the French, who no longer spoke.)

Drake nodded. "Okay. Yes, we got a three-page mission concept from your Colonel. He's right in suggesting a helo insertion is too much of a stretch – bird could get there, but not back. Not without refueling. Also too much danger of mechanical failure on a helo. So it's going to be a fixed-wing aircraft, and a combat jump."

"Right," Ainsley said. "HAHO." High-altitude, high-opening – after which the operators would steer their canopies to the target. "I'm told your air wing can support this?"

"Yes, you're in luck. One of the planes we agonized about, but ultimately decided to keep, was our C-2A Greyhound. It's a twin-engine cargo aircraft – generally used to move supplies around the strike group, or to shore bases. It's a big old bastard – about the heaviest thing ever to lumber off a carrier flight deck, and bang back down again – but it was too useful to scupper."

"Capacity?" Handon asked.

"About 4,500 kilograms, 26 passengers nominal. Should take your team, all your gear, and your chutes no problem."

"Plus a shitload of ammo," Fick added. "We assume that since you're jumping into Zulu Universe, you're going to want to jump with some big-ass resupply palletes. Set up some kind of local FOB, or at least supply cache."

"That's affirmative," said Ainsley.

"My guys can help you put it together and palletize it. I saw you brought an awful lot of your own hardware. But we're not too badly fixed for stuff like 5.56 rounds and linked 7.62. When we raided the U.S. Naval Base in Singapore, we *emptied* their ordnance stores."

"Top marks," said Ainsley.

With civilian firearms virtually banned in the UK, there hadn't been enough of a domestic armaments industry in place when the curtain came down. It had been ramped up as quickly as possible, but it was competing for industrial resources with absolutely everything – everything that Britain used to import. Of course, USOC got priority on ammo – but every time they pulled the trigger, that meant some poor bastard defending his neighborhood had to rely on an axe.

"And about that QRF?" Handon asked, referring to

the Quick Reaction Force.

Fick nodded. "Basically, you call, we come running."

Drake said, "They can insert in the same plane you went out in, as soon as it can be turned around. But probably a low-altitude opening to get in faster."

"Don't worry, we'll pull your bacon out of the fire," said Fick.

Ainsley let that sink in for a second, then spoke. "No. You'll pull our bacon out of the fire only if it conduces to mission accomplishment. If we're too bogged down, or torn up, or hard to get to, then you're to act precisely as if we're dead. You raise the banner yourselves and Charlie Mike." More slang: continue mission.

The Marine officer nodded, sobered. "Roger that."

Handon nodded himself. He had to give Ainsley credit. The man could be a bit of a tight-ass. But he was a brave son of a bitch and, like all the Brits Handon had served with, he definitely knew what his duty was, and damn well intended to do it.

Born to rule and sacrifice…

Fick cracked a smile again. "Well, if we do have to go in after you, I trust there'll be a hell of a lot fewer Zulus than when you landed."

Handon raised his eyebrows. "What, a hell of a lot fewer than three million? That might leave a few."

Fick kept on smiling. "Well… one nice thing. Once they're gone, they're gone. The dead never rise up a second time."

From the Marine's slightly demented grin, Handon got the sense he would be perfectly happy to go out and try to personally kill every one of the 7 billion undead abominations that currently ran the world. Like he felt no one was getting any younger, and this was a job that needed doing, and he'd prefer to be getting on with it.

Handon figured he could only respect that. Demented as it was.

"Okay," Ainsley said. "Let's get stuck into the mission parameters. At a high level, I want to make sure we're on the same page with logistics, comms, the air mission, waypoints for infil and exfil, branches and contingencies, ISR, map packs, essential tasks, operational timings. Once we've got our command ducks in a row, we'll bring in both teams and drill down on everything…"

BACK TO HAUNT YOU

Major Grews stood at the top of the slope, shifting impatiently, his mind jittering from one scene to the other. Below, in the yard, the last of the train carriages was being shunted along the track at an excruciatingly slow pace. It had taken the best part of the morning to clear them out in preparation for the tunnel's excavation. Even though he was weary of waiting, he was still extremely impressed by the speed at which the engineering team worked. Impressed would actually be an understatement.

He had witnessed a lot of deployments, a lot of temporary bases being erected in hostile territory, and he was always amazed at how quickly these things came together when they threw a few hundred skilled soldiers at the job. But this, this had been beyond that. He had watched for six hours as just thirty weary-looking soldiers of the Royal Corps of Engineers – arrived just that morning after being woken from their beds in London – systematically shifted nearly forty carriages with little more than a few engines and some forklift trucks.

The area had to be completely clear. A lot of heavy equipment was coming in to haul out the collapsed section of the tunnel – seriously heavy machinery that his bosses only dusted off on special occasions. They were gas guzzlers, these diggers, and meant for leveling an area very quickly. This time they would be digging out fifty cubic meters of rubble. Unfortunately, this would mean opening the tunnel right up, as well as a good chunk of the hill under which it sat.

Grews glanced over at the field, across the train tracks, at the two monstrosities that sat hulking in the blistering sun, waiting to churn the ground. He tracked his vision further over to the field, where pyres burned even now, eight hours after the last zombie had fallen. Nearly a hundred of the damn things had been on the loose in the end, most of them alive and sleeping in the Premier Inn a day ago. Now they were burning. The remainder, about two dozen, had crawled out of the hole that the first had made.

How the hell that thing had clawed its way out was something Grews didn't even want to dwell on. But he couldn't stop himself worrying that a few of them may have slipped by, out into the countryside. There was a large search party out there right now, scouring the forest and the scrublands, visiting every building no matter what its function. Drones and manned surveillance aircraft scanned the area tirelessly through video, IR, and synthetic aperture radar. And all of them just looking for stragglers who may have gotten away. As for the super-zombie... well, he hoped that it was only one of them. And that one had now been accounted for with a hundred bullets in its head put there by his troopers.

Though Grews still wasn't buying the super-zombie theory. He thought it more likely that damnable security guard had just been lying to save his own skin, along with the single remaining soldier from the hotel. Both damned useless. They would have had a lot to answer for if they weren't already on their way south. Best out of his way, thought Grews, who would have hung them if he could have. They should have used their own bodies to block up the hole instead of running for it.

The thing that was troubling him was how all of this had happened so quickly. The engineers from London and the diggers should have taken days to organize. They must have already had plans in place to do this, Grews thought.

Twenty minutes later and the diggers were at work. The first one took the tunnel entrance head on, eating away at the mass of solid stone – solid stone in all but a small passage that had allowed the creatures the night before to break through. The second digger was already slicing off massive mounds of earth on the hill above.

Digging. Had those creatures, the zombies, or at least this one fast one, really been digging away for nearly two years?

Grews turned to the junior officer, a woman, who stood nearby. "Check in with the Harbour barracks OC. I want to know if the second sweep of the town has been completed."

"Yes, sir," said the communications officer. She was young and inexperienced, but he couldn't take his two regular comms guys away from their desks. There was too much to organize today and he needed them on the radios to coordinate everything.

Grews looked down into the yard, fifty feet from where the digger was tearing the ground apart, and near where the first of the carriages had been parked just a few hours ago. A team of three dozen of his best men were gathered, checking equipment, loading weapons, and then rechecking. They were his elite – Royal Marine Commandos who had turned up in the Channel six months after the border had been closed, and months after Europe had become a graveyard. They had traveled all the way from Germany, and through all kinds of hell in between, stolen some fishing boats and rowed.

CentCom had wanted to move them out, reassign them to Hereford or London, but Grews had managed to delay that for months – long enough for them to become a permanent fixture in his barracks. They were his urban cleansers, used for storming coastal villages along the French and Portuguese coasts so that teams of scavengers could safely do their jobs. But this time they were going somewhere new. This time they were going underground to clear out the Channel Tunnel.

A shout went up near the tunnel, and the digger stopped. The ring of Marines, standing thirty yards from where the digger was munching away at the rubble, lifted their rifles and took aim. Shots rang out for a few seconds, and then silence.

More of the damn things being let out of the darkness.

Just an hour later and Grews stood and watched as the first team of Marines entered the tunnel – which was now a gaping maw at the end of a fifty-yard-long trench. The diggers had done their job at dazzling speed.

The first squad moved slowly, the lights on their weapons lighting up the tunnel ahead of them, glints flickering on the walls. Grews only wished that they still had enough working night vision goggles, but what few he'd had in stock had been packed up and shipped to Hereford for the golden boys of special operations. His men would have to use spot lamps, and their weapon-mounted tactical lights. At least they had been able to find a supply of oxygen canisters and breathing masks. He had no doubt that the air in that tunnel would be rancid at best.

The second squad entered the tunnel just thirty seconds later, followed by the final dozen that made up third squad. All moved as the first had, slowly and methodically, heads low and backs hunched over, their weapons never lowered.

Grews turned to his radio operator, now seated at a small desk with a laptop and large set of radios perched on top of it. Its noisy generator buzzed a few yards away. On a table nearby were three small LCD monitors showing the helmet-cam views of all three squad leaders. Shadows flickered across the screens and reflected off the water that was already ankle deep.

"Okay, give me a headset and keep open channels."

"Yes, sir. Hold on a moment… Harbour division confirms that the above-ground sweep is completed."

"Good."

Grews put the headphones on and tapped the microphone.

"One Troop, radio check."

"*One Troop here,*" came back the voice of the Marines' leader. "*Send, over.*" Grews knew that the other two squad leaders would also be listening on this channel.

"Okay. Keep your ranks tight, watch the flanks and cover every damn crevice that you see. No fuck-ups. Remember your orders: kill on sight. Anything that moves down there is a threat, no exceptions."

There was a pause, seconds passing as Grews waited. Now a new voice popped up on the command net. One that had been monitoring silently from almost a hundred miles away.

"*Good work, Major. I think I can leave this in your hands now.*"

"Thank you, Bob," said Grews, holding back the burning feeling in his stomach. *Interfering arse*, he thought.

Grews turned to another young officer standing nearby.

"Is that air pump going yet? Did we get the vents open? Fetch me a chair," he snapped, not waiting for answers. "And switch to the secondary squad net. We're ready to do this our way now."

The young officer grinned.

"Absolutely, sir."

INTERMISSIONARY POSITION

Deep in the bowels of the carrier, Handon stuck his head into a sleeping compartment as he and Drake cruised past it in the passageway outside.

"Mission briefing, all hands, one hour. Down the hall."

Predator nodded, and Juice saluted, ironically.

Handon started to withdraw, then paused. "You know where Homer and Ali are?"

"Nope."

"Tell 'em when you see 'em."

Drake stood behind Handon in the passageway. He leaned around him now. "You know, all ship's IDs have active RFID chips on them. We can find your guys from the bridge, or any deck's security station."

Juice's eyebrows had already gone north. "No need," he said, reaching into one of his hard cases and coming out with a handheld digital radio scanner.

"I think the frequency is—"

"Four-point-two gigaherz," Juice finished for him, pointing the scanner at his own pocket.

"We'll take it from here," Pred said.

"Carry on," Handon said, withdrawing and marching off with Drake.

"I assume you're thinking what I'm thinking," Juice

said to Pred, rubbing his hands together, then twiddling knobs.

"Yep. Not only are those two both always disappearing – but nearly always at the same damned time. Never realized it before. It's like never seeing Batman and Bruce Wayne at the same party… And now's our chance to bust them."

"Only if they're currently within about 200 meters…" Juice scrolled through a listing on a touchscreen on the scanner. "The IDs are broadcasting name and service number." He panned the device around the room. "Yep, got Ali. She's aft of here, probably a couple of decks up."

"Awesome. And Homer? 'Cause I'll bet you my last nutsack they're in the same spot. I *knew* it. On some level, I think I always knew it…"

"Got his card, too – looks pretty damned close to the same vector, but…"

"But what?"

"The signal strength." Juice stood and went to the door. Pred followed him out, down the passageway – and into the berthing compartment next door.

Pope looked up from his rack. "Help you boys?"

Juice stepped to the bunk on the other side of the room. He picked up Homer's ID card from where it lay on the bed, and looked at it forlornly.

"Sons of bitches," said Pred.

"Thought we had 'em," said Juice.

Pope gave them a serene yet uncomprehending look, and watched their backs as the pair withdrew.

* * *

Henno poured Ainsley a cup of coffee, Julie Andrews, as he always took it. (White nun, i.e. milk with no sugar.) Then another cup, Whoopi Goldberg, for himself. The two sat across the metal table in the dim and empty mess.

"You get through to the missus before we sailed?" Henno asked. He knew Ainsley's family, from long years of service together.

"No," Ainsley said. "Total commo blackout, after the first briefing."

"Jesus… Don't know what they think the gobshite zombies are going to do if they get wind of a mission. Moan on a different frequency or something."

"Well… OPSEC's a hard habit to break."

"It's gotta be tough for her," Henno said, holding his boss's eye, and thinking of the man's wife. "Not hearing a peep until we get back. That's *if* we get back." Henno had been a committed bachelor since his first divorce. It was a lot easier in the military, never mind in spec-ops. When you came back after unexplained six-week absences, and could only answer that you'd been "somewhere hot"… well, it was easier on a casual girlfriend, or one-night stand, than on someone you were supposed to be sharing your life with.

Ainsley shrugged. "She'll call Hereford and they'll tell her I'm deployed. She knows the drill. She's been through it enough times."

"Fair play." Henno's coffee was just getting to sub-scalding, so he raised it and drank deeply. He swallowed, paused, and looked up. "Do you think we'll come back from this one?"

"Don't worry too much about that," Ainsley said, straightening, and raising his mug with thumb and two fingers. "Worry about what kind of world we leave behind."

Henno was pretty sure his captain was thinking about his two little boys at that moment. But he let it lie.

* * *

Ali brushed her fingertips across his as she rose to leave.

Without a look back, she strode down the dim passageway, straightening her uniform slightly. Despite her best efforts, she thought anxiously about what the two of them had been doing – and what she'd say if they were caught. She could just hear Handon asking, "What were you thinking?"

Luckily, she had a good answer to that one: *I was thinking we all might be dead tomorrow.*

As to why she was with who she was with, well, that was a slightly more vexed question. She'd chosen him because he was gentle, and because he was good. As to why he had consented… well, he'd probably say it was because he was weak. And because he was a sinner. And Ali also knew of course that he was lonely, like all of them. The ZA was a damned lonely place, even in a family of special operators.

That also probably made it incest. Ali winced slightly as she slithered up a narrow ladder.

Worst of all, she knew that he considered himself still married. Married in the eyes of God. And he would still be married until the day his wife was put in the ground.

Which might not be until the end of the world.

Regaining Alpha's area, she stuck her head into her billet. Pope was on his rack, on his back, reviewing map packs on a tablet on his belly.

She smiled before asking, "Got time for some *Ji-geiko*, your Holiness?"

Pope looked up and smiled as well. Of course they'd brought their kendo equipment along.

And out on the flight deck of a supercarrier would be just about the baddest-assed place they'd banged swords yet.

RAPTURE

Homer lay where he was for a few minutes after she left, on their improvised bed of duffel bags in the corner of a nearly dark storeroom. But then he prodded himself to rise. It wasn't good to be idle. Too many thoughts. Plus that chapel service would be starting. At least there he could pray for forgiveness for his sins.

He rose, buttoned his shirt, and checked his watch. Though the true max cruising speed of the Ford-class carriers was classified, Homer knew it to be a blistering 40 knots. He also knew the distance of the Atlantic crossing from Portsmouth; and figured they had about 80 hours at sea. Most of that time would be given to mission planning and prep. But, as usual in the military, there was a lot of hurry-up-and-wait at the front end while things got organized.

He thought he could make his way to the chapel by memory, but ended up having to ask directions from a couple of aviation machinist mates along the way. When he slipped in the back hatch, about two dozen men and women were already seated and the service underway. He took a seat at the edge of the empty back pew. The chaplain was warming up.

"...and now, after a brief respite in a safe harbor, we are put to sea again. Amidst the storms, amidst the chaos, and amidst the Judgement."

The chaplain was a mystery to Homer – not like any naval chaplain he had ever seen. He was in uniform, a mere E2, a junior enlisted rank, with an apprentice steelworker rating. All this was evident from his shoulder insignia. He wore no clerical scarf, and he spoke with a deep southern accent – and with a palpable fervor.

"Yea, truly are we all judged. Mankind has been judged for its sins. And we will be judged for what we do here in these End Days."

Uh-oh – one of those, Homer thought, more amused than anything. The preacher raised an index finger to Heaven as he went on, picking up steam.

"Yes, verily, we have been judged, and afflicted with this plague. This plague of soulless who swarm across the land and the oceans. These soulless dead, whose souls are ascended to Heaven, while their bodies remain on Earth to finish God's cleansing…" He paused to wipe his forehead with his sleeve. "And yet still we thwart them – with our man-made warships and our weapons and our armor."

Now Homer's brow furrowed. This man wasn't just one of these – an End of Days type, who were common enough amongst those few believers who had made it this far into the ZA with their faith intact. No, this was worse…

"These swords and shields of ours were built to oppose Satan on Earth, his evil minions in the mortal realm. America and its military were a *great force* for God and for good." His voice soared now, accenting with abandon, as his open hands gestured. "For opposing those who blew up innocents in orgies of sin, and who worshipped a false God… But now – America itself has fallen, for its many sins. For hedonism, for gays in the military, for the abomination of so-called gay marriage, for licentiousness, for lack of thrift, for greed… America fell. It was God's will."

This was clearly a lay preacher of some type – and also clearly one of the fire-breathing Pentecostal sort. Homer wondered where the real ship's chaplains were – a supercarrier would have at least one each of Christian, Jewish, and Muslim faith. This guy was freelancing. Plus giving Homer a very bad feeling.

"How long, brothers? How long will we sail? Two long years we've been crossing the seas, staying alive, keeping the Final End of Days from coming, dragging out the Rapture, and keeping the faithful, including ourselves, from ascending to Heaven. How much more misery, how much more waiting?"

To survive long as a special operator one had to have, along with about 500 other skills, a pretty decent sense of folk psychology. And Homer was sensing a definite psychological aspect to these guys – assuming this congregation were in agreement, which from their nodding and humming, they seemed to be. And that psychological aspect was despair.

"And now, crossing the Atlantic again – God alone knows what for!" The preacher was near frenzy now. "To try to destroy all the soulless in America? To seek some kind of quote-cure-unquote? No cure will bring their souls back to Earth! This is God's will, these are supposed to be the End Days! Just finish it, and it will be over! Let God's cleaners do their last work on Earth."

Yep, Homer had it now. He knew in his bones these were simply people who just couldn't take the fight anymore – the fear, the hopelessness. The only way they could bear it now, he knew, was to decide that it was all supposed to be this way – and the only "problem" was our continued resistance and survival.

It was life under the ZA they couldn't face anymore.

Which was understandable. In fact, it all sounded awfully like guilty thoughts Homer had been having himself lately, in the privacy of his head. And, while hearing this said out loud might have been seductive for that reason… in fact it had the exact opposite effect.

It reminded Homer of his duty.

Because, while these people might have been free to give in to despair, and to capitulate, and to advocate surrender, if they were civilians on dry land… as it was, they were uniformed military personnel deployed on a surface vessel in a time of war. And this kind of shit was dangerous. Worse than bad for morale, it was borderline treason.

Homer slipped out the back of the room. As he did so, he could hear the sermon reaching a climax and then winding down. He looped back around to scope the area. He found the chaplains' quarters, tried the doors and found them locked. Toward the end of the same passage, and around the corner, he heard a door opening. Stopping dead, peeking around, he got a look into a room as the door closed. Inside, he could make out pallets, crates – and a rack of M4 assault rifles.

A voice spoke behind him.

"Greetings, brother." It was the preacher, with two other men standing beside him.

IN DARKNESS THEY DWELL

Four hours after he entered the Channel Tunnel, his feet drenched to the skin from standing in six inches of muddy water, Lieutenant Jameson turned his head across a full panoramic sweep of the tunnel blockage. The last few hours had pushed his Marines to the limit, as it had those behind him tasked with clearing up, filling the gaps in the line, and resupply. He had sent three of his men back with minor injuries – none of them, fortunately, from the undead they had put down. The tunnel was a danger in itself, with railway lines under the water and all manner of debris, most of which one didn't want to contemplate too closely, floating around their feet.

The battle of the last four hours had calmed somewhat, and Jameson's breathing was slowing to a steadier pace as his heart worked to catch up with the rest of his body. Not far away from him floated the decapitated head of the creature he had just killed. The rest of it was under the water, which still rippled from the splash the body had caused. The fight reminded him of his platoon's trek across Europe, mostly on foot, all the way from Germany. He had thought nothing could compare with what he had experienced during those months, but he had been proven wrong. This battle with the dead had been hard fought.

And they had killed a lot. Though still not as many as he had expected – not as many as the intel guys had predicted might be down here. The hardest part of the journey through the tunnels was trudging through the ankle-deep sludge and water. It slowed their pace and wore him and his men down faster than solid ground. Spotting zombies in the dark with only mining lamps to light your way was difficult enough without the terrain being against you as well.

The first sighting had happened barely a hundred yards inside the tunnel. Flickering lights highlighted the skulking figures of zombies moving slowly toward them – slower even than normal. At least the stinking sludge slowed the dead down as well, but another thing it did was hide those lying down in it. Several times he nearly lost a man as a hand came groping up from the murky waters to latch onto a leg or a boot. The first time, the creature had actually bitten into the squaddie's boot, but a shot to the back of the head had stopped it before its teeth could sink through the thick leather. From then on they were more careful, moving more slowly and in a straight line, watching the water as well as the darkness ahead of them.

That first encounter had fired Jameson's nerves and surged adrenaline through his veins, and it fueled him throughout the whole journey. Which was a good thing, since they would encounter many more groups of undead along the way. They didn't come in waves as the Royal Marines had experienced before; these creatures were somehow dulled and much clumsier, much slower than what were generally encountered on missions. It was as though the darkness and nearly excruciating confinement – the claustrophobia – of the tunnel had somehow stupefied even the already mindless dead. A ridiculous notion, Jameson thought, but he couldn't deny the difference. They didn't notice the living down there as quickly as they did on the surface.

They had moved slowly toward them, barely a dozen at first, and all in a rotten state like nothing he had seen in the last two years. The nearest, and the first to be cut down by gunfire, was barely held together. Stretched and pale sinews of what once might have been muscle covered it like a spiderweb; its bones clearly visible as they poked out of torn flesh. There was no skin on its face, and instead a grotesque moving skull stared at them through the darkness, the jaws twitching right up until the moment when several 5.56mm rounds slammed into its grin.

Mile upon mile of muddy tunnel had confronted them, until half an hour ago they had come across the barricade. It loomed out of the darkness and blocked the tunnel, standing nearly six feet high. At first, as the torn and broken metal frame came into view, Jameson had thought they had already found some remnant of the supply train they had been tasked, in part, to look for. But it was far too close to the British side of the Channel, and he was sure they hadn't covered enough ground to be near the midway gate yet.

Train parts, panels tied together with cabling, chairs and doors and seemingly any loose part of the train wreckage available had been piled together and stacked up high in a makeshift blockade that went the full width of the tunnel. The rotting dead were piled up high on this side, though very few of them moved.

First squad had approached very slowly, aware that at any moment the entire mound of dead things could rise up from its slumber and come crawling toward them. But that hadn't happened. As the lights from the soldiers' lamps lit the area more brightly upon approach, it became obvious that these creatures had already been dispatched.

These dead were dead forever.

From this initial assessment, they decided that the barricade was more of a trap than a defensive wall. And from the bodies entangled in the wreckage, Jameson imagined any survivors that had once lived down here must have visited this place regularly – to deal with the creatures that had stumbled into it and gotten caught amongst the wires and the sharp metal, entangled and desperately flailing around until they could be destroyed with relative ease.

Grews had nearly gone through the roof with excitement at this news, and Jameson had found himself grinning as well, as he used his helmet-cam to show the major the defensive wall. He imagined that the major would have given anything, well, almost anything, to be down there himself.

"*I knew it,*" Grews had breathed. "*I knew they'd done it somehow. Look at that. A defensive wall made of train wreckage. It means they survived long enough to put that damn thing up. Where did they find the tools, though?*"

Jameson peered through, to the other side of the wall.

"It's pretty rudimentary, mostly held together by cables. They would have had to work hard to keep the thing upright if faced with a big mass of the dead. It looks more like a way to trap the creatures than to stop them completely. I don't think it would hold a Zulu more than a few hours if it was determined."

"*How many undead so far, though?*"

"Maybe five hundred. Not nearly as many as we first suspected might be in here."

"*Why so few, I wonder? We expected thousands.*"

"No idea, sir," said Jameson, suddenly breathing heavily.

Grews frowned.

"*Are you all right, LT? Is everything okay down there?*"

"Yes, sir, but I don't think that air pump is doing much good. Maybe the vents are blocked or something. Seems that the further into the tunnel we get, the harder it is to breathe. There isn't a lot of oxygen down here."

"*Make sure everyone has their masks on. Those re-breathers should help you some.*"

"Roger that, sir."

Another hour later, and there was no sign of even a single zombie along the remaining stretch of tunnel. As Jameson stood scanning the midway defense gate, and the remaining framework of the train wreck, they had their answer.

"*So the gate did close,*" said Grews.

"Yes, sir, it would appear so. And it seems to have cut the train in half, quite literally. From what I can see, most of the wreckage had been compacted somehow, like it had been crushed before the gate even closed in on it."

Jameson cringed as an unwelcome stench flooded his nostrils for the hundredth time. The signs of survivors were everywhere. Piles of trash and human waste were dotted about on this side of the barricade. Grews was even more excited about that, but then he hadn't had to smell the damn stuff, or trudge through it. He also hadn't had to see the piles of zombie remains littered intermittently along the tunnel.

"*And the maintenance tunnel? The door that they opened?*" Grews' voice was quiet now, and the line crackled audibly. Evidence of old equipment gradually failing.

"We're just cutting it open now." Jameson glanced back down the tunnel, where he could see the glow of several welding torches burning. "Should be open in…"

The radio signal went quiet for an ominous moment. But then, instantly, Grews heard shouting from multiple voices on the squad net. The three screens that relayed the headcams of his squad leaders blurred with movement.

"Jameson. Sitrep."

Not now, thought Grews. Don't fall apart now.

Only Jameson's panicked breathing came back down the line.

Grews peered at the first screen and saw the doorway where two soldiers had been welding rushing up to meet him as Lieutenant Jameson sprinted to close the distance. More shouting, and movement from the darkness of the door. Muffled shouts as the world on all three screens went crazy for what was only a few seconds, but which to Grews was a lifetime of waiting.

Finally, Jameson's voice was back on the net.

"*Sir, we have survivors.*" More heavy breathing. "*Repeat, we have survivors here.*"

Grews sat back in his chair, stunned. The world was spinning around him and all he could do was try to take it in. *They survived all this time*, he thought. They actually managed to survive down there, even after we switched off the power, bombed the damn tunnel, and flooded it. They still survived. It was unthinkable.

"How many? How many are down there?" His voice cracked with urgency.

But Grews could already see the dirty face of a man in the doorway, speaking rapidly. His eyes were wide and glaring for a moment, before squinting against the bright light of Jameson's weapon-mounted light. The man wore some sort of jumpsuit, similar to the ones that the UK Security Services issued its officers. But this was different, with no logo on the front, no markings at all for that matter. The man's head was almost clean-shaven, as was his face, and there was a deep scar running down the middle of his forehead, like something had gouged him. Now, as Grews watched intently, almost standing up and out of his seat, the man spoke rapidly to Jameson – but also covered his eyes, blocking out the unaccustomed light.

Finally, the man nodded and smiled, showing a neglected set of brown and yellow teeth.

"*Thirty-eight survivors sir. I repeat, three-eight,*" reported Jameson across the line.

"Say again, Lieutenant," said Grews. "Was that

thirty-eight?"

"That's affirmative."

Grews shouted out loud this time, unable to restrain himself. He glanced around at his small command team, who looked back at him, their amazed expressions quickly turning to smiles that reflected his own emotional state.

"Lieutenant. Get them out of there, ASAP. Get them out before someone stops us. If we get them onto British soil then there is nothing anyone can do."

"Roger that, sir. Do we need to quarantine?"

Quarantine. Why hadn't he thought of that? Because he hadn't expected them to still be alive. Body bags were what was waiting for them outside the tunnel. But for once body bags wouldn't be needed.

"Yes Lieutenant, but I'll deal with that. Get them out of that tunnel. And exfil your team as well. Get your boys out."

"Roger that, sir."

"Thirty-eight survivors. My God."

"Copy that, sir. Actually, I can't totally make out the French guy, but I think he just said that one of them is only eighteen months old. A baby was born down there."

Deep in the tunnel, Jameson coughed, looked around at his men, and then addressed the dazed Frenchman in front of him.

"You say you cleared the maintenance tunnel all the way to the entrance?"

The man nodded. "But it was locked." It wasn't a question really, but an accusation. They had got so close to freedom, all the way to the entrance. And no one had let them out.

The Frenchman went on. "The doorway was not openable. We did try. We tried many times."

"Well we can fix that. Let's get a move on. Wait… is it safe to move around in there?"

"Yes. And it is dry."

Jameson turned to his squad leaders.

"Okay. Everyone into the maintenance tunnel. I'll inform Grews that we're coming out a different way."

Five minutes later, and Grews was still up and pacing the ground, barking orders to everyone who came within a few yards of him. There was a lot to do, but none of the staff carrying out the orders seemed to mind. They had seen a change in their commander almost instantly. He was himself again and he had a job to do and no one was going to stop him. Even if it meant that in a few hours he would be looking at a court-martial for disobeying orders.

"Get that damn maintenance tunnel open. And do it fast."

MOGADISHU OF THE DEAD

All of Alpha, plus the fifteen men of MARSOC Team 1, but minus their command elements, now sat in a larger briefing room belowdecks on the *Kennedy*. Predictably, the two teams sat on opposite sides of the room. But, for some reason, Henno made a special effort to plop down on the other side of the house. Maybe he was determined to meet some Americans he could fully endorse. He'd heard some damned impressive things about the U.S. Marine Corps.

"Henno," he said, putting his hand out to the Marine beside him.

"Reyes," the man answered, taking his hand. "Any news from the world?"

"Let's see. Last I heard, the Queen was touring the reconstruction of the East End, where the Olympic Park used to be."

Reyes laughed. "She still gets out? What's she, like 104? Amazing."

"Yeah. She learned it from her mum and dad in WWII. They refused to be evacuated during the Blitz." Most of the others in the room were talking quietly to their teammates, or reviewing pre-briefing notes.

Reyes leaned in. "I hear almost all of England's still got electrical power?"

Henno nodded. "Comes on and off. But reopening

and rehabilitating the coal mines in the north worked a treat. They've had to do modification of all kinds of shit to burn coal instead of oil. There's also the wind farms that the hippies and the bloody EU pushed for back when people gave a shit about the environment. They look pretty smart now. And, of course, we've twisted the dials on the nuclear power plants all the way to the right."

"I guess disposing of spent fuel rods is the least of our problems now."

"Yeah. The Eurozone makes a pretty good dumping ground for nuclear waste at this point."

Reyes laughed, but then his smile faded. "Tell me. Are you mothers seriously planning to do a run through a city of three million dead cannibals…?"

Henno just shrugged and nodded.

Reyes asked, "Are we even sure everyone there's dead?"

"Dead-ish."

"*Jesu Cristo*," Reyes said. Henno squinted and looked into the man's eyes – and recognized that look. It was the one they all got every once in a while – when it sank in that they might really be standing at the twilight of their species. That jolt of waking up into a nightmare.

Heigh ho, Henno always said at such times. May as well get on with it. Better than sitting around bemoaning the sorry fate of the world.

"What kind of tactics," Reyes asked, "have you guys developed against swarm attacks?"

But before Henno could answer, their commanders – Drake, Fick, Ainsley, and Handon – banged through the hatch and silenced the already pretty silent room.

* * *

"Good evening," Ainsley said, in his crisp and plummy British officer's accent. "Welcome to Op Secunda Mortem. Alpha has already gotten the high-level mission concept. Here it is for the MARSOC fellows, who are our backup and QRF." Handon had reminded him to make a conscious effort not to refer to them as "the B team." *No pissing off the Marines, remember…* "Our team call signs for the op are going to be Mortem One and Mortem Two. The air element is Grey Goose Zero." He sat on the edge of the table before continuing.

"This is a combat jump: high-altitude/high-opening over Lake Michigan, then we fly in on the prevailing winds – straight into downtown." He tapped at a keyboard on the table, and an overlaid street- and topo-map of Chicago came up on the projection screen behind him. "Our drop zone is the top of this building here: 290 West Lake Street, office and labs of NeuraDyne Neurosciences. Our target site." He flashed a laser pointer at a building – dead in the middle of downtown, just inside the point where the Chicago River branched.

"The good news is: we don't have to fight our way in on the street. We just touch down light as a feather on this nice flat roof, cut through the rooftop access doors, and descend – clearing and holding any levels of the building necessary to get where we're going."

Ainsley paused, put the laser pointer down, and pressed his palms flat on the table. He looked up, casting his gaze over the faces of the operators in the room. "The bad news is: particularly at this time of year, the wind off the lake can gust to 30mph – it can also send dense fog spilling into the canyons of the city streets. Meteorologically speaking, it's a closed-loop circulation pattern causing sharp updrafts under certain conditions. In foul weather it can also massively increase storm intensity."

"So that's us fucked, then," said Henno.

Handon took up the laser pointer. In gruffer tones he said, "You can see our drop zone here is ringed by both forks of the river… plus the 'L', or elevated train platforms… and about a dozen other skyscrapers on all sides." He clicked the laser off. "*That's* us fucked."

The briefing moved forward.

* * *

"And now a few words," Ainsley said, "about the new Zulu type."

Most of the Marines looked uncomprehending. This was news to them. Ainsley surveyed their expressions before continuing.

"We've only seen a handful, and only briefly, and never under sustained observation – never mind scientific controls. Luckily, we've got two gentlemen here with us who have." He nodded at Drake, who stepped outside and came back with two strangers in tow. The first wore the standard British Army

Temperate Combat dress – camo field jacket and trousers with beret. From his insignia, he was a captain in the Royal Corps of Engineers. The second man wore a blue jumpsuit, with the insignia of the UK Security Services.

"Captain Martin and Corporal Wesley," Ainsley said. "Both saw action in the Battle of Folkestone. And both had close encounters with a Foxtrot."

"Foxtrot, sir?" A Marine lance corporal had both his hand and his eyebrows raised.

Ainsley cleared his throat. "The designation for the new Zulu type is 'Foxtrot November'. Work it out in your own time." The heavy brow of the Marine started working up and down while Ainsley carried on. "It is believed that this represents a new adaptation of the virus – occurring in areas that have long been totally infested. So there's at least a chance we'll face them in Chicago. Martin and Wesley have kindly dropped in to brief us." He stepped aside.

The two newcomers, scanning the room, now looked briefly to each other. The soldier straightened up. "Well… they're fast – much faster than Romeos, or runners. Faster than any I'd ever fought. They also seem to have much more agility and body control. And they don't appear to feed – only to infect."

Another Marine raised a hand. "Don't feed, sir?"

Ainsley chimed in again. "The theory from the bio blokes is that it's an adaptation – when there are few enough living remaining, this 'infect-and-run' behavior gets the infection into the last remaining pockets of survivors."

"BOHICA," mumbled another Marine. *Bend over – here it comes again.* Several of his teammates laughed aloud.

Wesley, the UKSS non-com, took a step forward. He didn't look like he was finding any of this funny. "Just a single one of these things," he said, fighting a quaver in his voice, "took down both of the men in my station before they even realized what was happening. They never had a chance... And before we knew it, it had turned ten, twenty, fifty more…"

Under his breath, one of the Marines whispered, "Motherfuckers shoulda learned to duck… Security dudes, jeesh…" This drew barely stifled laughter from MARSOC and Alpha both.

Wesley gave the room a venomous look. Handon didn't look best pleased, either, and spoke sharply. "It's not just security service guys, you comedians. USOC's lost people, too. My team's PO attachment bought it when one of these things *leapt* onto a fast rope dragged by a moving helo. And they may be responsible for taking out the SEAL team that was wiped out *to a man* yesterday."

This seemed to drain the humor from the room.

Martin looked more circumspect, but added quietly, "I lost my whole platoon. One of these things got loose in our lodgings. Most of my men never made it out of bed."

Gunny Fick stood, removed a stub of cigar, and concluded: "So *you* motherfuckers be advised: field reports indicate that the difficulty of making a headshot on a Foxtrot is about like the difficulty of hitting a regular Zulu – *squared.* They're coming fast, they're running and jumping – and with the implacable intention of turning you into a flesh-eating freak, who will kill and eat your own friends, probably in seconds. Under those conditions, only complete dead-eye dicks, who also have pure liquid nitrogen running through their goddamned veins, can make that shot. Which had better describe you fucking smart alecks."

* * *

"…Another concern on this op is going to be the danger of 'Robert Neville' types still breathing air in Chicago." The commanders had been trading off for over an hour, and Fick was now taking a turn. Frankly, the Marines had a bit more experience zombie-fighting in more places, and in more varied terrain, than had Alpha. Also, since each group had lived its own personal ZA, their slang didn't match up perfectly.

Ali raised her hand. "Robert Neville types, Gunny?"

"Yeah, you know, from *I Am Legend.* That guy living all alone in New York. I think in that other book they called 'em *LaMOEs* – Last Man on Earth. A long-term survivor, holed up with a lot of firepower… and very accustomed to shooting first and asking questions never."

"Copy that, Gunny." Ali sunk low in her chair and pushed her hair behind her ear.

"Accordingly, it's going to be full body armor along with the bite suits and face shields…"

* * *

"Let's talk exfiltration and extraction," said Ainsley.

"Thank fuck for that," muttered Henno, along with several similar *sotto voce* sentiments.

"You all know how critical this target is believed to be. Frankly, it's a lot more important that we get the data out than that we get ourselves out." He let that grim reminder of their duty sink in for a few seconds. "The plan is this: we're jumping in with a powerful radio transmitter, with encrypted burst data capability, as well as the batteries to power it. When we've secured the NeuraDyne servers, we're going to try to send all the data out on the air straight away. But there may be paper documents, samples, chemical solutions, slides, X-rays, or other materials we need to get out as well."

Handon removed his soggy cigar stub from his mouth and jumped in. "Plus, some of you sons of bitches may have ideas about getting home yourselves." Most of the men grinned. The dynamic between Handon and Ainsley was actually a pretty good example of the complementary roles of officers and senior NCOs, with the latter as combination big brother and enforcer.

Ainsley went on. "As you'll have guessed, we can't just fly off the top of the building again. The closest place a fixed-wing aircraft can land to extract us is here." He lased the map at a little island just off the edge of downtown, sticking out into the lake, and connected by a thin land bridge at its northern end. "This is Northerly Island Park – formerly Meigs Air

Field. From 1948 it was a little single-strip airport. In 1994, Mayor Richard M. Daley announced plans to close the airport and build a park in its place. There was some sort of palaver involving the state legislature, and in the end Daley bulldozed the runway. However, in 2003, we know that a small commuter aircraft made an emergency landing on the grass next to the demolished strip. After effecting electrical repairs, it took off safely again."

Drake chimed in. "It won't be the smoothest take-off you've ever experienced. But my pilots have seen the sat imagery. And they're confident they can get in and out again. As you know, the bird for this op doesn't have the endurance to linger, and there's nowhere safe to land and hang out – so as soon as you jump, it's going to do a 180 and race back to the flattop to refuel. At the Greyhound's max cruise speed, it's a hair over 2.5 hours each way. So that's a minimum of five hours you're on your own. When you ring, the bird will go out again – empty, if you've got the goods and need extraction; full of Marines if you need assistance. Either way, it comes down on the island airstrip."

"Wait a second," Predator said, his palm making a move for his forehead. "There's still the small matter of getting ourselves to the freaking airstrip."

Ainsley nodded. "Two-point-eight miles over surface streets. You'll hardly notice it."

Predator went ahead and executed that face-palm maneuver. Juice joined him. Imagining that three-mile run out in the open, through an urban center, surrounded by virtually unlimited attackers, they were both pretty much thinking the same thing:

Welcome to the Mogadishu of the Dead – Population: us.

And around them the ship sailed on through the night, toward the Dead New World.

BOOK TWO

MOGADISHU OF THE DEAD

EVER ON

Andrew Wesley, former corporal with the UK Security Services, and one-time officer in charge of the night watch at the Channel Tunnel entrance in Folkestone, but now of no fixed abode, stood staring out at the night sky. He was off at the very edge of the gently rolling flight deck of the USS *John F. Kennedy*, as it churned the North Atlantic, steaming back toward its place of origin – the New World.

Now a Dead World.

The boat, a floating city really, was an American supercarrier that at one time had been the base of operations for over 80 combat aircraft. Now it held fewer than two dozen. It had simply turned out that air superiority was of no critical importance in the ZA. Also, pilots had gotten a little thin on the ground, in the two years since the fall of human civilization.

The sun was just now rising, and Wesley squinted into it, thinking fitfully about the unnerving events of the last week. There had been the terrifying outbreak in Folkestone, the death of his two rookies, and then the harrowing firefight in the town as an entire battalion of regular infantry had rushed in to quell the rampaging masses of the dead. And after that, the disorientation and vertigo of getting helicoptered out to the *JFK* in the middle of an endless ocean. It had all happened so quickly, there was no time to process any of it.

Now, as he stared into the first light of another

unsettling day, Wesley wondered what in hell they were getting themselves into. Word was that North America was completely dead, or rather undead, down to the last person. And here they were sailing straight for it, on what he could only think of as some mad and terribly ill-considered errand. Not that he had yet been given much information on which to form opinions.

A soft sound from behind startled him from his staring contest with the rising sun. It was Captain Martin, his fellow traveler on this perilous and incomprehensible journey.

"Hiding out?" Martin asked, though it was more statement than question. These two had only known each other a tiny stretch of time. And yet they seemed to know each other well, right from their first meeting – when Wesley had watched Martin emerge from an exploding hotel, just a few steps ahead of a herd of slavering corpses.

"Hiding out seemed much the best thing," replied Wesley. "Keeps me out of everyone's way."

Martin laughed, a warm and genuine sound, which considering recent events was a rare and welcome thing.

"Any idea how long before we arrive?" asked Wesley.

"Dunno, I haven't asked," said Martin with a shrug. "No one's talking about it, least of all the spec-ops boys."

"Hmm. They do rather keep things to themselves. You know, I've never been to America."

"Oh?"

"Nope. Never once. And to be honest I'm not sure I'm looking forward to it now."

"I'll second you on that," Martin said, shrugging. "I have actually been a few times. Though I suppose it's going to be rather less amusing this time around. Wouldn't care to brave the queues at DisneyWorld in its probable current state."

Wesley grinned at that, and the two lapsed into silence, both staring at the rising sun as it scattered dazzling flashes across the rough chop of the ocean's surface. There wasn't much beauty left in this world, but Wesley figured this qualified.

He also wondered what was happening back in Britain in the aftermath of the Folkestone incident. Shocked as he had been at the time, Wesley now figured: if it could happen there it could happen anywhere. And if Fortress Britain, the last significant bastion of surviving humanity, was still so vulnerable… well, then what chance did any of them stand? Then again, the odds that any of them on this boat would ever see Britain again were not something Wesley would care to rate. And if the sublime sight of sunlight on the water were all that were left to him… well, he would enjoy it in this moment that he still had left.

"I'm glad you're here," he said, looking across at Martin.

If there was still beauty in this fallen world, and if there could still be friendship, then maybe that was enough.

QUARANTINE

Lt. Colonel Bryan, Royal Army Medical Corps, vascular surgeon of 22 years experience, and ranking medical officer with USOC (the Unified Special Operations Command) at Hereford, flipped the page of the heavy book in his lap. It was the complete plays of Shakespeare, which he figured was as good a way as any to get through the long hours of the ZA. Seemingly longer still were these shifts in the Quarantine Shack, which sat adjacent to the primary helipad. It had to be manned 24/7 by a medical officer. And Colonel Bryan, OC of the base hospital, insisted on taking his shifts just like everyone else.

Hereford, former barracks of the British SAS, was now the home of USOC – the last, best few hundred special operators left, in what was left of the world. It was from here that these real-life superheroes worked to keep alive the last fifty million or so living humans, in what had now become Fortress Britain. It was only the incredible timing of a terrible terrorist attack, two years earlier, and just a few days before the zombie virus reached a tipping point across the world, that caused Britain to cancel all flights and lock down its borders. And it was those precious few days of isolation that allowed them to hunker down against the advancing rampage of the dead. Now, Doc Bryan and the USOC commanders just had to keep Hereford from going the way of virtually all the other military bases around the world – being overrun from within by infected soldiers brought back inside the wire by their brothers in arms.

The Quarantine Shack was a big part of this.

The facility consisted of one small building with two rooms. One of them was a waiting area for the attending doctor. The other was much larger, reinforced, lockable from the outside, and stocked with cots, food, water, limited medical supplies, and various items of minor comfort. Along one edge sat a cage with the sniffing dogs. An enclosed passage led directly from there to the base hospital, making the whole place basically a big conduit there from the helipad. A conduit that could be opened – or locked down and tightly controlled.

Bryan flipped another wispy page. Frankly, what he could only think of as the 16th-century slang of the Bard defeated him. The heavy annotations helped somewhat.

The phone on his desk rang.

"Bryan."

"*Incoming*," the voice on the other end announced. "*It's Echo team. They're back from over the water, with one litter urgent casualty. ETA five mikes.*"

"Nature of the injury?" Bryan thunked his book shut and pushed it across the desk.

"*Unknown at this time. Stand by.*"

Bryan hung up, dialed the hospital duty desk, and summoned two medical orderlies. They came trotting up within ten seconds, wide-eyed and expectant. Bryan nodded at them gravely, moved to the door that opened on the big room, worked the locks, then stepped inside. Turning again, he nodded to the orderlies through the thick plexiglas.

And they locked him in.

Less than a minute later, Bryan could hear the rotors and jet engines of the incoming helo. Other than pulling on some latex gloves and a face shield, there was really nothing to prepare on this end. Everything was all set up. It always was. He moved to the cages where the two dogs stood alert, sniffing, tails wagging.

"Hullo, lads," Bryan said, palming a couple of treats from the table and feeding them through the bars. "How are we this fine apocalyptic day? Good boys, good boys."

He heard the hurricane-like sounds of the bird flaring outside. A moment later, the outer door banged open, letting in the roiling wind and dust. A lolling and unconscious, or barely conscious, operator was supported from each sides by two others. One of them held an IV bag, the drip from which snaked around them into the casualty's arm. All three were dressed in full battle rattle – bite suits, Kevlar, tactical load-bearing vests, mags, grenades, sidearms, and short swords.

As they lurched in, the wounded man's feet drug on the floor behind them. He had a thick, blood-soaked bandage wrapped around his neck.

That doesn't look good, thought Bryan. He didn't just mean the seriousness of the injury.

Before he could ask, one of the Echo men said, "It's a ricochet, Doc. *Just a ricochet.*" They weren't putting down their burden, but merely angled him toward the exit door.

"Let me examine him," Bryan said. "Lay him down."

The two looked agitated, but complied. "He's bleeding out, Doc," one said as he laid his brother operator down. As they put him on the gurney alongside the cage, the two dogs started going apeshit, barking and snarling.

"He's half-covered in Zulu goo," the other Echo guy said. It was true – there was a lot of gore on the man's armor and particularly his boots. Some of it was black. If it was fresh, and it was, that would set off the dogs.

Gingerly but expertly, Bryan peeled back the bandage. It looked like his right common carotid had been severed. And from the man's color, he'd already lost an enormous amount of blood. The shape of the wound was consistent with a gunshot. It certainly wasn't a bite – though a scratch could conceivably produce something like this.

"See? Like we said. Stray round."

Bryan looked up. "What was the path of the bullet?" On at least one other documented occasion, a round had passed through a Zulu and into a soldier – with enough organic matter on it to infect the man. It was damned rare – a little like the apocryphal Civil War nurse said to be impregnated by the musket ball that passed through a soldier's teste – but it happened.

"It sparked off a car. We were all on the same side of the street." Frequently, in CQB (close quarters battle), shooters were on all sides of a structure – and moving 100 miles an hour. In those cases, a round passing through a wall or an enemy could be a hazard, hitting a teammate on the other side. But not in this case? Bryan frowned. Could a round have gone through a Zulu, then ricocheted back? Because these guys rarely missed entirely. And could it still carry infectious material?

The casualty convulsed on the litter, spitting up blood and bile. Shock from extreme blood loss. He was in fact bleeding out.

One of the Echo men put pressure on the wound. The other put his hand on his sidearm. "Colonel," the man said through gritted teeth. "Kindly open the door. This man's coming in."

Well, Bryan thought with resignation, *at least he's not holding the gun to my head*… He would just have to take responsibility – not to mention personally sit with the patient every second until he died, or until he recovered.

He made a thumbs-up toward the plexiglas. The locks clanked, the door banged open, and the two orderlies raced in. They unlocked the wheels on the gurney and raced out and down the hall toward the base hospital. Bryan followed at a trot behind them.

And the dogs carried on barking until they were out of hearing.

STAND FAST

In the wake of the long and disturbing briefing on their upcoming mission to the middle of dead North America, the operators of Alpha, officers and men both, had swung into action with mission prep work. There was a lot of it. The eight-man team was going to parachute directly into Chicago and try to get out with a vaccine developed there by a biotech called NeuraDyne Neurosciences. They were going to HAHO jump out over Lake Michigan, fly in on the prevailing winds, land on top of the target building, and fight their way down to the labs. And that was the easy part.

Afterwards, they would have to exfil overland, through a city of three million dead people, to a tiny airfield on an island out in the lake, for air extraction.

In all the intent activity, Homer, an Alpha operator and former Team Six SEAL, managed to buttonhole Commander Drake – ship's XO and Alpha's liaison and handler on the supercarrier. They now stood together in the shadows of one corner of the mess belowdecks. Homer needed a word in private – specifically, he needed to tell Drake about what he had discovered brewing down in the bowels of the ship. About the dangerous sermon he had overheard in the ship's chapel.

"Yeah, we know about those dudes," Drake said, as various operators and sailors cruised by in the adjacent passageway, or in one door and out the other. "We call them the Zealots. But you've got to understand – all three of our official chaplains quit those jobs, and took on other duties, after the fall. Well, two of them did. The third we think jumped ship. But, in any case, religion's strictly a volunteer activity these days."

Homer nodded. "I understand, Commander, but you need to be aware this man is preaching some fairly incendiary and seditious stuff. He's saying the Zulus are God's cleaners – and that *we*, the military, are the problem, messing up the End Days and holding up the Rapture."

Drake seemed to take this on board. "Yeah, it's not ideal, is it? But our verdict, when we last discussed it, was that it allowed the men to blow off steam. Nonetheless, I'll make a note to revisit it – send someone down to listen in on Sunday. That square you away, Chief?"

Homer said, "There's something else. I saw a lot of weapons and ordnance piled in a room near the chapel, by the chaplains' quarters."

Someone called Drake's name from the far hatch. He swiveled and made a one-minute sign, then turned back to Homer. "This boat's probably not as shipshape as what you might have been used to. We've got crap stored all over the place these days – hell, we've got a whole organic farm on the hangar deck…" He clapped Homer on the shoulder before heading off. "But I'll make a note to look into that as well. Stand fast, Chief…"

* * *

Four others who had also been in the briefing were Alpha team operators Ali and Pope. Ali was a former Delta sniper – now perhaps the most deadly long gunner left still breathing air; and Pope was a former paramilitary with the CIA Special Activities Division. They were taking fifteen minutes from mission prep and using it to pick the brains of the two British newcomers, Wesley and Martin.

The four of them emerged onto the five-acre flight deck, with its fresh sea air and bit of sun, and headed for the shade of the island. The towering structure, with its blast-proof glass windows and banks and arrays of antennas and dishes, rose up above them into a sky that had been crowding with clouds all afternoon. Either a weather front was coming, or they were sailing into one. The four sat down cross-legged, two with their backs against the steel wall.

"So the Folkestone outbreak was pretty close-run?" Ali asked.

Wesley nodded. "Yes. I remember thinking clearly: *This the end. We're all going to die*. But then the cavalry rolled in."

Martin nodded his agreement. "If an entire mechanized battalion hadn't rocked up when they did, I have no doubt both of us would be slouching and moaning even now."

Pope looked levelly at the British soldier, and clocked his insignia. "Royal Corps of Engineers."

Martin nodded once. "Fifteen years in. Mostly vehicle maintenance the last couple of years, but a lot of structural prior to that – bases, bridges, great big solid things. I miss all that, come to talk about it…"

Ali looked over at Wesley, still dressed in his UKSS jumpsuit. "What about you. Always been with the Security Services?"

"Yes," nodded Wesley. "Well, I have been since everything went to crap. I worked as a bodyguard before that, and for too many security firms to even remember. Started when I was eighteen, bouncing the doors of a nightclub in a small town in the Midlands. I was actually working in France when it all came down. Caught the last train back to the UK."

"Lucky man," Pope said. "Believe me. We've been back over there many times since."

Wesley looked down at his boots. "Is it as bad as they say?"

Ali nodded solemnly. "And not just France. The whole continent's a dead zone."

"Jesus." Wesley shook his head and squinted off into memory.

"We've moved through a lot of fallen Europe," said Pope. "And you always find the same last stand, played out over and over again – blocked hallways, first-floor stairwells torn down, lot of shotgun shell casings lying around. The odd chef's knife caked with that congealed black shit they have instead of blood. Usually, from the way it's laid out, you can reconstruct the whole battle, their last minutes, blow by blow. It's like a forensic jackpot. If any of that mattered now."

Ali shrugged. "Of course, we turn up far too late to do any good. You can see all this evidence of people desperate for someone to come and save them. But no one ever did. Horror stories that ended with absolute horror. Being devoured – and killed, if they were lucky. Coming back, if they weren't."

Wesley thought of Amarie with a shudder. She had been a woman he had grown close to, during those last weeks of civilization in France. They had only been together a month, but the after-image of that time burned bright in Wesley's mind. The horror that these soldiers had just described – had that been her fate?

Martin grunted. "What a state we've come to – where death is often the best gift you can give someone." He paused while squinting off into his own memory. Then, more quietly, he said, "I had to take off the heads of two of my best young soldiers. With a fire axe from the wall of the hotel."

The Folkestone outbreak had begun when one of the new super-fast zombies, which they called Foxtrot Novembers (for the "fucking nightmare"), had somehow dug its way out of the collapsed Channel Tunnel – and gotten loose in the barracks where Captain Martin's platoon had been billeted. All had been turned except him.

Pope reached across and put his hand on Martin's shoulder. "Hey. You did what you had to. For everyone's good."

Martin shook his head sadly. "And theirs, too. After the fast one had done the rounds, half of my platoon just laid into the other half, a very nasty fight in very tight quarters. No one made it out of that hotel alive. The upstairs was like some nightmare butcher shop that a tornado had just passed through. The floor was literally a pool of blood and there were bits of people everywhere. They didn't stand a chance. And I knew the best I could do at that point would be to just try and bring the whole building down. I didn't leave with any grenades."

Wesley looked across at his erstwhile partner. "I had to do both of my boys with a shotgun. They were just kids." These were his staff at the security station, who had been out on patrol when the Foxtrot scratched both of them, then disappeared in an eyeblink.

No one replied, but their expressions said it all. *That sucks.*

"With a single-barrel shotgun. I had to stop and reload."

Both Pope and Ali actually thought that was hilarious, and had to carefully swallow their mirth. Pope paused a respectful beat before speaking. "You both did your duty. And next time it might easily be you or me that has to be put down. No one gets a pass."

Ali kept her silence. And as she looked off the edge of the boat, thousands of yards away, toward the horizon, toward the edge of the world, she thought: *What if Homer were turned? Would I have the strength to put him down?* Privately, she doubted she did. She'd turned off hundreds, if not thousands, of living and dead both, in her career as an elite sniper. But this was one shot she could never take.

Would he have the strength to do it for me? she thought, thinking of their semi-secret, and perhaps very ill-advised, love affair. *Oh, God… have we made a terrible mistake – for which we're both going to pay later? Or, much worse, will the whole team pay? Or all of humanity?* A whole world gone down for one misjudged love. It was equally romantic and horrific to contemplate…

Pulling Ali from her reverie, Pope asked the others, "When did you last see the Foxtrot?"

Martin answered. "I saw it go head-first out a window on the top floor of the hotel and hit the ground running. I mean literally running, like it hadn't just fallen twenty feet onto its back. The last time I saw a human move at that kind of speed was when I watched the Olympic 100-meter sprint."

"Word was," Wesley said, "it was also in the battle in the village. But I never saw it. They said it took the concentrated fire of a whole battalion to bring it down."

Martin shook his head. "I don't know what you're all expecting to find in Chicago. But you run into more than a couple of these things at one time… man, you watch your arse."

* * *

Commander Drake appeared from out of a doorway to the island. He strode up to the group, without seeming to have to look around to locate them. (Pope remembered the tracking ship's ID cards that broadcast all their locations.) He addressed one of the newcomers directly.

"Captain Martin. I'm guessing you carry a UK DoD cell phone?"

Mobile, Martin mentally corrected, smiling inwardly at the Americanism. But he just nodded.

"Take a look?" Martin handed it over. "Hmm. High-grade encryption capability. This should connect seamlessly to the ship's packet data network." He began tapping. "Here are guest credentials to get you on… And here's my number." He handed it back. "You think of anything else relevant to this mission, you call me."

Martin almost said, "Aye aye, sir." But instead he just nodded once more.

Drake stalked off again – long, purposeful strides, like he had promises to keep. And nautical miles to go before he'd sleep.

HELLFIRE

Colonel Bryan (or "Doc" Bryan as the men almost always called him), flipped another page of *Coriolanus*. Though the grain riots and the assault on Rome in the story seemed eerily timely, his attention was even less on the book than before. Sitting in a bedside chair in an otherwise empty wardroom of the hospital, he put his bare hand on the grievously wounded operator's forehead again. The digital thermometer would have the last word on his temperature. But Bryan still felt like he could learn more through the touch of bare human skin.

Just so long as it actually remained human.

So far so good. The man was running a moderate fever – but that could be the result of any number of types of infection carried in by the deformed bullet and the gunk upon it. Infection in gunshot wounds was too common, ubiquitous really, even to remark upon. The unconscious operator had been put on massive doses of intravenous antibiotics, plus anti-virals. Aside from that, Bryan had been able to sew his severed neck artery back together, thus usefully keeping the blood in his body. So the patient actually stood a decent chance of surviving.

But, on this occasion, Bryan was a hell of a lot more concerned that if he died, he died properly, and completely. The man was held down with leather wrist and ankle restraints attached to the bed, but nonetheless... Bryan briefly opened one of the man's eyes to check color, dilation, and opacity. Leaning back again, he monitored the man's shallow breathing over the book in his lap. And he exhaled heavily himself.

This burden was his.

* * *

Back out on the helipad, the Black Hawk DAP ("Direct Action Penetrator") that had brought the casualty in was more than a little dinged up itself. The DAP version of the venerable Black Hawk had stub wings mounted with a 30mm automatic cannon, rocket pods, and various other armaments. It had been feared this firepower was going to be needed for the extraction of Echo team. In the event, the bird's pilots had been forced to land amongst a great deal of street debris in order to evacuate the badly wounded operator – during which one of its rocket hardpoints had been damaged by the edge of an overturned car. Two techs from the Aviation Maintenance Company wrestled with it now, trying to unmount an AGM-114 Hellfire laser-guided missile from the dodgy mount.

The two grimy and jumpsuited engineers hunched over the hardpoint, one supporting the missile from below, while the other used his full strength to try and pry it off. Between that, and all the dust in the air from the bird's recent landing, neither noticed the smoke floating out from the base of the stub wing – nor the sparking that was happening underneath the cowling.

There was no getting around that maintenance standards had taken a beating in the ZA – otherwise known as the post-industrial era. The maintenance guys managed to keep the birds flying. But, in this case, the lack of replacement and spare parts meant that the electricals feeding the weapons mounts were long past their expiration date. And the stress of the collision with the car pushed them into overload.

Due to the shorting electricals, one of the Hellfire missiles, which one of the techs still cradled in his arms, ignited. And then it launched.

The aptly named Hellfire, a 106-pound air-to-surface missile, has a shape-charged warhead which packs a 5-million-pound per square inch impact, defeating *all known armor* (back when the enemy could operate things like tanks). Now, as it sparked off, its burning propellant generated 500 foot-pounds of forward force, violently ripping it free of its hardpoint. Normally laser- or radar-guided, the blind and dumb missile simply plowed straight ahead – and directly into the enlisted mess on the opposite side of the compound. Its payload, a high-explosive shape-charged warhead, exploded a fraction of a second after entry, completely destroying most of the building.

And most of the people inside it.

* * *

Doc Bryan not only heard, but felt the explosion from where he sat in the hospital. It actually bounced him in his chair. His phone went off a few seconds later.

"Go for Bryan. *What…*? How many?" He listened gravely. "Understood. I can be there in thirty seconds. But I need an orderly here." He looked up from his phone and around the empty wardroom. "Orderly!" he shouted. "Nurse! Anyone!" A panicked-looking young woman in uniform ducked into the room.

"Sir?" she said, fear in her eyes. She already knew something terrible was happening.

"Watch this patient," he said. "Ring me any anomalies. *You do not leave this post.*" He didn't have time to brief her further. "Understand?" She nodded vigorously, but Doc Bryan was already leaping away down the aisle, and out of the room.

OVERRUN

Doc Bryan inserted a morphine syrette into the screaming, badly burnt man lying on the ground before him. He had to get him sedated to work on him – or even to assess him. All the thrashing and flopping around was a danger, to the man himself and to others nearby.

Bryan had set up a triage point 100 meters from the scene where the mess hall had been turned into a flaming inferno by the errant Hellfire. He had to balance precious minutes spent moving critically wounded people around, against the risk of secondary explosions or other hazards close to the blast site. For the better part of twenty minutes now he'd been doing emergency trauma care – most of which consisted of controlling hemorrhaging and airway management – and sending them off on litters to the hospital.

He was so engrossed in care and triage that he'd failed to notice his stretcher bearers had stopped returning to pick up more. He finished fixing a burn mask to the man before him, mentally pronounced him stable, and called out for a litter.

None came.

For the first time in several minutes, Bryan looked and listened attentively around him. Engrossed in life-or-death tasks, he'd nearly totally zoned out – hadn't even noticed the sounds or tumult of those fighting the fire, and others clearing rubble to pull out survivors.

Now, his vision expanding, and his hearing dialing back up, he caught wind of more – and much worse.

Over and above the screams and moans of the wounded nearby, he could make out shrieks from further away. That – and now the sound of gunfire, ramping up fast.

It was all coming from the direction of the hospital.

Doc Bryan squinted off in that direction as a terrible chill seized his heart.

* * *

The Colonel was himself personally pulling hunks of smoking rubble off a crumpled ragdoll of a soldier, around on the opposite side of the destroyed mess, when an MP hailed him, coming up at a gallop – with his sidearm in hand. The Colonel paused and looked up.

"What now, Sergeant?"

The man looked for a second like he didn't know how to answer. Finally he bit the bullet. "Some kind of outbreak, Colonel. Zulus in the hospital. It's complete bedlam, but I'm sure of it. I put one down myself."

"*Jesus fucking*… How many?"

The MP just shook his head, looking like he was fighting down panic.

And then the attack warning siren, a wavering tone across the base-wide speaker system, suddenly rent the air. The Colonel had never heard it – almost no one serving there had. It warbled up and down, chilling the blood of the already half-panicked garrison.

The Colonel dropped his hunk of rock where he

stood, and drew his own sidearm. "Roust your entire command. Get them out there setting up a perimeter."

"It's already being done."

"Take me to it."

But the Colonel was already racing off ahead. He knew the way to the hospital.

* * *

Doc Bryan had to fight his way to the hospital himself. It seemed like half the personnel on base were running away from it – and the other half toward. The latter carried rifles, pistols, swords, and in a few cases improvised melee weapons such as shovels. Nearing the main entrance, shoving and being shoved, Bryan pulled up short.

There were four or five bodies lying motionless in a jumble outside the double swinging doors out front. All appeared to be dead of head wounds. From the pallor of their skin… well, Bryan didn't think these people had been alive when they were killed.

He heard someone shout his name from behind. It was one of his young staff doctors – shouting at him to come back, to stay the hell out of there. Fear and guilt raged around in Bryan's breast, battling for control of his body and emotions, and he felt an involuntary sob rise up through his chest. He tried to master himself to take some action, to turn away – but then he looked again at the uniform and hair on one of the bodies. This one faced away from him, but was still bracingly familiar.

Gripped with horror, afraid to continue or to stop, he squatted down, leaned over… and rolled the body over. He couldn't recognize the face. Much of it, in particular the nose, looked like it had been bitten off. Also, the base of her skull was a large gaping wound, from a gunshot, or shotgun blast. But her name patch on her blouse was intact. It was the nurse he had called in to watch the wounded Echo operator, when he ran off to the scene of the disaster at the mess hall.

He found he could now see, so clearly, reconstructed in his mind's eye, though largely against his will, the nurse leaning over the patient, perhaps in response to him stirring, or convulsing… leaning over him close enough for him, or rather it, to snap its head upward, to stretch its neck out… and to bite. It must have gnawed through much of her face before she managed to pull away.

And then there would have been two zombies in the hospital. And only one of them tied down.

Unseen hands grasped Bryan by the arms and pulled him away.

On either side, flowing around him, four or five operators with assault rifles to their shoulders poured inside the hospital through the double doors.

* * *

"Sitrep!" the Colonel shouted, though not to anyone in particular. He was now the ranking officer on the scene. But, so far, no one really seemed to be running this battle.

An operator the Colonel recognized from Charlie team pulled his eye from his rifle sight and spoke in that inimitable ice-cool drawl of SOF guys in a crisis: "We've got something like a perimeter, Colonel. Could stand to firm it up, but I don't think anything's getting out. We've been putting down squirters as they appear." He snapped his sight back to his eye as a shadowed figure lurched past an upper-story window. But it was gone just as quickly. "On the other hand… I've seen a couple of groups of guys go in." He paused to spit on the ground, toward the building. "Haven't seen anyone come out."

The Colonel nodded and took a beat to process all of that. "Okay, spread the word. *No one* else goes inside. You hold here until relieved. Got it?"

"Roger that."

The Colonel took a few precious seconds to survey the shifting lines of the skirmish. He considered touring the perimeter around to the other side. But there was little point, and less time. He turned on his heel and headed for the helo hangars.

At a flat run.

* * *

Captain Charlotte Maidstone, British Army Air Corps, and ranking Apache pilot and gunner, jumped off the couch in the pilots' ready room when the door crashed open and banged against the wall. The rules for on-call combat pilots were clear: the world could be coming down in great sheets of shit, and she'd still have stay right where she was in the ready room. So there she'd sat, first hearing the earth-shaking explosion, then the shouting – then the firing and the wailing siren. No one had told her anything. Hardly anyone had answered when she tried to ask. She'd just had to sit there and listen to it.

Now, seeing the Colonel himself blast in behind the rocketing door, she could reasonably hope the moment had come to get her guns into the fight. Whatever the fight was.

"You fly that dragon?" the Colonel asked, jabbing his thumb over his shoulder at the nearest Apache parked up in the hangar.

"Affirmative."

"It armed and fueled?"

"Tanks topped – and Hellfires, rockets, and thirty mil topped off, too."

"You're on me," he said. "Get us airborne."

As they ran to the hangar, he asked about the rockets.

"Hydra 2.75-inch," she said. "Flechette loads."

As Captain Maidstone ran up the APC and began bringing the bird to life, the Colonel climbed into the front seat. When she climbed into the rear, pulling her full-face helmet on, he said to her, "I have full authority for what happens now. You understand me?"

She didn't understand, but she nodded her assent and got them taxiing out of the hangar. Fourteen minutes after the Colonel walked in her door, she had them rising and banking over the chaos of Hereford.

Below them, they could see smoke rising from several points.

And bodies running everywhere.

* * *

Doc Bryan struggled to master himself now, as the chaos finally subsided all around them. The outbreak was over.

Though, how they were going to deal with this many casualties was beyond him – never mind without the hospital. He had to struggle mightily to control his emotions – to stay effective and do his job in the midst of all this. The sounds of the most recent explosions, and the whizzing of zipping metal, still echoed in his ears.

One of the operators, smeared with soot and blood, holding his rifle low, was patiently explaining to him what had just happened.

"Flechette loads, Doc – 96 darts per warhead. The Colonel fired a spread of flechette rockets down the entire length of the hospital. I can guarantee you anything in there with a head had it skewered with a sharp sliver of metal. But a lot of people holding the perimeter were hit, too. I've got several guys with big-ish holes in 'em. Know you won't mind patching 'em up…"

Bryan shook his head to try and clear it. The hospital was of course a no-go zone, for the duration. The enlisted mess was out, as it had just been destroyed. The motor pool garage was probably the next biggest structure. He'd start setting up an ad hoc medical facility in there. There would be med supplies in various places – in vehicles, in aircraft, in medics' rucks. And he'd start medevac'ing everyone he could out to Bristol, Birmingham, or London… civilian hospitals, wherever could take them… He had a million things to do now, and lives hung on the balance of every decision.

But at least the living would live, or many of them; and the dead would stay dead.

For now.

* * *

The Colonel slumped behind his desk, the adrenaline finally draining out of him. He was on the horn to CentCom. Shit was very far from under control. But at least there was enough structure around him, a lot of ongoing crisis management, that he could pretend to be a commander again. And not some goddamned half-assed aerial rocketeer.

"It wasn't just a matter of saving the base, General," he said tiredly into the phone. "I put to you that this base is also the last best hope for humanity. As goes Hereford, so goes the world. Saving this facility was worth any price short of destroying it." He listened and nodded for a few seconds more. "Yes, I was up in the helo myself. And, yes, I directed the rocket fire into the center of the outbreak… Copy that, sir. Yes, you'll get my full report." He hung up the phone.

And he waved in the half dozen people at the door who needed something from him. Outside, the sun was going down; but the real work was just beginning.

In his last second before the chaos of command washed over him again, he thought:

This goddamned job was more fun before all the fucking zombies.

Making terrible decisions that cost men their lives never got any easier. But it seemed to be getting a whole lot more necessary lately…

LAUNCH

Several able seamen and a couple of flight deck ratings, plus the small aircrew, pitched in to help load up the plane that sat waiting on the flight deck. But Alpha team did most of the loading themselves.

This wasn't because they were overly precious about how their gear was handled. They were just accustomed to rolling up their sleeves and doing whatever needed doing. That they could make a headshot from a mile out, parachute into combat from 40,000 feet wearing SCUBA gear, speak Farsi, and hack computer networks didn't mean that they were too good to carry their own shit.

"Get it done," was one of the most commonly heard phrases in their world, the SOF world. Most often as in, "Right. We'll get it done."

Pallets of gear, ammo boxes, weapons, explosives, radios, parachute rigs, and crates and rucks of God knows what else got carried, rolled, heaved, and power-lifted into the rear half of the C-2A Greyhound. Its top-mounted wings, each with an underslung propeller engine, loomed over the ducking heads of the men. The flight deck was starkly lit with LED and sodium lights in the black middle of the night, shadows looming in every corner, all of it out in the inky blackness of the rolling Atlantic. Ordinarily, pre-Apocalypse, they would have been able to spot the lights of Norfolk and Virginia Beach off in the distance on the coast – at the edge of a mighty continent.

Now, of course, it was all black.

Heavy cloud cover also masked the stars and moon above. The wind foretold of a storm coming. The whole eastern half of the United States seemed to be socked in. But it was no good waiting for better weather – even if an accurate forecast could be produced. There was truly no time like the present. Especially when the present may be all you've got.

Two people who did not load shit were Commander Drake and Master Gunnery Sergeant Fick, the commander of the Marine Special Operations team onboard – who were also the B team and QRF (Quick Reaction Force) in case Alpha got in trouble. They stood with their bare arms folded, in a windy open area between the hulking island and the base of Catapult #3, the one at the starboard waist – or, rather, the Electromagnetic Aircraft Launch System (EMALS) that had replaced the traditional steam catapults. When kicked off, it would accelerate the 59,000-pound fully loaded aircraft from 0 to 160mph in two seconds.

As the loading finished up, and final flight checks were made… and as the seven men and one woman of Alpha team slung themselves coolly and emotionlessly into the front passenger section of the cabin… Captain Ainsley, formerly of SAS Increment, and commander of the team, stepped aside, and strode up to Drake and Fick, for a last word. Both the naval officer and the Marine senior NCO instinctively saluted. An habitual gesture, made for those going into harm's way, by those who have been there.

"Right. Thanks for the hospitality," Ainsley said with a serious look, saluting back.

"It's been our pleasure," Drake responded. "More where it came from, when you get back."

Ainsley's expression softened slightly at that, almost a smile, as if the idea of them coming back was funny. Then it faded. "You'll ring us immediately you hear from Hereford?"

"Absolutely, Captain," Drake said.

Ainsley reached out to shake his hand. "Just buggered comms again, no doubt."

Drake nodded, taking his hand.

Fick put out his. "We'll be on a short tether here. You fly safe." Ainsley raised his eyebrow but shook the Marine's hand, then turned on his heel and marched off again.

Fick looked across to Drake. "They can't reach Hereford?"

"Couldn't," Drake said. "Actually, we just got through ten minutes ago."

The pair were both having to yell now over the roar of the plane's prop engines, which were revving up to full power. The holdback bar at its rear held the trembling aircraft in place, while green-shirted flight deck crew attached the towbar to the plane's nose.

"And?" Fick shouted.

"It was an outbreak. Bad. They lost nearly 20% of their total strength – dead, wounded, or turned. Their colonel had to get in an Apache and rocket their own goddamned hospital."

"Jesus Christ's nuts on a hotplate. You're not gonna tell Alpha?"

"Negative," Drake said, shaking his head slowly. "There's not a blessed thing they can do about it from here. And the last thing these guys need is one more damned thing to worry about." He crossed his arms and squinted into the dazzling lights. "On top of saving the world."

With that, the catapult officer (or "shooter") did his final checks from the control pod, approved the pressure, and fired the release. The holdback bar dropped, the towbar yanked forward remorselessly – and the plane, and everyone packed into it, shrieked down half the length of the flight deck like, well, something shot out of a catapult. The bird dropped off the edge of the deck, briefly disappeared from sight, then reappeared, whining as it gained altitude.

And then its landing lights all went dark. After that, there was only a fading buzzing sound, heading for the greater darkness of land – for the very middle of the land of the dead.

And perhaps the last hope for the living.

FLIGHT

"Hey, wait a minute," growled Predator, the team's enormous and unkillable assaulter, in that voice that always reminded Ali of a professional wrestler doing a beef jerky commercial. "I saw exactly one of these cargo planes. So how do the Marines come bail our asses out if this one gets taken down…?"

Command Sergeant Major Handon, former Delta shooter, team's ranking NCO, and 2IC to Captain Ainsley, leaned back in the darkness of the cabin. Aside from a couple of low-level red combat lights, the plane was totally blacked out. He knitted his fingers together behind his head. For some reason, he was never so relaxed as in the hours and minutes before a combat jump, or combat insertion by helo. Any kind of flying leap into probable death and destruction seemed to soothe his nerves.

"Sea Hawks," he said, referring to the Navy UH-60-variant helos that lived on the deck of the destroyer, the USS *Michael Murphy*, which had sailed along with the *Kennedy*. "Big fuel bladders inside… and a one-way trip. It was all in the MARSOC briefing."

"What the hell kind of a rescue is that? *One way*?"

Pope looked up from a paperback volume of Dostoevsky he'd scored from the carrier's library, around which he was curled in a dark corner of the cramped cabin. "Escape and evade, big guy. It all goes south, we presume you'll hijack a monster car-crushing truck and drive us all to the coast."

Predator looked mollified. "Okay. That could work."

Juice, the team's signals and tech genius, bearded and puffy, formerly of the secretive spec-ops intelligence unit known as "The Activity," looked thoughtful. "I guess Mexico's out. Heh. Should have listened to the damned Republicans and locked down the border when we still had a chance to..."

Pope went back to his book.

Handon closed his eyes and dozed off.

* * *

Homer and Ali sat face to face in the row behind.

At this point, they both pretty much knew everyone else knew about the two of them. Somehow they didn't feel like going through any more contortions to conceal it. Maybe it was that their chances of survival had gone from slim, in their normal duties, to none, on this mission. And if they did somehow survive, well, everyone could just go on pretending.

Ali figured that even if they achieved their target and found the data on the vaccine, which seemed just about doable... well, after that, fighting their way through downtown Chicago to their extraction point was a *whole* other proposition. Three million Zulus (and Romeos, the runners – and maybe Foxtrots, the insanely lethal ones...) in a blighted and constricted urban space were going to make *Black Hawk Down* and the Battle of Mogadishu look like a sorority house pillow fight.

Ali, for her part, didn't know if it might not be better this way. Her whole life had been about trying to do something useful. And you didn't get to the Tier-1 level in spec-ops if you weren't totally ready to get killed doing it. She knew what Predator would say, about the looming spectre of the team's death, if she were brave enough to raise it with him: "Today's as good a day as any. Let's finish it right." Juice would probably make some noises about being smarter, not braver. But in the end he would stand and fight with Pred, and with all of them. Both Handon and Ainsley, despite their differences, would do their jobs until their last breaths. And probably a few seconds beyond that.

And Homer... well, Homer would be happy enough to go when God said it was his time. She didn't believe that meant anything, of course. Except in that it always gave him a reason to go on, and kept his spirits up even in their worst moments. That was real. She looked up into his eyes, glinting in the darkness. She reached out for his hand.

"Suppose," she said, quietly and carefully, "that you actually do loop through your whole life in the last second before you die. That it all flashes by. And then you wink out. How different is that, really, from looping through that one second over and over for eternity?"

Homer nodded and took this in. "Are you saying the soulless are replaying their lives over and over?" He thought immediately of Job, his Existential Zulu, standing forlorn on his Dover clifftop. Standing guard by his friend.

Ali shook her head slightly. "I don't know. I always

feel like I can see something in there. Behind their eyes."

Homer squeezed her hand. "Sister… just don't you ever find out."

She realized with embarrassment that a tear was forming at the corner of her eye. Homer had his God for comfort. And she had Homer.

And for that she would always be profoundly grateful.

* * *

For his part, Homer did not want to look away from her. But he did, out the window, and down, toward the endless continent that now loomed beneath them. He was also looking to the north. Little Creek, Virginia would be out there, maybe only 75 or 100 miles distant.

Which meant that his family would also be down there, somewhere. In some state, his family would be there.

When the reality of that fact hit home, it was all he could do not to grab his parachute rig, pop the door, and dive. To be so close, and to not know, to do nothing… all of it was insane.

Part of him also wanted to pull his hand away from Ali's.

Instead, he tightened his grip.

Wherever his wife and daughter and son were… they would be clinging to whatever they had left. Whether it was each other, or to the bosom of the Almighty.

If it pleases God to let me pass through this one last storm, he thought… *I swear on my immortal soul that I will go and find them. One way or another, whatever the outcome… I will go to them.*

* * *

Henno, the other Brit and SAS veteran, and a fierce Yorkshireman, slept through almost the whole flight. Operators spend a lot of time on long-haul aircraft, and have a well-honed ability to rack out quickly, anywhere. But Henno had taken kipping to an art form. It was his favorite pastime.

He came awake calmly and completely when the red cabin lights flashed the 15-minute warning. He yawned, grabbed his gear and rifle, and smiled out loud.

He'd been dreaming of a big fry-up, sausage and mushrooms and beans on toast, in his native North Yorkshire. He wondered if he'd ever see the beautiful North York Moors again.

Yeah, no danger, he thought. He always thought that way. With a childlike faith.

Ainsley clapped him on the shoulder, as they all stood and began to get rigged up for the jump. This included switching over to their oxygen bottles, and checking one another for signs of hypoxia. Also, every rig and connection needed to be triple-checked. The plane tilted and the engines screamed as the pilot coaxed it to its service ceiling of 33,500 feet.

The ammo cache pallet got shoved out the door first, into the screaming wind and rain.

After that, everything moved very, very quickly.

ON THE AIR

Thousands of miles back to the east, Alice Grisham nodded at the cameraman and then at the bedraggled man standing next to her, then raised the microphone. The wind was blasting across the field as her hair flailed around her, and she wished she had tied it back that morning. But they had been in a hurry. As one of only three television news crews still functioning, they had to move fast to get a drop on anything new, to get there before it was all over. And getting down to Folkestone as soon as possible that morning had been more important than good grooming.

"Are we on air?" she said, trying to focus on the wavering camera.

"Yes, we're go."

"Hello and welcome to Midland Central News. This morning I'm in Folkestone, where the most astounding story has been uncovered overnight. I'm here with Mr. Alderney, who is originally from Paris, but until recently has been a resident of none other than the Channel Tunnel. For the last two years, nearly forty people have been fighting for their lives inside the tunnel itself, and in the early hours of this morning troops from the barracks here in Folkestone initiated an astounding operation to clear out a zombie infestation threatening to break out of the tunnel and onto our streets. But what they were to discover inside was far more profound than zombies. No fewer than thirty-eight survivors have so far been recovered, including a young child who was in fact born inside. Mr. Alderney, how does it feel to be out of the tunnel?"

The man coughed, and stuttered before managing to speak.

"It's. Unspeakable. My English is not so good. I am not able to say how this feels. To be free and out from this place now."

"That's wonderful, Mr Alderney. Please, if you don't mind, we haven't been able to speak to the mother of the child, but could you tell us anything about her?"

"Oh the girl, she is so beautiful, she is what keep us all going all this time. Little Josie and her mother Amarie have been our driving to be free. So pretty she is and a lifeline to us all. I am sorry; my eyes are hurting from the light."

"And am I correct that she was born inside the tunnel, whilst you were trapped down there?"

"Yes. Yes. She was born in the back of a car in the maintenance tunnel. We had not doctor or nurse, but we had a... *paramèdical* with us. We thought that they would both die, because it was not a good birth, but they made it through."

"That is an amazing story. Please tell us what it was like to live in the tunnel. Were there many zombies down there?"

"Oh, God. Many of them. We had to fight with metal bars to keep them away. We lost some people as well. Those were the worst to have to kill. Then we managed to make a... *barrière?...* of the wreckage to keep them away from the supply train but still some manage to get over it. We were living in the maintenance tunnel. No zombies there and we had to always keep the doors shut."

"And you lived in the dark all this time, with only the food from the supply train?"

"Yes. But not all in the dark. One of the other men, he is an electrician from the train company and he find electrical points that are not switched off. We are able to make lighting in some places. Yes, we survived on the food from the supply train."

"I would imagine you are looking forward to eating and sleeping somewhere other than in the tunnel today?"

"Oh yes. So much. I don't mind what. Anything but tuna."

The cameraman panned the camera thirty degrees, focusing beyond the reporter, to the road. A soldier was pointing at the camera and barking orders to those around him.

Alice noticed this, glanced over her shoulder, saw the soldiers approaching, and then turned back to the camera.

"Thank you all for tuning in, we will try to report more news as we uncover it. Alice Grisham reporting for Midland Central News live from Folkestone, where survivors from the Channel Tunnel have this morning been rescued, including a small child born in the tunnel itself."

TO THOSE WHO WAIT

The bowels of the *JFK* were like an endless maze, with countless passageways and compartments spreading out across multiple decks. Two years ago, before the fall, the ship had been home to nearly 5,000 crew, and all of that space had been occupied and in use almost every day. But as the number of crew dwindled, more and more compartments on the lower decks became abandoned and disused. Many of these stored scavenged goods that the expedition teams had thought might be of use at some point, but much of it had proven unnecessary, and slowly but surely many of the areas were left closed, unlit, and untended.

In the very early days of the plague, even the ship's executive officer, Drake, hadn't realized the full extent of the risk – until it became apparent that just stepping on shore was dangerous, let alone failing to meticulously check those who came back.

That was how Brian Marlin had got back on board, days before they introduced the quarantine procedure of holding expedition members on the support ship. That was how, after the small skirmish that had left two of his team dead, Brian had returned to his duties, with no one even noticing the small scratch below his left ear that the undead creature had managed to inflict on him just as he smashed its head onto the pavement and crushed it with a trash can. Hell, Brian hadn't even noticed the scratch at the time, and when he saw it later, while shaving and trying to forget about the half dozen or so creatures that they had fought, he just shrugged it off and figured that he had caught himself on the furniture in the bar, or perhaps the dumpster in the alley.

He had been drunk after all; they all had. When the fight had broken out he had thought, like all of them, that their assailants were either also drunk or were street bums desperate to take advantage of a group of drunken sailors on their way back to ship after an evening of shore leave. They'd jumped them in the alleyway, appearing out of the dark before any of the seamen had a chance to clock them. Before he or any of his fellows could react, two of the group had been pulled to the ground, and blood splashed everywhere.

Of course, he hadn't just scratched himself on the rusty dumpster. From the moment that the zombie's finger, with its sharp and broken bone poking out of torn, dead flesh, had pierced his skin, causing a thin, half-inch-long line of blood to well up and dry quickly, Brian Marlin's fate had already been foreclosed.

The sickness had come quickly. He'd woken up and rushed to the toilet, hurling his guts up. *Oh God, too much beer*, he had thought – but then he had seen the color of the water in the bottom of the pan. It wasn't brown, or yellow, or just some mixture of his dinner the night before and eight large glasses of draught beer. No. The bottom of the toilet pan was splattered with black and red.

He'd flushed the toilet and walked away, telling himself it was just the wings turning a strange color with the beer, and stumbled out into the passageway. *I'll walk for a bit*, he thought, *maybe go up on deck and get some air and clear my head.* But that hadn't worked. He'd stood up on the flight deck and breathed in the night air and felt even worse.

An hour later and Brian Marlin was sitting in the storeroom two decks below his own berth, in the place where he and his shipmates would sometimes play cards and lose a few dollars here and there, out of the way where no one could see. He rocked backward and forward hoping that the sickness would pass. It had been the only place that he could think of at the time to sit quietly and not be disturbed; not be ridiculed by his fellows for not holding his drink. He hadn't locked the door, just in case he passed out and needed help.

His head swam and his stomach churned over and over, and he found himself focusing on the labels of the boxes that were stacked along one of the walls – 5.56mm rounds, many thousands of them.

Only his own team noticed him missing, but none of them had time to report it since the next morning they were back on shore, ordered to attempt to quell the rioting in the city. Not a single one of them returned.

Of course it had turned out not to be a riot at all, and the following morning, while Commander Drake was busy trying to put together all of the new information that was coming from all directions, and attempting to restore some kind of order to the shocked carrier strike group, Brian Marlin passed out in the darkness of storeroom 34 and never woke up again.

At least not alive.

Of course, it was not likely that a zombie could have stayed hidden and unnoticed on its own, on a warship, for two years, even locked away in a room on the lower decks that was rarely visited. It was Aaron Carson, a man who in the last year or so had started being called by another name – the Preacher – that found Marlin, or what was left of him.

Carson was young, and had only been on the ship for six months of his first tour when he found the creature in the disused storeroom. He was still in his apprenticeship, and at the time still thinking he was lucky as hell to be onboard the *JFK* so early in his career. The carrier was the goddess of the seas, the most powerful ship ever to sail, and he was one of the people responsible for making sure she was solid. He was a steelworker by trade and – until the reports of attacks in the city during shore leave came floating back – he had been content. He kept to himself, not paying much attention to the rest of the world or to the news. His strict religious upbringing had carved him into a quiet introvert.

Weeks after the quarantine procedure was put in place, he'd gone down to the lower decks, the storage areas, searching for fuel cells for a blowtorch. It had taken him six compartments before he found one in the locker of storeroom 34. The locker was a massive metal thing, about eight feet tall and six wide, and previously would have been used to safely store larger ordnance such as man-portable missile launchers. But it had been emptied at some point and all that was in it now was a case of fuel cells just like the one he needed. He took out the case, opened it, and began measuring it up when he heard the noise.

Thunk.

He frowned, put down the fuel cell and peered through the room, looking to the entrance. The door was still open, and he heard noises from the corridor, but they were faint; the normal sounds of the ship. This had been closer, definitely in the room with him.

He stood up, took a few steps forward and peered around the corner. The room was an L shape, curving around the back of the next storage area. He saw stacks of boxes, ammunition by the looks of them, but it was darker around there; the light must have been out.

"Who's there?" he asked, instinctively lowering his hand to his waist. Silly of him – only MPs and a few officers carried sidearms while onboard ship.

Thunk. The sound again. What the hell was that? He stepped around the corner, peering into the darkness.

"Is anybody in there?"

No answer. Maybe it had been a rat.

Then something moved in the darkness much closer to him. He felt his chest lurch as a shadow passed behind the stack of crates closest to him.

Carson grabbed for the nearest thing he had to a weapon – the blowtorch he'd laid down before him. He was too slow, and he knew it. He meant to call out, but whatever it was stumbled from behind the stack of crates and lunged toward him. He spun sideways, swinging the blowtorch, and managed to dodge a clumsy attack, smacking the unknown assailant around the side of the face. The creature's cheek burst open with a crunch, splashing black gunk across the floor, and then it fell forward into the locker.

Carson was faster this time, and stepped forward, pushing the zombie hard so that its whole body fell into the bottom of the locker. It tried to fight back, reaching for him, and managed to snatch the cuff of his shirt. But Carson panicked and flailed and its grip loosened, just for a moment. It was enough for him to grab the open locker door and slam it shut.

He fell to the floor, breathing heavily, nearly retching at the stink that now assaulted his nostrils. It was too much. He emptied the contents of his stomach onto the floor.

As Carson sat there, trying to recover from the shock of seeing an actual zombie on the carrier, he heard a dull thud from inside the locker, then another. It was very quiet. Those lockers had thick walls and the thing that he had trapped inside was apparently very weak.

What the hell would he do now? Would he tell his commanding officer? He had to, didn't he? Or did he? If the chain of command found out that there was a zombie on board, the ship would become chaos as they quarantined everything and everyone nearby, anyone who might have come into contact. That included him. *Oh God, no.* Quarantine drove him nuts. He couldn't do that again. He would just leave it in there for a while, while he decided how best to deal with it.

That had been nearly two years ago.

Carson had kept it all to himself, in the end. The creature in the locker. God's cleaner. After a week it had already been too late to tell anyone, he belatedly realized – he'd have been court-martialed, if not lynched. Anyone who opened the locker would have been able to figure out that the thing had been in there longer than a few minutes; they would have discovered it and that would have been the end of him. It would have meant exile – out into the blossoming ZA.

Of course, once he opened the locker and tied the thing up – a task that had proven nearly as dangerous as the first encounter – it had been more or less safe. Once it was bound and gagged with thick layers of duct tape it could barely move. The bumping against the side of the locker stopped. People rarely went down to storeroom 34 unless they wanted 5.56 ammunition, and he moved some of that to a room nearer the section entrance. He'd used the locker key to lock it up, and kept it with him, around his neck on a chain, so that no one else would be able to open it and discover what he had done.

After a few weeks, his curiosity started to itch. What could he find out from the fell creature? How had God allowed such a thing to exist? Could he discover something from that rotting, undead but walking corpse that no one else had been able to fathom?

Over the months that followed he examined the zombie repeatedly, marvelling at how a creature with no living organs could still be alive. All things are equal in the eyes of God, are they not? Surely this thing must be a creation of the Almighty? Surely its presence here was some kind of miracle? As the weeks passed, Carson began to spend more and more of his time off duty sitting facing his captive. There were answers in those eyes, he was sure of it.

Slowly, but inevitably, Aaron Carson's mind began to twist. His sanity ebbed as the days passed. He was still able to do his job, but more and more he went to the chapel, to where the chaplain would give his sermons, so he could listen. He asked questions about zombies, pushed and prodded the chaplain, whose faith was already waning, with constant theories that made the man peer at him like he was some sort of leech.

How dare he look at me like that? Carson had cursed, and he became convinced that the chaplain was not worthy of his position. The man was blatantly gutless and weak, and the idea that he could preach the word of God an insult.

When the chaplain didn't turn up to mass one day, people talked. There was a search, but they never found him, and the last time he had been seen by anyone – at least, anyone who would speak up – he had been spotted heading for the fantail deck late at night. A lot of people knew that was where he spent some of his off-duty time, quietly and in prayer. It was presumed that the man, who had recently shown many signs of stress and strain, had simply jumped from the ship, into the cold waves of the Pacific. And in a way they would have been right. The chaplain was indeed floating in the waves many miles away and just below the surface.

But he hadn't gone there voluntarily.

Without a Christian chaplain to lead prayer,

meetings had been reduced to quiet contemplation for most. There was no one to speak the word of God, or no one willing to take up the book and attempt to guide folks. Until one evening, when there was a particularly low attendance, Carson stood up, walked to the front, picked up the Bible from the small table, opened it and began to speak. He didn't speak from the book itself, instead feeling that he was driven by God himself to speak his own words, channeling the thoughts of the Almighty, the thoughts given to him when sitting staring into the eyes of his undead guest in the locker of storeroom 34.

"In the End Days, when the Rapture was upon the Earth, the last remaining pure souls would be called upon to fight one last battle, one great battle against the most evil of enemies…"

And people had listened. Two years had passed since the Apocalypse began, months of prayer and preaching to his followers, those amongst the crew that felt their world was lost. But he had changed all that. He, Aaron Carson, now the Preacher, was a guide to the lost. Slowly his audience had grown, and so had those that he could trust. Those who also believed that they should welcome the will of God, that they should return to their homeland, return to their homes and die, and then ascend, as they were intended to.

From a few, to a few dozen. Then more, many more. By the time the carrier left on its journey back to the USA, its first such homecoming in six months, his following numbered nearly a hundred. On the night when the special forces from the UK flew off, over *his* native soil, his country, a place where they didn't belong, Aaron Carson decided that it was time to go home.

"This day, my brothers and sisters, we watched as the avatars of evil flew into our homeland for some secret purpose that we are not privy to. What are they looking for, I wonder? To steal what should rightfully be ours? A gift from God to those who are faithful, guarded by millions of his followers?"

A murmur went through the assembled crowd, and nods of agreement.

"You all noticed, did you not, how they even sent one of their own amongst us? A spy sent into our ranks, like they thought that they could fool us. That we are stupid?" He meant Homer – who had come down simply to pray, but had become alarmed and taken a probing look around the compartments of the Zealots.

Louder murmurs and angry faces looked back at Carson.

"But we are not stupid. We are not fools. And so long as they believe that we are, we have the advantage of surprise. We are, for the first time in many months, merely yards from our home shore. Our homeland. It is time that we make a stand and take what is rightfully ours. In the name of God. And this is how we are going to do it..."

ZEALOTRY UNLEASHED

Now Carson stood once again in storeroom 34, looking at the locker, while next to him were two of his henchmen. He had never called them that, but these were his most trusted followers. Right now, others would be moving into place, and in less than fifteen minutes their uprising would begin. All on cue, and all according to schedule, his followers would take up key positions, by deadly force where necessary. The ship's nuclear reactors, the weapons caches, and the bridge. With many of the officers and sailors in the island busy with preparations for the plane's return and its refueling, few would be watching the other areas of the ship, and certainly not the movements of a hundred or so of Carson's faithful.

"Do not be fearful, my brothers," he said as he opened the locker and revealed the zombie. Neither of the other two moved; both looked at the creature with mild alarm. They had not run, as he been worried they might.

"This, my brothers, is where I have gained all of my answers. Fools may believe that these are monstrous creatures, but as we know they cannot be. For were they not originally made in God's likeness? Did he not create each one of them? This change has been his will, and by long study and contemplation, God has told me his will.

Now we shall release this creature and guide it toward our enemies."

They hauled the zombie out of the locker and stood it up. The stench was overpowering, but neither of the men showed any signs of weakness.

Carson stood facing it, reached forward and pulled off some of the duct tape that had kept it incapacitated all these months, just from its legs for now. Then they began to walk it ahead of them through the dim passageways. Around them, the hum of the ship, the background noise that was always there, disguised the low groaning that the zombie now made. The henchmen held one arm each, with Carson guiding it by a rope tied around its neck. They took it up two flights of stairs, quietly avoiding the few sailors who worked nearby. Carson had carefully checked the duty logs, and knew exactly which berthing compartment to go to. The carrier required staffing 24 hours a day, and that meant people sleeping at all hours.

He peered through the door that was slightly ajar, then turned and nodded. The nearer henchman pushed the zombie forward and began to cut the duct tape that bound it. It started to struggle, to reach for them, but they pushed it into the room as the last of the duct tape gave way. Carson reached forward to pull the strip from the creature's mouth, just as a sailor in one of the nearby bunks began to stir.

What no one was expecting was the speed with which the zombie moved. Carson had always believed the thing to be one of the slow-moving ones. He had no information, and no way to consider that the fast ones, the new nightmares that could spread the virus like lightning, were actually an evolution of the earliest victims. This creature had been dormant for two years, hidden away in the locker. Its body had not deteriorated nearly as much as those that walk the Earth – but its behavior had evolved dramatically.

Carson stepped back out the door as the follower on his left pulled it shut. They would close the door and listen while the creature turned those in the room. It wouldn't matter if people awoke. They would not be quick enough to realize they had the walking dead in their midst.

But that wasn't what happened next.

As the henchman pulled on the door he felt a pain in his wrist. Black and filthy fingernails dug into his arm as the zombie tore into him, shredding the skin and bursting the veins. Blood squirted out as the artery was sliced open, splattering Carson and the other man, blinding them both for long enough to leave them dazed as the zombie rushed back out the door. In a flash, it raked its other hand across the face of the second henchman, at the same time lunging forward and sinking its teeth into Carson's face. All three men lurched backward, shock and fear incapacitating them as the creature bit and clawed. Carson reached for the gun in his waistband, drew it and fired, but he couldn't see clearly, and the round tunneled straight through the chest of the first henchman, who stopped clutching at his wrist and fell to the ground.

And with that, the zombie was gone, rushing back into the room behind it to attack the twenty sailors asleep in the bunks. Carson staggered backward, stopped himself from falling to the floor, and stumbled away down the corridor. He glanced back at his men, unable to speak even a word. At that very moment, the dead henchman began to twitch. Carson ran. He ran all the way to the hospital ward on the floor above, passing several people on the way, but not saying a word. At least one person called out to him, but he didn't stop. He just kept running until he could lock himself away.

He yanked open the door, forgetting to shut it behind him, pulled open a cabinet and came up with a fistful of bandages. The blood from his face was pouring down his neck fast and, as Carson looked into the mirror beside the cabinet, he noticed the skin around the wound – a gaping hole that made him faint to behold – was turning grey and mottled. Small tendrils of dark coloring were already spreading from it. He panicked, grabbing hold of the mirror to steady himself, now revealing claw marks on his arms. More pale skin and spiderweb lines of darkness were appearing, as he watched the virus spread and take hold.

Carson's chest heaved as he struggled to breathe. The asphyxiation, he thought. The lack of breath. His heart thumping slower and slower. All were signs of the infection, but this was too fast, much faster than he had known it could be.

Aaron Carson slumped down onto the floor and stared at his hands. Around him, the distant sounds of gunfire began to echo through the halls. His followers had begun their mutiny. Soon the ship would be in their hands, but now… now he would not be there to lead them in the way that he had envisioned.

How could this be? he thought. This was not the will of God, not what was promised. This was wrong. He was supposed to lead the chosen few home, not become one of God's cleaners.

THROUGH GLADDEN FIELDS

Corey Westrow prodded the soil and frowned at the wilting potato plant in front of him. He stood up, stretched, and shook his head in disgust at the spreading patch of dying plants. He was completely puzzled by it. Up until the last few days, this hangar had been the ideal place for growing crops – even more so than his father's fields, and that was saying something. Everyone thought of Idaho for potatoes, of course. But Washington state, with its gorgeous soil plus the wet and chilly weather everyone complained about, had the most productive potato fields in the world. Well, used to have.

But now that same soil, dug from the ground not far from the fields his father had tended, and hauled in sacks onboard and then down to the cavernous hangar deck of the *JFK*, had given no fewer than four life-saving crops to the thousands aboard the surviving ships of the strike group. It had taken the work crews a week of going backward and forward to the mainland to gather enough soil and wood to build the farm – a week that Drake had not wanted to spend with the carrier sitting so near to shore. But it had been worth it. Corey looked across the dimly lit deck. He glanced up at the racks of UV lighting that they had installed, all taken from a warehouse on the outskirts of Seattle, and then over the endless rows of crop beds packed with spreading plants.

It had worked a treat so far, but now something was amiss. He guessed that it was the drainage, or the sea air, or maybe the water filtration was failing somehow. His father would have gotten to the bottom of it quickly, no doubt. And Corey wished that his father were here now to berate him for not airing the soil enough, or not turning it over a third or fourth time. It's all in the preparation, that's what his dad had drilled into him from the moment he had grown old enough to walk and watch his father on the farm. As he had approached manhood, though, Corey became convinced that it was a hopeless profession, farming the fields while most of the other Irish immigrant families to the region had long ago taken up work as bankers, merchants, publishers, politicians, mine owners – anything to escape the grip of the single crop that had devastated Ireland. Like them, Corey longed for something else.

In spite of his current troubles, he laughed loudly at how ridiculous it all was, really – imagining the look on his father's face if he had lived to see the world's most powerful warship with its aircraft hangar deck full of potato beds. He laughed bitterly at how he had left his father and that farm on the hillside to run off and join the Navy. The catering corps had been ideal for him, the escape that he had needed and a means to travel the world and see places that he had only dreamed of. A way to forget the hurt and disappointed expression on his father's face when he had told him he was leaving the farm. He never imagined that he would end up on an aircraft carrier, not only cooking the meals but growing the damned potatoes as well.

Corey laughed aloud, even though he couldn't hear the sound himself. The CD player that he had scavenged from the electronics shop three weeks ago, when he was told to collect batteries, was turned up full blast, Iron Maiden hammering at his ears. Another little something surviving from the Auld Sod, the British Isles. It was his secret guilt, that player, and it meant that he could tune out of the hum and bustle of the carrier; shut away the loud noises that echoed belowdecks through the monstrous behemoth.

Unfortunately for Corey it also meant that he hadn't heard the door in the south of the hangar deck creak open and then bang against the outer wall. He hadn't heard the slow footfalls of the visitor approaching him. If he had turned a few seconds earlier, he would have seen the dim UV lights casting shadows across the torn face that had once belonged to Aaron Carson – as the undead Preacher lumbered forward, dragging his left leg heavily across patches of spilt soil.

When the song that was playing on Corey's CD player ended and didn't jump to the next track, he looked down and tapped the device a few times, wondering if the batteries were finally going. It was then that he heard it – a low rattling rasp that cut through even the muffling of the headphones.

Corey spun around at the noise and took a step back, instinctively holding up the only weapon available to him at the time – a trowel – and felt his heart miss a beat.

This... it wasn't possible... not on the ship, not belowdecks. Not after all this time...

He took two more steps back, and stared straight into the dead face of the Preacher, who in turn glared back at him with a burning hatred that made Corey feel a chill down to his bootsoles. The Preacher. The one who took up the post of the disappeared chaplain. But this wasn't the same man. This was the dead version. This one had a gaping hole in his face and claw marks across his arms. This one opened its mouth and hissed, a sound of pure malice.

The creature reached for him, now only a few feet away, and Corey swung the trowel, hitting it in the neck just above the collarbone. Black blood splattered across the already wilting potato plants. The zombie lashed out, grasping Corey's shirt and pulling hard as he tried to escape, to clamber through the plant bed – but the weight of the corpse pulled him back and sent him stumbling. He tripped, called out, and dropped the trowel as he flailed his arms and tried to break his own fall. But he only had one hand to do it with.

I miss you, Dad, was the last thing that went through Corey's mind as his head hit the wooden edge of the plant bed, knocking him cold instantly. Corey would not wake up again, at least not as Corey. Thirty seconds later his system began shutting down and going into shock, as the virus spread rapidly through his system. He hadn't even felt the bite in his arm that had been the catalyst, hadn't even noticed the clumsy figure stumbling away across the hangar toward the north door. He also didn't sense others pass him by as he lay there dying.

Ten minutes later, Corey Westrow rose, sniffed at the air, and started shuffling in the same direction. Around him others staggered through the plant beds as the sound of gunfire began echoing through the corridors. But now he barely heard those noises. All that went through Corey's dead mind was pure instinct, pure hatred, and a single impulse.

Feed.

JUMP MASTER

The wind and stinging rain slapped Captain Ainsley in the face like it had gotten a good wind-up, and lightning flashes rippled in 360 degrees. He was immediately disoriented in the black cloud soup, tumbling and trying to maintain his breathing through his regulator.

This was the worst weather he had ever jumped into. Never mind from high altitude.

He had of course gone out the door first, leading from the front. Anything else would have been unthinkable for a combat leader – in USOC, in the SAS, or in any regiment.

As senior NCO, Command Sergeant Major Handon would be jumping last, tail-gunner Charlie, riding herd on his flock.

But even now, the others would be tumbling out right behind Ainsley, and despite the horrifying conditions, he had to be effective, and he had to hit his marks. He spared one look for the altimeter, none for the GPS, and deployed his canopy. Within a few seconds, he began to spot the flashing IR beacons of the others, which made bright and pretty green fireflies in his night-vision goggles.

With a little luck and timing, they'd be ditching the NVGs within half an hour. By the time they hit Chicago, coming in west from across Lake Michigan, as well as down from the sky, sunlight should be breaking. Or maybe, once underneath the cloud cover, there'd at least be gloom they could see through.

Visuals were dodgy, so Ainsley did a radio head count. No one below would be listening. Everyone sounded off. He checked his instruments again, and everything checked. So, following his compass, he turned his canopy on the proper heading, and felt as much as saw the seven others maintain formation around him.

And right now all they had to do was fly thirty miles to Chicago… but it was after they hit the ground that things would get tricky.

* * *

Handon didn't much like it. But, then again, as so often, he didn't have to like it – he just had to do it. The weather was a bastard. But he and his people could make it happen anyway.

He felt the weight of his leg bag hanging beneath him. When he hit the drop zone, the parachute canopy would come off – and the leg bag would convert to his ruck. For now, to ensure a common rate of descent of all the gliding paratroopers, gear had been carefully apportioned to keep everyone the same weight.

If all went well, they'd cover the 32,000 or so feet of descent to the height of their target structure, and the 30 miles to downtown Chicago, in about 34 minutes.

But it couldn't be said that everything was going well so far.

Just maintaining formation was a nearly full physical and cognitive load on all the operators, as they were buffeted mercilessly by the storm. Plus, with the temperature lower than predicted, and the higher wind chill, hypothermia was becoming a real risk – they lost about 2.6 degrees Fahrenheit for every 1,000 feet of altitude. And as the extremities began to go numb, their ability to manipulate the canopy, or any other equipment, dropped toward zero.

Handon saw one of the IR beacons ahead of him begin to veer dramatically, the operator it represented sucked off course by a rogue gust of wind in the storm. He was pretty sure he knew who it was.

"Ali, sitrep," he said into his throat mic.

Since she weighed the least of anyone in the group, her leg bag was the heaviest – which left her with the lowest power-to-weight ratio of any of them. She was having to battle her steering lines, with her lesser upper-body strength. And as the storm picked up, and the cold sucked her strength and dexterity, she was losing the battle.

"*I've got it*," she said. Sure enough, the wayward beacon began slowly, tremblingly, to merge with the group again.

What Handon had forgotten, but never should have, is that strength is a puny factor compared to the one that defines a special operator:

Resolve.

And which Ali had in greater measure than any other soldier Handon had ever met.

He thought he could now begin to make out the edge, of dark on slightly less dark, where the shore of the Great Lake met the Windy City. Somewhere a few hundred meters inland would be the tiny rooftop upon which they had to land.

Some fucking aircraft beacon lights, he thought, *would come in handy right about now.*

Instead they were going to have to rely on GPS.

And, if that went out, on visual landmarks and dead reckoning.

Hell of a way to start the day, Handon thought.

Below him, in his imagination, the city seemed to moan.

INSURRECTION

Wesley was already waking drowsily, when he woke violently to the sound of an explosion. Surely it was only in his dream? His dreams had been getting worse, not helped by the claustrophobia of sleeping in a sailor's berth. Worst of all, opening his eyes did nothing – the world was just as black on the other side of them. The sound of gunfire – rattlingly, crashingly, pummellingly loud and echoing in the steel confines of the ship-city's belly – told him that the explosion had not been in his dreams.

Thank fuck, the lights now came on – revealing Martin in his skivvies, standing at the switch, by the door. The two men shared a disbelieving look. The sound of gunfire, in at least two calibers, shook the room. Martin reached for the door handle. Wesley's mouth went wide, trying to find the words to make him stop, but it was too late.

Martin pulled the door wide enough for them both to see angry green tracers skipping down the hall in both directions, like lethal fireflies at light-speed in the near dark.

Martin pushed the door shut again, then retreated back to his bunk, and began shakily pulling his clothes on. Wesley mimicked him. *Better to die dressed, I guess*, he thought… Captain Martin also found his sidearm, drew it, chamber-checked that there was a round loaded, then wrapped the belt with the holster around his waist.

Wesley sidled closer, and found his voice. "What in hell's going on?"

"I have absolutely no idea," Martin said. Then he did have an idea. He found his mobile and speed-dialed Drake. It rang through to voicemail. Martin rang off and dialed again. On the third attempt, it answered. "*Go for Drake!*" The man was shouting – over gunfire.

"Drake, Captain Martin. What the bloody hell is going on?"

There was a pause, with more gunfire, before an answer came. "*Mutiny! It's the fucking Zealots. They've got numbers, arms, and surprise. They've taken the goddamned Bridge and are trying to run the ship aground.*"

"Where are you?" Martin asked, his face a mask of dismay.

"*We're in the island, mostly scattered around the Launch Ops Room and the Flag Bridge. We're trying to retake the Bridge. Fuck it. Never mind. Stay put. Arm yourselves if possible. I'll come for you when I can. Out.*"

The line went dead. Martin regarded the phone before him.

The door to the room flew open. Martin dropped the phone, raised his sidearm, and nearly shot the man who came through it. It was one of the MARSOC Marines, cradling a .45-caliber H&K UMP sub-machine gun and appearing slightly wounded. After almost shooting Martin in turn, he surveyed the room. "You're the Brits."

Martin and Wesley both nodded.

"You loyal to this vessel?"

They both nodded again, more vigorously. "God, yes," Wesley stammered.

The Marine nodded his acceptance of this. "Stay put. Don't open this door." Then he stepped back into the passageway, one hand on his weapon, the other on the hatch handle to pull it closed. A round took him in the head and knocked him over backward.

He lay dead and still on the deck before Martin – who suddenly got an overwhelming sense that this deck wasn't in fact going to be retaken. "Come on," he said to Wesley. "I think we're going to be overrun if we stay here."

Wesley had to swallow an enormous bolus of fear before he could make himself step out that hatch.

* * *

They went the direction the Marine hadn't gotten shot from. Soon they were amongst running throngs of sailors, and the odd Marine, who were scrambling, loading weapons, shouting at one another, and trying to figure out what the hell was going on.

"Well?" Wesley shouted over the tumult. "What now?"

"I say let's go find Drake. I think I can get us to the island from here."

Wesley wasn't sure that was the best idea he'd heard all morning, but that route at least seemed to take them away from the fighting belowdecks. Or so they thought – the route Martin knew took them first up to the flight deck, which they'd then have to cross to get to the island.

Martin poked his head up over the ladder first. He could hear gunfire from the direction of the island – and every few seconds a stray tracer would flash off into the dimness of the gray and heavily overcast morning. From the wind coursing over the flight deck, and the sound of the surf, the ship seemed to be moving, and moving briskly.

Just as Martin gave Wesley the (more or less) all clear, and they both clambered up onto deck, a raucous and terrifying explosion rocked the outer edge of the deck, knocking them halfway back down the hatch again. Much of the world to their right went up in an orange and white inferno, which briefly lit up nearly every inch of the deck like stage lighting, tore a hole in the cloudy sky, and totally seared the vision and hearing of the two refugees.

"What the fuck was that?!" Wesley shouted, looking away and covering his eyes.

Martin was no expert, but he clocked the location as being that of the starboard Sparrow missile launchers. "A weapons magazine, I think!"

"Jesus Christ! Is this safe?!"

Martin realized that was very much a question worth considering.

But then he spotted the flaming figures lurching toward them across the deck – from right out of the flames at the site of the explosion.

For just one second, he thought they were wounded and burning sailors.

But then he recognized that walk.

"*Ruuunnn!*" he shouted, pulling Wesley up the ladder, and both of them into a headlong flight toward the island.

Wesley went with it and came up running, hand over head – but he spared a look over his shoulder trying to make out their pursuers. "What?" he stammered, "what is it?"

"*It's the dead, you fool…!*"

A long hundred meters lay between them and that island.

Bullets began snapping the air over their heads.

And urgent moaning grew louder behind them.

DROP ZONE

Ainsley's GPS fix was coming on and off. On the upside, the storm was starting to blow itself out, clearing from in front of a strong wind off the lake – or what was really a large inland sea posing as a lake. The captain and Alpha commander squinted to get a visual on the target building. He began flaring his chute and hauling on his steering lines to get himself and his team on a heading that would intersect it, before he was too low and on an express elevator for the probable wild west of street level. The others, slightly behind and above him, had a little more space and time, and thus a little more room to maneuver.

Ainsley fought a stiff tailwind from off the lake, as it tried to push him past the drop zone. The rooftop was coming up fast, and Ainsley, and all of them, were still too far to the north of it. Ainsley's biceps strained against his lines like the reins of a runaway stagecoach, and his face beaded sweat, despite the chill air. He, and the others, had all ditched the oxygen masks as they passed through 7,000 feet.

He spared a look behind him. The formation was slightly ragged, but they all seemed more or less on the same vector. As to whether he was going to be able to master both the wind and gravity in time to make the drop zone... The cluttered rooftop raced toward him on three axes – left, forward, and down – and Ainsley hauled on his left riser for all he was worth.

The wind slackened slightly and the building finally lined up under him. They were going to make it. Ainsley flared his canopy at the last second to slow his rate of descent; a broken leg or other serious landing injury would really mess up everyone's day. But his descent instantly slowed *much* more than he'd intended – reversed in fact, lifting him back up into the sky.

It was a massive updraft, driven by the low-pressure zone left by the storm, fed by the warm air off the lake, and coming up the vertical cliffside of the building. Ainsley found himself rising radically, while still moving forward – the updraft was going to take him right over the edge of the building. He was going to miss the rooftop entirely.

Nothing else to be done, and no time to do anything else anyway. Pulling the quick releases on his canopy, he fell from the chute and plummeted straight down, more than twenty feet to the hard rooftop. On landing, he still had forward momentum, and rolled into it, hoping to absorb the force across his side and shoulder. While desperately trying to survive his landing, he was also completely aware that he had no idea what was happening to the rest of his team.

Until, that is, everyone started shouting into their team radios at once.

The squad net had gone completely hectic.

And Ainsley tumbled toward the building edge end over end – a tangle of man, equipment, and webbing.

* * *

Predator initially kept his mouth shut and off the radio. He wasn't one for sending traffic when things in his sector went to shit. It was too much like whining. He preferred to deal with a crisis and then bring the others up to speed as and when. Of course, there was a fine line between operating independently and neglecting team comms and coordination. But very often there was just no time, and that was the case now.

The same updraft that blindsided Ainsley caught him – but higher and farther from the target building. He tried to steer to correct, but after the towering wave of air took him to its apex, a crosswind caught his big body and bigger canopy, and slung him off to the side like a rock in a sling. For the moment, he was basically out of control, and watched the next rooftop, maybe five stories lower than the target, race at him at train-wreck speed.

He figured now might be an okay time to radio something in. "Uh… Pred going in hard. Mayday, motherfuckers…"

The surface of this other building's roof was a tangle of antennas, satellite dishes, and duct pipes. One particularly tall radio tower, which probably had the building's aircraft warning light, back when there were lights, looked like having Predator's number on it. As he whirled in a spiral beneath and outside of his canopy, he thought to himself:

Yeah… this is gonna hurt.

* * *

Juice had been descending less than twenty meters behind and above Predator. But due to the vagaries of micro-weather and low-pressure systems, the updraft that caught his friend left him in peace. He was still working hard to control his flight and descent, but he was on a solid vector for their drop zone – when everything went to shit.

He saw Ainsley, in the lead, head up toward the troposphere – then drop right out from under his canopy. He lost track of him after that, as his gaze snapped to the right – where Predator was doing some kind of para-gyroscope routine, spiraling down into the next building over. His final rotation took his lines dead across a tall radio tower. After that, his rate of spin increased, wrapping tightly around it. He stopped when his body smacked into its side with a crack so loud it was audible above the wind, and a hundred yards away.

He came to rest hanging upside down by his lines, fouled in risers and soggy chute. The weight of his kit bag levered his leg at a sickeningly unnatural angle.

And that was as far as Juice had time to follow it. Because he also had to decide on his own course of action in an instant, and did so – hauling on his right steering line, coming around, passing over the edge of the target building, and soaring down toward its neighbor. He flared two seconds later, coming to rest perfectly upright, both feet planted, a textbook landing, totally squared away.

Just on the wrong building.

His big reddish-brown beard twitched beneath his black tactical helmet as he sniffed loudly, once, then paused in that spot for a single second.

Then he shrugged out of his harness while drawing a six-inch Spyderco knife from his chest harness, used it to cut free his leg bag, then advanced with the knife through the gloom toward his friend. If there turned out to be any Zulus up here with them, well, he figured he'd just have to deal with them the old fashioned way. He flipped the enormous knife up onto the back of his hand, then palmed it again.

Overhand grip – right down through the top of the skull.

* * *

Ali's final approach was going pretty well, actually – until Ainsley's released and now free-flying chute came flapping back at her through the damp gloom like Mothra in some kind of gray and storm-tossed hell. Only a decade and a half of intensive training and operational experience in disaster management allowed her to keep her cool.

If that chute hit her anywhere – her body, her lines, or especially her own canopy – she'd be fouled and mostly likely fall out of the sky like a meat rock. She yanked on both lines with every ounce of her strength, flaring and turning. At the last second, she tensed and pulled both her knees into her chest. (*Thank fuck for all that ab work…*) The snapping, splashing, whistling mass of parachute slipped beneath her with inches to spare.

Having survived that, and getting her bearings, her next crisis was obvious: having slowed her descent to dodge the chute, she'd overshot the target building. She sailed now into the canyon of skyscrapers with no building tops of any sort any longer in her line of sight… and beneath her nothing but the major artery of West Lake Street.

Nothing but the near death-sentence of street level.

She got on the squad net, speaking normally. "Ali to Command. I have overshot drop zone. Repeat, overshot drop zone. My new location is about to be, uh… *downtown*. Stand by."

No, scratch that about there being only the street below. There was also the Chicago River, which was only now resolving to her through the near darkness. And also the elevated train platform, providing a complex hazard thirty feet *above* the hard street.

And both of those were coming up pretty damned fast, too.

* * *

Homer was perfectly in the pipe himself, set to hit his marker with precision.

But then he saw everything go wrong. He saw it all: Ainsley's rise and fall, Pred's whirl-a-gig, Juice's diversion – and Ali's death-defyingly close call. And then her sailing off toward downtown. It was all laid out before and below him, like box seats to an opera of fatal errors.

And he decided his own fate in a second as well. Their orders from the pre-mission briefings were completely clear – force protection was *not* a mission priority. Nobody went back for anyone else. Everyone went forward toward the mission objective – no matter what. But…

There was no way Homer could make himself leave Ali on that street alone. Not at this point, not after everything. No, he'd much sooner die down there with her, than listen to her die from the safety of a rooftop. This loved one he was coming for – no matter what.

Heck with it, he figured in his own head. *Guess I'm just not in an order-following mood today…*

He flared early, overshot the rooftop with plenty of room to spare, and followed her down.

He figured he'd update command on that one when he got where he was going.

* * *

Handon, Henno, and Pope, at various points up on the actual target rooftop, got out of their harnesses, charged their weapons, and got to Ainsley at about the same time. There was a wire fence that ringed the rooftop, and protected anyone up there from a 24-story fall. But Ainsley had crashed through it – with his helmet.

Now his head and shoulders stuck out into open air, hundreds of feet above the cement. He seemed lucid, but not quite ready to try moving. Henno and Pope each grabbed a leg and pulled him back in, while Handon faced behind them, took a knee, put his rifle to his shoulder, and pulled security. Parachuting accidents didn't mean the enemy wasn't going to show up, or would give you a time-out.

"Sitrep," Ainsley said, sitting up and shaking his head. He also rubbed his left shoulder, where he had taken much of the force of the fall.

The four of them pieced together what had happened, and worked out everyone's current, or probable, location. This project was aided when Juice and Homer reported in from their improvised rescue ops.

"Right," Ainsley said, climbing shakily to his feet. "So I guess it's just disobey fucking orders day, then, isn't it…"

Pope and Henno dealt with distributing the combat load in the leg bags, while Ainsley and Handon tried to put together a plan to salvage the mission.

Or at least to keep all their people alive through the next few minutes.

ALL OVER THE PLACE / NO PLACE

"Roger that, Top," Juice said, after briefing Handon over the radio, and getting general instructions from him in turn. "What I'll do is strongpoint here for now, while I see about Pred's mobility – and then look at options for getting down off this building." He grabbed the top of his head to scratch his scalp with his ballcap – but found only his tactical helmet, which was strapped down tight and didn't shift. "Yeah, we're always careful. Yeah, just like church mice… Juice out."

He went down on one knee, just in front of where Predator lay flat on his back. This was after Juice had cut him free, lowered him to the ground with sheer arm and back strength – and then straightened his right leg out for him. The brittle cracking sound had only been audible because Predator had declined to scream. He'd also declined morphine.

Juice waggled a syrette of morphine sulfate in front of his face, which was drenched with sweat. "Ready for some of that sweet fruit of the poppy now, tough guy?"

Predator snatched it and crushed it in his hand. The oozing liquid did smell sweet, like vanilla. Pred tossed it away and wiped his hand on his assault suit. "You show me another one of those, you son of a bitch, and you and me are going to have words."

Juice wasn't surprised. Giant unstoppable badasses

like Predator generally preferred to bull through pain, rather than dull their senses and reflexes mid-mission. Though it was looking an awful lot like Pred's mission was over before it had begun.

"All right," Juice said, knowing it was totally pointless to argue. "You sit tight. Gonna check the roof access." As he hefted his SIG assault rifle, he saw Pred draw one of his .45 pistols and lay it across his chest. Juice stepped off into the sooty maze of the rooftop. The sun was just cracking on the horizon somewhere out there, and the morning lightening.

After doing a full circuit of the roof, rifle at low ready, he quickly found the two roof-access doors, most likely to emergency stairwells. Circling back to the first one, he tried rattling the doorknob. Locked. That of course could be fixed. He tried knocking lightly. Nothing. Back to the second door. He rattled the knob. Locked. He pulled back his gloved hand to try knocking.

The doorknob rattled, from the other side.

As he leapt backward like an electroshock victim, eyes going wide, the whole door began shaking violently in its frame. Juice stopped his backward lurch, solidified his stance, and used biofeedback techniques to bring his breathing and heart rate back down.

As much as he and Pred wanted off this rooftop… clearly, someone badly wanted in.

Predator came in over the squad net, from across the rooftop. The noise of the rattling door had obviously carried. "*Dude, what the fuck? Over.*"

* * *

Ainsley and Handon stood off to one side, in conference. Their situation was slowly clarifying. And it seemingly got worse with every revelation, with every decision point they had to consider.

"So what's your call?" Handon asked.

Ainsley looked grim. "I think we need to get the QRF moving." Handon raised his eyebrows at that. Ainsley persisted. "We've got one wounded, one missing, and two separated, at exactly H-hour plus zero seconds. We're already down to half strength."

Handon shrugged. "True. But on the other hand, we're not in contact yet. And we're guaranteed to be if those Sea Hawks come screaming in here." If the QRF launched now, they'd have to do it in the helos – their prop plane wouldn't reach the carrier again for another two hours.

Ainsley nodded. "We could execute the waterborne infil option." This contingency plan called for the MARSOC team to put down in rigid inflatable boats a mile out in Lake Michigan, then motor in.

Handon didn't look impressed. "With the storm over, plus the wind off the lake, I'm afraid the engine noise would still carry. And if it didn't, those Zodiac engines would when they got near the shoreline. I say we just get on with it."

Ainsley seemed as if he was starting to see it his way.

"And I can't raise the *JFK* anyway."

"What?" Ainsley's eyebrows went for his helmet.

"Just now, trying to radio in our status. No answer to my hails. Nothing."

"No signal – from the top of a 24-story building?"

Handon just held his gaze. They both knew this was another very bad portent.

* * *

Parachuting right down through the skyscraper canyons of a major city was actually the extreme-sports experience of a lifetime. *Wish I were in a position to give a shit*, Ali considered.

She also considered the Hobson's choice that now confronted her. On her current heading and speed, she was going in the drink. Ditching it in the Chicago River in late November would without question mean dicing with hypothermia. When she got out of the water – that's if she could cut loose from enough gear to swim, plus find a section of embankment not too sheer for her to climb up – she'd have maybe an hour to get undressed and dried out. After that, she was a goner.

And before that, out on the street, alone, with all of her weapons and equipment gone, she was also a goner.

Even braking her forward momentum against the tailwind, and speeding her rate of descent as much as she dared, she didn't think she could get down on the main drag. And her forward speed was too high, and her turning radius too wide, to try and just turn down a side street.

What did that leave? That left the 'L' – as they called the elevated train platform that circled the Loop, right near the edge of the river. It perched over the street, directly between her and the water. Normal skydiving instincts had led her to steer away from this at all costs – wildly uneven surface, dangerously high above ground, electrified. Fucking *trains* coming. On any normal, non-apocalyptic jump, this would be the absolute worst conceivable place to land.

Now it was looking like her only hope.

Hell, it's actually looking pretty sweet, she amended. Up off the street. Probably no longer electrified. And certainly no trains coming.

Now – all she had to do was avoid snapping part or all of herself off in the tracks while landing.

* * *

Homer worked out what Ali was doing too late. Coming over the top of the target building with more control, he'd had time to think about avoiding both the water and the 'L', and to brake himself toward a street landing in front of both hazards.

And not only had he failed to mentally re-evaluate the implications of landing on the train platform, but he'd also reconciled himself to facing whatever he would find down there on the street. In his own mind, he was already dead. And now he'd already lost too much altitude to bring it back up and follow Ali.

The street was in deep darkness – the sun hadn't cracked the horizon down here yet – and all that black space now loomed, racing up at him, with whatever it held, and all it hid.

* * *

The half of Alpha team that had actually made it to the intended landing zone now stacked up outside the rooftop-access door of the target building. This meant the four of them stood in a tight line down the side of the wall, Pope in the lead. Ordinarily a door stack and dynamic entry would mean blowing the door with a small charge, shooting it off its hinges with shotgun slugs, or bashing it in with a mechanical breaching tool. Also, a couple of flashbang grenades would precede their entry – which would then turn into a swirling maelstrom of controlled chaos. They would pour in and clear the structure, making shoot/no-shoot decisions, executing four-box shots on the shoots, and taking down and controlling the no-shoots.

That was how they'd done it back in the world.

In this after-world, though… everything they faced would (almost) definitely be a shoot; flashbangs didn't really work; and noise just brought more of them. So Pope squatted down, withdrew two small tools from a small folding leather case, and picked the lock. He pulled the door open quickly but quietly.

The other three, NVGs seated on the fronts of their helmets again, slithered into the interior darkness. Pope followed, pulled the door shut… and locked it behind them.

* * *

In the final moment before impact, Ali saw what she hadn't before: a blessed train station. It was two bits of roof over the platform, and looked a hell of a lot more promising as a landing surface than the bare tracks. She hauled for all she was worth, brought it around at the last instant, and executed a running, sliding landing on the tiled but nearly horizontal surface.

She skidded to a stop, well pleased with herself.

As she reached for her chute quick release, the ground (i.e. the roof) opened up from under her. She fell with a crash, right through the rotten structure, and twelve feet to the hard wooden platform below. On her way through, a spike-shaped shard of wood went in one side of her left bicep and came out the other. She landed on her back, stunned, bleeding from the arm, and vertebrae screaming. Her rifle was wedged painfully beneath her. Her leg bag came down on top of her in a spray of dust and rotted wood, knocking the remaining wind out of her.

She drew a lungful of air with spectacular difficulty, rolled off her rifle, charged it with her right hand, and dragged both it and herself away from the center of the platform and up to the outside wall of the station office. She then sat still, in complete silence, amid crashing waves of pain, tuning into the environment and waiting.

Waiting to see what would come for her.

* * *

Pope, Ainsley, Henno, and Handon now stacked up a second time – this time outside the emergency stairwell door on floor 18. Behind it would be the offices of NeuraDyne Neurosciences. They had encountered no resistance on the way down from the roof. This was surprising, but they didn't show it. Their job was to be completely ready for anything. And that included when they faced absolutely nothing.

This time Pope had to jimmy the door's one-way locking bar with a thin metal rod. It gave with a metallic pop. Ainsley pushed his way in, rifle barrel and binocular NVGs pointing ahead of him like the prow of a military spaceship. The other three slithered inside after him.

In three minutes, they had cleared the level.

There was nothing there.

No living, no dead. Just a small bit of detritus that seemed to indicate people here had cleared out in a hurry. And two years of dust on the carpet and desk surfaces.

"And no fucking computers," Handon said, flipping up his NVGs and yanking the blinds away from the exterior windows, which let in a bit of thin early-morning light. From the large-screen LCDs and docking stations at most of the desks, it was obvious everyone here had worked off laptops. Which were now just as gone as the people were.

Pope stepped back into the main office area. "I've scoured the labs. No machines, no servers. And it looks like most of the samples and slides have done a runner."

Ainsley cursed silently under his breath. *All this way, and a dry hole…*

Henno called to them from the reception area. "Oi. I found some e-mail."

Ainsley was opening his mouth to ask how the hell he could have found e-mail when there were no blighting computers for it to be on… But Henno was already walking into the room. With his gloved hand, he held out a single piece of A4 paper. Ainsley took it.

It was a one-page e-mail print-out.

DEAD CITY

After a perfect two-point landing in the dead middle of the street, Homer trotted to a halt, reeled in his chute, shrugged out of his harness, wrapped the latter in the former, and shoved the whole bundle down an open street drain. He then unslung his weapon, charged it, grabbed his leg bag by its strap with his left hand, and got the hell off the street.

This meant ducking into a recessed doorway. He immediately took a very careful gander through the windows for any sign of movement inside, then put his full attention back on the street. His patrol boots, sleek and form-fitting assault suit and load-bearing harness, short-barrelled assault rifle, and hockey-style tactical helmet melted fluidly into the dim recess. He looked out, pivoting from his left, to his right, to directly across the way. Nothing moved in the lightening gloom.

That's not so bad, then. He almost smiled at his good luck so far.

But then he grimaced again. This was supposed to be a city of three million dead people. Where in God's name were they all? He should be neck-deep right now. He felt reprieved. But he also felt a sense of deep foreboding. Something was very wrong. And it couldn't, in the end, turn out to be good.

All around him, littering the street, were the telltale signs of a struggle for survival long lost. There were no fresh bodies. Two years of Chicago weather had seen to that, and all that remained were rag-covered bones littering the ground. A few feet away, in the next doorway along, were two adult-sized skeletons clutching each other. Homer stared at them for a moment and wondered what this place had been like the day those two huddled in that doorway for shelter.

He scanned the area, looking a second time for movement. But apart from the bits of trash that littered the street, skittering in the slight wind, nothing moved.

He pressed the transmit button built into the foregrip of his assault rifle and hailed Ali.

She hadn't been quite so lucky in her landing, he learned in short order. She was working to keep the pain out of her voice, with some success. But the effort was costing her.

Homer told her to stay put, signed off, and immediately picked up her grid location from his forearm-mounted Blue Force Tracker. The transponder in her BFT unit was talking seamlessly with his. She was close – but not close enough for comfort, and also elevated. The moving map in his forearm-mounted display drew out a route for him.

He moved out smartly, hugging the walls and building fronts. Back in the world before, this was a no-no – bullets also hugged walls, sometimes skimming along them for hundreds of feet, making them an excellent place to get shot. But now, of course, no one was shooting back – and the great thing was to stay out of sight, and silent. This was often made easier, as it was in this dead city, by the abandoned cars and garbage that lay everywhere.

The streets were quiet through his short journey, as Homer skirted his way along the sidewalk, ducking behind cars, posts, and trash cans, and keeping to doorways – though only the ones that were still more or less intact. Open doorways were to be avoided at all costs, especially if the building they led to was in darkness. Which all these were.

He'd had a few close moments making that mistake back in the early days. Zombies didn't tend to deliberately hide themselves away – they weren't clever enough for that – but they often wandered into a building when catching the scent of the living, and then stayed there in the dark if nothing else caught their attention. With walls around them, they seemed to find it hard to navigate their way out. All of this meant that the open front of a house, shop, or other structure represented a pretty high risk of something coming sprawling out at you. And standing in the doorway, with sunlight in your eyes and low visibility into the building, was a good way to get yourself jumped and chomped.

Homer moved swiftly from cover to cover, still wondering why the hell there weren't any signs of the dead – signs of anything for that matter. But within a block, the silence gave way. He squatted down, frozen, making himself small, as soon as he heard it. It was just up ahead, and unmistakable – but so out of place that he struggled to comprehend it.

Finally he realized: it was music.

He blinked hard and stayed where he was, willing himself not to go mad.

* * *

"Roger that, I'm not going anywhere," Ali said, in response to Homer's hail. "Walk safely. Out."

Jesus Christ, Homer… This was some damned unprofessionalism right here, following her down in her missed drop. Still, all things considered, she couldn't say she minded the assistance. She was in a bit of a bad way.

She popped a handful of analgesics from her med kit. She'd already pulled the wood splinter – "spike" was more like it – from her arm, let it bleed freely for a bit, then disinfected and wrapped it up. It hurt like hell, and the arm felt out of commission for the duration. Luckily, sniping was mostly done one-handed – with the off hand resting across the shooting arm for stability. She followed the Diclofenac pills with a jab – full-spectrum antibiotics, also from the med kit, and directly into her impaled arm. There was no telling what disgusting shit was on that roof after two years. Pigeon crap might be the best of it.

She'd also wrenched her back badly. But outside of a hospital, or probably a sports rehab clinic, there was nothing she could do but endure it. Now that she was basically squared away, she had to decide whether to sit tight and wait for rescue – or get up and make herself useful.

Well, she thought, clenching her jaw, *I guess that one answers itself.*

* * *

Homer faced a decision point as well, and it was also

auto-answering. However spooky the next few meters, they had to be crossed. He leg-pressed himself up out of his deep crouch, rifle at his shoulder, and started taking one padded step after another.

Dear Lord, he thought. *What madness was this?* Chicago was supposed to be a dead city. There was *no way* there was power generation still on here. Not two years later. And he figured a live band had to be out of the question.

Step by creeped-out step, he heard the music grow louder, until it was clearly audible.

"Wait 'til you're locked in my embrace," the velvet voice crooned. *"Wait 'til I hold you near… Wait 'til you see that sunshine place…There ain't nothin' like it here…"*

Homer knew the song well: Frank Sinatra, "The Best Is Yet To Come." Maybe that was even more ironic than "My Kind of Town" would have been? Who could say. Not Homer.

On closer approach, he found it was floating out of a storefront jazz joint and cocktail bar. He stepped slowly through a set of swing doors that hung from the entrance, broken as though someone had tried to rip them off the wall and failed. One of the doors was covered in black stains that could have been zombie or dried-up human blood. He couldn't tell. Moving inside, he scanned all the dark spots and covered positions as he advanced. Nothing moved, but all over the floor were desiccated human remains, much of it chaotically scattered.

They really tore this place apart, he thought.

In short order, he determined that the music was

coming from satellite speakers along the walls – and found them all connected to a digital jukebox behind the bar. The jukebox was plugged into the same socket as a nearby fridge. Slowly pulling its door open, Homer found that it was full of beer bottles – full beer bottles, not opened ones. And the fridge was still on, though the light bulb had long since burned out. Also plugged into the socket via a three-way adapter was something that looked like a mini vehicle battery, though it was too small to be a standard car battery. It was wired up to a standard plug, as if being recharged. Homer wondered if someone had come here after the city had fallen, or if this had been here before. He would never know. Nothing else lived in the establishment. And nothing else had power. It was just a complete mystery.

Homer paused at the front door before leaving. *Not a mystery*, he thought.

A miracle.

* * *

Ali cleared both train platforms, as well as the Chicago Transit Authority offices on either side, in four minutes. Her arm hurt like hell, and her back a lot worse than that, but she retained most of her mobility. She held her rifle by resting it on her left forearm. When she got back to her starting point, and her leg bag, she flipped down the rifle's bipod, and popped the cover on the big scope.

And she had a think about where she might emplace to best effect up here.

* * *

The Miracle of St. Frank, Homer thought, back on the street now, and beyond bemused. The real miracle, of course, and as he well knew, was that the music had not drawn zombie one. It should have been like catnip for them at this point. Where were all the dead? As he moved out and forward, on a hair trigger, ready for anything… still he encountered nothing.

When he reached the 'L' station, only a minute or so later, he had to stop to recalibrate. All of the stairwells leading up to the platform had been destroyed. This was not unusual. Alpha had been on the scenes of very many last stands. In addition to the bullet casings, the wide splashes of blood, the broken windows and toppled doors, one great hallmark of a human last stand was destroyed first-floor stairwells. Anyone smart enough to think of it, and with the tools or strength to manage it, did this. It was one of the best strategies for keeping the dead away the longest.

He reported the lack of access to Ali. "But be advised, I'll find a way to climb up…" He was already up and moving along underneath the platform, looking for egress. "Just stay put."

"*Negative*," she transmitted back. "*This is actually an excellent sniper's OP. And if you can sweep and clear the street directly below me, I think we can be pretty effective.*"

Homer stopped where he was, his eyes narrowing. "Effective at what?"

In answer, Ali's suppressed rifle chugged twice from over his head.

He spun in place and took cover. He couldn't see what she was shooting at. But it wouldn't be nothing… "*Contact, due south*," came her inevitable report. "*Visual on multiple Zulus, approx one-zero, in ones and twos. And they are closing distance.*"

* * *

Ainsley scanned the printed e-mail, the other three standing still in the dim and dusty room. It was addressed to roughly fifty recipients. About half the addresses sounded like other biotechs or university labs, about half perhaps personal contacts. He read it aloud:

> I pray to God most or all of you receive this. If you're still online, I don't have to tell you how bad things are. Virtually all of my colleagues have gone now - back to their families, or their homes in the country, or to whatever fate awaits them out there.
>
> I can actually see the fighting going on in buildings across the street. And I know it's only a matter of time before they are here as well.
>
> I have stayed, to continue the work. We're so close, to either a vaccine, or an antidote, or both, so close I can taste it... the samples we have are excellent, and I know we can do it, given enough time. But I don't think I can stay here. To do so would simply be to wait for death.
>
> Some of you know my brother-in-law, Al,

who is an IT contractor. After 9/11, they put in a bunker beneath the Chicago Mercantile Exchange, beneath the trading floor. It was supposed to allow them to keep operating during a natural or man-made disaster. They've got generator power, food and water, I don't know how long for. Maybe weapons, too, I don't know. I know all this because Al worked on the project, on the security and IT systems. I also know there's a backdoor – literal, and figurative. There's a tunnel entrance that comes out in the basement of the Hyatt, across the street from the Mercantile Exchange Center. It's behind an unmarked steel door with a keypad, card reader, and thumbprint reader. It normally requires both a smartcard and a recognized thumbprint, in addition to a code. But Al programmed in a backdoor: if you just type 19 zeros in a row, it opens up. Obviously, I'm not supposed to know any of this. If I make it there, and I get in, maybe those already inside will shoot me. But that actually sounds much better than the remaining alternatives at this point.

The Exchange is close, only about six blocks from here. Maybe I can make it. I'm taking a laptop with all of the research data, as well as the samples, and some instruments, in a backpack. If you're in Chicago, and alive, and you get this, and you can make your way there, and you don't have any better options... well, it's a chance. And if you're a colleague elsewhere... if I make it there alive, and can continue working, and can somehow convey any results to you from there, I will.

May God protect you all.

Simon

"Well," said Henno, his palm on the butt of his sidearm. "That's some good luck, then."

Pope just shook his head at him. He had to hand it to that guy… everything always coming up roses in his world.

"Give me a map," Ainsley said, snapping his fingers at Handon, who pulled a digital map pack from a thigh pouch and handed it over. Ainsley powered it up and put it on the table, then zoomed and scrolled with thumb and forefinger. "Six block radius," he said, making a circle with both hands. "Chicago Mercantile Exchange Center… Hyatt…" he recited aloud while scanning. "Here." His finger came to rest on a spot four blocks south of their position, and two to the west. He keyed his transmit button and hailed Ali. Her traffic with Homer had been coming in loud and clear on the squad net from down on the street.

"*Ali here, you are Lima Charlie, send traffic,*" she answered.

"Interrogative: where are those Zulus of yours coming in from?"

"*The south, and a bit west. But they're not Zulus.*"

"What are they then?" Ainsley looked impatient.

"*I think they're Foxtrots. They've gotten extremely feisty since they've twigged to my presence up here, and to Homer down on the street.*"

"Copy that. Interrogative: how many Foxtrots, over."

After Ali pressed transmit, but before she answered, they could hear her suppressed rifle firing non-stop in the background. "*All of them, I think. Gotta bounce, Cap, these are SERIOUSLY hard shots to make. Out.*"

The three men looked to their officer. None of them looked worried.

But Captain Connor Ainsley sure as hell was. He nodded at Handon. "Okay. *Now* we call in the QRF. Do it." He knew that if it was a matter of fighting their way through the streets to a new location, they were going to need every gun they could get in the fight.

Handon twiddled his channel selector to the command net and hailed the *JFK* again.

And then again, and a third time. He just looked back up at Ainsley.

Nobody had to be told the new state of play.

They were on their own.

INSURRECTION][

Drake steadied his M4 rifle on the gunwale. He was kneeling on a balcony platform of the Flag Bridge, the second of the four habitable levels of the island. Directly above him was the Bridge; above that, Primary Flight Control; below him, at ground level, was the Flight Deck Control and Launch Operations Room. Drake was currently covering a rear sector in an unlikely battle, watching the flight deck below and behind them, as a mixed unit of sailors and Marines pressed forward to try and retake the Bridge.

But, frankly, it wasn't happening. The Zealots, the mutineers, had superior position, elevation, full control of the whole Bridge level of the island – and they had a lot of grenades. That made fighting their way back up there a tough row to hoe.

But Commander Drake knew they had somehow to do it. Only a few minutes after the bridge had been stormed and lost, the nuclear-powered steam turbines had blasted up to their full 320,000 horsepower, causing the whole vessel to vibrate. And then the four bronze screw propellers (each 22 feet across and weighing 68,000 pounds) began to spin. And then the whole mammoth vessel, all 110,000 tons of her, began to turn and to move.

And now she was steaming directly toward land. In what could be no more than twenty minutes, they would be run aground. At high speed, this would also likely rupture the hull, flooding the lower decks – and almost certainly putting the *Kennedy* out of action for the rest of time.

Clattering gunfire and throaty explosions shook the whole island. The bastards had come out of nowhere. No one had been expecting it. Standard shipboard security protocols had been in place for a combat mission in hostile waters, but these guys must have been planning this forever. And of course they knew all the security protocols, just as they knew everything else about how the ship was organized and run.

There had actually only ever been one mutiny in U.S. naval history, before this. And it had happened in 1842.

But, Drake considered, *I guess every damned thing's different now.*

Now he seemed to recall the SEAL, Homer, say something to that effect – that the interesting thing about a zombie apocalypse was what it did to the living. How they either worked together to survive – or else turned against each other, and clawed themselves to bits. With a painful twinge, he also remembered Homer trying to warn him about the Zealots. *Just too many damned things to worry about at once…*

And that's when the fore starboard Sparrow emplacement went up. *Jesus Christ…*

He saw two figures, backlit by the flames, sprinting across the flight deck. Was it a Zealot counterattack, in their rear? Drake had secretly been relieved to not be on the front lines – it had been a long time since he qualified on the M4, though he kept up his pistol qualification. He pulled the assault rifle into his shoulder and took a bead on the lead figure down there… Oh, God, it was the British soldier… he eased up on the trigger, breathing hard.

And then he saw the burning figures behind them. And, like Martin, he soon recognized their motion – never mind that they weren't dying despite being covered head to toe in flame.

Mother of God, he thought, raising his barrel and taking a bead. He had no idea how it could possibly have happened, but now the dead were here. Out at sea, and in the middle of a raging insurrection. Fuck it. His first rounds caught one of them in the torso, slowing but not dropping it. He struggled to pull off a headshot. Underneath his barrel, he saw the Brits make it into the cover of the island.

While out on the flight deck, fires burned and the dead walked.

Drake frantically tried to figure out how they were going to keep them out of the island – while they were all still in the fight of their lives with the living for control of it…

* * *

Wesley and Martin leapt up the stairs, after a couple of the loyalists one deck down directed them up. They found Drake out on his balcony, still sniping flaming corpse heads.

"I thought I told you to stay put?" he said.

"Apologies, Commander," Martin said. "Got too

hot belowdecks." Wesley nodded rapidly in frantic agreement.

"Oh, hell." Drake's M4 stovepiped, and he stopped to try and clear the jam.

"Help you with that?" Martin asked. He took the weapon, promptly cleared and charged it, and took a couple of measured shots himself. He paused to hand his sidearm to Wesley, who seemed to know how to handle it. But now there were too many figures running around on the deck below: the mutineers, the loyalists, and the dead – who were loyal to no one. Some people shot others at close range, while others dove on and devoured them. It was complete and total chaos. Drake flinched and motioned them all inside.

"Look. We've all got to get in the fight upstairs," he said. "If we don't take the Bridge back within fifteen minutes, we're all completely screwed. We'll be run aground. Maybe sunk."

Martin nodded and took this in. He seemed fairly unflappable. "What about shutting down the engines?"

"The nuclear reactors?" Drake asked. "I can't reach any of the engineers down there. I don't know if any of them are alive, driven off, what."

"I'm an engineer," Martin said jauntily. "Corps of Royal Engineers."

Drake almost laughed. "That's great. But this isn't sapping, or pontoon bridges."

"Doubtless," Martin said. "But my degree is in nuclear. And I certainly know how a nuclear fission pressurized water reactor works. Enough to shut it down, anyway."

Drake gave him a look, half in awe, half in disbelief. He had no time to decide, so he just did.

"Okay, let's go. I'll see if I can get us a Marine escort."

But as he turned toward the ladder, a sailor came running up it, from the Launch Ops room. "Commander! Incoming aircraft, twelve o'clock." He pointed over Drake's shoulder out the porthole. *Oh, shit*, Drake thought, stepping outside again. It was the C-2A Greyhound – back from inserting the USOC team in Chicago. And here to land, refuel – and return to extract the team.

Without it, there would be no extraction. And no extraction, no cure. No cure, no last hope for humanity…

Drake cast his eye over the manic flight deck – flames, debris, living, dead, and undead.

The plane buzzed around in an arc.

The pilot no doubt seeing the same thundering shit-storm below.

STREET BATTLE ROYALE

For this mission, Ali had selected as her primary weapon a Mk 12 Special Purpose Rifle – what was sometimes called a "designated marksman weapon." Not quite a sniper rifle, it was still very effective out to 600 or 800 yards (more like 1,000 with Ali driving). And not quite an assault rifle, it was still very handy when things got hairy up close and personal. It looked like an M4 on steroids, with a large scope, bipod, suppressor, straight magazine, and air-cooled upper receiver. It allowed Ali extreme flexibility – and allowed her to carry only one rifle, which was much more pleasant when jumping out of a plane.

With one eye to the Mk 12's 3.5-10x tactical day optic, and the other wide open, she tried to track targets. There still were quite a few of them. And, moreover, they were just *jackrabbit sons of bitches*. At first, they seemed to take it easy and stagger around like your normal workaday Zulus. But when one of them got a whiff of Homer on the ground, or caught wind of Ali's shots chugging from up above, they just went batshit crazy – moving a hundred miles an hour, jigging, wheeling, and finally *leaping* upon their prey – whether that be Homer down below, or the bottom of the 'L' platform where Ali was laying up.

She took a headshot on one that hadn't been

activated yet. Cake. But then her other eye registered movement, two of them, coming in fast. She swiveled on her bipod trying to track. The first one she caught with a round in the center of mass – and this slowed it enough for her to *just* make a headshot. The second got by her totally. She could hear Homer's rifle going cyclic down below.

So far, two had totally slipped by both Ali's overwatch and Homer's patrolling of the ground below, coming from unexpected directions. And these ones had enough vertical juice to leap up and *grab* the bottom of the train platform. Both had been killed while trying to haul themselves up – one by Homer below, one by Ali above (with her sidearm). Luckily, having to climb had the effect of both slowing and steadying them.

But it wouldn't take too many more of these to swarm up, over, and across the platform, overwhelming Ali's position. And with overwatch gone, Homer would probably go down shortly after. That level of threat wasn't here yet. But Ali could see it coming, as the bastards multiplied. She was starting to think very seriously about moving inside the target building, and up top with the others. But Handon hailed her first.

"*Ali, Handon, how copy?*"

"Ali copies, send it."

"*Yeah, stand by. We're coming to you.*"

She blinked heavily. "Repeat your last."

"*It's a dry hole. We're all moving overground to a secondary target. Down to you in five mikes.*"

Ali swallowed heavily, squared herself up – and addressed her full attention to trying to clear the street for her team, before they were all down and neck-deep in it.

* * *

Homer had no problem operating on his own. SEALs were a little more comfortable in pairs (swim buddies and all that), but they were totally modular, configuring into groups of one, two, or four, up to multiple platoons of 16. The problem today was that these Foxtrots were *fast.* And having someone to watch his back, literally, would have been very welcome right about now.

The issue wasn't so much dealing with the handful that got curious and made their way up the street toward him. The problem would be arousing the interest of those thousands most likely behind them. Every time he or Ali fired a shot, and every time one of the soulless had time to emit a moan in response to prey, it increased the likelihood that the dam would burst.

And then they'd be awash in the three million missing Zulus. Or perhaps three million Foxtrots, God preserve them.

Correction: Homer, alone down on the street, would be awash in the three million.

He pictured himself being washed out to sea on a literal tide of the dead, like Noah in some horrifying Biblical Story/Zombie Apocalypse mashup…

* * *

In the end, Juice hadn't seen any reason to go looking for trouble. If the building they sat on top of was full of dead… well, that was a fantastic place for them, safe behind a locked door, and he and Predator would very happily leave them the hell alone. Seeming to validate this intuition, on his way back, he got his marching orders from Handon – or rather his lack of them.

"Yeah, we're gonna try and consolidate with Ali and Homer on the ground, and all move together to a secondary target site. You two take it easy for now. We'll figure out how to get you down off of there later."

"Roger that. Good hunting."

A few seconds later, he turned the corner into view of Predator, who was lying where he'd left him – and who of course had heard the whole exchange on his own team radio. He was also busy manufacturing an improvised splint, made up of a section of two-by-four which he'd snapped in half with his bare hands, and which he was now duct-taping to his fractured leg. Around and around he wrapped the heavy tape. The agony this cost him must have been soul-scraping. But he didn't make a sound, and only gritted his teeth in concentration.

"*Oh*, no, man," Juice said – knowing this was useless even as he tried it. Pred didn't even look up. So Juice just sighed and started gathering up their gear. When Pred was up on his feet – or rather on one foot, the other stuck out like a drumstick, silently belying the torment this too must have caused – the two hobbled together back to the access door. Before Juice could address the matter of breaching it, Pred shredded the lock with a buckshot round from the Metalstorm shotgun slung under his rifle.

And without a pause, he went straight into the darkness ahead, firing and cursing, and hobbling on one agonizing drumstick.

Juice took a breath and went in straight behind him.

They would simply fight their way down. Hardly for the first time.

* * *

After Alpha hit the ground, consolidated, and got moving, it quickly became obvious where the Foxtrots were coming from.

They were coming from exactly where Alpha was *going* to. With each block the team covered, the opposition they faced increased. It seemed that every Foxtrot they dropped brought four more. And they were expending a lot more ordnance per kill than any of them were accustomed to, so difficult were the damned shots. It was truly turning into some *Black Hawk Down* shit. Including the dwindling ammo.

All eight of them had hit the street at the same time – Ainsley, Handon, Pope, and Henno down from the target building… Homer half-catching Ali as she dropped by her fingertips from the platform… and Predator and Juice stumbling out of the building across the street. The storm was well over now, but the streets still slick, and the sky still a low and oppressive gray.

Synchronized movement had long been part of

their playbook. They were more like a dance troupe than shock troops sometimes – even if Juice and Pred were cutting in today. When Ainsley and Handon saw them, they just shook their heads. Ainsley briefly considered trying to order them back. Handon instantly knew that to do so he'd have to *fight* Predator. And they all had more than enough fight on their hands as it was.

Ali had rigged up a nylon sling to help elevate the barrel of her weapon. Pope and Handon passed a few rifle magazines over to Homer, who was already running low. Ainsley got a bearing and took the lead. And they all moved out.

Bounding overwatch, the old fire and movement routine when moving to contact, was right out. Now it was just haul ass – and make shots on the hoof. It's only with tens of thousands of hours of training and drilling in close quarters battle (CQB) that soldiers can make shots on moving targets, while also moving themselves. (While a staple of blustery Hollywood dreck, it's actually one of the most difficult feats of arms imaginable.) Luckily, every member of Alpha had that level of training – plus thousands of hours shooting in operational situations.

And this was a good thing – because battling through swarms of Foxtrots, they discovered, was like being tossed into the Velociraptor pen. They came from everywhere – but more often from nowhere, fell flashes of mottled flesh, bared teeth, and cracked, filthy, slashing nails. Where they got the energy for this, none of the living could imagine. Then again, the dead seemed to violate most of the known laws of biology.

The eight moved in a staggered line, each responsible for an overlapping sector, 360-degree zombie warfare. Ali, with her superior vision and situational awareness, spotted two of them coming dead from the front ("zero angle on the bow" as Homer would put it), at full speed, and well before Ainsley did. She steadied her rifle on her half-dead left arm. She fired twice. Both went down. Their dead-on approach did mean they jigged less.

As they passed a crap-strewn alley on their left, Pope swiveled to cover it. But he was a little too close to its mouth, and they were moving too fast, and two of them blasted out and were on him before he could bring his rifle around. The three figures tumbled into a maelstrom of living and dead flesh, Pope's rifle wedging up in between them and clanking on the blacktop. Henno reacted and turned in to help. But Pope already had two knives out, one in each hand. In less than a second of flashing butchery, one dead arm had been cut loose, a hand off, and two brainstems speared – one from above, one from behind. Henno pulled Pope to his feet, and they both accelerated onto the back of the column.

Ainsley clocked all this. "*How's he look, Henno?*"

Henno eyed Pope up as they ran. There was a fair bit of gore on his chest and left thigh. But, in addition to being bite-proof, the suits were pus-proof. "He's good," Henno said. *He'll want to be hosed off later,* he thought, *but we can deal with that if we live long enough…*

After three frantic blocks south, Ainsley led them in a jog to the right, one block west. Without any kind of overhead surveillance to find them the clearest route, Ainsley was just going full out. Keeping the turns down to two, but otherwise just going hard and fast.

Handon, still tail-gunner Charlie, actually felt like he was having an okay day of it. He sure wouldn't want to be as dinged up as Predator or Ali and try this. But for his part, and with the spiritual kick he got from dire peril, he was having a good outing. He spared some of his attention for the sectors of the wounded, in case they got overwhelmed. But otherwise, it was a little like a day on the CQB range – motorized pop-up targets zanging up and racing by, or lurching straight at him. The cardboard versions wouldn't chomp your neck, killing you and then reanimating your corpse as a monster which would then kill your friends… but otherwise. His adrenaline was up. He just had to look out for his people. It was complete madness. But in a good way. He was in the zone, in a perfect state of flow.

But just when he was getting sanguine, that's when he saw one *fall* on top of Homer up ahead. As Handon moved to react, a second one came out of a window, right on his arm. *Fuck*. Wrestling is not a recommended tactic for zombie warfare – and neither Homer nor Handon had Pope's laser-gun knife skills. Homer let his rifle fall on its sling, and came around with his boarding axe, putting it straight through the mottled and worm-eaten face of his attacker. Handon held onto the pistol grip of his rifle, while drawing his second .45 and rapid-firing point blank. The zombie's head turned into a canoe, and brain matter and black pus splashed Handon's face shield. While regaining his feet and resuming the mad run, he pulled the fouled plastic mask off and tossed it. Dripping with infectious material, it was more of a hazard now. Though the next such splash might be lethal, ruining Handon's good day out – and switching his allegiance for good.

Thank God, they were finally approaching the Hyatt from the rear. Through the cross street, they could make out the twin cylindrical towers of the riverside Chicago Mercantile Exchange Center.

Virtually only the towers themselves were visible.

Because the lower stories were encased in a writhing skirt of meat – dead but animated bodies piled dozen upon hundred, clawing to get deeper in, climbing to get higher, pulling off pieces of themselves and others, wriggling like a plague of maggots in some Lovecraftian hell.

Ainsley actually had to swallow the contents of his stomach back down, when he caught sight of it. Now the entire group caught the stench. It smelled like what it was – an enormous pile of thousands of rotting dead bodies. And the dead out on the edge were starting to catch scent of the living. *Fuck the hotel entrance*, Ainsley thought, shooting out a large pane of groundfloor glass, and leading the group straight inside the hotel at a gallop. In the rear, Handon turned around and started moving backward, making rapid single shots on the scores of swarming, enraged, starving, hyper-powered soulless, who were now moving to follow them in.

Within thirty seconds, they found a service stairwell. *Down, fuck it, down*, Ainsley thought. They were so close – but playing it way too close to the bone.

There were also a few strays inside the building, in their own patch of turf, converging on the noise. The operators put them down in close quarters in whatever way seemed to hold most hope of keeping themselves on their feet. But behind them, through the shattered glass, a much greater mass of undead were sluicing into the building, filling up the space behind Alpha like air into a vacuum.

Juice spared a lightning look back to make sure his battle buddy was still with him. He caught a strobe light flash of Pred flyingly unscrewing the suppressor off the end of his rifle barrel and letting it fall. Without asking, Juice instantly knew why: the suppressor slowed rounds, and Pred wanted his full muzzle velocity; also, it was already so tight in here that bringing your weapon to bear was tricky – the shorter the barrel length the better; and, finally, who the goddamned hell else was the noise going to attract? The entire former population of Chicago already seemed to be on them. Juice made a mental note to take his off, if he happened to get two seconds to rub together at any point during the rest of his life.

Which floor? Which fucking floor? Ainsley gritted his teeth. There were several below-ground levels, and he didn't have any better intel than "in the basement." *Fuck it*, he thought – *in for a penny, in for a pound.* He'd take them all the way to the bottom. If there was no secret door there, well, it was a perfect place to be buried.

Buried under the weight of thousands of dead.

"*Room clearing drill!*" he shouted across the squad net. It was the quickest way to scour every part of every room on the level. "*Looking for a secure door!*" Out of habit, he instantly went to the heavy side – the one with a pair of Foxtrots coming to life and leaping down the dark and dirty corridor. Indoors, thank fuck, they couldn't dance around so goddamned much. On the other hand, it was so tight they were on you in fractions of a second.

Handon took the light side – but it didn't stay that way long. He knew the other six would be dynamically making decisions about movement and fire, based on a hundred factors, including visible opposition, the layout of the structure, and what the guy ahead of him was doing. They flowed through and across and around the floor in a slithering flash, dropping attackers at fast-forward speed, passing in full view of other operators and holding fire, a supremely controlled chaos. This was what they were very, very best at.

It was only twenty seconds later that Homer announced: "*Found it! North edge, beyond the boiler room.*" By the time the full group converged, Homer had the dummy code entered and the door open. But by the time they were all through it and inside, the great mass of dead were on them.

Juice and Predator, the two biggest men (and Predator was strongest, even on one leg), pushed on the door with all their strength, while the others fired out the slit into the mass of hissing mouths and undulating dead flesh outside. Finally, Pope got a tiny look at open air and tossed two grenades through. "Frags up!" he shouted and everyone hunkered down. The explosions didn't even kill the ones against the door, shielded as they were by the bodies of others. And the sheer mass of corpses was too much now – animated or not, they were keeping this door open.

While the others held the dyke, Handon scouted frantically forward. Dim blue LEDs illuminated the floor – it was only twenty meters of corridor, running alongside a scooped-out enclosure of chugging machinery, which Handon clocked as a large diesel generator, and then terminating in another door at the end. This one was steel, and solid, and had no keypad or reader. The long lever handle wouldn't budge – locked from the inside. *Fuck*. Handon was reaching for a shape charge to blow it when his peripheral vision registered movement. He came up with his sidearm in a blur – but only found himself aiming at a mini-CCTV camera above and in the corner. Its active red LED was lit. And Handon was sure it had moved.

Fuck it, he thought again, holstering his pistol and pulling out the shape charge. *No time.*

But then… the door simply opened. A youthful man with short dark hair and brown-framed eyeglasses stood behind it. For a quarter second neither seemed to know what to say. Then they both spoke at once:

"Get in!" shouted the man.

"Make way!" shouted the sergeant major.

BENEATH THIS DEAD EARTH

Juice and Pred stayed in the rear, now covering the fighting withdrawal. They stepped backward down the dark hallway, Pred dragging his badly swollen and immobilized leg, both of them firing incessantly. They got in sync – each reloading at the midpoint of the other's magazine, empties dropping out with a scraping sound, and hitting the cement floor with a clunk. Ejected shell casings hit the walls and the floor with a tinny sound. And the rifles roared.

The dead flew at them with ravenous single-mindedness. None of these could have fed in months or years. All were driven to frenzy – though whether by hunger, or merely hunger to infect, was a question no one had time for. As they leapt forward, levering by the destroyed ones in front with their stringy arms, Juice actually thought they might start using the walls and ceiling to come at them. It was all already *way* too much like the teeming-horde scene from *Aliens*...

As they neared the back end of the corridor, Pred emptied the remaining four buckshot rounds from his underslung Metalstorm launcher – then jammed in a pack of five high explosive (HE) rounds. Juice gave him a look – in this enclosed area, the overpressure caused when the rounds exploded could *seriously* fuck them all up. As in kill them. But there was nothing else for it. As things stood, the horde was too close, virtually on top of them – the dead would be on the inner door at the same time the last humans tried to go through it. Then they wouldn't be able to close that one, either – and then all of them would be doomed.

As Pred slammed shut the receiver on the five round munition tube, an unseen hand grabbed his collar and pulled him backward. He almost tumbled ass over teakettle, and as he staggered backward, his assailant pulled his rifle out of his hands. It was Ainsley. He pivoted and gave Juice a mighty shove with his strong right arm, then turned away, into the horde. Pred and Juice tripped over each other – falling right through the doorway and into the others inside.

The first HE round went off only a few feet down the corridor. It ruptured the eardrums of both Juice and Pred, and sucked the air out of the lungs of everyone behind. The overpressure also slammed the heavy, handleless door closed with a whump.

Behind it, four more explosions sounded dully.

* * *

"Simon Park," the young man said. He was trembling badly. "Doctor Simon Park."

Handon took his hand. Even as completely unhinged as the world had gone… it still must have been a bad shock for this guy to find seven heavily armed commandos, dripping blood and zombie gore, suddenly standing in his secret bunker. "I was expecting someone older," Handon said.

"Yeah, I get that a lot." Park pointed at the heavy inner door. "Your... your friend... Jesus..."

"He's gone," Handon said, repeating a scene he'd acted out a hundred times. He turned slightly toward the others. "And we pick up his banner and carry on. While there's breath in our bodies." The others nodded. There hadn't been any real need to say it. But it served as a passing of the torch of command. Ainsley had made his choice, spending his life gloriously. And they were all alive because of it.

Predator turned away and staggered into the main room, looking for and finding a couch. Blood dripped from his ears. "Not sure there *is* breath in my fucking body..." he said, too loud, and collapsed. Juice followed to look after him.

* * *

It was an underground complex of more than twenty rooms. Several of them, most of the larger ones, were filled with computers, desks, network gear, phones, and large display screens. Most of the rest were one type or another of living quarters – bedrooms, bathrooms, a kitchen, an enormous supply closet (really a mini-warehouse), and the large living room in which Alpha, or the remainder of it, sprawled out now. They peeled off sweaty assault suits – several of them after being hosed down in the shower – dropped their heavy rucks on the floor, shrugged out of assault vests, unchambered and safetied weapons, tightened bandages, and chugged down bottles of water.

Park talked directly to Handon, who was also

gearing down. The others listened.

"They built all this after 9/11," Park said. "When they saw how long the New York Stock Exchange was out of action after the attacks, they decided to make sure they could continue trading through any kind of disaster. Natural or man-made."

"Yeah," Handon said, sitting and loosening his assault boots. "We saw your e-mail."

The young scientist's eyes went wide. "You were at NeuraDyne?"

Handon nodded. "That's what we came for. Your research data."

"So… there's someone left out there? Somewhere?"

"Britain. It stood when everyplace else fell. Listen – how long was this bunker designed to hold out for?"

"Three months. But that was with a full staff of traders, techs, managers, executives – everyone vital to operating the Exchange. With just one man, me, the food and water looks like lasting for years. As for the diesel generator… well, I conserve power, and only run it when the batteries need topping up. I'm about halfway through the fuel."

Handon perked up. "Juice," he said. "Get to the trading room. Get on their radio set, if they have one. Or try to hook one of our radios into an aerial or repeater, if they've got that."

"On it," Juice said, rising with his ruck and striding out.

"Pope. Check the perimeter. Especially the other

door, and outside via the cameras."

Pope nodded and glided out.

Handon slumped down a bit on the couch again, and pinned the young man with his eye. "And so where are all these people who are supposed to be here?"

Park shrugged. "They never turned up. I'm guessing the dead swept the trading floor before anyone could make it down here. It's just me."

"Well, bully for you," Henno said, levering himself up. "I'm gonna recce the kitchen."

"I'd murder a bacon sandwich," said Predator – who'd finally consented to taking a half gram of morphine sulfate. He lay diagonally on a large loveseat, taking up the whole thing.

"Okay. How do we get out of here?" Handon asked.

"I don't think we can. You must have seen – the building is literally covered with them."

"Why is that?"

Park shook his head quickly. "I don't know, not for sure. I think maybe it's because I'm the last living person in Chicago."

Ali snorted with laughter. "A LaMOE! We found one."

"What?" asked Simon.

"Never mind," said Handon. "How do the dead know you're in here?"

"That's been a matter of some speculation on my part. I thought maybe it was because of the toilet flushing. It would be the only one."

Homer looked up. "Where does your garbage go?"

"Um. I don't know. It gets sucked out a pneumatic tube, about once a week."

"That's probably it right there. It will have organic matter in it, and they'll smell it. Like ringing the dinner bell."

Handon nodded, looking intent, and looking like changing the subject. "Your research... Have you cured the plague? *Do you have a vaccine?*"

Simon drew breath. "Yes and no."

Handon worked to swallow his irritation. He refrained from pointing out that what they'd all just gone through to get there probably at least merited a straight answer. "*Go on.*"

Park nodded. "I don't know how much you know about vaccine research – or care to. There are several types of novel vaccine strategies that presented themselves as possible candidates for the zombie plague – for a double-stranded RNA virus. I focused my work on a possible recombinant vector vaccine. Using data from the dsRNA interference technique we worked out, I was able to combine the physiology of one microorganism and the DNA of the other, creating immunity against an organism with as complex an infection process as this one has."

"So does it work, or doesn't it?"

"Yes," Park said, finally. "It works against the early samples of the virus I have here. But the virus is clearly mutating. Hell, it's mutating in here, in test tubes, in isolation. But out *there*..." and he tossed his head toward the steel doors. "With two years, and the whole world as a breeding ground… look, I've got a lot of external cameras. And I can see the changes in their behavior, even from in here. But I wasn't going to open that door, not just to get new samples. Plus… I didn't really think there was anyone left in the world to immunize…"

Handon blinked. "So you're saying it wouldn't protect anybody from the virus as it is today?"

"I believe it could be *made* to work on current strains of the virus. I'm sure of it. All I need is to understand which features of the virus are transitory, and subject to significant mutation – and which aspects are enduring. Look, all organisms have DNA that stays basically the same over time. I target my technique to *those* genes and, blammo, we've got a universal vaccine."

"Okay," Ali said, from across the room. "How do you find out which genes have endured?"

Park paused before answering. He looked like he was worried how his next statement was going to go over.

"I need patient zero."

Handon snorted, shaking his head mordantly. *Isn't that just like the ZA*, he thought.

With this, Juice returned to the main room.

"No go, Sarge. I've got long-range radio transmission capability. But it's like the *JFK*'s just not there. Or everyone on it's asleep… or dead."

Now Predator snorted. "I'm gonna take a shit."

Juice moved to help him up.

Drake bounded down the stairs of the island to the *JFK*'s Ops room. "*Status!*" he bellowed.

One of the duty officers, puffy headphones on, answered, "It's the Greyhound. She's coming in on final approach, whether we're ready or not. Running on fumes, sir."

"Can you get her down?"

"It would help a lot if we controlled Pri-Fly," the officer said tightly, referring to Primary Flight Control, on the top level of the island. "But we can do it from here. Especially since we've got no choice…"

Just as Drake felt he was reaching maximum cognitive capacity, Master Gunnery Sergeant Fick stomped into the room, reeking of cordite, and streaked with soot and droplets of blood. His scarred and scowling face was a mask of frustration. "God*damm*it," he said, striding up. "Sir. Those bastards are dug in like Alabama ticks. I've got multiple casualties. And now my men are desperately needed to try and control this zombie outbreak. If we don't deal with that, we're all done for."

Drake remembered to draw breath. "And if we don't stop the ship from crashing into land, this vessel is done for… And, fuck me, if we don't refuel this plane to extract the away team, the human race is probably finished…" He felt as if his brain were stewing in its own juices. But he took another breath, mastered himself – and gave orders.

"Gunnery Sergeant Fick – redeploy all your men here to battle the zombies. *Get the outbreak under control – whatever that entails.* They fight as a team."

"Sir." Fick started to turn.

"But they fight without you. You're going with Martin and Wesley. You get them safely to the reactor room." Fick knew as well as Drake that this was a heavily armored, heavily restricted area dead in the middle of the ship. But he didn't seem daunted.

"And you, Commander?" Martin asked.

"I'm going to get that plane down – and, God willing, back up again." The others looked at him. "We might make it here, and we might not. But if we get that bird in the air, then at least those men in Chicago have a chance. And so does humanity."

He was already turning away toward the operator at the control station.

* * *

After dashing upstairs, leading his men as they withdrew and broke contact with the Zealots, and retasking them to assault the burgeoning ranks of zombies, Fick returned to the Ops Center and rounded up Martin and Wesley. He'd rearmed out of a weapons locker, 18 full magazines of 5.56 for his M16. He gave four of them to Martin, who still had Drake's rifle, and who shoved them in his pockets. Nobody had any spare ammo for Wesley's pistol, so Fick gave him his sidearm, with two spare mags. He squared up and gave orders to his new two-man command.

"Listen up. We're going to be moving hard and fast – and fluid. *Stay on me.* Stop for nothing. Your sector will be everything between my eight o'clock and four o'clock – that's behind me. Okay? If you have to take a shot, take it with authority and move on. You should know whether a headshot is required. If you shoot a loyal sailor by mistake, that will suck for him, and also for you. But it doesn't matter. We are moving to save the ship. Everything else is secondary – including and in particular us. Understood?"

The two Brits nodded.

Fick paused and seemed to grow thoughtful, then looked to Martin. "Well, not you, actually. You're the only son of a bitch who knows how to stop this crazy thing. Okay – on me! *Go, go, go!*"

The three of them spilled down the exterior stairwell of the island and onto the flight deck.

MARSOC Marines were already pushing out a perimeter. The dead were mostly down; and any sailors who might have been Zealots were suddenly acting like they weren't. (*One problem with a fucking mutiny*, Fick thought. *No real way to tell who's who…*) The three crossed a hundred meters of deck in a tight knot, then descended through the same hatch from which Martin and Wesley had so recently been greeted by fire and death.

Fick had his rifle pulled in tight to his shoulder, eye down to his EOTech holo-sight, swiveling at the hips, covering almost 180 degrees. *Every Marine is a rifleman*, they say. The other two did their best to stay close behind him.

And to make sure no one else did.

* * *

"You can *do* this," Drake uttered into the desk mic, leaning in over it. He was talking to the Greyhound pilot still circling above. "Arresting wires are up. And the deck is mostly clear. You're just going to have to catch the first wire. It's the only way you'll have enough clear deck to stop."

"*Copy that*," said the Navy pilot, perfectly poised and professional, as military aviators tend to be even in the most nerve-shredding circumstances. "*We're coming down one way or another. State zero plus zero-one to splash.*" This meant he had *one minute* of fuel left. "*But negative on deck landing. Seas are choppy – and if I go for the first wire, and the boat rises so much as two feet on a swell, we'll be eating stern. No, we're going to punch out and ditch it.*"

Drake jammed the transmit button. "*Negative, NEGATIVE*. Be advised – you are the *only* aircraft with the range to extract our team in contact. You are going to put that aircraft on the goddamned deck, we are going to tank it, and you are going to go get those men. Acknowledge!"

There was only the shortest pause on the other end.

"*Aye aye, sir. We are inbound on short final.*"

Drake swatted the desk mic away from him, and it tumbled over.

He stepped out onto the balcony to check their

position in the water.

North America was coming at them *way* too fast.

* * *

Fick took a round right between his shoulder blades, luckily in the ceramic plate in the back of his tactical vest. He spun on a dime and snap-fired one into the head of the Zealot behind them. A dead man lurched out of a cabin and fell on the man he'd just shot. Fick drilled it in the head.

He gave Martin and Wesley a look like: *What the fuck are you guys doing back there?*

But the passageways were narrow and twisting and dim, and very perilous. And despite being responsible for the Marine's back, they couldn't really keep their gaze turned around behind them. They were simply moving too fast. Fick did a lightning tactical reload and took off again. The other two dashed off in pursuit before he got out of sight.

They reached another ladder and descended. And again. This new level looked deserted.

But when they got in the vicinity of the reactor, they quickly determined that it hadn't been taken by the Zealots.

It had been taken by the dead.

At least they won't know how to sabotage it, Martin thought mordantly.

The three of them spread out and started trying to clear the area.

Now, this, Wesley thought, almost happily, *I know*

how to do.

Zombie fighting. It was becoming old hat for him now.

* * *

A carrier landing deck has four arresting wires, one of which a pilot must snag with his tailhook in order to bring his aircraft safely down and to a stop – on a strip that would otherwise be far too short for it. There are four wires because they are damned hard to hit, more so in rough seas. And even more so with a three-way mutiny and zombie battle going on all over the ship.

Pilots almost always go for the third wire – because the first two are uncomfortably close to the edge. Undershoot one of those, or have the ship rise on a wave, and you'll crash into the stern. But a bunch of even worse alternatives were making this one look pretty appealing. The pilot caught the first wire, on his first pass – which was good because he wasn't going to get another one. The bird screeched to a halt amidst clouds of white smoke. Deck crew dashed out to assist the pilot, secure the plane, and start the refueling.

The two pilots came tumbling out the cabin door, helmets still on, looking in every direction like they were in a fright house – which they were. Fires still burned, shots rang out, and the dead could still be heard to moan, amidst the screams of men. They raced through smoke to the island, just to take shelter until the Greyhound was ready to launch again.

They moved like men being chased.

* * *

Okay, Wesley mentally amended, turning a corner with his pistol held outstretched in both hands. *Maybe not exactly old hat.* In fact, he'd never fought zombies in what was basically a dungeon.

He heard shots ring out periodically – the hard snaps of the 5.56mm assault rifles. He hadn't fired his pistol yet. He was responsible for clearing the area closest to where they'd come in, on the fore side – which was basically already clear. Martin was aft. And Fick was right in the reactor center. Wesley thought maybe their shots had drawn them all from the entire deck.

"*Wesley!*" He jumped three inches at the sound of his name echoing down the deck.

"Yes!" He craned his neck, and peered down the hall.

"*Are you clear th—*" A gray face resolved out of the darkness, four feet in front of his head, mouth open, arms outstretched, and translucent eyes shining. It was on him in a fraction of a second. Wesley brought his handgun up and triggered off four rapid rounds. They caught the dead sailor across the chest and midsection and knocked it back a foot – enough room for Wesley to master himself. And make the headshot.

"*Wesley! You there?*"

He shook his head to clear it. His mouth was almost totally dry, and his voice cracked when he tried to yell back. "Ye— yes. I think I'm clear."

He stepped over the twice-dead corpse, and ran to

the sound of the others. By the time he arrived, Martin was bringing down first one reactor and then the other.

"Starting a nuclear reactor is quite complex," he narrated, moving from one station to the other. "And running it in production can be demanding, and dangerous. But the designers and manufacturers make shutting them down pretty easy." He used a key to open up a covered switch. It read "Emergency Shutdown Enable". He flicked it. Then he pulled a large, conspicuous, two-stemmed red lever on the wall.

"For reasons that might be guessed."

* * *

Drake was debriefing the two Greyhound pilots when he felt it fading away beneath them – the immensely powerful rumble that always seized the ship when she was underway, the thrum of the enormous engines. He stuck his head out the door. The wind was slowing. And the rate of their approach toward the spit of land started to slow.

But he didn't think it was slowing enough.

Never mind, he thought. He looked to the fuelers out by the plane, with their enormous articulated hoses, and the hazy penumbra of jet fuel vapor around them. He caught one's eye. The man gave him a thumbs-up. Drake ducked back inside.

"Gentlemen," he said. (Naval aviators were always, by proclamation, officers and gentlemen.) "You're good to go." The two rose in their flight suits and followed him out. Drake stopped on the second-floor balcony and watched them descend. They hit the flight deck and began to trot out toward the waiting aircraft.

And then something else caught his eye. No, he heard it first.

It was one of the three enormous deck-edge elevators, which were used for moving aircraft from the hangar deck up to the flight deck and back down again. Drake racked his brain for why one of these would be coming up. God knows they weren't scheduled to move any aircraft.

And then he saw. The elevator was covered with the dead.

Scratch that, there were a few living – mostly being fed on. Those were probably the ones who had actuated the elevator – using it to try to escape. But they hadn't gotten away quickly enough. Fast these elevators were not, and the dead had followed them on. Now it was a hydraulic charnel house. As it came into view, almost level with the deck, one of the living tried to haul himself over to safety – but was pulled back down from behind. As the platform came level, the dead there sensed the living on the flight deck.

And they all clambered out.

Shots began ringing and zipping – from both the loyalists, and the Zealots on the bridge.

Drake turned his gaze to the two pilots. They were *very* aware of what was going on – and now running flat out toward the (relative) safety of their aircraft. Drake ducked back inside, grabbed a rifle and went back out. All was madness – even more confused and panicked than it had been before. He made out the aviators – still on their feet. He looked for zombies.

Oh shit, he thought, seeing one that had clocked the pilots. He tried to draw a bead, through the roiling smoke, through the adrenaline, over the rolling deck. He fired – missed. Fired and missed again. Now the zombie reached the co-pilot, and grabbed with both hands and bit. *Fuck!* Drake fired again. The zombie's head turned to spray. The co-pilot fell down along with it. The pilot, who had been looking back, turned forward again, put his head down, and reached the plane. He climbed in and slammed the door behind him.

"Thank God," Drake whispered. And thank God it only took one to fly that thing. And mostly thank God that, with no men or equipment aboard, that plane could get off the deck without the catapult. Both prop engines spun up, and the pilot rolled it out, right over the wheel blocks. He turned, taxied, looking for a clear lane down the deck. He didn't quite find it and so instead went straight into two zombies, shredding them through the propellers. He accelerated rapidly after that, dropped off the edge of the deck, rose again, and turned his nose inland.

Drake lowered his rifle and smiled.

The horrifying, cosmic grind of the bottom of the ship smashing and scraping into the sea bottom stopped everyone in their tracks. Drake's smile melted away.

The *John F. Kennedy* had floundered.

They were run aground.

CONTACT

Down in the basement bunker, deep beneath undead Chicago, Handon re-tasked Juice. Instead of helping Predator take a dump, he went to work with Dr. Park in trying to transmit all of his research data out of there and back to the *JFK*. The two had disappeared to the trading room, carrying Park's laptop and the team's long range radio transmitter. Now they returned to the living area where the others were tabletop-gaming ideas for getting out of the Exchange Center alive. Which they'd actually only need to bother with if they managed to contact the carrier and arrange their air extraction.

"No dice, boss," Juice said. "I don't think anyone's receiving on the data channel, either. At least, I got no acknowledgement. There's no way to be sure any of it went out. I'll keep trying. But right now it's looking like we're just going to have to walk this stuff out of here."

Handon took this in. He was used to missions where things frequently went from bad, to worse, to "you're fucking kidding me." But now, not only were they buried under a sea of the living dead – but so was the last, best hope for the world, a chance at a cure. And so now the operators' fates were tied to that of every other living person left on the planet. And Handon needed to do what he'd done so many times before: dig down deeper.

It just felt like there wasn't much left down there anymore.

Well, he thought, *it's just one more goddamned thing. And it's not like it's the end of the world...* This last thought amused him and raised his spirits. Also, he remembered, twenty minutes ago they thought they were all dead. Now at least they were safe in this bunker. For a while.

"What's that smell?" It was Park, looking around, and looking worried.

Then Handon noticed it. "Smells like engine exhaust... $C0_2$."

Juice stepped over to an air vent. "Yep. Coming from here."

"The diesel generator, out in the hall," Handon said. "Could it be malfunctioning?"

Juice snorted. "What, after five HE explosions in close quarters, and now an army of smushed zombies pressed all around it? Yeah, maybe." He turned to Park. "Where does the exhaust from that thing normally go?"

"I don't know—"

"Never mind," Handon said. "Shut it down. Now!"

Park nodded and dashed off. When he returned, he said expectantly, "Done. Better?"

But it wasn't better. Now they could all smell acrid smoke. And within a few seconds, they could see it visibly drifting in through the vent.

"Too late," Juice said. "It must have shorted. And maybe sparked something flammable nearby..."

"Zombie clothing?" Ali suggested. "Or Ainsley clothing. What happens when it hits Ainsley's ammo, or grenades?"

"Forget the grenades," Juice said. "There's a whole

depot of diesel fuel out there."

Handon went to the door and pressed his hand against it. It was stove-top hot. "Where's the other entrance to this place?"

"On the other side of the bunker," Park said. "But we can't get out that way either. It leads up into the Exchange. And the building's completely enclosed in dead."

"Fuck," Handon spat, looking around helplessly.

"*Mortem One, this is Grey Goose Zero. How copy? Mortem One, Grey Goose Zero.*" This leaked out of the radio earpiece hanging on Handon's chest. Everyone in the room heard it. Handon jammed the earpiece back in and pressed his transmit button.

"Grey Goose, this is Mortem One Actual. Interrogative – what is your location and status?"

"*Mortem One, Gray Goose. I am inbound for extraction point Alpha, Chicago Miegs Airfield. ETA 35 minutes. But be advised – I have just enough fuel to touch and go. After about one minute on the ground at engine idle, I will be at bingo fuel. So you had better be on the spot and ready to get out of Dodge. How copy, over.*"

Handon's expression stayed neutral. "Mortem One copies all." That was great – their ride was inbound on a totally do-or-die schedule. And there was still no way for them to get through the army of dead outside to the extraction point. Oh, and they also couldn't stay where they were, because the building was burning down.

"Fuck," he repeated.

A not-quite-muffled explosion rocked the back

door, from out in the hall. Probably one of Ainsley's grenades. The smoke coming in through the vent grew thicker and darker.

"Fuck."

Now several people were saying it.

But everyone was thinking it.

* * *

Henno wasn't given to speechifying. But now he stood, picked up Dr. Park's laptop, pointed toward the back exit, and spoke.

"The man just outside that door sacrificed himself – and he didn't do it to save *you* lot. He did it for the whole world. For his children. So just maybe they'll have a world to grow up in. And we fucking well *will* get this vaccine out of here and back to Britain."

No one spoke for a second.

"He's right," Handon finally said. "So saddle up. Take everything. We're moving out."

"Where to?" Homer asked.

"Far side of the bunker for now – if the fuel tank out in that hall goes, I'm not sure I see the inner door holding. We'll think of something else from there."

"Hell," Predator said, levering his huge bulk off the couch with three limbs. "I'm not sure I see this side of the structure not collapsing…"

As the commandos began an accelerated process of strapping everything back on, Pope sidled over to Handon. "Quick word with you, Top?"

The two of them led the exodus down the hall, then stepped off alone into the kitchen, as the others filed by. Suddenly Handon noticed that Pope wasn't looking too good. He clocked the sweat beading on Pope's forehead. The temperature in the bunker was rising now, but was still relatively cool. And when Handon squinted, focusing on Pope's face, he saw the early signs – those tiny black lines spreading out from the eyes and the mouth, faint red spots around the face and neck, and that strange glazing of the eyes.

"Ah, shit, Pope," Handon cursed, shaking his head.

"Yeah," sighed Pope, flexing his right hand and peering at the white dots already appearing on his fingernails. Body proteins being destroyed.

Handon looked Pope straight in the eyes. "Why didn't you say anything?"

"I didn't know until just now. Thought I was still just out of breath. Something. But that roll-around, during the run here, must have splashed me. On a bit of mucous membrane probably."

Handon held the other man's eye. "Do you want me to do it? Or on your own?"

"Neither." Pope spoke levelly and carefully. He knew that there was no one else that he would have wanted to end it, but he had another plan. "Use me. To get out of here."

"How?" asked Handon.

"Diversion," replied Pope, nodding in the direction of their blocked exit. "Send me up out the main exit."

Handon frowned. "You can't. It's overrun up

there. A mass of meat."

"No," Pope said, shaking his head. "The *outside* of the building's meat. But the inside, the trading floor and whatnot, I think has just got a few from the internal outbreak. The outer doors must have held. I saw it on the security cams. Maybe a few dozen wandering around. However, if I go up there and *open* the outer doors…"

Handon nodded. "Then the ones outside will pour in. And maybe the ones in our back tunnel, and clogging up the basement of the hotel, will follow them."

"Exactly. They'll follow the frenzy and decamp, giving the rest of you a way out."

Handon thought seriously about this. He didn't have much time to ponder, but it depended on the dead doing exactly as predicted, and they weren't always predictable.

"And what if they don't?"

Pope smiled. "Well, you'll have nearly a half hour to think up a new, better plan."

"Jesus." Handon shook his head – 98.5% of humanity dead, and yet they still managed to produce heroes like this one. Right now, though, Handon would have given all of those others to hang on to this one for even just another day. For two years they had been the only team in USOC – perhaps the only deployed military unit anywhere in the ZA – never to lose a man. Now they'd lost two in the space of ten minutes. If felt like the world, or what was left of it, or maybe just their little sane corner, was falling to pieces. Handon pushed the feeling away, shoving it deep down inside him.

"You're ready to do that?" he asked, knowing the answer already. It was a stupid question.

"Oh, yes." Pope held up his hand and showed Handon the lesion that had appeared on the back of it, a long thin line that had already turned black, the edges starting to seep and grow raw. "I'm on my countdown anyway, and I don't want to be around long enough for the bell to toll. Let's do this."

Handon paused for the briefest of moments, held Pope's gaze again, and then nodded.

"Okay," he said.

KI KEN TAI I-CHI ("SPIRIT SWORD BODY AS ONE")

Pope had a minute or two to prepare. He wiped his sword down with a soft cloth, then sheathed it again. He cleared the chamber of his assault rifle, reloaded it, and slung it across his back. Then he did the same with his sidearm, re-holstering it. He catalogued the magazines and grenades on his assault vest by touch, along with others on his belt and in thigh pouches.

Briefly, he'd tried to take off his bite-proof assault suit, and put it on Dr. Park instead. After all, the scientist was a lot more important now. Also, suddenly, getting bit was much less of a big deal for Pope. But the others wouldn't hear of it. They made noises about being able to perform close protection just fine, thank you very much. But to Pope it was transparent that they just refused to send him out to his end looking, for a Tier-1 operator, naked.

Now the others were milling around the far end of the compound, by the main door, which led up to the Exchange Center. Someone had gathered up four large fire extinguishers, both CO_2 and dry powder varieties. Handon and Park were checking video feeds – trying to clock the location of everything upstairs, and as much of their outdoor exfil route as they could see.

Very soon, it was time. Because there was no time.

Handon and Pope nodded at each other, as the door swung open.

Without looking back, Pope began the climb up. The stairwell was clear. When he reached ground level, he pulled his sword with his right hand, and opened the stairwell door with his left.

There were three there. Pope dispatched them methodically with the blade. Pivoting, lunging, and striking, using the footwork and combination techniques of kendo, the ritual movement of it all soothed him. He felt so much as if he were back in the dojo at Hendon with Ali. Those were beautiful times. Beautiful memories. He suddenly remembered what he'd overheard Ali saying, to Homer, on their flight in: something about looping through your whole life in the last second of your life.

Maybe he'd get to experience it all once more.

Emerging from his brief reverie, he moved out of the stairwell, stepped over the headless bodies, and made his way forward. Within a minute, he found the main lobby and atrium of the south tower. It was like nothing he'd ever seen – the dead outside blotted out the sky. Literally every inch of the two-story-high glass, from one end of the lobby to the other, was pressed with writhing, dead flesh. It was something beyond a horror show.

"Well, no time like the present," Pope said aloud to himself, then moved to take up a position a little further out in the middle of the lobby. He removed an HE grenade from his vest, pulled the pin with his teeth –

then whirled suddenly at footsteps behind him. It was Ali.

And also Handon, and Pred, and Juice. And Henno and Homer. The whole team. They walked up to him in silence in a line, then split in two, and formed a loose ring around him.

"Okay," grunted Predator. "You gonna throw that thing? Or make me stand here all day?"

Pope smiled out loud, turned around, and gave the grenade an easy underhand toss over the main desk. It hit the outer glass wall, dropped, and rolled a foot or two. The short, percussive blast took out the glass panels above and to either side, and for twenty feet in all directions. And in came the dead with their own rumbling explosion of moans. They *literally* spilled in. And, in a frenzy, those that could still locomote rushed the circle of the living. As they approached, the operators could hear the moaning being picked up outside, and repeated down the block.

"FPF!" Handon barked. "Two volleys! On my signal!" Final Protective Fire – an unrelenting volley of full-auto and grenades, generally only used in the most desperate situations. When the dead were ten meters out and closing, Handon gave the signal. In a fraction of an instant, the whole room lit up with a galaxy of muzzle flashes, and explosions of grenades further out. Those with MetalStorm launchers fired all five rounds of HE or buckshot. Those without chucked hand grenades. Everyone emptied their magazines in seconds, reloaded, and went again.

After the second volley, the dead were piled up in a

semicircle halfway to the ceiling. With little delay, the dead behind them could be heard scrabbling over the barricade of their fellows. Nothing slowed the dead. Nothing dinged their self-confidence. The dead didn't ruminate.

"*O-karada o daiji ni*," Ali said quietly, kissing Pope on the cheek as she passed him by. A beautiful Japanese phrase, it meant "take care of yourself." But, literally translated, it was "your body is precious." The others shook Pope's hand, nodded, or clapped him on the shoulder as they went by. Homer was last.

"I'll see you in the next place, my brother," he said, looking warmly into his eyes.

And Pope thought to himself: *I am a very lucky man. I am blessed.*

Then he gripped his sword, drew his sidearm, and turned back to face the room.

Time for one last dance.

SALVATION

Homer pulled the stairwell door closed behind him and raced down to keep pace with the others. Just as they were spilling back into the bunker, a terrible explosion rocked the walls and floor, and hot gases rolled over them in waves. Homer instantly knew it was the diesel fuel tank from the back hallway. He also knew something else: God was watching over them. Because that explosion, timed so perfectly, would have cleared out that hallway of the dead, both the animated and squashed varieties.

It cleared their escape path.

Now, if Pope's sacrifice worked, and Homer didn't doubt for a second that it would, those that had crushed down into the hotel after them, would be reversing course, and following the noise, and the smell, and the general frenzy toward the lobby of the Exchange Center across the street.

Homer let his rifle fall on its sling, hefted one of the CO_2 extinguishers and hauled ass through the bunker, knowing the others would be right behind him. Sure enough, the inner door was gone from its frame, and flame and smoke poured in from outside. Homer gave it a long rolling blast from the extinguisher, then paused a second to let the gases clear.

"Everyone ready to go again?" Handon barked. He had his left hand wrapped around the thin bicep of Dr. Park, who had his laptop bag slung around him, plus clutched in both arms. The others stood poised like sprinters at the starting line.

"'Til the roof comes off, boss," Juice said.

"'Til the lights go out," Ali added.

The lights in the bunker went out. *One down*, thought Ali, pulling down her NVGs.

Predator spoke in the dark, as he did the same: "'Til my leg give out, then."

"That'll be never," Juice said, coming up in the others' vision as a puffy fluorescent green.

Homer pulled his *shemagh* up over his face, hefted the extinguisher, and charged.

* * *

The group burst out into the street, after fighting through moderate opposition in the hotel. Pope hadn't died for nothing – most of the dead had withdrawn. Homer spared a look back up the cross street, where the Exchange Center had turned from a meat wall to a meat funnel, sucking in the dead from all directions. *God lets no one die in vain*, Homer thought. He then turned the opposite direction, east, and led the team in their last run.

Pulling up the rear again was Handon – who also rode herd on Dr. Park, shoving him, and his laptop, out ahead of him. As they took off, Handon spared one quick look at his wristwatch. They now had 21 minutes to get across town, down the lakefront, and out to the airstrip on Northerly Island. It was 2.6 miles, as Handon had earlier measured it. This required only 8-minute miles of them, slower than their conditioning runs, and would have been completely manageable – if they all didn't happen to be encumbered with weapons, armor, and ammo, plus fighting their way through an entire city of Fucking Nightmare zombies. Plus running for their lives. Also, there was zero leeway on the timing. It was sudden-death, do-or-die.

Predator mocked up a plummy English accent, and parroted Ainsley: "'Two-point-eight miles over surface streets. You'll hardly notice it.' Easy for that son of a bitch to say, he doesn't have to do it now." Henno made a mental note to kneecap Pred later, if they lived.

This time the running street battle was like their earlier one, only more so – plus at only 75% of their previous strength, and also with one helpless passenger. They all ran, shot, reloaded, stabbed, dodged, and parried. Every zombie in the city not already there was now clearly headed for the Exchange Center – which meant that every zombie between the airstrip and them was headed directly their way. They cut through them with whirling blades, and mag after mag of 5.56mm, 7.62mm, .45-cal, and shotgun shells. Some were starting to conclude it was easier to pulp and dismember them, than to make headshots on these jackrabbit sons of bitches. Or maybe they were just too tired now. They painted a rich black smear of zombie blood across the urban heart of Chicago.

As they finally emerged from the forest of buildings, spotting ahead of them the open expanse of Lake Shore Drive bordering the water, they were all sucking wind and critically low on ammo. But Chicago still had zombies to burn.

As he ran and changed out magazines, eyes and ears scanning in all directions for threats, Homer heard something from an unexpected direction: up. It was the prop-engine buzzing of the Greyhound, already banking and descending, coming in from over the broad expanse of the lake.

Thank fuck, Homer thought. He slightly startled himself with this, realizing he'd probably been hanging out with Brits, not to mention heathens, for too long now. He tweaked their path, toward the north end of the island, which connected with the mainland via a narrow spit of road and footpath. He gasped for air, and steeled himself to race the final distance.

Hope was dangerous. But there was no way to avoid it. The appearance of the plane was making all of them start to believe that they *just* might get out of this alive after all.

DAMNATION

"*No, no, no,*" chanted Major Lee Vesbost, sole surviving pilot of the Greyhound transport aircraft. Early forties, big lean frame, short curly hair, and wry manner, he was an extremely experienced naval aviator, with a variety of challenging flying assignments behind him. He hadn't gotten as far as he had by being a mushy-headed dreamer, or wishful thinker.

"No, no, no," he repeated, trying to hold the plane on the long banking track that would line it up with the long narrow grass edge of the island, which was formerly the airstrip. His words were now like a totemic incantation. They didn't mean anything, had no affect. He was just denying it, ritually.

The first two hours of the flight from the charnel house of the *Kennedy* had been fine. Of course, he had been equally horrified to lose his long-time co-pilot, as he was blessedly relieved to get the hell out of there alive. It had been a terrifyingly close call, and of course only one of them had survived. But some unseen sniper had taken off the zombie's head, giving Vesbost the time he needed to hurl himself into the cabin. After that, finding enough clear deck to take off had been another miracle.

For that first two hours, he'd just focused on the flight and the mission. He had paused briefly to wipe off the viscous gunk that had splashed from the exploding zombie's head. It had only caught him on the shoulder. Mainly. He'd left it at that.

Including when he started getting headachy and dizzy later on. But when the fever hit him, he realized. But still he denied it. There was nothing else to do. He thought maybe he could bull through. Maybe the infection wouldn't take him. He was the only one left to fly the plane, to make the extraction. This simply couldn't happen to him.

The gray of the city and sky, and the steel blue of the lake, started to go hazy and dark in his fading vision. It all began to go out of focus. And holding himself up over the yoke and flight controls was becoming impossible. But he was beginning not to care about that...

Down he went.

* * *

Juice had Pred's arm over his shoulder now. How the man-mountain had just *run* nearly three miles, on a leg that was mostly lumber, was beyond him. He was physically failing now. But it was okay. They were going to make it. They were halfway across the land bridge to the island – and they could see the Greyhound lining up for approach.

Coming onto the island proper, they turned right – heading south down the grass strip and straight toward the descending aircraft. It drew them all on in those final 200 meters. But then a strange wobble appeared in its wings. And then its altitude dropped – too low, way too low. As Juice exclaimed aloud, "Oh, no, no, no –

no!" the twin-engine plane plowed nose-first into the south edge of the island, coming apart in an ugly pirouette of dismemberment, wings and tail and fuselage and aileron separating, and then the fuel tanks went up in a pretty orange explosion. The sound of it, and warm wash of air, reached them a second later.

The group slowed to a trot, then a stop.

They turned back around.

Out in the open now, they could all see, literally plain as day, the hundreds of Foxtrots racing after them, lurching, sprinting, tumbling, ravening, rasping. They'd be across the land bridge in less than a minute.

The six commandos and one civilian stood in a loose knot, all trying to catch their breath.

"Swim for it?" Homer suggested.

"Fuck that," Predator said. "I'm exhausted. And they'll just follow us out."

"Plus there's nowhere to go," Henno added. "I'm with the big man. Let's finish it here."

Homer knew that he could, like any SEAL, swim any distance, however winded he was. But Henno was right. There was nowhere to go. And, even if there were, he'd much prefer to stay and die with his team. With his brothers.

They formed a skirmish line, bowing it at the flanks, some taking a knee, others laying out their few remaining magazines before them. Pred actually sat down. He grunted in satisfaction, the relief of taking the weight off. He swiveled his head toward the others. "And I don't want to hear any of that 'It's been an honor serving with you' bullshit, either."

He wouldn't hear it. They all knew it already. And nobody had to say anything.

"JFK Combat Control to Mortem One. Mortem One, how copy?"

Handon could hardly hear – the others had started shooting at the advancing horde, which was also moaning and shrieking. He pressed his finger to his earpiece and squinted in concentration.

* * *

Commander Drake sat in one of the swivel chairs in the combat control center, leaning back, radio headset on. It felt *good* to have taken back their bridge, the whole island in fact. And it had felt particularly nice to kill or capture what had to be most of the rest of the living Zealots. But he quickly realized he had little time for feeling self-satisfied. He had critically urgent things to do. He pressed the transmit button and hailed again – hoping against hope.

"JFK Combat Control to Mortem One. Mortem One, how copy?"

He released the transmit bar. Tapped his finger.

"*Mortem One Actual copies, five by five.*" Drake sat bolt upright.

"Holy shit! Outstanding. Mortem One, what is your status? Do you have the mission objective? Have you been extracted?"

"*That's affirmative on the objective. But negative on extraction. Grey Goose has splashed down. Repeat, Grey Goose is down. Total loss. Over.*"

Drake boggled. They got the vaccine? But the plane had crashed? How? He pressed the transmit button. "What is your intent, Mortem?" There was no answer for a second. Drake thought he could hear resignation in the silence. Not surrender, and not quite defeat. But definitely resignation – to approaching death. Drake began punching at a bank of touch screens, calling up a map, and sliding the display over across North America. "Mortem, how copy?"

"*We're here,*" Handon's distant voice answered. There was firing, explosions, and moaning behind it. "*But probably for only another minute or two. Over.*"

Drake pulled at the map and zoomed with two fingers, then zoomed out again.

"Handon, listen. You and your people need to get on a boat, and you need to get out onto Lake Michigan. How copy?"

"*Copy that. You know where we might find a boat?*"

Drake leaned forward, intense. "Handon, the whole leeward side of that island is one big marina. Can't you see it?"

More silence. But this one had a totally different flavor.

* * *

Handon stood up to his full height. The others blazed away around him. Ali had gone dry, and was out front with her wakizashi, spinning and slashing. Homer was down to his SIG 226. Park cowered behind them all, beyond terror, watching death surround and fall upon them. Handon went up on his toes. Sure enough. Just over the hill. Fucking masts.

"*Displace!*" he hollered. "Everyone on me! *Go, go, go!*"

Predator didn't look like he wanted to get up, so Handon joined Juice in hauling him up by his elbows. In seconds, the whole group was tumbling east, over the hill, and toward the edge of the island that faced back toward the city. In seconds they saw it: row after row of smart wooden slat piers stretched out over the water, branching into individual berths for small boats. Most were empty. But at least a dozen vessels were still tied up.

"*Which one?*" Ali yelled. "*Cabin cruiser?*" She held her black blade and sprinted ahead.

"*No!*" yelled Homer. "The engine will never start! No time to get it running…" That they had no time was obvious from Homer firing over his own shoulder at the nightmarish pursuers who clawed at their heels. "Sailboat!" Homer scanned ahead, assessed the vessels in an instant – then holstered his weapon, put his shoulder down and sprinted ahead in a primal burst of speed, toward his chosen ride. By the time the others were all out on the pier, he had cut (not cast off) one of the two lines, leapt aboard, and was now cutting away the sail cover from the main mast.

Ali leapt aboard to help him. Handon shoved the scientist aboard, then joined the others in pushing out a perimeter to defend the dock. Sprinting corpses streamed down it, reaching them in seconds. They were shot or decapitated, and went in the water to either side, or piled up in front. Handon pulled his .45 and started firing, while he pressed his radio earpiece to hear over the moaning and gunfire.

"*This is what you've got to do!*" Drake was yelling, too – he could hear how frantic it was on the other end. "*You need to chart a course and sail north to Beaver Island. It's nearly at the top end of Lake Michigan. How copy?*"

"Copy that!" Handon dropped his mag out, slapped another one in, and resumed firing quickly but evenly. The Foxtrots kept coming. They climbed over the growing pile of those destroyed. They would never stop coming. Handon thought, *On any other day, sailing the length of Lake Michigan might sound like a pain in the ass…* "What do we do then?"

"*There's a small airport on the island. There can't be too many dead there. By the time you reach it, I hope I'll have worked out some way to extract you. A helo full of fuel, mid-air refueling then ditch the refueler. Something.*"

"C'mon! Board!" This was Homer and Ali, hailing the defenders. While Handon watched, Ali slashed through the last mooring line. The boat began to drift out. Homer was running up the mainsail. The wind of the lake was still blowing hard. They'd have to tack. But there was wind.

"Roger that!" Handon said, walking backward, reloading, and continuing to fire. The others were behind him, climbing aboard. Handon holstered his empty .45 and drew his own short sword. "Top!" Predator bellowed. "Fucking c'mon!"

Handon could sense his radio battery beginning to

fade. They'd need that later.

"This is Mortem One Actual," he said, turning, running for the boat, then jumping five feet of open water onto the moving wooden deck. "Signing off for now…"

* * *

Commander Drake pushed away from the desk. He could hardly believe it, and whistled aloud. He heard steps, and Gunny Fick appeared in the doorway. The two Brits stood behind him. Fick saluted. "Commander. Captain Martin here requests permission to join the damage party ashore. Thinks just because he knows how to shut down a nuclear reactor, he can refloat a beached carrier."

Drake nodded. But instead of answering, he just stood and walked past the men out onto the forward-facing balcony. Craning his neck, he could see the security perimeter the Marines had set up – but not the men of the work parties underneath the overhang of the flight deck, who were assessing damage to the hull. Others, mainly officers, were trying to formulate a plan that might get the supercarrier off the sandbar, and back out to sea. Frankly, at this point, Drake wasn't at all sure it would be possible.

Then again, he thought, *I used to think it wasn't possible for the dead to walk the Earth.*

He also never thought this mission would succeed, or that any of the insertion team would survive it. For that matter, he'd never really believed the *Kennedy* would last this long into the ZA – never mind discover a whole nation of other survivors.

Hope had been beaten to within an inch of its life.

But it wasn't dead yet.

BOOK THREE

THREE PARTS DEAD

ADRIFT

Humanity on its raft.

The raft adrift on the sea – empty, Godless, endless, depopulated.

And surrounded by darkness.

Dr. Simon Park, bioscientist and amateur hack survivalist, stared emotionlessly across the deck of the Catalina 40-foot fiberglass sailboat that had recently become his entire world. He shared this drifting capsule of life, this single-species arc, with a half-dozen other human beings. These six others were not scientists. They were "operators," or so they called themselves.

To Park, they were soldiers – strange, violent, foreign. But at least recognizably human.

Together, these seven fragile vessels of flesh, packed onto this small boat, and adrift on a staggeringly wide inland sea, represented way too big a proportion of the world's last 50 million people still breathing air. Overshadowing even that was their relative importance, and that of the secret they carried with them. In that boat, and in the mind and on the laptop of Dr. Simon Park, resided what might be the first, last, best, and only hope those other 50 million were going to have to survive.

So it could almost be said that humanity was *literally* on this raft.

As for the other seven billion humans with whom

these seven had, only two years ago, shared this wet, whirling hunk of rock… well, those people were not technically *gone*. Much to the misfortune of the living, they were very insistently hanging around. They just weren't breathing air anymore. Instead, they were slouching and moaning.

And hunting the living – remorselessly.

It had occurred to Dr. Park that what had befallen them was a lot like any other really bad global pandemic. Except that in this one the already infected people *hunted you down*.

And he was afraid.

Dr. Park – thirtyish, boyish, lean, bespectacled, with a manner both careful and precise – knew terrible fear. He'd been afraid for a very long time, and the problem had gotten worse in the last few hours. Now, he let his eye wander over the other figures arrayed around him on the dark and nearly silent deck of the sailboat. These newcomers had, in the space of a few seconds, massively expanded the scope and scale of Dr. Park's social universe – which had long been, and had looked as if it would be forevermore, a universe of one.

These six, these operators, had now shucked their helmets, their face shields, their load-bearing tactical harnesses. But they all still went armed. And they could be distinguished from Dr. Park in a fraction of a glance. The posture. The musculature. The lean and powerful lines, and economy of motion. The coolness, and unflappability, which bordered on some kind of monk-like serenity, and which Park could not really fathom.

And, of course, their total lack of fear.

Fear was one thing Simon Park didn't lack. It had subsided somewhat from the galloping panic that had enveloped him, and threatened to subsume and extinguish him, as the seven had escaped at a dead run, with not even seconds to spare, from a city of three million very fast-moving dead guys, all of whom wanted to eat them. Chicago itself had seemed like it wanted to eat them.

It had nearly succeeded. It had taken a bite, in fact.

Alpha team, as Park had learned this unit was called, had originally been an eight-man team. But it had lost a full 25% of its strength in a few very bad minutes in downtown Chicago. That was after two long years of non-stop battling in what the military, it seemed, called the "Zulu Alpha." Two years and not a scratch on them. And then this debacle – two down, including their commanding officer – worse than decimation, in minutes.

Until that moment when these men, and one woman, had turned up, Dr. Park had every reason to believe that everyone else on Earth was dead. For those same two long years, ever since the fall of human civilization, Park had been holed up in a basement bunker, deep beneath the Chicago Mercantile Exchange. Two years, during which he had come to believe he was truly the Last Man on Earth. He'd continued doing vaccine, antiviral, and genomic research… but found it much harder to take seriously after he concluded there was nobody left anywhere to vaccinate.

But in his heart he was a man of science, so he had kept working with the research results and bioengineering and genetic models that he had first produced – during those frantic weeks between the first global outbreaks and the final fall. Back when every biomedical researcher in the world had been working round the clock to try and save humanity, as it teetered on the brink.

But Dr. Park had beaten them all. Maybe.

Humanity fell anyway.

Now Park monitored the black, featureless, rippleless surface of the lake. The great gusting winds of Lake Michigan, which had carried them on their privateered craft away from Chicago and to safety, or what seemed like it, had now abandoned them. Now they were adrift. They floated – if not aimless, then temporarily helpless.

They floated and waited. And got into their own heads.

Dr. Park saw the one they called Homer emerge from the hatch, from down below. He was the one who seemed to have most of the nautical skills and experience. Park gathered he had been a Navy SEAL, back in the world. This gentle-seeming and measured man wiped black grease on his black clothing in the black night, and spoke quietly from halfway out of the hatch.

"Could do with a second pair of hands."

Homer had been trying to get the boat's gasoline engine running, since the wind failed.

Handon, the one who was clearly in charge, in every manner a man might indicate such a thing, nodded toward Dr. Park. "Robert Neville here will give you a hand." They'd been calling him that, on and off. That, and "Hey, lame-o." He didn't get either joke. But he rose carefully on the lightly swaying deck, and readied himself to follow Homer down.

Before he could take a step, though, the woman, Ali, popped to her feet.

"I've got it," she said.

Handon nodded, but gave her a look out of the corner of his eye – as did one or two of the others. Park gathered there was something between Homer and the woman.

"This toy sailboat's not giving you trouble, is it?" she asked, as she stepped below.

As the pair receded, Park could hear the man's answer fading off into the muffling darkness of the cabin. "Well, the battery won't hold a charge because its plates have sulfated, there's water from condensation in the tank, the hoses and belts are all shot, most of the fluids are now solids, the cylinders are gunked up, and the spark plugs corroded. But, other than that, she's shipshape…"

* * *

Command Sergeant Major Handon, senior NCO of Alpha team, and its commander since the death of Captain Ainsley in the foyer of Dr. Park's apocalyptic residence, rose to his feet, all smoothness and power. He followed the other two down into the cabin, stopping just inside thc hatch. Then he inclined his thick neck and lit a cigar.

He'd gone belowdecks for this purpose, but cupped his hands around the flame anyway. *Good old noise and light discipline*, he thought to himself. Those were two tactical principles, at least, that had carried over from the old world, and the old wars.

In the Zulu Alpha, light and noise were definitely not your friends.

The flaring waterproof match made chiaroscuro, dramatic light and shadow, of Handon's heavily stubbled jaw, his brow-shadowed steely blue eyes, and his wavy black hair. He puffed once, contentedly, and let the sweet rich smoke exit his mouth at its own pace.

The grizzled sergeant smoking a cigar was a cliché. But at least it was *his* cliché.

The interior of the Catalina 40 sailing yacht was plush, without being spacious. There were fabric couches and hardwood fixtures, a forward sleeping compartment wedged into the V of the prow, head and shower behind that, a small salon and galley amidships, master sleeping compartment in the rear. Cockpit up top and aft – around which, and out on the surrounding deck, sprawled most of Handon's team as they passed the time.

Spec-ops guys, most military personnel actually, tended to be good at killing time as they got shuffled from one place to another. Or, as now, when they were stuck between one place and the next.

With most everyone on deck for the air, a little privacy could still be had down below. Handon could hear, and almost see, Homer and Ali doing wrench work, half swallowed up by the engine hatch. This sat amidships, beneath the galley sink cabinet. He let them get on with it. He knew Homer's griping about the state of the engine was only to make Ali laugh. Handon's people rarely complained.

And Homer never did.

If Homer were storing up any grief, Handon knew, he'd hash it out with his Maker on the Day of Judgment. Total faith in a Creator, and the righteousness of his Creation, conferred a lot of damned serenity. Or so it seemed to Sergeant Major Handon.

Nonetheless… two years into the Zulu Alpha, and everyone left alive, including the people on Handon's team, was feeling the strain. And none of those under his command were as young as they used to be. None were in their twenties. These guys all came from Tier-1 special operations units – the most capable, committed, and indispensable commandos ever known on the planet, pre- or certainly post-ZA.

And Tier-1 operators had always been older – for the simple reason that the skills, expertise, reactions, intuition, and especially experience required at that level were not picked up in a couple of years. There were few if any shortcuts to combat wisdom, and the people in Delta, in Seal Team Six, in SAS Increment, in the Air Force 24th Special Tactics Squadron, had been doing it, and surviving it, and endlessly training and honing their techniques to the point of perfection and beyond, for at least ten years. The most senior of them had been doing it for twenty.

But, in the world that had been, they'd at least been able to look forward to retirement, if they lived that long.

But now there was no retirement. The money they'd socked away existed only as inert bits of magnetism on hard drives that had spun down long ago, in banks staffed by the dead. The organization that owed most of them a retirement pension, the U.S. Department of Defense, no longer existed. The highline private security contractors that begged to hire former special operators for big bucks during the counter-terror wars no longer existed.

Hell, money barely existed.

And of course it now looked like there would never be any end to it.

Unless... unless, somehow, they could get this scientist, for whose rescue they had paid such a heavy price, to some kind of a viable extraction point. And thence back to the aircraft carrier, the USS *John F. Kennedy*, which sat off the Atlantic coast waiting for them. And, finally, back to Fortress Britain. And then *if*... he could produce a working vaccine, and *if*... they could manufacture enough doses for all 50 million survivors, and get it distributed.

And after all that, they would still have the small problem of a world teeming with seven billion ravening dead guys. And even if those mean, ugly, dead bastards couldn't any longer infect, they'd still be perfectly happy to rip you to bits and eat you. With regard to which immunity from the virus would be small enough consolation.

And then if they somehow put down all the soulless, or maybe just waited for them to fall apart and rot away, they still faced the crushing and monumental task of rebuilding all of human civilization. Starting from one little rainy island in the North Atlantic.

It was exhausting just to think about.

Handon snorted quietly, twirling his cigar in the dark. *But you know what?* he thought to himself. *It was at least something.* And it was a hell of a lot more than they'd had to look forward to yesterday, which was nothing.

Especially as a combat leader, Handon knew that hope was a funny old thing. It was a bit like a virus, actually. It could infect the most resistant of bodies. It could spread rapidly and widely, given only the chance of a little human contact. And, finally, however little of it you had, however tiny the traces that remained, it was still enough to nurture, to grow – and to infect the whole world. After that… who knew what might happen?

Hope. It had to be enough – to hang onto, to keep taking the risks.

Because something had to keep them going.

Somehow, life had to still be worth it.

Handon put out his cigar with thumb and forefinger, replaced it in his shirt pocket, and went back out into the clean night air. There he would try again to make radio contact with the carrier. This had been going in and out, but mainly out, since they'd gotten on the water, and as another weather front crawled heavily into the black sky above them from the east.

* * *

The great black body of the night pressed down upon them from above. But it was from below, and to every side, that the great lake, this immense inland sea, menaced the seven on their tiny craft. Nearly 60,000 square kilometers it stretched around them – and almost a thousand feet straight down at its deepest abysses.

More troubling was the thought of what lurked on its 1,600 miles of shoreline.

In the unpopulated stretches of forest that made up much of it, well, that was perhaps just trees. But in the populated sections… the great metropolises of Chicago and Milwaukee, the heavily industrialized southern tip, the small towns that dotted the shore, and the isolated but numerous waterfront properties and developments… well, wherever people had lived, now the dead ruled.

Every population center had become a death zone.

For this reason, they had steered a course near the center of the lake. That was when they'd had wind, and the ability to steer. Now they drifted.

Dr. Park continued to monitor the still surface, which sparkled faintly with starlight and a tiny sliver of moon. But it was not the water or the reflections he saw. In fact, he looked beyond the still surface, into memory, which now reflected back at him from those black depths.

While he had some time here, and since he couldn't seem to stop it anyway, he decided to try and review the last two years, to put them into some kind of sequence. And to try and make sense out of what had become a jarring, flashing, careening car crash of images in his head.

* * *

The bright flashes of the TV news spots scrolled past his mind's eye. Initially they had been broadcast from exotic locales – and he'd watched them with the detachment that always attended disasters in faraway places. Life went on, the channels flipped. But then, terrifyingly quickly, those places got less far away… faster than anyone could believe, faster than those in charge could react.

He remembered the vise of fear that gripped his chest when the seriousness of the virus started to hit home – its contagiousness, its virulence, its treacherously long incubation period… not to mention the fact that there was no cure, no vaccine, and a 100% mortality rate.

He felt the bone-deep fatigue as he'd found himself working 12-hour days, then 16, then more… Pausing only to register news of outbreaks in bigger and closer cities, the rioting and the breakdown of public services, always growing closer – while a cure seemed just as far away…

And then the surreal view out the glass walls of the lobby of NeuraDyne Neurosciences, during the first outbreaks in Chicago, where he was safe up above it all – for a while. The panic in the streets, martial law, the National Guard with their machine guns and armored vehicles… Through it all, Park had stayed on station, as had his colleagues – at first.

But then there was the profoundly creepy sensation of the company's employees slipping away, just disappearing, in ones and twos… He remembered the unnerving silence and emptiness of the labs – contrasted with the apocalyptic chaos down below. His colleagues had gone to be with their families, or to try to escape (to where?)... But Park's closest family had been in Korea, on the southern island of Chedju, where he imagined they would be safe.

He could hear the cracking of fear in their voices, for themselves, and especially on his behalf, in those last phone calls that went through... It was a universal, constricting fear – a sensation of impending doom, which can only feel so total and consuming when the threat is existential, everywhere, when the danger is to the whole world and everyone in it. When no one is going to come and save you.

Because no one can.

Then, at the very end, when personal survival finally fell heavier on the scales than his scientific labors on behalf of humanity, and he ran for it. That kinetic disorientation and blurring of his panicked, nightmare dash across six blocks of disintegrating Chicago, the sick and the healthy clashing in the streets, screams and sirens and gunfire, the streetlights going out as the power failed... Trying to get to the one place he thought he might have a chance – to the bunker that he, and perhaps he alone amongst the living, knew existed beneath the Mercantile Exchange.

And into which he alone made it alive.

Somehow the next two years blurred together into only a few frames... the dull beige walls, the canned food, monitoring of the radio and television until they went black for good... Then shepherding his power and resources, and doing desultory research, when he could find the energy and motivation. Mainly he remembered the silence, and the soul-scraping loneliness, and the tedium... Until, one day, this very morning, when there came the utterly unexpected sounds of gunfire, then shouts, then moaning, all leaking in through his two-foot steel and airtight back door...

And then the operators of Alpha crashing the party… The next two hours were somehow more vivid and traumatizing than the prior two years… The failure of the generator, the fire and smoke, the explosions, the desperate flight… And then that endless, nightmare, horrifyingly perilous sprint through the heaving surface streets of Chicago… When all he could hear was non-stop gunfire, and grenade blasts, and the howling and moaning of the inexhaustible ranks of the dead… The operators had fought like vengeful gods, down to their last bullets, down to their swords and knives, to get him to the airfield at the shore of the lake…

And then when the plane sent to recover them fell out of the sky and blossomed into a transfixing bloom of fire tumbling along the dry grass… And the seven of them finally stood utterly helpless and hopeless and fatally breathless and drained, with nowhere else to flee to, and the entire former population of Chicago bearing down on them… until…

* * *

Park startled, his reverie interrupted, when Homer emerged from the hatch again.

"Okay," he said, delivering his report mainly to Handon. "It's going to be eight hours at best, and that's if we're lucky. Ideally, I'd want to leave some oil in the cylinders overnight, before even trying to start this thing – and all we've got is gun oil. Either way, we risk it seizing up. And I've also got to get the condensation out of the gas tank, and there's no quick way to do that."

Handon nodded, expressionless. "How about improvising oars? Or paddles?"

Homer shook his head. "Realistically? Look at the freeboard on this thing – even with all of us aboard, it's 30 inches above the waterline. And this thing displaces twenty thousand pounds. Oars would have to be fifteen feet long to get any traction. And we can throw our backs out trying to lean down and paddle – but it's not going to get us anywhere." Homer smiled. "But it's not all gloom. The wind can't hide forever. She always comes back."

Handon didn't smile in response. In fact, his expression darkened. "That may be. But right now we're drifting into shore. The current's slight, but it's perceptible – at least to GPS." He glanced at his watch, then at the shore. "And those look like buildings. Maybe a marina."

Everyone onboard, even Dr. Park, knew the score.

If they drifted into a section of forest, no problem. Virtually everyone on this boat was an expert hunter, tracker, pathfinder, and wilderness survival expert. But if they drifted into an area of human settlement… well, wherever there had been humans, now there were the dead. And, at least so far, the dead in fallen North America didn't look to be loner types.

And now the tiny group of the living all felt the dark body of the sprawling shore grow closer.

Whether they could see it coming or not.

JARHEAD

Commander Drake looked across the small table and scratched his chin, regarding the man opposite him. Drake was XO, executive officer, of the USS *John F. Kennedy* – the biggest, most powerful, and most complex warship, or *machine of any sort*, that had ever been built by the hand of man.

Across from him sat Master Gunnery Sergeant Fick, acting commander of the platoon of Marines that had previously been attached to MARSOC – the Marine Corps Forces Special Operations Command. Now they worked for Drake as the designated ground combat and security detachment of the *JFK* – and for the entire surviving carrier strike group that it led.

"Let me go get them," Fick said intently, referring to the currently lost Alpha team. "I'll bring them all back, gentle as you please. Vaccine and all." With this, he tried on a smile. But this merely creased the dramatic scars down the right side of his face, which already looked like it belonged in a Paleolithic diorama, and basically gave him a horror mask visage that would frighten small children.

And probably big ones, Drake thought.

He already knew well that the thirty men under Fick's command were some of the baddest hombres fighting anywhere since the world ended, and probably before. And he knew that if any team could fight their way through half of fallen North America, it's was

Fick's.

But that was a huge *if.*

Drake checked his wristwatch, exhaled, and looked back up at the Marine. He thought of their small transport prop plane, which had inexplicably gone down while trying to extract Alpha from Chicago. And that was after surviving, and somehow taking off in the middle of, the ship-wide mutiny and outbreak that had spilled out across the carrier's flight deck – all as the ship was being run aground at speed. That plane had been the only aircraft they had with both the capacity to lift a whole squad, and the range and endurance to get to Chicago and back.

After taking a sip of coffee from its hurricane-proof mug, Drake spoke across the table again. "With the Greyhound splashed down, all we've got to move you in are the Sea Hawks. And, as you already know, those helos can make it there but not back. Which is no good to me. That just means we'll then have the lot of you humping overland, or up Lake Michigan, trying to fight your way home. And anyway, they've already got what they went for, and they're out of the Chicago death zone. It's transport they need, Gunny, not fire support."

Fick started to object again, but Drake cut him off.

"No, what we need is some kind of workable extraction plan to get them out of there. I've got the surviving air wing commanders reporting here in ten. And we're all just going to have to sit here and brainstorm until we come up with some options. We're going to have to get creative." With this his voice lowered a notch. "Though I'm very much afraid we're going to end up trying to sail something right up the goddamned Eerie Canal."

Fick stared at him evenly. "The locks won't work without power," he said. "Sir."

"Goddammit, Gunnery Sergeant, I need solutions. Not fascinating new problems."

"Yes, sir." Fick paused, and his dark eye developed a certain gleam. "Okay, then. With respect, and pardon me speaking frankly, but the air wing commanders are going to be about as helpful as a dick sandwich on this one. We already know what our existing air capabilities are. What we need is bigger aircraft."

Drake nodded once. "Go on."

"*Oceana Naval Air Station.*" He said it with careful emphasis. Drake gave him a sharp look. Fick went on anyway. "It's *right* there. Practically on the water. I could piss on it from here."

"I have no doubt you could," Drake said, not showing any amusement at Fick's creative distance-reckoning. "But you could also get your entire team infected or eaten there. It's not only onshore – it's *right* in the middle of Virginia Beach, and all its suburbs. It's practically a downtown airport."

"I readily admit the risk," Fick said. "But I say it's worth the stretch. You said it yourself – we don't recover Alpha, we don't recover the vaccine. And, with no vaccine, maybe that's humanity itself smoke-checked."

Drake knew Fick was using Marine slang for, basically, getting dead. He also knew Fick was probably right. *This is the bit*, he thought to himself, *where the dumb-looking jarhead surprises you for the hundredth time with how shrewd and cagey he actually is…*

Drake looked up and locked eyes with his ground commander. "Okay. Get it in motion. Put your team together, and put together a mission plan. A short one. Five-paragraph op order."

"Sir."

"I'll get a drone in the air, to recce the airfield. See how bad it looks. And we'll see if we can spot any aircraft still on the deck."

"Very good, sir." Fick rose to leave. Drake stopped him with a raised hand.

"This is not an ordinary scavenging op. And this will *not* be an ordinary shore party. You're going to war. Take anyone you need who is not absolutely critical to the repair effort, essential fleet ops, or shipboard security. I want you out there in sufficient strength to be survivable. And I want you to make sure and get the goddamned aircraft we need."

"Roger that, sir. We'll make it happen."

Drake slumped slightly in his chair. "And make it fast, too. Despite the radio silence, we assume Alpha is alive and en route to their extraction point. We assume that they're going to make it. And we're damned well going to be there to scoop them up."

Fick was thinking that was a lot of assumptions. But he just nodded.

Drake started to look down and check his phone. "Oh, and – good thinking, Gunny."

"*Semper Scrotus*," Fick said, saluting and exiting.

Drake, head down in his messages now, didn't need to be told what that meant.

Always on the ball.

EYES IN THE DARK

Elham, East Kent, England

Walter Jennings had lived in the lodge for four years now. He owned a house, or presumed he still owned a house, in the older part of Ashford, some ten miles away. But he hadn't been there since the day they had buried his wife, Melanie, in the old church grounds. He'd never liked living in the town anyway, but Melanie had, so he had put up with it for her. He hadn't even liked the house, but again, she had, and whatever Mel wanted, she got.

The lodge was tucked away in Acrise Wood, a mile or so from the town of Elham, and that was the way he liked it. It was ten miles to the nearest big towns – Folkestone south on the coast, and Canterbury to the north; and, beyond that, a million miles, or what happily felt like it, from the teeming and crime-ridden capital of London.

When they had bought the place from one of the local landowners, a few years before Mel passed away, they had intended it to be a getaway, someplace not too far away from Ashford, but far enough that they could relax and forget. It had been his thing, and he knew that Mel only let him buy the place because deep down she knew how much he tolerated just for her.

The day after they covered her coffin in dirt, he woke up, feeling more empty than he ever had in his life, packed some bags, closed the door of the house in Ashford, and never went back. He had made sure that he had everything he needed to remember her by – photographs, diaries, and all the keepsakes they had collected over the years – and he also took everything from his shed in the back garden.

That had been four years ago.

He had a small radio on the countertop in the tiny kitchen he'd built himself, by hand, and he had a television. Not that he had ever watched the TV. No, that had been Mel's thing. At least it had been until he found himself alone, in the lodge, with no one to talk to but the birds outside. The birds he liked, and he thought he would like the quietness of the lodge, but the being alone bit was the trouble.

A week after he moved into the lodge, he switched the television on and started to watch the news. It was strange. He had never been interested before, but now he needed something to focus on. There was his garden, which was now expanding after a week of heavy toil; in fact it had probably just exploded beyond the tiny patch of land he actually owned. But in the evening there was very little to do, so he took to watching the news and reading Mel's books.

These became his obsessions.

Over the next two years Walter would watch the news on every channel he could, learning more about the outside world than he had ever known, ever cared to know.

Then two years ago the terror had begun. He had watched it all unravel over such a small amount of time, on every news channel he could find. Moment by moment Walter watched as the world fell apart around him. He saw the dead folk that walked on his screen many times, and also the horror that often followed in those short, terrible clips. He watched it all, right up until two months into the terror, when the TV channels, one by one, started to become nothing but static fuzz.

Then nothing.

He hadn't gone into town immediately. No, he only wandered down to the tiny store in Elham once every couple of months to stock up on things that he couldn't grow in his garden or trap in the woods. He waited a few days before he did finally go. And when he got there he was surprised how quiet the town was. The shop was open, but the young girl who normally served him had been replaced by her elderly grandmother.

He'd asked about the girl, and the grandmother said that she had rushed off to London to be with her father in the troubled times. He asked if the old woman had heard anything about the news and the terror, but the old lady just shrugged.

"I don't pay a lot of attention to world doin's," she'd said.

Walter bought out everything of use he could find in the shop and left. When he got back to the lodge he went to the small storage box at the back of the structure, took out the three woodcutter's axes that were propped up against the side of the tiny space, and carried them inside. One he left at the front door, one at the back, and the other, a much smaller hand axe, he attached to his belt.

He had killed three of the creatures in the last two years. Two of them had been dressed in fisherman's overalls, and they had wandered in off the road a hundred yards away, maybe attracted to the small outside light on the front of the lodge. They had been so slow they might just as well have been comatose. And he supposed that in a way they were.

After they both lay dead on the gravel drive, he had sat on the wooden steps and cried.

The third he killed had been the old woman, the next week, when he went to stock up again.

It was then that he realized that the world around him had gone awry, and that it had done so right up to his front door. He suddenly knew that the only way he would survive was if he cut himself off completely. The lodge, his home, was distant enough to do that, especially now that Elham, the nearest village, was deserted. In the last four years his garden had grown to a considerable size. He'd also taken up hunting rabbits, with some success. This was something he could do, he decided.

That was, until he met the fourth creature.

He'd sensed it approaching through the woods, and was standing ready for it when it stumbled out of the treeline. It was dark, lightless apart from the small lamp outside the front of the house, and Walter could see the thing lumbering along, completely oblivious to him. In fact, as it traipsed through his vegetable patch and carried on heading toward the drive, and the road, he wondered if he wouldn't have to kill it. Maybe it wouldn't even notice him. He stepped backward, moving into the heavier shadow at the side of the house, deciding to let the creature pass by.

Then he felt a pain at the back of his head, and felt a trickle of blood run down onto the collar of his shirt. His head swam with dizziness for a moment, and he stepped back, spinning round to see what had struck him.

The crunching of gravel on the drive. Fast footsteps, heading away. Walter's eyes were blurred, but he could still make out the receding figure, running with a limp, he thought. He hurried back into the house, shutting the back door as quietly as he could, and stopped for a moment to lean against the porch wall, before heading quickly to the bathroom.

It was a cut, or a deep scratch, barely two inches long, and it was bleeding a lot. He couldn't make it out clearly in the small mirror, and it was difficult to line up Mel's tiny make-up mirror with the equally tiny toilet mirror, so that he could see the back of his head. It hurt a lot, he knew that much, and he felt tired, very tired.

Whatever it was that attacked him was gone now, as was the creature that had stumbled through his vegetables.

Walter took a bandage from one of the first aid kits stacked up in the kitchen, and stuck it to the back of his head, then went to lie down.

He'd get some sleep. The place was locked up and the creature, or creatures, had gone. He was fine. Sleep was what he needed. Maybe the headache would go away, and in the morning it would be warm again and he wouldn't feel so cold.

Walter Jennings slept like the dead.

* * *

The creature ran onwards into the night, driven by a base, mindless urge that never faded or grew weary. It had an evil energy that burned bright. It was not flesh that it sought, nor hunger that drove it. It was blood – and the need to infect. Its burning, dead eyes bored into the darkness, scanning for anything that lived and breathed. It had touched many since it had first crawled from the darkness of the Channel Tunnel.

And the lights of the larger town in the distance beckoned it.

ON THESE FELL SHOALS

Earlier, when Dr. Park had asked Juice, the big bearded one, who seemed to be the team's resident geek, why they couldn't just radio the carrier for help, he'd said:

"Well, Doc, radio communications are a bit of a black art. A good military HF radio can in theory reach anywhere in the world. However, getting it to work in practice requires graft, calculation, skill, luck, and patience. First off, the little stub antennas you see in the movies won't cut it. An antenna capable of bouncing signals off the ionosphere and reaching around the world generally needs to be a massive, oddly-shaped series of cables strung up across trees, buildings, or Clark masts. Now, we're lucky enough on this boat to have a kind of mast, plus a boom. But said antenna needs to be cut to the length appropriate to the frequency, pointed in a precise direction, given enough power, and finally blessed with suitable weather."

Now, hours later, and as they'd started to drift into shore, Dr. Park saw Juice clambering up around the cruciform mast, stringing copper wire he'd scavenged from the boat. Perhaps related to this, he also saw Homer cross himself.

Handon stepped to the boom and spliced the end of Juice's improvised antenna into their portable long-range radio. "Mortem One to *JFK* CIC, how copy?" He spoke in quiet but intent tones, then released his transmit bar, pausing two seconds. "Mortem One to any call signs receiving, acknowledge." Only silence came back, settling on them in the ominous darkness.

And the shore came closer.

* * *

Ali clocked the discomfiture of the scientist as she and a couple of the others casually swung by the resupply pallet to palm a few extra magazines and grenades. She guessed there was no way to soft-pedal this kind of thing, not on a boat this small.

But reassuring their joyriding civilian was not real high on her list of concerns right now.

She jammed a couple of 30-round STANAG magazines in her thigh pouches, grabbed an energy bar and a bottle of water and a few more paper packets of painkillers, and padded silently back toward the prow. She then lowered herself gracefully to the deck, fired down the painkillers, then peeled open the food bar's wrapper and started getting that down. One lesson of military life was that the best time to eat is generally now. And, particularly in spec-ops, you usually had to just fight through the pain. Her perforated bicep and wrenched vertebrae, from the combat jump gone horribly wrong, weren't going to be healing anytime soon. And she didn't have the luxury of bedrest.

She watched some of the others also top up from the pallet. After they had first sailed out of the city-side marina, tacking like Ithacan sailors possessed, with dozens of howling animated corpses leaping off the pier literally into their wake, the first thing they did was make a beeline for their resupply pallet. With its own cargo canopy, this had gotten shoved out of the plane at the beginning of their original insertion, with the eight human parachutists diving headfirst behind it.

Setting up a resupply cache, to allow them to rearm and refit with ammo, radio batteries, water, and all the other essentials that urban combat burns through at a dizzying rate, had struck everybody as a good idea. But putting it down in the lake had been the stroke of genius of Gunnery Sergeant Fick, who assisted with their mission planning and logistics.

Not only had they needed to avoid overflying the city and thus waking the dead; but Fick had discerned that there was no safe place to put it on the ground in Chicago anyway – every square foot was a no-go zone, and prone to being overrun at any second. But at least the surface of the lake was guaranteed to be dead-guy-free. So the pallet had been configured on a semi-rigid raft that auto-inflated just before splashdown, with an onboard radio transponder to locate it.

Picking up the floating cache on their way out of town had radically increased their odds of eventual survival. Ali had even been out of pistol rounds by the end of the Battle of Lake Shore Drive, as she'd come to think of it. Not that she minded using her sword. It soothed her in a strange way, the ritualistic motions of kendo, and it reminded her of her friend, Pope – with whom she used to train in their dojo back at Hereford, and whom they had left behind in Chicago.

It was he who had dug the team out from under the mountain of Zulus beneath which they had gotten buried – though he'd only done so by volunteering to be buried under them himself. The best Ali could hope for him now was that he had found his final rest.

Anyway, the entire team had effectively been black on ammo by the end of the street battle. Now they were at least dug out of that particular hole. But, unfortunately, it sat way deep down inside of several other kinds of perilous holes.

For instance, they were still a damned long way from help, never mind safety.

The motion of the boat was imperceptible. But the treeline loomed a little higher every time Ali looked up at it. From where she sat, she could make out the silhouette of Homer, up at the very prow of the boat. From his posture, she also knew just what he was doing. He was praying. Watching him quietly, and with affection, Ali remembered the line from that great atheist John Fowles: "We all drift on the same raft. There is only one question. What sort of shipwrecked man shall I be?"

She chamber-checked her rifle, double-checked the safety, then lay down and racked out.

Now was also always an excellent time to get some sleep.

* * *

Homer stopped reciting. He found prayer was a little like meditation – you had to have the discipline to drive the other thoughts out. And he wasn't succeeding tonight. One thought kept intruding, as it had more and more over the last weeks and months. It had become like some invader, or homunculus, in his brain. Some kind of virus. The thought abided, and grew, and he couldn't make it go away. And he didn't entirely want it to.

This thought was of his family.

Ever since the fall, and being stranded in the UK, he had gotten by the way he always had: by keeping his faith, and by doing his duty. But his faith had clashed with the near certainty that his wife and his children were dead, or worse – a crushing certainty that his faith could not overcome. And his duty to country, to unit, to humanity, had meant that he could not fulfil his duty as a father and a husband. He could not go to them. He could not find them.

And, whether or not he could still save them, or ever could have… still there could be no explanation, no excuse, no solace, for not having tried.

When he had been on the other side of the ocean, when he had been head-down in operations, and working for the survival of what remained of the species… well, it had felt like a long way from the New World, and further still from the old living world. An uncrossable distance.

But now, against all possible odds, they had crossed that distance, as well as an entire ocean – and here he was back in North America. The carrier itself was, even at that moment, moored off the Atlantic coast not 100 miles from his old home in Little Creek, Virginia – the last place he had seen his wife and children alive. When the team flew off the carrier's deck, into the maw of their impossible mission, Homer had sworn an oath:

If it pleases God to let me pass through this last storm… I swear that I will go and find them. One way or another, whatever the outcome… I will find them.

And now, also against inconceivable odds, he *had* survived that mission, at least what it had thrown at them so far. The near catastrophe of their busted air drop, the hour he fought alone out on the streets… Then their first rampage through the streets to get to the underground bunker… The fire and explosion, the second, even more desperate, running urban battle to the water… And then, finally, when all hope was gone, and they had resigned themselves to a last forlorn stand, dying side by side as brothers…

Well, then that marina had appeared over the hill like Zion, and the sailboat like the angels that rescued Lot, and verily were they vomited out of the belly of the whale. All of it against impossibly long odds.

But there was a word for a triumph over impossible odds: *a miracle.*

Homer wondered: would he be worthy of this one?

The weights of his irreconcilable duties were starting to shift.

* * *

Predator only grunted and growled softly in the dark as Juice worked on his leg.

His friend had finally convinced him that the time

had come for the lumber-and-duct-tape splint to come off. This was what Predator had improvised after the lethal winds over Chicago had wrapped him around a building-top antenna, bending his leg all the way back the wrong way. Luckily for him, the much bigger medical pack in the resupply pallet had a military-issue fiberglass moldable splint. It only required a little water, which was one thing they had plenty of, and it could be fitted perfectly around his knee.

Predator sat and caught his breath while it hardened. He also caught the scientist watching him from across the deck, which gently rolled and glittered with starlight. It felt like they were floating alone in a tiny pool at the center of an endless, empty void. Which was exactly the case. Predator addressed Park in his growly basso, which carried across the night air even at low volume.

"So, Doc – this business about you needing to find Patient Zero, to get your vaccine working. Is there even such a person? And how can we possibly find one dead guy among billions?"

Dr. Park nodded and touched the corner of his glasses, composing his reply. "I just need a sample of the virus from a very early-stage victim. Not necessarily the first one, but the earlier the better. As to where… well, I was head-down in an electron microscope at the time, so I didn't follow the epidemiology or disease etiology very closely. But we do have a good idea about the point of disease emergence: eastern Africa, in northern Somalia. It's always Africa, by the way."

Predator grunted again as Juice poked at the

firming cast. "Why is that?"

"I'm not entirely sure, to be honest. Not my field. But it probably has to do with the very poor public health standards, as well as the large and diverse animal populations. Almost all emerging human diseases are zoonotic – that is, originating in animal species, and then crossing over to humans. Usually via animal husbandry – livestock, slaughtering, breeding, food contamination with dung, that sort of thing."

Sitting in his dark corner of the cockpit, Henno snorted quietly. "Yeah, though people started doing a good little line in creating new diseases themselves." Henno had previously done WMD counter-proliferation work in the SAS. And that included hunting human-engineered bioweapons.

"So now we have to fight our way into darkest Africa," Juice mumbled, wrapping Pred's leg in heavy tan gauze. "Never thought I'd get out of that region alive the first time." In his previous unit, the shadowy Intelligence Support Activity, Juice had done several tours of the Horn of Africa, fighting and disrupting al-Qaeda affiliates in the region.

As Juice taped down the gauze and splint, Predator dug out a pouch of rough-cut chewing tobacco, and held it open for his nurse. Juice took a wodge and jammed it in his cheek. Predator followed suit and spat messily over the gunwale. He grunted again. "I don't know. Starting to wonder whether any of this is really worth the battle. Even if we cure the disease, the world's still shot to shit. Maybe we just keep going because we're hardwired to survive."

Juice frowned, sadness obvious on his face even in the dark. He hated to hear his friend talk like that. And it was true that all of this, the whole ZA, was a damned miserable waste. But it definitely wasn't pointless. Not as long as friendship remained. That was what it had always been about for him, anyway. Fighting for the man next to you. Dying for him, if need be. He didn't see that it mattered what got you – a Zulu, or a Tango (terrorist).

It was all about the love that made you willing to make the sacrifice.

At this point, Handon emerged from below. He looked down at Predator. "What you're hardwired to do is kick ass, Master Sergeant. Just focus on that, and you'll be fine. Anyway, who are you kidding? You'd have no idea what to do with yourself without the fight." He looked around at the others, and spoke gruffly. "Plus we've already done all the hard work on this one. We've got the package, and we're out of Undead City. The rest is just a pleasure cruise." None of that needed saying, not to guys on this team. But, as commander, it was Handon's duty to spread around some motivational pabulum now and again.

He wasn't sure he believed it himself, at least not at that moment.

But it was his job to say it – and sound like he meant it.

Dr. Park sat up straighter in the dark. He peered into the blackness, trying to make out what exactly was on the shoreline to their east, their evident direction of drift. Of course there wouldn't be any lights on in structures. He'd left electricity behind in his bunker, Alpha had left it in Britain, and humanity had left it in its past.

In any case, Park couldn't make anything out. It was all black on black.

But it was definitely getting closer.

The whole boat jolted beneath them, and a loud bump echoed through the hull.

"What the hell was that?" Predator rumbled.

Homer stood. "Relax," he said. "It's just submerged debris. There will be branches, rocks, maybe whole submerged trees, as we get closer in to shore." He paused to peer over the side, the whites of his eyes shining slightly in the starlight. "In fact, this one's doing us a favor. We've run aground, but it's stopped us drifting any closer in to shore. Now tell me we're not watched over…"

"Terrific," Predator grumbled. "First the *Kennedy* runs aground, now whatever this piece of shit is called."

And the boat had in fact stopped.

For a few seconds.

But then it lurched violently – and Homer, the only one standing, was hurled out of the cockpit. Sliding away, he clawed at a cleat and line to stop himself going over the side.

Bloodless fingers gripped anything within reach, all around the cockpit and deck. Saucer-wide eyes flashed from person to person. None of them had the vaguest idea what was happening, nor quite how to react.

The whole ten-ton boat rolled and bumped beneath them like a theme-park ride.

AGROUND

Commander Drake still hadn't made it out of the small officer's room off the flag bridge, where he had met with Gunny Fick. He'd started out reading messages on his phone – but then after that, the cursed thing wouldn't stop ringing. As ship's XO, and in the wake of a large number of simultaneous catastrophes, Drake had about ten thousand problems to deal with.

And he had to deal with them simultaneously. Or so it seemed.

"If they can't get them resealed in the next twenty minutes," he said into the phone, "pull everyone from that duty and reassign them. We've got a whole lot of other crap we need those ratings for, most of it a lot higher on the tasking list. If it's not a quick win, shit-can it. Good. Out."

Seemingly on cue, the door leading out to the flag bridge knocked, then opened. A man stuck his head in, looking friendly yet respectful.

Drake swiveled his head to clock him. "Captain Martin," he said. "*Entrez, s'il vous plaît.*"

The man hesitated – trying to figure out if the American was taking the piss. Martin was British, a captain in the Corps of Royal Engineers. He had also been the only one aboard and still alive who knew enough about nuclear reactors to be able to shut down the *JFK*'s – when they had needed to do so quickly, as the mutineers, known as the Zealots, tried to run the ship aground. Due to Martin's last-second heroism, the ship had avoided smashing into the coast any more catastrophically than it actually did.

So Martin had saved the ship from sinking – but not from wedging itself firmly up on the shallows off Virginia Beach. Since then, he'd spent most of his time out in the shoals with the damage parties, trying to work out their prospects for refloating the beached supercarrier.

"Sit," Drake said. "Report."

Right, Martin thought to himself, pulling out a chair and sliding into it. *Americans – no nonsense. And straight to the point.* "Well, sir, the bad news is that we're well aground – the keel is wedged like hell into a series of large sandbars."

"How wedged?" Drake asked, not looking any more thrilled than he sounded.

"Five meters deep. A bit more at some points."

"I presume you've got good news to go with that?"

"Yes," Martin said. "The hull's intact. Bent in a few places, subject to a bit of stress warping. But not actually breached anywhere. That we've been able to find."

"Thank God for that."

Martin nodded. "Yes, quite. Given a full-blown mutiny, an outbreak belowdecks, explosions and fires, and intentionally being run aground at speed..."

"Yeah," Drake said. "I get it. It's a miracle we're still here at all. But Big John is a tough old tub."

"Just so," Martin said. "But I'm afraid there's some

more bad news to follow the good."

"Just as long as it doesn't go on like that forever, Captain. One of those good-news/bad-news jokes. Back and forth."

Martin squinted in mild confusion, but then just carried on. "It's to do with refloating the ship. Getting us off the sandbar. Simply… we can't do it without power."

"What's the problem with power?"

"We don't have any."

Drake looked up at the overhead lights, which were burning bright enough.

"Ship's batteries are still charged, and holding strong at about eighty percent. So no problem there, not with mains power for the ship. Not for a while. But, as you'll know, our propulsion depends on the nuclear reactors. The steam they generate drives a turbine – which, in addition to recharging the batteries for electrical power, is then coupled through a gearbox directly to the propellers."

"Thank you, Captain, for that lesson in nuclear marine propulsion."

"Sorry," Martin said, looking ill-at-ease in that special way the English had. "Of course. But, the point is, you'll also remember the bit yesterday where I shut down the reactors."

"Yes, that does sound familiar," Drake said. "So start them up again."

"That's precisely the problem," Martin said. "I knew enough about their operation to shut them down.

But that's much the easiest part – they're designed to be simple to shut down, as a safety measure. But starting and running them safely is a whole different ball of twine."

Drake mouthed the word *Shit*, without saying it aloud. He looked up. "And we lost most of the ship's nuclear engineering section in the insurrection, and the outbreak."

"Afraid so," Martin said. "The crew on duty in the reactor compartments at the time were almost all killed by the mutineers – who were then almost all killed by the dead. And their commander died beside his men." Martin knew this, in part, because he'd had to fight his way down there, with Fick and Wesley, to retake those compartments and shut down the reactors.

Drake continued for him. "Died defending his post, alongside his men. Which seemed pretty courageous at the time. Looks a little less smart now. Also, that starboard-side explosion took out much of the engineers' quarters and some of the workshops. *Fuck*." This he said aloud.

The XO had already known all these facts. He just hadn't been attending to them, and hadn't put them all together. He currently had so many damned problems to deal with, most of them critically urgent, that he'd forgotten the implications of losing almost all of his remaining senior engineers. *One damned thing after another...*

He muttered, "Great, so we're basically an airport now. Stuck out on the edge of Virginia." But then he looked back up at Martin – and suddenly saw his great white hope.

"Wait. What's it going to take for you to get the reactors spun up again?"

Martin exhaled heavily. "About a month in my cabin with the operations manuals, I think."

"You've got the documentation?"

"Downloaded it all an hour ago."

"So get on it. You're also authorized to shanghai any surviving engineering ratings who might be able to help you. Meanwhile, I'll see if there are any qualified people left alive in Britain, and if so get them in the air. And we'll see who wins the race, you or them – and just as long as it's not the dead. Oh, and, for the moment at least, I think you also just became my Chief Engineer. With all that entails."

Martin looked concerned. "What tasks do you want me to prioritize?"

Commander Drake gave him a hard look. "Everything. Do everything. Just like everyone else around here. You're dismissed."

Martin got up wordlessly, saluted, and walked to the hatch. Before he could open it, though, it opened from the other side. After moving aside to let Martin exit, an ensign stuck his head in.

"Commander, the CIC Watch Officer needs you. Downstairs, sir."

"Want to give me an advance preview, Ensign?"

"They think they've picked up a storm system, sir."

"Severe enough that *I* need to worry about it?"

The ensign looked slightly flustered. "They think it

may be a… a storm of the dead. Um, sir.”

AN EMPTY LAND

Andrew Wesley, former corporal with the UK Security Services, stood now at the passenger side of an oversized American 4x4, the door wide open, and looked down the street. His side arm was in his hand, loaded and ready to go if necessary, but the safety was still on, and it didn't look as though he was going to need to change that in the next few minutes. It still boggled his mind: here he was, actually on the ground in America – on the coast of Virginia and at the periphery of what used to be U.S. Naval Air Station Oceana.

A sharp wind blew through the buildings, cutting along the wide boulevard and ruffling Wesley's two-week beard. It was a strange feeling, and one that he knew would take time to get used to. Rain-worn sheets of two-year-old newspaper drifted by, followed closely by shreds of cloth that had once belonged to… he shrugged off the thought, deciding it was best not to dwell on their origin.

"Where the hell are they all?" he asked, more to himself than anyone else.

Anderson, Wesley's driver, a young seaman with freakishly unkempt hair and two missing front teeth – both lost during a scuffle on the lower decks during the Zealot uprising, to the butt of an ammunition-depleted M4 in the hands of a mutineer who had completely lost the plot – squinted through the dust that caked the windscreen, and he shrugged.

"Not a clue, sir," he said, keeping his hands comfortably on the steering wheel – and all of him safely in the vehicle.

They'd pulled over, at Wesley's insistence, at the crossing of the Dam Neck Road and General Booth Boulevard, and into the parking lot of a 7-Eleven. Two other SUVs, also appropriated from the endless car parks that surrounded the air station, itself surrounded by Virginia Beach, were pulled over behind them. From inside of each of these, the faces of the shore patrolmen who Commander Drake had sent out with Wesley scanned the area. Only Derwin, Wesley's new second-in-command, had gotten out of his vehicle.

The stout man walked over, but didn't say anything.

"Not a single sighting for the whole of today," said Wesley as he saw the sailor standing beside him.

"Yes, sir."

Sir. A new form of address that didn't sit comfortably with Wesley, and another decision forced upon him. It seemed to him they had a lot of sailors and soldiers left on the *JFK* and the *Michael Murphy*, the destroyer that had sailed with them, but he had still been promoted. He'd actually overheard the complete deliberation on the matter, while holding up a wall outside Drake's office:

"This guy's got zombie-fighting experience. He was at Folkestone."

"Fine. Send him."

"He's only a corporal, though."

"Well, promote his ass. Give him a field commission. But get his ass out there. We need live bodies."

And thus had Andrew Wesley been given a rank, Second Lieutenant, that he considered well above his station. Captain Martin, his friend from the Royal Engineers, and with whom he had survived that nightmare in Folkestone, was different. Martin was a professional soldier, and already an officer. Rising in the ranks, considering the situation and the value the man obviously had, made perfect sense. But Wesley? One night fighting on the streets of a small coastal town did not a commanding officer make.

Wesley looked back to Derwin, the team's Master-at-Arms. Wesley knew the man's real commander had been killed trying to put down the mutiny on the carrier. It had subsequently been explained to Wesley that this shore patrol team, or Naval Security Force (NSF), was tasked with LE (Law Enforcement) and ATFP (Anti-Terrorism Force Protection) duties. That was too many acronyms by half, Wesley felt. Of course, now that all the terrorists were dead, these men were mainly tasked with zombie fighting. And now all of them were looking to Wesley – British, out of his element, vaguely ill-at-ease – for leadership.

He tried to square up to his duty.

"It doesn't make any sense," Wesley said crisply. "We've seen… what? Three of the damned things since we set foot on the ground here, all of them trapped in some way. Just three."

Derwin frowned. "To be honest, sir…"

"The name's Wes, mate."

"Okay… Wes. To be honest, we haven't been in any of the buildings yet. There may be many more of them around here."

Wesley turned to regard the young seaman, wondering how he felt about being under the command of a security guard. He tried to shrug that off.

"That's not how they work though, is it? They move on, drift around, and others wander in. It just doesn't make sense that the only ones left around here would be stuck inside buildings or trapped under a car."

Wesley looked over at the 7-Eleven.

"We're going in there."

Derwin turned toward the building, his military training already kicking in. Entry points, exit points, lanes of fire, cover and concealment, potential hazards.

"Do you mind me asking why this particular building, sir… I mean Wes?"

Wesley pointed across the road.

"Lots of space around it. There's no other buildings within spitting distance, so we don't have to leave more than one person out here to cover us and the vehicles. I don't think we'll find anything of use in there, apart from long-rotten food, but I want to know if there are Zulus inside."

Wesley smiled. He'd begun to pick up their military yabber. And, just conceivably, maybe he even had a bit of a knack for this whole tactical lark…

"I want to prove you wrong," he said, grinning at Derwin.

Derwin frowned back. "How so?"

"I don't think there are many in the buildings. I think they have all gone. Look, It's just a gut feeling, but I just don't feel the same oppressive presence that there was back in Folkestone. There are supposed to be 350 million dead people wandering around the USA, and this is a pretty built-up area. It should be teeming with them, but it just doesn't feel like the land of the dead."

Derwin nodded his understanding.

"It feels like the land of the lost."

Anderson seemed to have no problem with serving as their watchman, as Wesley had expected. One trait that he had noticed about Anderson was that he had no shortage of reluctance when it came to anything that might put him at risk. Maybe he'd had his fill of risk in the mutiny. So far, Wesley had only met example after example of military people who were willing to put themselves out, and into harm's way, for their fellows. He guessed there was bound to be an exception to this rule, and Anderson was it.

Derwin and the other three sailors, men who Wesley had only met that morning as they loaded up the Sea Hawk helicopters that had ferried them to shore, now fanned out around the entrance to the shop. They held their M4 assault rifles to their shoulders but pointing toward the ground, eyes everywhere at once, and waited for Wesley to lead them in.

He tentatively pushed open the left entranceway door, his handgun raised – safety off now – and peered into the darkness inside. Normally these places were easy to see into; huge plate-glass windows allowed light in to showcase the cheap goods. But this building had been sitting here for a long time, unattended and uncleaned. Where all the dust came from, Wesley could only guess, but it had completely covered the inside of the windows, blocking the light and leaving the interior submerged in near darkness.

The door protested loudly as it opened, surely alerting anyone or anything inside that they had visitors. But as Wesley stood there for the better part of a minute before stepping into the dimness of the store, he heard not a sound.

Nothing came rushing out of the darkness to attack him.

Then Derwin, Scott, Melvin, and Browning were inside, moving swiftly through the aisles, gun-mounted LED beams lighting up the dark places as they covered one another methodically, stepping quickly and flooding through the building. For just one moment Derwin stopped dead, raising his hand. The other three froze as well. But then a second later he lowered it, nodded, and they moved on.

Wesley followed the squad, impressed with their timing and coordination. He kept a few paces' distance, giving them the space they needed to work the place. These guys knew far better what they were doing, and he wasn't going to get in their way.

Perhaps one day there would be someone on hand to tell him that this was actually one of the very best traits of a commanding officer.

As Wesley stepped in behind his men, he saw that they had found bodies. Three of them – but these corpses weren't getting up and wandering around anytime soon. They were barely recognizable as human. They were victims of the dead, rather than Zulus themselves. If the three dead people – for Wesley couldn't discern their gender, age, or anything else about them – had ever turned or come back, there was so little left of them that all they could do was thrash around for a while.

But Wesley doubted they had ever come back.

"This place is chock-a-block with scoff," said Melvin from the next aisle over. Wesley's ear tripped on the man's strong Scottish accent – and up until this moment, when he first heard him speak, hadn't even known he wasn't American. Melvin had been one of the replenishment troops sent to join the *JFK* when it had stopped at the UK to pick up Alpha team. He was a sailor sure enough, but not a US swabbie. He was Royal Navy.

Now that the initial nervous tension had dissipated, Wesley took a moment to look around. His eyes were adjusting to the low light now, and he saw exactly what Melvin was talking about.

Row upon row of goods were stacked upon the shelves. At some time in the last two years the perishable goods had baked, rotted and slowly turned to mush, which dried in the moistureless air inside the store. Now all that was left were the dry goods and tinned food. But there was a lot of it.

"You were right," said Derwin, scratching the stubble on his chin, as he and Wesley stepped back outside. "Empty. Completely empty."

"Yes," replied Wesley, nodding and taking a deep

breath of the open air. Even though the fresh produce had long ago passed through its foulest stage of rotting, the mustiness and dankness still assaulted him and he was glad to be outside again.

He looked at Derwin. "That's only one building, though. I could be wrong. Hell, that huge place over there," he pointed at the monstrous hangar north of them, "could have a heap of them hiding in it."

"True," agreed Derwin, "But somehow I still think you're right. I don't know where all of the Zulus have gone to, but they've gone. Shit, I'd hate to be the poor asshole that bumps into them if they are all in the same place somewhere else."

"Tell me about it," said Wesley, and he was about to say something else when Anderson cut in, calling loudly.

"Wes. I've got Gillan on the radio. He says it's important."

Wesley's heart skipped a beat in his chest, and he could see from Derwin's expression that the man was thinking the same. Had the team up at the airfield proper discovered where all the Zulus were? Was Gillan the poor asshole?

Wesley ran to the vehicle and grabbed the handset.

"Wes here. Gillan, what's up? Is everything okay?"

Radio silence for a second.

"Copy, Wes. Everything's fine. Too fine, in fact. Not a whiff of the enemy up here. But you need to head back ASAP – Fick's orders. Anyway, you'll wanna see what we found up here. Fick is already on his way."

Wesley frowned, and looked over at Derwin, who still looked concerned. The other sailors were already bundling back into their vehicles, obviously expecting to rush off to support their fellows. *Bless them for their willingness*, thought Wesley.

"They're all fine up there," Wesley said to his men. "Panic over. Gillan, what did you find?"

"Um... everything," Gillan said into his handset, from a couple of miles away, inside the warehouse. *"Just get your sector done ASAP and get back up here. See for yourself."*

"On our way. Out." Wesley turned to Derwin. "Okay, just one more building, picked at random, and then we haul back to the center of the base. Fifty quid says it's just as empty this place."

From Derwin's expression, Wesley gathered he wasn't totally clear on what a quid was.

* * *

Gillan handed the radio handset back to the young woman standing next to him – Hersey was her name, the group's RTO (radio telephone operator) and another newcomer from Portsmouth. He then took a deep breath and scanned the whole panorama of the warehouse, which they had only just opened the doors to a few minutes earlier. The second squad of Marines under Fick's command were still moving through the vast building, securing aisles of tall metal racking as they went.

Fick had brought his entire platoon out to the base

and they had been given a single, incredibly important task. Go ashore and secure Naval Air Station (NAS) Oceana, and the adjacent Dam Neck Naval Air Station – and find something, anything, that could fly to the north end of Lake Michigan and back, and that would hold eight men. In short, a way to extract Alpha team, along with their invaluable cargo.

Teetering as they usually were on the brink of subsistence and survival, they also had standing orders to keep an eye out for anything else they might eat or otherwise make use of. But the aircraft was the important thing, and the *anything else* was relatively minor.

The shore party had expected to find ranks of fighter planes on the runways and in the hangars of the airbase – and with luck at least one long-haul transport aircraft. But so far they had found the place completely barren of flying metal. At one point there would have been enough air power sitting here to refit an entire wing if necessary, probably two.

But now it was looking increasingly hopeless, and unlikely that they would succeed in their mission. Best guess was that everything that could fly had been flown out of here right before the fall. Where to was a whole other vexing question…

But Fick's Marines had found something else in the shut-up hangars they'd hoped would contain flyable aircraft.

Not planes, but guns. Thousands and thousands of square feet packed and racked with weapons and ammunition.

THE STASH

Fick and Wesley stood in the entrance to the warehouse, each looking as dumbfounded as the other.

"Shit, this is some serious hardware," said Fick, walking over to the nearest pallet, which at a glance appeared to be packed up with unblemished assault rifles, still in sawdust. Fick lifted one of the boxes and turned it over.

"Rifles?" asked Wesley.

"Not just. XM29 Prototype. Dual 20mm smart grenade-launcher, with underslung 5.56 assault carbine. Plus a computer-assisted sighting system with integrated laser rangefinder, thermal vision, and night-vision capabilities. Basically, a whole armload of complete whoop-ass. Still in development when everything went to shit. Must be twenty crates on this pallet. And how many more in this place?"

"Enough to equip an entire regiment, I'd say," said a voice from behind them. It was Coles, the *JFK*'s Store Master. He'd arrived with a handful of his crewmen while Wesley had been busy clearing buildings on the periphery.

Wesley turned to Coles.

"You can tell that just by looking at it?"

"Of course; that's what I'm trained to do."

Fick glanced at the pair of them, and then back down the first aisle, where he could see one of his four-man fire teams finishing a security sweep.

Coles said, "I also noticed a pair of helos out on the tarmac further up the field. Sea Knights. Medium-lift."

"Will they fly?" asked Fick.

"No idea. I'm no wrench monkey, but they aren't packed down, so that suggests they were ready to go a couple of years ago. Then again, if they were ready to go, why haven't they went?"

Wesley took a deep breath. "Sea Knights. Can they fly long-distance?"

"No," said Gillan. "But they'd make good donkeys to move all this stuff back to the *JFK*. If they'll fly."

"Or a way to bring people back and forth," suggested Wesley.

"Wesley. Be useful now. What did you find?" Fick asked.

Wesley nodded. "Nothing but empty buildings. This place seems like a ghost town, though there's a lot left to check."

"No shit. I want your team assisting my Marines in the hangar searches now. This time you're starting five hundred meters from the center here and working your way out. We've come up totally empty on our primary search targets. Unless there's something hidden away in one of the outlying hangars, we are basically eating a huge horse-cock sandwich here, as regards finding our goddamned plane."

Wesley nodded. "Roger that. One question. If we come up empty, should we move out and look at the other airfields, maybe even a nearby airport?"

Fick nodded. "You mean a civilian jet, something like that?"

"Yes," replied Wesley. "Back in the UK we had countless smaller airfields with civilian aircraft and helicopters. Do we have to be picky? It's all very well looking for a military plane, but anything that can land and pick them up on… what's the place called?"

"Beaver Island."

"Yes, Beaver Island. Well, if all we can find is some dinky private jet, but it can make the distance, then we're go aren't we?"

"True enough. Maybe you're not as useless as you sound."

"Something else," said Wesley. "If we make contact with Alpha and they are on Beaver Island, maybe they can check the airstrip there to see if there's any fuel. That way we can go for a plane that can just make the distance there. Should expand our options a lot."

Fick squinted at Wesley. "Huh. A shiny good-conduct medal for the Brit. Good thinking. Okay, everybody listen up. We expected a battle when we got here, so we didn't plan on staying, but now we know the area is clear, we're gonna put a temporary base down here. Secure the area, and get this set up as a jumping-off point to expand our search. Let's get those helos checked to see if they'll fly… Coles, get your people to start shipping this stuff back to flat-top… weapons, munitions, fuel, everything. We've still got a job to do, but I for one am not leaving all this beautiful shit here."

"Roger that," Coles said, turning away.

As Wesley also turned to leave, he heard Fick mutter, "Though if our aircraft search keeps coming up empty and we're stuck here long enough, eventually we're gonna need the guns and ammo ourselves…"

SCUTTLED

On the deck of the suddenly rocking sailboat, near the prow on the port side, was where Ali had racked out – how long ago, she couldn't immediately say. Now she came to quickly but smoothly, and in perfect silence. It was how she always woke, whether due to the alarm clock, a firefight, or breakfast in bed.

She also paused before reacting, instead simply taking stock and tuning in to the darkness. She didn't even sit up. Not yet knowing what needed doing, there was no point in moving in what might turn out to be the exact wrong direction. Also, with the boat bucking underneath her like at a funfair, it seemed to her being flat on the deck had some tactical advantages.

She listened, swiveled her neck to look around, and drew a steadying breath.

And a hand flopped wetly over the gunwale in the near dark – ten inches from her face.

Now Ali stood up – like an electric cat on a glowing stove.

The hand had only been in front of her for a fraction of a second. But the image of it lingered – massively swollen, mottled with gangrene, a rainbow of nightmare colors, covered with floppy sores... and smelling of bottom-feeding fish left to rot for a hundred years in some underwater hell.

Her wakizashi, or samurai short sword, appeared in

a bright flash as starlight reflected in its sleek blade, and whatever the hand was trying to pull up over the gunwale fell back into the water. Ali kicked the hand after it. It splashed dully.

"Multiple contacts, submerged!" Homer reported crisply.

Yeah, I could have told you that, Ali thought to herself, looking peeved as she pivoted around her sword in the dark.

In her peripheral, she also clocked motion as somebody shoved the scientist through the cabin hatch; he crashed down inside with a yelp. The others now fanned out to the black edges of the boat, their backs all to the center. No one fired. And no one else spoke. Silence reigned again. Silence and darkness.

The boat merely continued to rumble and bounce, because of something underneath, in the perfect midnight of the lake's invisible depths.

Ali thought balefully of the many feet of gunwale that surrounded them in the dark – and of how very many hands might at that moment be coming over it in other places.

She edged out toward the water again, covering her sector, which was afore on the port side. Leaning out and craning her neck, she peered down into the much blacker blackness of the lake. The water rippled and rolled, reflected stars riding the little swells. Something was definitely moving down there. She smoothly drew her Surefire tactical light from her belt with her left hand. This was the side on which she'd taken a wooden spike through her bicep, after parachuting through a windstorm onto the Chicago elevated train platform. But the damaged arm managed the flashlight well enough.

Pausing one beat, swallowing dryly, she steeled herself and clicked it on with her thumb.

As one, a hundred rotten heads all swiveled to look up at her, their rheumy, gelatinous, or rotted-out eyes locking in on the beam of light. They all stood perhaps a foot below the surface of the water, some a bit more or less, based on height or missing feet. And now, as one, they began to wade, paddle, scrabble, grope – and climb one upon the other trying to reach the surface and the edge of the boat deck.

Within seconds, a watery hill of dead was self-organizing in front of her.

She clicked her light off, and scrabbled for her NVGs.

She knew the others around her would be doing the same.

* * *

Henno got his on with no drama. As the world turned bright green around him, and all the detail resolved from gloom, he saw only two hands, in just two spots, grabbing at the edge of the boat. *Thank fuck for that*, he thought, mentally exhaling.

But with that, and no other preamble, Sleestak-like melting appendages flopped over the gunwale in a dozen other places, interspersed with one or two waterlogged chins and faces and missing noses. Henno took a step back, and held his fire, as he heard the first couple of suppressed shots chuffing out around him. For his part, he simply stepped over to the edge and kicked all the Zulu hands and heads back in the water.

Job jobbed, he thought, contentedly. For now, anyway.

One eye still on the water, he looked over his shoulder and spotted Handon.

"Oi, boss," he said. Handon seated his own NVGs, then pointed them back at Henno, expectant. "Hate to point this out, but we've got no options here. We're gonna have to swim for it – and the sooner the better."

"Negative," Handon said. "Too dangerous for the civilian, too far from shore. And this might be an isolated concentration, from a sunk boat or something." He raised his voice slightly. "Fire discipline!"

"Bollocks," Henno muttered, as he shook his head and roughly drew his cricket bat from his ruck, which lay near his feet. He rarely got to use this; but he never went anywhere without it. As he stepped to the wicket and started batting heads, he thought, *Soon enough, we're gonna have a Zulu singularity right in our laps – and nowhere to retreat, advance, or escape to…*

Gritting his teeth, he teed off on a few more rotten faces. They gurgled as they broke the surface, expelling fetid lake water and bits of mouths and tongues as they tried to moan in frenzy. As Henno swung, their heads collapsed and exploded like long-rotten melons. The trick was to make sure they sprayed seaward – it was too much infectious organic matter to have splashing around the deck. Henno paused swinging to take stock around him.

Fire discipline was still being maintained. *But*, he thought, *sooner or later the shooting is like to start – and it'll avail us nought, because the minging dead will just keep on coming.*

And not long after that, he knew, they'd be out of ammo and overrun.

* * *

On the opposite side of the cockpit, Juice looked down to Predator and said, "Well, at least the *Kennedy* didn't run aground on the dead."

Predator snorted and then rocked himself upright on his drumstick. Juice offered him a hand up, but he ignored it. The whole point of the new cast was that he could get around on his own now, albeit still in great pain. Once upright, he hauled up his tactical vest, shrugged into it, put on his helmet, shouldered his backpack, drew his sword, and stood back to back with Juice. Juice clocked all the gear and gave him a look.

"Gotta be ready to move, man," Pred grunted.

"Move? Where to?" Juice said, making a wide gesture with his arm. They were adrift on a small boat and completely surrounded by a lake full of the dead.

Predator spat over the side. "One problem at a time, man. One problem at a time…"

* * *

Ali and Homer worked in tandem at the front of the

boat, keeping its edges clear of hissing would-be boarders. They also had their vests back on, and their rifles slung, also ready to move to nowhere. They had their NVGs but not helmets on. Ali still had her sword out, and Homer wielded his unique, and now uniquely suitable, melee weapon – a boarding axe. He jabbed its top-mounted spike through rotten skull after skull.

The destroyed ones fell back, but also contributed to the mound the others could try to climb. The moaning and hissing on all sides of them had reached a frenzy such that civilians or lesser fighters might have fallen to their knees and covered up their ears. From all the movement underneath, and the grabbing hands, the prow was now swinging out toward the middle of the lake and away from shore. But the deck was still clear.

"This could be going worse," Ali said over her shoulder.

Homer paused and gave her a quick grin in response.

A flying body, trailing moonlit water, streaked through the air between them, screaming.

Homer dropped to a crouch to get under it, and Ali pivoted, bringing her sword around, as Homer's smile melted away. A shout of warning formed in her throat: *Foxtrots!...*

But before she could vocalize, and before either of them could react, two more rocketed out of the water and landed between them, both fixed on Homer. He brought his axe up, but he didn't have leverage. It lodged in the groin of one of them; he gave it a tug, but it stayed stuck – and all three of the dead were collapsing on him now. Mentally, he flashed back to how their friend Pope had died – infected in a tussle, rolling around with two Foxtrots.

As Ali swung desperately and decapitated one of the three, but otherwise looked on helpless, Homer clenched his leg muscles, pivoted away, and dove – low, horizontal, long, and strong – straight off the boat and into the teeming lake.

It was the only direction he had to go.

* * *

Handon, trying to monitor all sides of the battle, had just been thinking it was going okay himself. "Look," he said sidelong to Henno. "They're maxing out. The pile's not getting any bi—" but then went wide-eyed as he suddenly realized the front of the boat was being overrun by flying corpses. He stuck his sword in the deck and brought his assault rifle up from its sling. He had to shoot around Ali, but in two seconds he had the mess cleared up.

Just beside and behind him, Henno muttered, "Fuck the cricket," dropped his bat, and pulled an HE grenade from his rig. "Frag up!" he shouted, pulling the pin, and cocking his arm toward the edge of the boat. *THIS'll wake these dead bastards up in the morning…*

But something launched out of the water right at his face, crashing into his body and knocking him onto his back. The grenade floated up into the air like a mis-juggled egg – and only Predator saw its arc. He took the long step needed to get under it, snatched it out of the air, cocked his arm to baseball-throw it toward the horizon – at which point the tussling Zulu and Yorkshireman rolled into his bad leg, which collapsed, folding under him. Predator went down like the ton of bricks he was, and the live grenade skittered across the deck, zipping straight through the open hatch, and down into the cabin below.

My bad, Predator thought, laid out flat, electric pain firing up his leg.

Handon pivoted where he was, dropped to a squat, and put four point-blank 5.56 rounds lengthwise through the head of the one wrestling on top of Henno. Opening a Zulu brainpan over his team member's face wasn't good news, but Handon had a hundred other problems. Luckily, one of them auto-resolved when the little scientist hauled ass out of the cabin like the Road Runner ahead of exploding dynamite, legs almost windmilling on the deck. Handon tackled him and kicked the cabin door shut with one boot as the explosion inside rocked the boat.

One door closes, Handon thought, prone and draped over Park. *And another opens…*

* * *

But at the same time, he realized he was also staring straight into the dead eyes of several attackers coming over the stern, not ten feet away.

"Good to go," Henno said, rising to a crouch, when Handon gave him a look. There was a lot of liquid on the Brit, but it seemed like lake water to him.

Anyway, he knew it didn't matter what he said – Handon would be watching him like a hawk for a day at least, for any sign of the turning. Henno shrugged it off and forgot it. Either he'd be fine, or he wouldn't.

And, either way, he'd just have to get on with it.

Shooting, swinging, splatting, and minor acrobatics were going on in almost all quarters of the small and shrinking surface of the deck around them. The sound of rapid firing approached as Ali backed across the deck toward the cockpit, her Mk 12 Special Purpose Rifle to her shoulder, barking incessantly, spitting a hail of close-in precision lead toward the prow. She was retreating to tighten up their formation. She was also abandoning Homer, alone down in the lake, as she couldn't forget for a second. But still she figured, or tried to tell herself, she knew what she was doing.

And, mainly, that *he* knew what he was doing…

In her last sight of him, he'd been doing a smooth and strong combat sidestroke, straight out into the middle of the lake and toward deep water – too deep for anything to grab him from the bottom. Or so Ali hoped. He had also been struggling against the weight of his gear. But staying above water with thirty pounds of gear on was one of the first tricks they taught Navy SEALs.

Or, again, so Ali hoped.

In the middle of the cockpit, closest to the cabin, Handon heard a noise underneath the firing, shouting, and moaning. He pulled open the hatch and took a step down and inside. Sure enough – rushing water. The grenade blast had, naturally enough, opened a gaping hole in the hull, on the starboard side and just below the waterline.

Emerging again, he saw Henno had already seen it.

"Sodding told you so," he didn't resist saying. *Now* they'd have to fucking swim for it.

Handon assessed. Since they now knew to expect flying bodies leaping out of the water like some kind of spawning zombie salmon, they could at least react. There were also plenty of slow-moving attackers still just trying to haul themselves up over the gunwale. Rifles chugged, melee weapons whistled and thunked, and body after body hit the water again.

But it was hardly even like water now. It was turning into a corpse pit, or open grave. And still they came.

While he did a quick mag change, Handon looked down to see that water was now ankle-deep in the cockpit. They'd all be swimming in another minute, whether they stayed or went.

"On me," he barked. "We use grenades to clear a path to shore."

The others, in their shrinking circle, assimilated that while they fought.

"And then swim through Zulu soup?" Predator said. "No thanks."

"We're only in eight feet of water," Ali said, still facing and firing toward the prow, out to sea. "If we keep our heads above water until we touch bottom we might be okay…"

Juice said, "Close your eyes, get your ear protection in – *and do not open your mouth.*"

"Roger that," Pred said, reloading.

"Do it," Handon said, and then turned around to Park, at the very center of their ship's last stand, in the center of the cockpit. The water was now mid-thigh. Handon drew a knife, cut a piece of rigging line in two places, and tied one end around Park's belt buckle. "You get all that? Eyes and mouth closed?"

Park nodded rapidly, looking too panicked to speak, mainly trying to gulp air. Handon looked down and saw he held his laptop satchel clutched in both arms. "That waterproof?"

"No."

"Screw it. They can take the plate out of the hard drive lat—"

The rest of his sentence was cut off by the first whumps of grenades, walking from the stern of the sailboat in toward shore. Whump after crump sounded, as the Alpha operators coordinated a perfect walking artillery strike, geysers of body-part-sodden water launching thirty feet into the night sky. As the last explosion settled, Handon pushed Park toward the landward edge of the boat – which was now the stern. The water looked far from healthy. But it did at least seem to lack animation.

"Wade out," Handon said to Park. "Go!"

The deck of the sinking ship was now below the water, making this easier. Anyway, there was no place else to go.

"Go, go, we gotta go!" Ali said, she and Henno holding the rear, which was closing in on them hellaciously quickly. Slinging their weapons, splashing through the water, the operators also frantically grabbed last pieces of gear and ammo – weighing the odds of drowning, versus being infected by the hundreds of liters of zombie guts in the water, versus being eaten alive later for lack of weapons and ordnance… Then they slid one after another into the water.

The lightest of them was way too heavy.

And, as their heads went under, they paddled blind.

Ali and Henno fired unceasingly behind them, pivoting in an growing arc, covering the withdrawal. The deck was filling with dead, the weight of them swamping the boat more quickly, as it was overrun and pulled under. The momentum of an advancing pair of them took them right into the cockpit even as they were destroyed, landing right at Henno and Ali's feet, further crowding the evacuation.

Ali was last out. Before she went, she stood on tiptoe, trying catch a last glimpse of Homer. But he had disappeared. And now a half dozen of the dead, and then a dozen, had heaved themselves up onto the sinking and nearly abandoned craft.

Ali let them have it. She slid into the water and swam for it.

NEARER

Lower Hardres, Kent, the South of England

John Gutteridge slammed his fist against the wheel arch of the tractor and cursed. He was a mile across the field, and it was a damned long walk to go and fetch his tools. He was cursing himself more than anything. He had known the knackered old machine was in trouble for two weeks now, but that didn't stop him from lashing out at it when it finally failed.

It had been juddering as of late, mostly when traveling slowly, and the bend at the top of the field was usually the culprit. And that was where he was now, standing with the engine cover open, peering into the dirty mess at the heart of the machine, and wondering if he had enough pipe-and-hose tape left to fix the thing. It certainly wasn't going anywhere at this moment, and was even then spewing its fuel onto the hard ground and over his boots. He also realized that he had nothing to tie it off with, so gravity was going to lose him half a tank of fuel at least.

He cursed again and began to trudge across the field, back toward the yard. He'd barely days to go before he needed this field ready and it was nowhere near that. Ten days from now a truckload of seed potatoes would arrive and he would need to get them into the ground.

He shivered against the chill of the wind, pulled his

collar higher, and tried to walk faster across the uneven ground. This field hadn't seen a plow for over six years, and he never thought it would again, but then the soldiers from Folkestone had come by the month before and told him he needed to increase his output to help provision the growing garrison. They'd even supply the seeds. This was just when John had been starting to wind things down, hoping to retire and sell off the land.

Damn zombie apocalypse had to scupper his plans, didn't it?

He was about halfway across the field when he heard the first scream. Initially, he thought it was the distant sound of some bird of prey that had discovered an unguarded nest, and so he only stopped for a moment before carrying on his trudge across the uneven ground. Ten yards later the scream sounded far from avian, and it wasn't letting up. It was coming from the houses behind the yard, on the main road.

John Gutteridge began to run.

As he sped across the open ground, dodging molehills and plow furrows as best he could, the sound of the screaming rose. More voices now, then a gun started firing, shot after shot. The gun kept on until John pushed through the gate that led into the yard, and then a louder, deeper scream joined the others.

He ran onward, his chest heaving and boots crunching on the graveled yard. He ran straight for the drive that led around the main building, wishing he had exercised more, as his body protested at the strain he was putting on it.

He never did find out who was screaming.

Gutteridge barreled around the corner at a speed he couldn't control, and ran straight into the middle of the street, overtaking at least two of the staggering figures that now lined the road.

It wasn't the zombies, of which there were at least a hundred moving along the main thoroughfare and forcing their way into the houses that lined it, that put John down. It was the Ford Mondeo driven by Samuel Neale – the local convenience-shop owner – moving in excess of fifty miles per hour that did that. John didn't have time to slow down, and the car hit him head on, launching him thirty feet further down the road, where he landed right at the shuffling feet of one of the zombies. The car had swerved at the last moment, but not quickly enough. It also now went spinning out of control and crashed into the front of an old Victorian cottage that had once been a rented holiday home.

John Gutteridge was eaten alive over the course of the next five minutes, trapped in his broken body, his spine shattered in a dozen places. He was unable to defend himself and couldn't even raise a hand toward the creatures that fell upon him. By the time they had finished with him there wasn't enough of him left to be recognizable as human, let alone to turn.

Samuel Neale, a man who all of his life had endured bad luck, met his end much more abruptly and mercifully. He had been in such a panic that he hadn't put his seatbelt on, and when the Mondeo collided with the solid stone structure of the cottage he was sent flying forward at fifty miles per hour, headfirst through the windshield, and into solid stone. He was dead long before John's screams ceased and the village fell silent.

A hundred zombies lumbered their way through the now-quiet hamlet, heading north – always north. Less than an hour later, thirty more stumbling figures clumsily made their way out of the houses of Lower Hardres and followed after the others – and following the one that moved much faster than them, the one that even now sensed another place not far away where there were more to be infected.

The city of Canterbury.

HUNTRESS

The female of the species, free now of responsibility for the less-deadly male, as well as her vulnerable offspring, moved through the night-time forest in silence. The starlight and bit of moon failed to penetrate the canopy of trees, and she made her way mostly by memory and touch, as she followed the disturbing and unfamiliar sounds. Was it the sound of prey? Or more fearsome predators than she?

She was determined to nose her way forward until she found out.

She had sent the male and the cub back as soon as she'd sensed something was wrong. The three of them had been out hunting together, mostly because the female judged it safer, on a night like this, not to go out alone. And since she also much preferred not to leave the young one by himself, that meant they all went together.

But any anomaly or danger she would face on her own.

The blackness of the thick forest gave way to the heavy gloom of the town. This was the place of greatest danger. This was the area that always drew her back, but which she stayed out of when at all possible. Tonight, she couldn't keep herself from following the sounds of this unlikely fray. It was the sort of noise she hadn't heard in the better part of two years.

Human sounds.

Voices – whispered hisses, but recognizable, or nearly so. And then shouts, unmistakable. And the puffs and snaps of gunfire. And finally the explosions. The dead made a lot of trouble, but she knew they rarely blew up. And there was little if anything left in the human settlement that might go boom. All of this could mean any of a number of things for the female, and for her family – but most of the possibilities were very bad news.

Though it was just conceivable…

Either way, she had to know.

She circled around the perimeter of the small and rustic lakeside town, stealing peeks through the wooden-slat structures onto the packed-dirt main street, and across to the small marina – and finally out onto the great sprawling body of the lake itself. Sure enough, there was a craft on the water, outlined smudgily in the tiny amount of ambient light.

And there were men upon this boat. And they were fighting – with the dead.

Much worse, at least for these humans, was that the noise of the scuffle had carried into the town itself. And the dead on land had perked up and were moving out. Even if the men on the boat survived the maritime assault, an amphibious one was lined up right behind it. Unless they could get moving back out onto the lake, to the safety of deep water, they were done for.

Crouching a bit lower, set back in the deeper shadow in a gap between buildings, the female smoothly unslung her Ruger Mini-14 rifle from across her back, wrapped the strap tightly around her forearm, pulled it in to her shoulder, and sighted in through the Leupold scope on top. Feeling her way through the magnified and jerky darkness, she walked her crosshairs out from the pier to the boat, which was less than fifty meters offshore.

Her view came to rest just in time to be obscured by a great heavy plume of water rising like a beast from the deep. It was from one of the explosions, which turned out to be the last. But they already had plenty of real beasts coming up from the deep – the former acquaintances and neighbors of this human female, whom she'd hoped would have found their rest at the bottom of the lake's shallows.

But then here came the living, being a pain in the ass, riling them all up again. At least the dead could be counted on to quiet down after a while. And, generally, she found that if she left them alone, they left her alone. They were also pretty predictable.

The living, of course, were capable of absolutely anything.

* * *

The walking explosions under the water at first took her by surprise. But she worked out pretty quickly what they were doing – clearing a path through the water – and she knew she was right when they waded in near the spot of the first explosion and swam for it. She could also see that their boat was listing, and probably sinking, so maybe desperation had inspired genius.

Or maybe it had only inspired more desperation.

They might make it to shore, but that would avail them little. Because their welcoming party was already wading out to greet them.

The woman withdrew and swung silently around the back of two other buildings, to improve her observation of the point where they'd emerge from the water. She moved warily – with the whole town riled up, the dead might pop up anywhere. But she got where she was going without incident. When she crouched again and settled in, she reached down just to touch the autoloading handgun on her belt, and the hand-held radio nestled beside it. She wished she had some of her old colleagues from Metro with her tonight.

But they were all gone now. And best not thought about.

A few seconds after reaching her new position, she got her second surprise: the hapless pleasure-boaters came out of the water shooting – and shooting *well.* They cleared their beachhead in seconds, and waded ashore with authority.

But the woman knew there were plenty more dead behind those first ones. They could be seen stumbling into town from either end. Not to mention trying to claw their way out of structures.

When the woman and her husband, and their son, had built their cabin, six miles up a rutted dirt road from the village, they had selected the spot very carefully. The weekend vacation cottage was also intended to serve as their BOL ("Bug Out Location"), so they'd sited it far enough away from other people to be isolated, should they need to disappear, or defend their patch. But also close enough to be a source of supplies, or support, if they needed that.

Of course they hadn't seriously considered the possibility of something like… what had actually happened. *If we had*, the woman thought mournfully, *we would have put it in the middle of the Canadian boreal forest… or maybe the Canadian Arctic tundra…*

The sound of gunfire, suppressed but still audible, grew louder now – as did the noise of grunts, spoken commands, and moaning and hissing, as the group of newcomers fought their way into the town proper. Watching them move, she counted seven. And it suddenly dawned on the woman that they were actually displaying pretty outstanding fire and movement. She was no expert, but she had buddies on the Emergency Task Force, and she'd gotten them to let her sit in on some of their tactical training. And this group moved with authority.

But then they made their fatal error. They fled into the church.

Suddenly, the woman had no idea how these guys had survived two years into the Crunch – which, let's face it, was really almost certainly the EOTW. Anyway, one thing you *never* did was hole up in a structure – not once the dead were on to you. No, they'd just hang out forever, drawing more and more with every frenzied moan, and there would be your last, eternal stand. There you'd be entombed. The woman knew that much.

As she watched the group file into the square, squat, and not-terribly-big wood and stone structure, with most of the deceased local population hot on their heels, she figured that was it for them. And that was probably a good thing.

No, it was definitely a good thing.

Because, as noted, the living were utterly unpredictable. And, this far into the Crunch, the resources needed to survive – food, clean water, ammunition, fuel, batteries, spare parts, medicine – were so thin on the ground out here that they were without question worth killing for. Which, basically, made the living every bit as dangerous as the dead – *more* dangerous, really, because the living had guns and tools, knew how to climb over obstacles and open doors, and could also drive vehicles. And, very worst of all, the living could trick you.

They could lie to you. Pretend to be your friends.

Until they took everything you had.

No, in the state of nature, in this post-civilizational hell into which they had descended, interacting with other people was just way too tense – and encounters with strangers far too dangerous. Even if you found yourself facing another person as good and decent as you, he would almost certainly be as heavily armed as you. And you could find yourself in the Hobbesian trap of having to shoot that person, just to keep him from doing it to you first… who might only be doing it to keep you from doing it first… and on and on into death, or at least insanity.

Yes, the woman was relieved by this outcome. The group would disappear into the church, and they would never emerge. With a little luck, they'd even thin the local undead population a little first. But, at any rate, now she didn't have to make an agonizing moral decision: whether to let other, possibly innocent, people die – and they were after all seven of the probably tiny handful of her fellow humans still left alive anywhere. Or else to endanger herself and her family – to go out of her way to worsen odds that were already horrifically against them.

No, it was better this way.

She had just unwrapped her rifle sling and started to slip away, when something stopped her. It was something strange about the way one of them moved. It was anomalous. She pulled the scope back to her eye, just in time to see the last of the group step backwards into the doorway of the church, squeeze off a last few careful shots, take a final look around, and then pull the door closed – on her thin and graceful silhouette.

It was a woman, or girl.

Shit.

LAY YOUR BURDENS DOWN

"Sarge, we go in that church, we ain't comin' out."

So had said Henno, sidelong, when Handon ordered them in there. He was just Mr. Gloomy Pants today. And Handon knew he might be as right as he'd been before. But there was little or no choice. They couldn't conduct a running firefight through an unfamiliar stretch of wilderness, with one mobility casualty and one terrified civilian, plus one man detached and unaccounted for.

Mainly, they couldn't do it drenched chin to toe in probably infectious goop.

They had to consolidate. And this was as bad a place as any.

Now, with the slamming of the church's heavy wooden door still echoing, and competing with the moaning and banging outside, the team fanned out into the nearly pitch-black interior, through the entryway, and down the aisles between the pews into the church hall.

"Ali, Henno," Handon said, "sweep and clear. Everyone else on me, to clean up." With that he pulled out the tube from his hydration sleeve and rinsed his own face and eyes. He then pulled and cracked a fluorescent glow stick and dropped it on the ground; then produced a bottle of water he'd stuffed in a pouch.

Roughly, he tipped Dr. Park's head back, got busy pouring, and told him to shut up and settle down while he did it.

Park felt like he was being waterboarded.

"Maybe the lake water was okay," Juice suggested. He was thinking that the whole point of the grenades had been to clear out the dead... although it also liquefied a lot of them.

Ali had been able to keep her head clear of the water – though, with her helmet off, her hair had come down, and was soaked and matted below her chin. This was not a matter of fashion; that hair could now kill her. Pushing this thought aside, she moved out to the left side of the building, NVGs still on and rifle to shoulder, while Henno moved to the right. In thirty seconds, they both trotted back up.

"Structure's clear," Henno said. "Either it stayed locked up through the fall, or someone cleared it out later. And cleared it out properly. No signs of Zulus or a scrap."

"Water?"

Ali shook her head. "Both the boiler and the toilet tank are bone dry."

Juice looked up from where he was trying to wipe down both himself and Predator with antiseptic wipes from his aid kit. "How about bleach? Is there a janitor's closet?" Ali nodded and took off again. The others crouched around the little green glow in the center of the church, the darkness pressing in on them – and the dead pressing in around that. They seemed to rattle the very structure with their heaving against the door and exterior walls.

Handon looked up at Ali. "Homer?" He knew she would have already tried to radio him.

She shook her head. "He's probably still in the water."

Handon wasn't worried. Everyone knew that the safest place for a SEAL was in the water, the deeper the better. They always seemed to be trying to fight their way back to it.

Something cracked from the back of the church, sharp and loud. Handon looked at Henno. "Got it," he said. Coming back seconds later, he said, "Stained glass. In the, the watchacallit, the short bits of the cross the church makes. The windows are at ground level. They won't hold."

"How long?" Handon asked.

"Ten minutes? Two?" Henno shrugged.

Ali reappeared, toting a bucket and a white jug. Coordinating with efficient language, they got all of their remaining water into the bucket, then poured the bleach in after it. Then they got busy wiping and scrubbing. Wretchedly, where they most needed the bleach – around their mucous membranes – was where it burnt most savagely.

While they scrubbed, Predator and Juice did their old-married-couple routine.

"Hey," Predator said, "remember that old zombie TV show, where people were *constantly* covered in the guts of zombies, episode after episode—"

Juice cut in. "—and yet were in absolutely no

danger of infection?"

"*Exactly*. The tiniest scratch or bite, and they're doomed – but they could be gargling with Zulu guts, and they're fine."

Juice laughed, as he dunked his NVGs entire in the bleach solution. "What did they think the infection actually infected? And how did we ever buy into that?"

"They probably just figured it looked edgy with everyone covered in gore all the damned time."

Handon wanted to tell them to shut the fuck up and focus. But he didn't have the energy.

Instead, he directed everyone to divide and swallow the anti-viral meds from their aid kits. There was no compelling clinical evidence that these prevented contraction of the virus. But it couldn't hurt – and it was what they had. As the guys on the very front lines, they always carried them. It was something.

Dr. Park got a double dose, which he had to swallow dry. Their water was gone.

And now, if they'd been lucky enough to survive a close call with infection, they'd still have to try to avoid touching their wet clothes, or their faces, at least until they were able to clean up properly. Which was looking like it might be never.

Handon looked around at his team, huddled in the middle of the nave, in the green glow of the single light stick, dead in the center aisle between the rows of pews. His immediate impulse, a stupid one, was to try to radio for support. But of course he knew that absolutely no support was coming.

They were utterly on their own.

This was nothing new, of course. But it was starting to feel uniquely bleak. After all this, after everything… would Alpha go down in a country church in some backwater lake town? Had the odds finally caught up with them?

Shoving the blanket of hopelessness off him, reaching down again, as he'd done a hundred times before, Handon had the others do a quick catalog of weapons, ammo, and supplies they'd salvaged from the boat. It didn't add up to much. Whatever hole that resupply pallet had dug them out of had itself been engulfed and swallowed up by Lake Michigan – the lake of the dead.

Now they had only what they carried.

And what they carried – rifles, magazines, grenades, radios, vests, helmets, NVGs – varied from man to man. Nobody had everything. It had all happened too fast. Handguns were about the only universal. Oh, and they were also down another team member – hopefully temporarily.

And then there were five, thought Handon.

The noise of cracking glass, from up in the transept, turned now to crashing. The snuffling of the dead sounded clearly, no longer muted by the wood and stone walls. The church was breached. As much to stall for planning time as out of necessity, Handon sent Ali and Henno forward to hold the line.

Juice helped Pred to his feet, pausing to tell him to fuck off when he tried to shrug him off and do it on his own. Dr. Park bounced to his feet, eyes wide and shining. Handon took a deep breath. *Oh, well,* he thought. *We'll just have to shoot our way out of here. It worked for Butch and Sundance…*

"I've got a horrible feeling," Juice said, "that it's not gonna be any better out there than it was when we came in."

Predator grunted. "I've just got a horrible feeling."

As Handon chamber-checked his HK416 – taking care not to eject the round in the chamber; they'd need every cartridge – his radio did something extraordinary.

First it squelched. And then it spoke. In a woman's voice.

"Hey, you." It then squelched off, and paused. *"The dumbasses. In the church."*

Handon ground his jaw and looked at the others circled around him. He almost cursed aloud. This was beyond stupid, beyond even comical, and pretty much beyond enduring. But then he exhaled heavily. *Oh, what the hell…?* he thought. He pressed his transmit bar and spoke.

"Dumbasses receiving five by five, send traffic."

The others busted out laughing, and Handon tried to hush them with his hand so he didn't miss the response.

Even Ali guffawed. And she was up at the front of the church, battling the dead.

* * *

The woman suddenly had no idea why she'd said that, spoken so flippantly. She knew radio protocol as well as anyone – maybe not their specific flavor of it, but still. But when the sound of their laughter came through her radio earpiece – including, she'd swear, the laughter of the woman she'd seen – she had to admit that was a pretty good omen.

She was now half the length of the village away from their location – where the newcomers had basically advertised a free dead-guy festival up at the church. She had to keep her distance to avoid all the fun. But it was still easily within radio range.

She pressed her transmit bar again, then raised the radio to her lips and spoke quietly. "This is Five-Five-Eight Tango Papa receiving. Listen to me if you want to get out of there alive. Over."

She took a steadying breath. Now she was *really* committing.

God, let me not have cause to regret this…

* * *

"Standing by, Five-Five-Eight," Handon said. He pointed his radio speaker outward. He figured everyone may as well hear this, if only to save time. And they were about out of that. Again.

"Okay. Listen carefully, and do not mistake me. I can get you out of there. And I can get you to safety. But you do EVERYTHING I say. When I say it. Including when I say it's time for you to go. Understood?"

Handon spoke seriously in response. "All received and understood. It's your party, Five-Five-Eight."

"Okay. That church you're in is of colonial vintage. Which

means it's built on a root cellar. You won't have seen it, because last I checked it's under a rug, but there's stairwell access through the floor behind the altar. Got that?"

Handon tossed his head at Juice, who darted off toward the altar.

"Dumbass copies all. And does that get us out of the building alive, over?"

"Affirmative on getting you out of the building. Alive will be trickier. Most of your dead are clustered around the front doors where you went in, and the windows of the transept. But they're pretty much on all sides at this point – and they aren't getting any fewer, so listen up. Because I'm an idiot, I'm going to do you a diversion, on the front side of the building. If you're lucky, that will draw the ones from the back. On my signal you break out. Got it?"

"Roger that. Moving into position now."

"Not so fast! No shooting when you break out. You do it as damned close to silently as you can manage. Because if I see the dead are still on you when you get back outside… you are on your own again. You got that?"

"Roger that," Handon said, looking around as they all moved down the aisle and around the altar. This took them past Ali and Henno's positions in the two transepts. All the front-facing windows there had now been shot or smashed out. The two defenders fired methodically, every time one of the creatures seemed like it was about to claw around the others and drag itself inside.

"Noise discipline," Handon said, and reached for the rug at their feet. But as he grabbed a handful and started to yank, another hand stopped his. It was

Predator, grabbing him by the wrist. Handon swiveled his neck and pinned the giant's squinted eyes with his own. He just waited for it.

"Any idea *whatsoever* who's on the other end of that line?" Predator said. His tone implied a certain doubt in Handon's decision-making right this second. "And any particular reason we trust her?" He let go of Handon's wrist and let him answer.

"No idea. But there can't be as many of them as there are Zulus, and if it goes south we'll just kill them, too. And I'm a little more trusting precisely because it's a 'her'."

Predator nodded, his expression saying *Okay, fair enough.*

Handon now gave the rug a yank, revealing a trapdoor in the floor beneath it. *Huh*, he thought. *With a little luck, the Zulus won't be able to get this open behind us...* He held it up for Dr. Park, Juice, and Pred – then whistled for Ali and Henno, who backed toward him, their rifles slung and melee weapons out. They disappeared into the black maw of the basement, and Handon followed them down. He could see dead piling into the building on either side as he did so.

As a last brilliant maneuver, he tried to pull the rug back over the trapdoor as he shut it.

But it wasn't necessary. Within five seconds, he could hear the Zulus walking all over it. Their own stupid dead weight would keep them from ever getting it open.

Handon clicked on his weapon-mounted light, took a few steps toward the rear of the building, and cast around until he found another short set of stairs. It rose up and terminated in one of those slanted cellar doors they're always taking shelter from tornadoes behind. Or so Handon remembered from the movies. With the others stacked up behind him, he pressed to transmit, hoping like hell whoever it was was still there.

"Five-Five-Eight, Dumbass is in position, how copy?"

"That's received. Stand by." She sounded like she was moving. She came back on a few seconds later. *"You ready for that diversion?"*

"Good to go. On your signal."

"Well, this is your signal. The coast is clear – all your dead are now inside the church, or trying to fight their way in. No diversion required. Thank fuck. Over."

Handon made a *Silence* hand signal, extinguished his light, worked the latch, and *slooowly* pushed open the cellar door. Outside, it looked like empty churchyard and clear night air to him – though the dark was now starting to lighten slightly. Dawn was almost breaking. Handon led the way out, head on a swivel, the snuffling and scrabbling sounds of the dead coming around either side of the building behind them. There was a treeline to the rear, on the other side of fifty meters of churchyard, and Handon made for it. The others followed.

As soon as they were what Handon would call a safe depth inside the wooded area, about a hundred meters, he came upon the woman. Or she came upon them. She was of average height, proportional build, with what looked like shoulder-length dark hair pulled into an efficient ponytail. Early thirties Handon guessed.

Attractive. She wore synthetic hiking pants – they'd stay warm, wear tough, and dry fast – beneath a thigh-length hunting jacket, with a tactical belt on the outside of it. She also carried a Ruger Mini-14 – not quite pointed at them, but not quite lowered either.

Handon lowered his weapon completely. He put out his hand.

"Handon," he said.

"Later," she said, eyeing the rest of the group. "This way." She led them at a smart jog up what looked to Handon like a deer trail. After another two hundred meters, she angled them off it, taking them through thick underbrush, which finally emerged onto a somewhat washed-out dirt or clay road. Then she carried on, still at a vigorous jog, west along it – away from the lake, and up into forest of higher elevation.

Only when they were a good mile out did she slow her jog to a brisk walk.

Walking side by side with Handon, she stuck her hand out this time.

"Sarah," she said.

Handon took hers. "How'd you know our radio frequency, Sarah?"

"Not hard to work out," she said, keeping her eye on the dirt road and the gloom that spooled out ahead of them. "You're obviously military. Ex-military, I guess." Her voice was rich and feminine, but smart and professional. Serious, Handon thought. Grown-up. She looked back behind them – and saw, perhaps for the first time, Predator's half-crippled, lurching gait. "You didn't tell me you had wounded," she said.

Before Handon could answer, Pred said, "Screw you, lady," as he accelerated to a stiff-legged fast-walk and overtook them all. Handon shook his head. The problem with giant unstoppable badasses was that they dealt very poorly with injury, limitation, or incapacity.

"Parachuting accident," Handon said.

Sarah raised her eyebrows at this, and turned on her heel and started walking backward. As she did so, she eyed the others in the group more closely. They all looked intact. Moreover, she probably just had to trust here. This group looked serious enough not to keep bit or scratched friends around. If they were like that, they never would have made it two years in the first place.

Handon worked out what she was doing – as well as the conclusion she reached. As she turned on her heel again and faced forward, Handon smiled slightly, intrigued. Whoever this woman was, she was all business.

And she was very clearly in charge.

Good enough, he thought, settling in to the walk. This suited him at the moment. And he knew enough to always defer to the person who knew the ground.

Local knowledge was powerful mojo.

As the terrain gently rose and forested hills swelled up around them, Handon looked sidelong at her again, and considered asking her where they were going. But she'd done enough already, and he decided to leave it for now. She'd tell them in her own time.

Sometimes demonstrating a little faith was tactically proficient.

AT THE GATES

CentCom Exchange, London

Elise Bridgeton, exchange operator, leaned back in her chair and took a mournful breath. She grabbed her coffee cup and fired down a swig, grimacing at the cold, sharp liquid. Around her, the office was buzzing; thirty other operators chattered into their headsets, answering emergency calls or patching military comms from one location to another. This was an average day at the CentCom first-line call center.

Elise had joined CentCom a year before, having been in telephone sales for five years before everything went bad. She used to love her job, sitting in a high-rise office not far from Westminster, cold-calling London banking and finance firms, and selling them computer hardware and software. It had been easy.

This, on the other hand, answering distress calls and patching military updates, gave her a level of deep-down good feeling that sales never had. There was something very satisfying about telling someone that help was on the way, or just saying the words, "Received, CentCom out" to a squad of soldiers patrolling the coast, or maybe some inbound flight coming back from a mission and making their hourly call in.

CentCom was very strict about those hourly call-ins, and when one didn't happen it made everybody nervous.

That was what was happening now, and Elise was frightened as hell. She'd only had a few incidents where a team hadn't reported in at the correct time, and that usually just meant they were occupied at that moment, or were having a comms outage. A quick call from a CentCom operator, or a few minutes' waiting, normally resolved the issue. But occasionally the call went unanswered, as had the one she just made to a Rural Mobile Team patrolling south of Canterbury. Patrol 15, Canterbury Border Division were now twenty minutes over their call-in time.

She was just about to flag down her superior officer, the call center supervisor, when the incoming-call light on her screen began to flick on and off.

Elise breathed a sigh of relief. It was the team's radio signature. Crisis over. She opened the channel.

"CentCom. Go ahead, Team Fifteen."

But the voice that answered was not the one she expected.

"Hello? Hello? Do you hear me?"

Elise's heart jumped in her chest. The voice on the other end sounded strained, frightened.

"CentCom Exchange, please state your unit designation."

"I'm at the hospital. Chaucer Hospital. We've just picked up your soldiers. I mean the patrol. They came in and they're all…"

The voice trailed off. There was a noise in the background, but Elise couldn't make it out. Someone in pain, maybe?

"Please state the condition of the patrol," said Elise, at the same time as she flicked an alert switch on the board in front of her – the one that said *Urgent Alert.*

"They came in about ten minutes ago," said the voice. "Four of them are hurt really bad. Two died before they got here. They've been— oh, God, what's going on back there?"

Elise heard a scream echoing in the background across the radio.

"Oh, God, they're up."

Elise jumped to her feet and waved both arms at her supervisor, who was already on his way over. He started hurrying.

"I think Chaucer Hospital have a possible outbreak in progress."

The man's eyes widened. "What?"

The hospitals had been where it all began. *Oh, God, not again…*

Elise pulled the headphone cable out of the switchboard and pushed the volume to the top.

The voice on the radio spoke once more before the line went dead.

"We have an outbreak at Chaucer Hospital. Please, we need help." Just before the radio went silent the entire CentCom Exchange room heard the final scream.

The supervisor turned to the operator next to Elise, his expression grave.

"Alert Folkestone barracks, North Canterbury barracks and Faversham barracks. Tell them that we need full mobilization and a lockdown on the entire grid square around Chaucer Hospital, and we need it now."

STORM OF THE DEAD

Commander Drake had just taken the stairs down to the Combat Information Center (or CIC, but sometimes still called the Ops Room) a half a flight at a time. He'd also given a couple of shoves to the hapless ensign assigned to bring him down there, in order to maintain his sense of urgency. Now he looked down on the radar console, one hand on its operator's shoulder. The officer of the watch, Lieutenant Campbell, stood at his left shoulder, along with another pair of CIC techs.

"What am I looking at?" Drake asked Campbell.

"That was pretty much my question, sir," Campbell said. She held Drake's eye levelly.

"C'mon, LT," Drake said. "Do I look like a man with time on my hands? It's a storm system, right?"

Campbell nodded. "Looks to be, at first glance. Like a classic hurricane or heavy storm pattern, with a big mass circling around a relatively still center, and arms spiraling out from there… But it's also unlike any storm I've ever seen."

"How so?"

"Much lower to the ground. Thinner. Basically weirder."

"Are you saying the ZA is producing new weather patterns? Why don't we send out a UAV? Get a close-up view and figure out what we're dealing with."

"Already done, sir." She paused before continuing.

"But not a drone. A Prowler."

The Boeing EA-6B Prowler was an electronic warfare aircraft, this one originally part of Electronic Attack Squadron 130, which had been fleet-deployed to the *Kennedy* at the time of the fall. But there wasn't a hell of a lot of electronic warfare to be done lately. There weren't a hell of a lot of working electronics, for that matter, and the Zulus didn't have them. But the Prowler also made an excellent surveillance/reconnaissance platform, so two of them had been spared from getting dumped in the ocean, when the carrier's hangar deck got repurposed as an organic farm.

Drake turned to face his CIC chief, his demeanor now even less friendly than it had been when he entered. "A manned sortie? Without my authorization?"

Campbell cleared her throat quietly. "The Captain authorized it, sir."

Drake didn't even know how to respond to this. The Captain had not been involved in the day-to-day running of the ship, commanding either tactically or strategically, in over a year. Hell, he'd hardly been spotted out of his quarters in months.

"Where do you think the JP-8 for this is going to come from?" Drake meant the military-grade aviation fuel that their jets gulped like marathoners did Gatorade. They had little enough in stores, and generally reserved it for critical missions.

Campbell kept a straight face as she answered. "Should be plenty in the tanks at AB Oceana. Sir." She was practically standing at attention at this point.

"*Je*-sus Christ..." Drake said, shaking his head. The

very fact of their scavenging op was supposed to be need-to-know. And they certainly weren't going in there for the purpose of siphoning jet fuel. They were trying to find an aircraft to extract Alpha, and thus maybe recover a vaccine to save the whole human race. Drake pinned Campbell with his unamused eye. She straightened up further, if that were possible. "Be advised, Lieutenant. No more fucking mission planning *based on scuttlebutt*. You read me?"

"Aye aye, sir. Lima Charlie."

"Good. Now where's your bird?"

"Feet dry over the homeland, and reaching the edge of… the anomaly… any second."

"Video?"

Campbell snapped her fingers at a tech, who powered up a large overhead video display.

"Wait," Drake said. "Where the hell is this thing, actually? Zoom the map out."

Campbell showed him on the console screen. "North Carolina," she said. "The center's about a hundred and fifty miles northwest of Raleigh."

"The *center*? How big is this thing? Shit, that is big. It's moving this way?"

"Aye, sir. Since we started tracking it."

Drake looked up now to the streaming video on the overhead screen. Thick Carolina pine forest zipped by beneath the Prowler's underwing-mounted targeting pod, which housed the camera. The plane was cruising at low altitude, maybe a couple of hundred feet. Suddenly, the great stretches of forest gave way to farmland – those distinct, multicolored rectangles of cultivated crop plots.

And then, almost as quickly, that gave way to something else.

First, Drake thought he saw figures moving on the ground, in ones and twos, zipping by too quickly to track. But then suddenly the camera was skimming across…

"*What the hell…*" Drake muttered.

LT Campbell stood erect, in a wide stance, arms crossed, but also leaning closer to the screen. No one in the room spoke for a few seconds.

"*Is that…?*"

Campbell picked up a desk mic from the station beside her. "Prodigy Five-Four, this is Alpha Whiskey Actual. Interrogative: what are we looking at here, over?" She flicked a switch that put the channel on room speaker.

"Alpha Whiskey, Prodigy. I am visual on what looks to be… a whole shit-ton of Zulus. All the way out to the horizon. Over."

The LT touched the transmit bar. "Prodigy, Alpha Whiskey, that's received… with thanks."

"It's a fucking herd," Drake said, his voice devoid of affect or emotion. And it was a herd – but numbering in the hundreds of thousands. Or millions.

Campbell and Drake looked at each other for a moment, then back to the screen. The depth of the image was starting to resolve. It wasn't just a staggeringly large crowd of bodies. It had a third dimension to it. They were somehow… *roiling* – particularly as they rolled over everything in their path, trees, rocks, ridges. As the mass moved, it was somehow more than one layer of bodies deep, a great heaving ocean, with depths to it. The individual bodies were heaving and leaping upon one another as it surged forward, limbs and heads and torsos thrashing and legs going ass over teakettle, and somehow…

"Alpha Whiskey, Prodigy, I'm descending for a better look, over."

The LT looked concerned. "Copy that, Prodigy. Let's not put it right on the deck."

"Roger that. Hang on… they seem to be reacting to my engine noise. Coming around…"

From the video view in the CIC, the Prowler had already descended more than half the total distance to the ground, and now that view banked and swerved as the jet came around at high speed…

"Holy shit…" Lt. Campbell said, involuntarily.

Coming back around on its original path, and a lot lower as well, the plane now faced a *much* more riled up and roiling ocean of bodies. Thousands of them now scrambled up on the backs of others as they relentlessly tried to get at the noise that had just blasted overhead, all of them totally heedless of the crushing of their own bodies in the pursuit and the pile-up, and the whole wave crested dead ahead, as one, now ten, now a hundred were leaping into the ai—

Something blacked out most of the camera view, and the remaining sliver of light twisted and dove…

"Alpha Whi—!"

And that was it. The screen was black, the channel dead.

"Prodigy Five-Four, Alpha Whiskey Actual, sitrep. Acknowledge." The LT spoke the words into the microphone. But she spoke them mechanically. The pilot had been way too low. There'd been zero time for him to react.

And it had taken less than a second for his aircraft, smashing into dozens of leaping bags of dead meat, to drop out of the sky and plow nose-first into… whatever *it* was.

* * *

Commander Drake now sat again in his little conference room up on the flag bridge, with Lieutenant Campbell and a handful of other officers. He damn well wished Gunnery Sergeant Fick were there. But Fick was out on the ground – along with virtually everyone who represented the carrier strike group's accumulated ground-combat experience.

We're spread too damned thin, Drake thought. Especially after the fucking mutiny and outbreak. The ship was coming apart at the seams. He did have the ship's Senior Medical Officer (SMO) in there, a surgeon and lieutenant commander named Roberts.

Drake looked to him now. "I thought we understood these things to shut down and go dormant when there was no living prey around?"

LCDR Roberts, serious and senior with his decades of service and salt-and-pepper hair, spoke evenly. "We did understand that. But then this wouldn't be the first time they've evolved a new behavior pattern."

"I don't think I like this one," Drake said. He struggled to maintain his calm and professionalism. He spoke again now, but almost to himself. "It looked like not all of them were Foxtrots, with the speed and the leaping… but some of them sure as hell were." He looked back to the doctor. "Can this be related to the ghost town the shore party found at the air station? The total lack of Zulus there?"

The surgeon shrugged. "Maybe. Maybe they're clumping or clustering in some way we haven't seen yet. Perhaps all the undeveloped open space in the U.S. allows them to range more freely, or more of them to clump together in the same spot. I don't know."

"Something like this idea of the zombie singularity?" Drake said. "When they all follow the same prey, and the ones further out follow the moaning of the closer ones?"

Roberts had nothing else to add, so he didn't.

Drake looked to LT Campbell again. "How long? Until it's here?"

"Twelve to fourteen hours, at current heading and speed."

Drake shook his head. "But why would the accursed things be heading *right* toward us? Of all the possible goddamned directions? With all of North America to rampage through?"

"Dunno, sir," Campbell said. She paused fractionally. "But we did just ram a hundred and ten thousand tons of aircraft carrier into the edge of the continent."

Drake inclined his head slightly down, squinted, and sat there with his lips parted for a full ten seconds.

"Fuck me," he said, finally.

"Yes, sir."

THE ROAD

Ali walked behind the rest of the team, in the decreasing dimness, serving as Tailgunner Charlie. She was generally the only one Handon trusted with this duty, other than himself. From the back, she noted Handon's failure to ask the woman where they were going. And another thing he'd chosen to leave for now was the matter of trying again to radio Homer.

It was conspicuous by its absence.

And Ali also knew intuitively why he was doing it. For this mystery woman, Sarah, it was going to be unsettling enough to have six strange armed men turn up turn up right in her patch like this. If they also started radioing friends and reporting their location, it might be too much for her. She might well ditch them.

And she might be smart to, Ali considered.

And, anyway, by this point Ali had worked with Handon long enough – they'd all worked together long enough – to generally know what the others were doing, and why, almost before they did it. Explanation was rarely necessary. And Handon's cautious and deferential air with the woman made it obvious to Ali what his objectives were.

Foremost of which was obviously not freaking her out.

So she followed his lead, and refrained from trying to radio Homer herself.

Though, as she mechanically placed her assault boots over and around the ruts in the scarred dirt road, and as she set periodic mini-ambushes behind them to make sure they weren't being shadowed… well, she damned well couldn't stop herself *thinking* about Homer.

He was in her thoughts a lot these days, so her specific feelings at this moment took some teasing out. But self-reflection, and self-analysis, were long-established habits of mind for her. And pretty quickly she worked out it was that she had left Homer out on that lake alone – less than a day after he had so gallantly *not* left her on the streets of Chicago. He had followed her straight down in that botched parachute drop. He hadn't hesitated.

But she had let him just swim out to meet his fate.

The asymmetry was stark, or appeared so.

But Ali also knew the tactical realities of the two cases were totally different. There had been little or nothing she could do to support him while they were both swimming. And she knew, and he knew perfectly well that she knew, that he'd be totally fine out there on his own. Probably better off, given their relative swimming ability.

So why did she still feel so heavy?

She turned, stepped ten meters off the road into the bush, and concealed herself. A full ten minutes of ambush would reassure her about whether they'd really gotten away cleanly. And maybe it would be time enough to push her feelings of guilt, of forlornness, deep down where they wouldn't distract her. After that, she'd double-time it until she caught the group up.

Wherever the hell they were headed.

* * *

By Handon's calculations, they were four miles into their road march before the woman spoke again. At that point the sun was up, but still below the tops of the trees. The air was crisp and clean. If vehicles ever used this road, they didn't do it often. They were in a truly wild place – original-growth forest pressed in on them from both sides, and healthy ground-level vegetation nibbled at the road. Not far off, to the south, Handon could hear a good-sized stream, rushing down to the lake behind and below them.

"You seem a bit incurious," the woman finally said, "about where I'm taking you."

"Figured you'd get to it in your own time," Handon said.

The two of them walked side by side. A few paces behind, Henno kept an eye on the scientist, with Juice and Pred behind them, and Ali alone in the rear.

"So I'm guessing you're from Britain," she said.

"Yes," Handon said. He didn't ask how she knew, but guessed she'd picked up one of the radio beacons. And from that, Handon guessed that wherever they were going there would be a decent radio receiver. Perhaps even a long-range transmitter.

"And what military did you say you'd served with?" Sarah asked.

Handon hadn't said. But he simply answered, "Originally the U.S. Army, in my case. Same with

Predator there, as well as Ali in the back. That strange bearded thing, Juice, worked in the U.S. intelligence services. Henno there was British Army. And Dr. Park is a microbiologist, civilian."

Sarah seemed to like these answers well enough. She certainly noticed that all of them presented with a definite military bearing, with the exception of the last one – the smaller, much more timid, and unarmed Park – who definitely didn't.

"And did you serve?" Handon asked.

"No, not in the military," she said. "Metropolitan Toronto Police."

Handon nodded, impressed. "First responder. All respect. But Toronto's some distance from Lake Michigan…"

"That's by design," she said. She stopped walking, turned to face the group, and raised her voice enough to be heard. Simple efficiency, Handon figured – like she'd given more than one briefing, and didn't believe in giving them twice.

"Okay. Where I'm taking you is to my cabin. My husband and son are there now. It's a safe location – as much as any place is safe anymore. You're welcome to consolidate there, hole up for a bit, try to contact your chain of command, or whoever you need to contact. We've got a good radio set, and power to run it. We can even get you fed, for a meal or two." She paused, pinning each of the operators with her eye. "But then you're off. Got it?"

Handon nodded, and the others let him answer for them. "As agreed," he said.

"Good," she said. "And maybe along the way you can tell me what you know. From out there. About what's going on in the world. What's left of it, if anything."

Before starting off again, she looked into Handon's eyes to try and take his measure.

And she suddenly found herself slightly flustered – though it didn't show up on her in any way. She simply realized she had perhaps never locked eyes with anyone so solid and unflappable. This guy was like an ivory statue – one that extended four stories below the earth. Not cold. But utterly solid, and at ease with himself and the world – and she guessed unyielding and unmovable, when he wanted to be. And unbreakable – there was an obsidian-like hardness to him. But something more than that, underneath. She didn't know what.

Wresting her eyes away, she also guessed that, solid as he was, he could also move damned fast when he needed to. She turned and resumed walking, trusting the others to follow.

"The cabin was our weekend getaway spot," she said, in part to cover up her reaction. "Until there stopped being a world to get away from. Now it's – what did the taxmen used to say? – our primary domicile."

Handon considered the cabin's "by design" location, far from civilization. He refrained from asking whether it had intentionally been stocked to withstand a major disaster – or perhaps the end of the world. He had a feeling it had been. Something told him this was a woman who thought ahead.

"So what's that, about four hundred miles? To Toronto?"

Sarah eyed him sidelong. "Four-thirty-four, if you take the highways. Longer if you avoid them. Why? You have plans to visit? I don't suppose we're ever going back now."

Handon smiled gently. "No, I guess you won't." He looked across at the woman's belt – at the radio and side arm clipped on it; and then at the rifle, which she carried over one shoulder, with her right hand easily on the strap. Basically, she looked tightly wired. He said, "So Toronto Police – one of their specialized units? Emergency Task Force? Gangs and drugs?"

She looked back at him briefly. "Nope. Just a good old street copper – constable first class, Fifty-Two Division, Central Field Command."

"That downtown?"

"Right downtown, station house on Dundas Street itself. But if you've ever been there, you'll know that mean the streets of Toronto ain't…"

"I have been there," Handon said. "But not for many years. It was beautiful. I remember it being the cleanest city I've ever seen. Like you had elves sweeping up the dirt at night."

Sarah laughed quietly. "Well, much good the elves did us." She gave Handon another look – wondering why he might know about things like their force's ETF. Americans would call it a SWAT team. Maybe he'd been some kind of special forces soldier, and kept up with such things. He certainly didn't seem like a grunt.

And he *definitely* wasn't stupid. Even while he said

little, she could see that behind his eyes.

With that, they reached a bend in the dirt road. Sarah didn't go around it. The others pulled up in formation. Sarah said, "You wait here. I've got to brace the crew for boarders."

Handon figured her family probably hadn't seen living people in a long time. They'd be unnerved, at best. As she turned to go, he said, "Thanks for bailing us out. Back in town."

Sarah paused, then tossed her head toward Ali. "Thank *her*." Then she turned and was gone.

"Huh," Predator said, looking bemused, and looking at Ali, while getting the weight off his bad leg. "Why you?"

Ali took a couple of easy steps forward. "My guess is she was going to leave us to our fate. But then she saw me, and changed her calculation."

"And why do you add up differently?" Handon said.

Ali blinked once, seeming pretty relaxed as always. "A male hominid in the presence of a female is, almost by definition, better news than a male or males alone."

"Why's that, then?" Henno looked skeptical.

"Four reasons. One, he's less likely to rape, since he already has sexual access to his own female. Two, he's less likely to steal – which for men is usually about gaining wealth and status, and thus sexual access to females. Three, he probably won't try to kill you in a dominance contest."

"The winner of which," Handon said, getting the

drift now, "gets sexual access to the women."

Ali nodded. "And four, basically, he's a lot less likely to start any shit – and risk the safety of his woman, and the child she may be carrying." She checked her watch. "Basic evolutionary psychology."

"But there's six of us," Juice said plaintively. "And only one of you."

Ali shrugged. "Guess I'm better than nothing."

Sarah reappeared without fanfare. "Okay," she said. "Everyone inside the wire..."

THE CABIN IN THE WOODS

And there was in fact a literal wire to get inside – a sturdy wire fence, rising to just above head height, around the forest clearing in which the cabin sat. The fence looked to Handon to be Zulu-proof – not locked, but with a latch that would defeat anyone without a working brain. Sarah held it open while the team entered, then closed and secured it behind them. The cabin itself was a one-story job, with a peaked roof that might hold a storage attic. Handon guessed four rooms, maybe a thousand square feet.

A man and a boy stood on the tiny porch, both with hands in pockets. They wore camping or hunting clothes, hiking boots, no visible weapons. They looked a little frayed around the edges, but no worse than what a long camping trip might do to you. They both looked wary, which seemed natural enough to Handon. But, underneath it, the man looked somehow glum, and the boy, fourteen or fifteen, looked surly. Somehow this made the two of them seem more like father and son – as if you could see what the surliness would turn into after twenty-five years.

Handon nodded carefully and respectfully at the two.

Sarah said, "This is my husband, Mark, and our son. Guys, this is Handon, Predator, Juice, Henno, Ali, and Dr. Park." Handon whistled internally at her perfect recall. But then he remembered that being a cop was awesome for the memory – the ones he'd known effortlessly absorbed license plates, phone numbers, custody numbers, and then kept them in their heads for years. Sometimes whether they wanted to or not.

Ali surveyed the scene – and then she clocked the look the man gave her, which was way less subtle, and way slower to move on, than he probably imagined it was. This was a common failing with men, and Ali wasn't so long out of the world as to have forgotten it. Worse, she saw that the wife had *also* clocked the look the man gave her – and Sarah gave both of them a quick look of her own. It was somewhere north of sharp but south of withering. And she was subtle about it, much unlike her husband.

The man, Mark, nodded to the group, but didn't venture anything like a smile. Then he said, in an aside to his wife, "Quick word inside?" She nodded, made a one-minute gesture to Handon, and then the whole family disappeared inside again.

"And then again," Ali said breezily, as she scanned the forest around them, "there's also a certain kind of woman who doesn't readily like or trust other women."

"And what makes you think she's one of them?" Juice asked, his gloved hand resting on the pistol grip of his rifle.

Ali answered deadpan. "You can tell them because they spend all their time around men."

"And because you're one of them," Handon added.

Ali shrugged.

The door opened again, and Sarah reappeared, without her rifle this time. "Come on in, gentlemen." She paused a half a beat. "And Catwoman there." She turned and went inside, leaving the door wide for them.

Ali exhaled mournfully as she mounted the stairs. "Everyone's always gotta be hating on the assault suit. It's not my fault you can't do this job in baggy clothes…"

* * *

There weren't enough chairs at the little breakfast table in the alcove kitchen, but there were enough places to sit in the main room taken as a whole. So Alpha sat, and they accepted the Camerons' hospitality. That was the family's name, as Handon worked out from a framed cross-stitch on the wall, which also welcomed them.

The tired, hungry, grimy, and battle-weary operators accepted bowls of homemade stew, which they now spooned up. They learned that this had been made with beans from cans, kale from the garden, and venison from the forest – or rather, Handon figured, from Sarah's rifle.

"This is excellent, ma'am," Juice said, with his usual bearded babe-in-the-woods innocence. The others made echoing noises, from their various points around the room. There was something surreal about the world's deadliest squad of commandos suddenly on their best behavior as luncheon guests.

The interior of the cabin was halfway between country-home cozy, and apocalypse-bunker practical. A full kitchen bulged off the main living room, and two bedrooms, one bigger, took up the back of the structure. A wood-burning stove glowed in the corner – Handon guessed they kept it burning continually – and a rotisserie, grill, and Dutch oven in the fireplace indicated it was also a hearth, used for cooking. There was a refrigerator in the kitchen – but Handon imagined a basement did for most of their cold storage. He'd seen a good-sized diesel generator outside, but not running; as well as solar panels on the roof. But the room was also dotted with oil lamps, so he guessed they minimized their power usage.

Handon turned his soup spoon. There was barley in there, too. He'd also seen some big mylar casks to the side of the cabin. He guessed that was where the grains came from.

The Camerons didn't eat. The stew, from a huge pot, had evidently been their dinner last night. Sarah sat at ease at the head of the table, at Handon's right side – or, rather, with him at her left. Mark Cameron sat on a stuffed chair on the far side of the room, regarding the others, and the boy held up a wall, looking like he was too cool to stay, but too curious to leave. His hands hid out in his pockets, and a sweep of brown hair didn't quite cover his eyes.

Handon put his spoon down and looked at Sarah. "Looks like you're extremely well provisioned," he said – and immediately regretted it. Admiring their provisions wasn't exactly the way to come across as non-threatening.

The woman arched an eyebrow, but only for a

second. *Screw it*, she said to herself. *They're already here, better or worse.* And she felt like she knew enough to know these guys weren't marauders. Another thing being a cop did for you was give you an instant sense of when people were up to no good.

And also a sense of when they were the sort who were *dangerous* to those up to no good. Sheepdogs, rather than wolves. But definitely not sheep. They were still a bit of a puzzle. But Sarah would bet the ranch they weren't bandits. Hell, she'd already bet the ranch – her home, her family, and her very life…

She smiled warmly, if tiredly, at Handon. "We're not fixed as well as we were two years ago. Of course, we long ago went through the cached food – it was originally supposed to be a year's worth, for the three of us. Only lasted ten months, in the end. Never really thought we'd put that to the test." Her gaze grew a little wistful before she went on.

"The garden has helped some, and we're just now tilling a proper field nearby, to put in grains for the spring. And there's still plenty of game. Fish in the river, though we don't trust the lake anymore. God knows what's running off into it at this point. Or, as you saw, living at the bottom of it. The forest provides plenty of fuel for the stove – if not for the generator, which needs diesel. We've inevitably had to do some scavenging, from the town you saw – and from farther afield. But it's dangerous. If we ever led them back here…" She shrugged.

Handon glanced out the kitchen window, through which a big vehicle could be seen. It looked to Handon like a 90s-era Ford Expedition.

Sarah saw him looking. "That was actually why we were back in town today, before first light. Timing belt's about shot. And there are a lot of vehicles in town."

"Did you get a replacement?" Handon asked.

She laughed. "Are you kidding? With you nutjobs shooting up the place, and riling up the dead? Rambo himself wouldn't have ventured into that."

The boy spoke for the first time. "I can go back and get the belt," he said. "I know right where that Ford is parked."

Sarah shook her head slowly. "No one goes into town alone, kiddo. You know this."

He retreated slightly beneath his flop of hair. "*You* go alone…"

"That's because Mom's an idiot," she said. "But everything will still be right where we left it later. Believe me."

Handon saw the boy go back to what he was doing before – staring with naked hunger at Alpha's weapons and kit. He evidently thought he'd landed in a Boy's Own Adventure, but with more serious small arms.

"Anyway," Sarah went on breezily, "yes, we're decently provisioned, and we've got all the critical stuff: tools, med supplies – including antibiotics, weapons, and a lot of ammunition…" Handon clocked a shotgun on a rack by the door – a very sleek Mossberg Tactical with fixed stock and pistol grip, side by side with the Mini-14. "…cooking utensils, fishing gear, radios, chargers. A lot of salt, seeds. Warm clothes. I imagine you know the routine. The usual doomsday manifest."

"Usually," Handon said, "we carry all of that on our backs."

She laughed, more warmly now.

Handon nodded at an elliptical trainer machine in the corner, beside a small rack of free weights. "We left the cross-trainer at home this time."

She laughed again. "I expect the guys wish I had. They wake up to it clanking most mornings. The worst thing about the apocalypse is that I can't go out running safely." She leaned toward Handon conspiratorially. "Don't tell them, but I sometimes get up really early and do it anyway…"

The boy looked even more embarrassed at this, and removed himself now to his room. Come to notice it, actually, Handon didn't think either of the Cameron "guys" was thrilled with the rapport he seemed to be developing with their wife and mother. He made a note to tone it down. Shakespearean family drama was about the last thing he needed right now. And amiable female companionship was hardly why he had come.

"About that radio set…" he said, putting his neutral face back on.

"Right," Sarah said, pushing herself up and away from the table. Handon started to see the effects of the free weights, with her jacket off. But just as she got up…

The cabin door knocked. Three times, strong and steady.

* * *

Everyone in the room briefly looked at everyone else, at a loss.

"Neighbors?" Juice asked.

"Well, it's not the bloody postman," Henno said. But even as he was saying it, Ali was springing lightly to her feet. She knew who it was. Before anyone could move to stop her, she opened the door.

Homer actually did look a bit like the mailman, or maybe a gentleman caller – tentative, polite. He looked like he ought to have his hat in his hand, except that he'd lost it. Ali forgot all protocol, not to mention the subterfuge around their love affair, and leapt into his arms. The reunited couple stood holding each other in the doorway for… well, Handon figured it was not quite as long as they would have liked, but a little longer than senior non-commissioned officers usually hugged one another.

Handon noted that the one who seemed to be made most uncomfortable by this display was actually… the husband, Mark Cameron. He squirmed where he sat, and looked away.

When Ali dared let go of him, Predator spoke, from his position on the couch, where having his right leg stretched out was obviously making him very happy. "Late to formation as usual," he said.

"Yeah," Henno said. "Care to fill us in, mate?"

Homer nodded as he stepped inside. He quickly worked out who the owners of the cabin must be, and nodded to each of them.

"About like you'd guess," he said. "Swam out to a safe distance and depth. Then I paralleled the shore for a mile, swam back in where it was clear. Then patrolled back into town. Saw the remains of the party you obviously threw at the church. Then I picked up your trail in the woods behind it. Tracked you here."

"You're lucky I didn't shoot you on ambush," Ali said.

"Hey, swabbie," Predator said. "Come here." From his tone and posture, it was obvious Predator had no plans to get up off the couch – perhaps ever. Homer followed his instruction. As soon as he was in range, Predator firmed up and punched him in the gut, evacuating the air from his lungs. "*That*'s for running out on a goddamned firefight." He hit him again, less hard, in the arm. "That's for screwing off for so long. Welcome back."

Predator looked across at Sarah. "Begging your pardon for the language."

She stood and walked to a radio set in the corner of the kitchen. "Mark, would you mind firing up the generator for us?" Her husband looked like he was worrying how many more soldiers, or sailors, were going to walk through his front door. But he nodded, rose, and exited. "No problem," he said over his shoulder on the way out.

When he'd gone, Sarah looked back at Predator. "Don't worry about it. I'm sure I would have kicked his ass myself for running out on a goddamned firefight." Handon, following her into the kitchen, smiled again despite himself.

Ali stole a glance at her team leader. By her unofficial count, this made four more times that

Handon had smiled today than in the entire rest of the Zulu Alpha before today.

Careful, boss, she thought to herself. *These in-theater romances can be damned awkward...*

OLD TIMER

Wesley and Derwin stepped out of the small hangar and into the sunlight, both of them looking tired and disappointed. Their search had not gone well. Between them and the other Marines that Fick had assigned to the task, they had searched what they believed to be every hangar on the naval air base, and found nothing. To top it off, the engineers who arrived with Coles had confirmed that only one of the helos they'd was in working condition, and only just. They had been left on the tarmac for a reason.

"That's all of the hangars empty, isn't it?" Wesley asked.

Derwin nodded.

Wesley looked out across the vast plain of grass that was the center of the sprawling facility. "You would think, with an air station this big, that there would be *something* lying around of use."

Derwin shrugged. "I guess they used everything available to get the hell out at the end. They would have had a lot of pilots on base, and no reason for them to leave any aircraft behind."

"They left the munitions dump behind."

Derwin regarded him with a wry smile. "Everything they could take with them. That dump is massive."

Wesley scanned out to the horizon, or what he could see of it. What had likely once been a carefully manicured field of grass was now two years overgrown and up to waist-level in places. There were a heck of a lot of buildings on the base, and even more if you went out into the areas surrounding it. There were research facilities, administration buildings, and everything that had popped up to support them, but none of those was going to help. Even if there were records of some sort inside some of the buildings, it would take them months to search, and they didn't have the time.

He was about to turn and start walking back over to the main building, where Fick would still be running his show, when his scan of the surroundings stopped on a large, sheet-metal warehouse in the distance. He frowned. It wasn't a hangar, or at least not like any of the other ones. It looked to be just inside the perimeter, but didn't appear to have a runway leading up to it.

"What do you think that place is?"

Derwin followed his gaze, and frowned. "No idea. No tarmac up to it so it's unlikely anything flies out of there."

Wesley was silent for a moment. "I think we should check it out."

Derwin sighed. "Okay. Looks like a dud to me, all the way out there. But you're the boss on this one."

The building was farther away than they had thought, and after over ten minutes of trudging through the overgrown grass and across broken roadway, they finally stood outside the main doors.

"Well it's got something like hangar doors," said Wesley.

"Yep. But look at the place. It probably hadn't

been actively used for years before the ZA." Derwin rubbed at one of the panel windows that were coated with grime and dirt. The dirt didn't come off.

The main doors wouldn't open even with both of them pulling, but they found the entrance to a small office at the side of the building. Inside, desks and a cabinet had been turned over. Paperwork and files lay strewn across the floor, covered in mold. Both men drew their side arms, and Derwin stepped inside first.

"Maybe we should call back and get the others over here?" asked Wesley.

Derwin scanned the office, his handgun pointing at spots that could provide cover. "You want to wait twenty minutes while they saddle up and conduct large-scale maneuvers to this position?"

"No, thanks," said Wesley, stepping into the doorway and making his way carefully across the floor, avoiding the debris.

The door opposite, which he guessed must lead into the main part of the warehouse, was slightly ajar. Derwin stood to one side as Wesley gave the door a light kick, then stepped back. The warehouse was almost in darkness, with very little light breaking through the dirty windows, but they could see clearly enough to know what was sitting directly in front of them, gathering dust.

The sleek wing of a fighter plane.

"This place still has power," said Derwin, nodding in the direction of a panel on the support column a few feet inside the building. Wesley peered at it, recognizing that it was an on/off switch. The red button was lit up.

He stepped towards it, reached out and pressed the green button, and an audible click echoed across the vast empty space. It was followed by a loud clanging sound as the nearest hangar door clunked to life and started retracting upwards.

"How come it still works?" asked Wesley, frowning.

"There must be a big-ass UPS battery around here somewhere," said Derwin. "Maybe it was charged up before the power was lost and it's just been sitting here ever since. I doubt it'll last long."

Wesley nodded, and they stood there watching as the massive door rose, sunlight gradually inching into the building – and slowly revealing not one, but a half dozen fighter planes crammed into the space in the middle of the warehouse. They were all covered in thick dust, and obviously had been there for a long time.

"Well," laughed Derwin, "I don't think this is quite what we were looking for, and they aren't a lot of good to us, but at least we can report back that we found aircraft."

"What are they? Why are they here?" Wesley asked.

"F-14 Tomcats. The whole fleet was retired in 2006, if I recall. Hmm, they *are* two-seaters… if there were just a few more, actually…"

He turned toward Wesley, and stopped smiling. The other man was now frowning at something, and deep in thought. Then he started walking, heading through the middle aisle of the warehouse, towards the back. Derwin followed, scanning around the edges of the echoing space as they went. In every corner the remnants of stored equipment lay stacked in great piles. From the state of the crates and boxes, it was evident that whatever was stored in them had been there for years – even before living people ceased to tread the grounds of the air station.

"Talk to me buddy," said Derwin.

"There's something out the back there."

They moved slowly past the row of mothballed fighter planes until they reached an archway two-thirds of the way into the warehouse. Behind that another large bay opened up, and this one was almost completely empty – empty apart from one enormous object that sat like an ancient behemoth, some hulking god or idol, dead in the middle of space.

It was a B-17 Flying Fortress – the legendary World War II bomber.

Derwin looked over at Wesley.

"Please tell me that you are not thinking what I think you are thinking?"

Wesley just smiled.

THE LAST TALE OF CANTERBURY

It swept through the southern part of the city before anyone even knew to be afraid. And it didn't matter that the sirens blared out their ear-piercing wail of warning for the first time since World War II. Most people in Canterbury, even in an age where the rest of the world had fallen because they hadn't been prepared, still didn't heed the warnings and follow the procedures that had been drilled into them for two years.

Starting with: *stay inside and lock your doors.*

At the sound of the siren people came outside, wondering what was wrong. Was it some sort of drill? Was there a fire? That was how a single lightning-fast zombie singlehandedly spread the plague to the point where the balance tipped. It moved amongst them at a speed no one had expected. As far as everyone in the town knew, the creatures didn't move that fast. But this gray, bedraggled thing almost flew past them in a frenzy, never stopping as it scratched, clawed, and bit its way toward the center of the city.

At the roundabout of Watling Street and Old Dover Road, an ATV sat humming, doors open, parked half off the road and half on. Caulton, Berry, and Wilson, three members of the Royal Anglian Regiment, stood their watch, as they had every day for the last three months since their posting to the south. They could hear the siren blaring, but until the radio buzzed and they got the call to move, they just waited.

Caulton, a tall man, six-foot-six and barrel-chested, sat on a concrete water mains marker a few feet away from the vehicle, smoking a cigarette and listening to his companions debate the football league and its five remaining teams. He wasn't too bothered about sport, at least not watching it, and in his opinion the downfall of the sport world due to the apocalypse rendering most athletes dead was not a life-threatening issue. His buddies disagreed. They were furiously arguing about the upcoming last match of the season, when the creature came running down Old Dover Road straight toward them.

Wilson saw it first.

"What the fuck is that?" he blurted, football forgotten in an instant. The creature was still two hundred yards away but it was closing damned fast.

Caulton frowned and then dropped his smoke, grabbing as fast as he could for his side arm. Berry still hadn't spotted the thing, and was still peering out the dirty windscreen with a look of confusion.

Then someone stepped out onto the road between them; an old man, perhaps in his eighties, who also hadn't seen the creature. He hobbled onto the tarmac and began his slow crossing, not even once looking to his sides for signs of traffic, let alone anything else. In some ways that might have been a blessing, for the Foxtrot was not one to aim or discriminate, and certainly had no concept of respecting its elders.

It passed the man while still in a full-speed gallop

toward the ATV, raising its sharp, clawed hand as it went by and tearing out the man's throat, gouging him deeply and severing his carotid artery. The old man stumbled a short distance further into the road before it even dawned on him that something was wrong. Then he fell forward, hitting the ground hard and knocking himself out instantly.

The fell creature sped onwards toward the Anglians. A hundred and fifty yards, then a hundred.

The soldiers sat in their spots, disbelieving, as the gap between them and their looming deaths shortened with every millisecond. If it hadn't been for Caulton finally snapping out of his daze it would all have been over in seconds.

The crazed dead thing raced to close the last twenty yards as Caulton hefted his handgun, raised it to level, and fired. He only had time for one shot, and it had been a long time since he had aimed at anything that ran that fast.

But luck was with him. The bullet hit the creature in the mouth, blowing a spray of flesh and dark liquid in a cloud behind it as it tumbled forward to crash onto the ground just three feet away from him. Caulton lowered his weapon.

The Foxtrot that had crawled out of the Channel Tunnel was now gone, but the infection that it had brought to Canterbury was alive and well, and even now spreading further.

Mission complete.

ONE FOR SORROW

"Sorry," Sarah said, holding the cabin's front door open for Handon, then pressing it closed behind them. "The battery's going to have to charge for a while if it's going to put out the kind of power needed to reach your ship."

"Understood," Handon said.

"We don't make a lot of long-distance calls lately. We can go in and try again in twenty minutes. Meanwhile, I thought you and I might sit and talk for a bit."

"Sounds fine," Handon said. "Here?"

He looked to a rough wooden bench on the porch. But as he did so, the front door opened again and Mark Cameron emerged – holding an axe. He paused, nodded at Handon, looked at his wife, and adjusted his grip on the axe handle. "Could use some firewood," he said, then stepped off and moved toward what Handon could see was a woodpile nearby. As he left, Handon could now also see a conspicuous bald patch on the back of his head – and also noticed the cable-knit sweater the man wore.

Sarah looked around. "We get our water from a stream nearby," she said. "It's nice to sit by the banks."

Handon gestured. "Lead on."

* * *

"Christ, mate," Henno said, looking over at Juice. "You trumped again, didn't you?"

Juice, by now used to Henno's exotic Yorkshire-speak, knew what that meant – he'd just been accused of farting. "Screw you, man. I'm innocent." Everyone there also knew that Juice had on many previous occasions been guilty.

"Well, something cleared the room. Everyone's skived off."

And this was true, even if somewhat garbled. Handon had left with the woman. Ali and Homer were on the porch, probably cuddling. The scientist was in isolation in the parents' bedroom – frantically reviewing his research notes, now that it looked like saving humanity was back in play – and the boy was off sulking in his. God knew where the husband was.

Only Predator, Juice, and Henno remained in the main room of the cabin.

"May as well use the time for weapons maintenance," Juice said. He pulled a cleaning kit out of his ruck and started to break down his baby – a Swiss Arms SG 553 assault rifle. Since its last cleaning, it had been frozen in the upper atmosphere, pawed at by jackrabbit zombies, dunked in the lake – and, moreover, had put out nearly a thousand rounds of high-velocity 5.56mm. In fact, none of that was likely to slow it down, much less jam it.

But Juice couldn't have it thinking he didn't love it.

He briefly eyed Predator. "Don't give me that look," Pred snapped. "*I'm* going to use the time for sitting still for just five fucking minutes. For once."

"Aye," Henno agreed, nodding. "Doing fuck-all is the way forward."

Juice shrugged. He couldn't fault them. It had been non-stop and a thousand-miles-an-hour lately. And while Tier-1 guys weren't known for sitting on their asses, still it was a military axiom that one ought to rest when one may. Because the opportunity may not come again soon.

Or at all.

* * *

"One for sorrow," Homer said, pointing up and to the west.

Ali followed the ray of his finger, but didn't see it. "What am I looking at?"

"A magpie," Homer said. "See the black and white? With the flash of iridescent blue?"

"Got it. Beautiful bird."

"Smart, too. They're of the corvid family, with ravens and crows. Very clever creatures. Once, in London, I saw a raven cracking open a nut on the corner of a CCTV camera housing."

The two warriors sat now on the bench on the front porch, having landed on it a few minutes after Handon and Sarah passed it up for more privacy. For these two, though, it was enough. To withdraw any further would draw comment.

The sun was fully up now, though the sky was mostly cloudy, and the air very cool. They had been getting more northerly, starting from Chicago – which was already no beach holiday in November. And both the lateness of the season and the increasing latitude meant that the days were getting very short, and the sun hugging the horizon.

"Why sorrow?" Ali asked, squeezing his hand.

"What?"

"You said, 'One for sorrow'."

"Oh. It's an English nursery rhyme. There's an omen associated with whatever number of magpies you might see. Unfortunately…"

An easy and peaceful half-smile lingered on Ali's face now. She was feeling alive and whole, and more so with every moment Homer was back. Though this good feeling was not totally without reservations. She had absolutely zero desire to feel that much dependency on another person. She had certainly never been that way before – and it was especially dodgy now, when people could be, and often were, taken away from you in one bad blink of an eye.

The ZA had not been good for human intimacy.

"Unfortunately what?" Ali said, prompting him after he trailed off.

He looked up at her, and slowly recalled what he'd been saying. "Unfortunately… magpies are very solitary. So it's most often just one you see. One for sorrow."

Ali laughed. "Good thing we don't believe in omens. What are the others?"

"Let's see… 'One for sorrow / Two for mirth / Three for a wedding / Four for a birth…' Though some say 'Four for death'. I gather there are different versions of it. I forget the rest."

Homer paused and pointed again. Sure enough, a second bird had appeared, striking and sleek, both of them swooping to the ground, and closer to the cabin now.

"Two for mirth," Ali said.

And as she said it, deep and raucous laughter erupted right behind them, muted by the thick wood walls, but still very audible. Homer twisted to face Ali, and gave her a look that she wanted to find smug… but it just seemed cute to her. She laughed, reluctantly. Now was probably not the time to give Homer the lecture about coincidences – and about humankind's troublesome propensity to find cosmic significance every time two events in the world matched up in any way whatsoever. About how luck was an imaginary concept.

Then again. It was certainly luck that they were both still alive – as their friends Pope and Ainsley were not. And luck that they were still together. But Ali imputed no cosmic significance to these facts – they were just random outcomes of contingent fate in an arbitrary and uncaring universe.

But, while their survival, their finding of each other, had no cosmic meaning… still it held a hell of a lot of meaning *for her*.

And that was enough.

* * *

"We reserve use of the generator for really critical

things, and of course for emergencies," Sarah said, from ahead of Handon. The two walked now down an overgrown trail, blanketed with damp leaves, and menaced by hanging branches above and undergrowth below. If it had once been a deer run, the deer had abandoned it. Visibility was about fifteen feet. Handon touched his side arm. He'd left his rifle inside, just as his guide had left hers.

But she, too, wore a handgun.

"And it's just gotten too dangerous going out to siphon fuel," Sarah said. "Takes too long, makes too much noise. And at this point, we've used every drop to be had in the village. So now it means a trip further afield."

"I know just how you feel," Handon said. "Our missions keep stretching farther and farther out. And the risks mount. I see you've got the generator and fuel tank positioned away from the house, up against the fence. Smart."

"Yes, even with the dead running around, fire safety is important. More important, come to think of it. And I really try not to let the fuel tank get below half empty. The last thing we need is to have to stage a scavenging mission right in the middle of an emergency – a medical crisis, or if we need the radio for some reason."

Handon smiled. "Once again, welcome to our world. Military logistics and planning – with scare quotes around the 'planning' part."

Watching her walk ahead of him, he also noted that Sarah had left her hunting jacket off, revealing a long-sleeve synthetic T-shirt with the sleeves pushed up. The cold air didn't seem to bother her. And Handon could see better now that she was slim, or slender – though by no means petite, or vanishing. Mainly, she looked healthy, and extremely functional.

She also looks pretty damned good, Handon couldn't stop himself thinking.

But very quickly, and luckily to his way of thinking, the two emerged into the open, on the banks of a small stream. It tumbled quietly over smooth stones as it wound its way back toward the town, and down into the lake. Sarah led him to a fallen tree, perfectly positioned for a view of the water, and the top of which someone had carved into a wide flat section.

A bench seat, for two. They sat.

Sarah looked across at Handon levelly. "Okay," she said. "Now why don't you tell me why you're here. Or, at least, whatever of it you can tell me."

Handon nodded. He appreciated her acknowledgement of their need for operational security, or OPSEC. He certainly wanted to tell her what he could. And something about the way she made him feel had him wanting to tell her everything.

Though, like most temptations, he reminded himself, *that one is to be resisted.*

While he was still planning his answer, she said, "You already said you're based in the UK."

"Yes," Handon said. "And, from your guess, I figured you must have picked up one of the beacons."

Shortly after Britain had stabilized its borders and

tamped down internal outbreaks – and also figured out that no other country in the world had done so – they had started broadcasting worldwide on a variety of radio frequencies. The messages repeated day and night, on a loop, explaining that there were survivors in Britain – and that humankind was still in the fight. It also listed frequencies that they monitored, which other survivors could use to make contact.

"Did you radio in?" Handon asked.

"Yes," Sarah said. "We're on their registry. I can't say that's made much difference to our day-to-day struggle."

Somewhere in CentCom, Handon knew, they maintained a list of all known pockets of survivors around the world. He thought he remembered the biggest one was a few thousand. And the smallest were single dudes. LaMOEs.

"I know it's not much," he said. "But the idea is: *some day*. When we beat the virus. When we figure out some way to destroy the dead. One day, when we fight our way back, they can use the registry to go around and police up survivors, everyone who made it."

"It's a nice dream."

This made Handon a little sad. He said, "You're right there's nothing we can do for those people right now. But it takes little enough power to send out the transmissions. And they say it helps us hang on to our humanity. By not abandoning others to their fate. Wherever they may be. And whether or not they ultimately make it."

"Okay," Sarah said, monitoring the plashing waters

as they burbled by. “That’s all nice enough. But if you can’t rescue people… then what *are* you doing, actually? Your team is clearly not sitting around making cave paintings.”

Handon smiled. “Back to your original question.” He was still pondering how to answer it.

Sarah turned in and pinned him with her eyes, which he now saw were a rich, forest green, with tiny flecks of exotic black. They also seemed to be some unlikely combination of flinty and kind. Like they could flash with either boundless compassion or ice-cold malevolence as the situation required.

Also, deep down beneath all that, was something like vulnerability. But well buried.

And, in that instant of looking into her eyes, Handon decided: he trusted her. He knew he’d trusted her, for some reason, the minute he laid eyes on her. And that made it reciprocal. Because Handon knew perfectly well the risks she had taken. Not just in rescuing them – but in bringing them back to her sanctuary. She had risked everything. So she must have felt like she knew something about them, as well.

Or maybe just about Handon.

“We’re scavengers,” he said. “Ranging outside of Britain, but solely in Europe – until now.”

“Scavenging for what?”

“There are other teams, out looking for all kinds of things society needs to run: food, seeds, manufactured things. Industrial parts, electronics. Medicine. Fuel.” He paused, still holding her gaze. “But our team is single-purpose. What we’re searching for is a cure.”

"A cure?"

"Or pieces of it. Research. Samples. Chemical or genetic models. Clues, roadmaps. We launch these ops over the water to the labs of pharmaceutical companies, biotechs, university research labs… Anyplace we think might have been on the trail of a cure. Before the fall."

Sarah looked very intent as she processed this. "And so what would a cure look like?"

"From what they tell me, most people think it will either be a vaccine, or a serum. Or some kind of gene therapy."

"And did you find such a thing? Out on Lake Michigan?"

Handon looked back to her from the stream. "Our target was Chicago. A biotech, downtown."

"Jesus," Sarah said. "What was Chicago like?"

"Crowded."

She laughed. "You still didn't answer the question. Did you find it?"

Handon looked across at her again. For some reason, their conversation was zero small talk, and all cutting right to the heart of things. Maybe there was no time for anything else. "I'm not sure," he said. "We found Dr. Park, and we got him out, along with his research materials. And he's got hold of something."

Handon tossed a stem he'd been winding into the stream.

"He thinks he's close."

THE AIR BETWEEN THEM

"How were things in the town?" Homer asked, finally stirring them both from the sweet reverie he and Ali had been enjoying on the porch. It was so pleasant to be out of doors, out of danger, alive, and there together. "It looked hairy around the church."

Ali shrugged. "I don't know. Every time you think it's gotten as bad as it can get, and still have anybody survive… Every time you think we've taken it right down to the wire…"

Homer smiled, puzzlingly to Ali. "Well, it couldn't have been worse than Chicago. Could it?"

Ali softened. "No. You're right. You've got me there."

"And we survived that." He paused again.

"*Please* don't tell me it must have been for some higher purpose."

Homer was imperturbable. "Well, I don't know about you," he said with laughter in his voice. "But I didn't make that trip for no reason."

Ali spluttered. "That was *our* purpose! Not a divine one!"

Homer nodded, serenely. "Maybe. And maybe you can tell the difference."

"Goddammit, Homer." But she immediately

regretted saying it. She reached across and squeezed his right bicep with her left hand. She changed the subject. "What's your take on the situation here?"

"What – in the cabin, with the Camerons? You tell me."

"Okay." Ali generally hesitated long before speaking ill of people. She also took a look around to see if anyone was within earshot. *Screw it*, she thought. "I think the kid is trouble. Just a sense I've got. I'm afraid he's going to bring the swarm down on us."

"Teenage boys usually are trouble," Homer said. That struck Ali as uncharacteristically uncharitable. Or maybe that was just him trying to be funny.

"The husband is obviously the weakest link," Ali added. "But probably harmless. Now Sarah… she's amazing, as anybody can see. But I don't think she likes me very much."

"Why not?"

"Mostly because her husband *does* like me too much."

Ali shrugged again. She was basically dismissive of domesticity, and she knew it, without being proud of it. Sarah's were choices Ali never made – never had the opportunity to make.

Homer said, "I wouldn't be too hard on the husband. He probably hasn't laid eyes on another living female in over two years. I'm sure he means well."

Ali blinked once, heavily, but kept silent. Homer always thought everyone meant well. He always thought the best of everyone. Come to consider it, she had no idea how he was still alive at this point.

Maybe it *was* God looking out for him.

It had to be something.

* * *

"That a waterproof pouch for your cleaning kit?" Henno asked Juice.

"Yeah. I've gotten soaked to the skin on what turned out to be a long-ass mission, just one too many damned times."

Predator looked over from the couch. "How many times was that?"

Juice looked up at him like this was a strange question. "Once," he said.

Just as he was sliding the upper receiver of his rifle back onto the lower, the boy emerged again from his bedroom. Juice guessed he'd heard the discussion, as well as the clacking. He got a strong sense the kid was interested in weapons. Then again, at this point, pretty much anybody interested in going on living had better be.

Juice nodded seriously to the adolescent, as the boy entered and resumed holding up a wall. "What's your weapon of choice, then?" Juice asked. He was thinking the kid was more than old enough to go armed. *Hell, there was arguably no such thing as too young anymore. Especially not out here.*

The boy nodded toward the gun rack by the door. "I know how to use the shotgun."

Predator perked up at this conversation. "Is that

what you carry when you go out?"

The boy looked at his shoes. "Not really. Most of the time, Mom doesn't let me."

Henno and Predator laughed aloud at this – and, before he could stop himself, Juice chuckled as well. But, trying to be conciliatory, he said, "Must be rough living in a world with one woman."

"We live in a world with one woman," said Predator.

"Yeah," said Henno, "but she's his mum!"

They both shouted with laughter.

Juice saw the kid's face going beet red. He cleared the chamber of the rifle, locked the bolt back, and waved the boy over. "C'mon, I'll show you how to use this one."

* * *

Handon and Sarah had now sat in companionable silence for a few minutes. She was clearly absorbing everything he had told her, the implications and importance of it. About the possibility of a cure.

Finally, Handon said, gently, "I'm sorry you lost your dog."

She looked at him, surprised. Handon gestured back up the trail behind them. "I saw the metal eye screwed into the porch. No chain, but no other obvious reason for it."

Sarah nodded. "Yes, there used to be four of us."

"How'd you lose him?"

"The usual way. He got eaten." Handon gave her a stage reaction – the scandalized look. "Not by us!" she said quickly. "Jesus. We loved that dog."

Handon smiled. "I know. Of course you did. Why the chain, by the way, if you had the fence?"

"Built the fence after we lost the dog."

"Good thinking."

"It's necessary, but not sufficient. You don't want to get trapped in there. But I figured it to save us from a lone one or pair, wandering in while we're sleeping."

"Has that ever happened?"

"I've seen one or two go by in the dead of night. We were lucky they didn't catch scent of us. If that's how they do it."

"Our experience has been it's more sound than smell."

"Agreed. That's why I've religiously avoided gunfire anywhere within five miles of the cabin – and worked hard to avoid it elsewhere. So far, the secret of our location has been kept."

Handon rested his forearms on his knees and leaned forward. "What brought you all out here? Why the bug-out location?" He took the risk of trying on some of the survivalism lingo, offering it as a shibboleth. She was clearly a survivalist of some type – you could tell because she'd survived. Also, everything in the cabin screamed of it. Including the existence of the cabin itself. And, at this point in time, it hardly looked like a radical fringe movement anymore.

"I suppose it's a hobby," she said. "A bit like any

other. You start off storing some bottled water and a first aid kit, and it kind of goes from there. Also, I think it was in part the police work that shaped my view. When you deal with the worst examples of human behavior, day in and day out… well, it's easy to develop a pessimistic view of the prospects for human civilization."

Handon nodded. He knew what she meant. Though he had generally killed the bad people he dealt with before getting very close to them. He didn't do a lot of restraining suspects, searching them, or booking them into custody. But he guessed she had.

"Also, there were the debt-to-GDP ratios," she added. Handon arched his eyebrows at this. He didn't get it. She elaborated.

"The math stopped working. The public debt in most western countries, the U.S. and Canada included, well, it got so high that, mathematically, it could never go down again. With all the social spending that was set in stone, there was no way to tax enough of a surplus to pay down the debt. Not without cratering the economies of these countries. The best long-term scenario was something like Greece. In the worst, major currencies collapsed, governments defaulted on sovereign debt – and the U.S. and Canadian governments basically folded."

"So you were ready for a breakdown in government services. Maybe a major civil unrest."

"Yes. But we weren't ready for this."

"Nobody was. And you were a hell of a lot better prepared than most."

She smiled sardonically. "Well, I certainly don't regret the five hundred dollars I dropped on that Mossberg."

Handon smiled. "Excellent zombie-fighting weapon. As any video-game player back in the world could have told you." They both chuckled. "And is that why your cabin is in the U.S., rather than across the border? To keep the heavier hardware?"

"One of the reasons. The gun laws are certainly laxer here. There was also the location – distant from major population centers, isolated. But also within striking distance of a town, if we needed supplies or support. It's also a good spot for fish and game. And only a day's drive from Toronto. Finally…" and with this she looked around her, with obvious affection. "The Manistee National Forest is totally beautiful. This was our weekend retreat, before all of this."

Handon took a second to look around as well. "Is that where we are?"

"Actually, we're just off it. You can't build in the national forest itself. But a lot of property on or near the lake is privately held. And the forest stretches out behind us, and to the north and south, for forty miles in every direction."

Handon piped down, and just enjoyed the silence for a minute. The stillness. The peace. Something they'd known damned little of lately. Finally, he shook his head and said, "Yesterday morning we were over the Atlantic, packing our chutes and getting ready to jump into Chicago. Everything seems to happen so damned fast in the Zulu Alpha."

"The what?"

"Sorry. Military phonetic alphabet slang. Zulu Alpha – the Zo—"

"I get it from there," she said, gently. "But I don't know that I agree with you. The spread of the disease, and the collapse, of course they happened unbelievably fast. But, since then… well, actually, everything has seemed to take forever."

She turned to face him, and he dared look back into her eyes.

They sat this way, breathing, and feeling electricity pour out into the moment, until the air between them was swollen and raging with it.

* * *

Ali and Homer had been sitting in happy and intimate silence themselves. But it had now started to go on too long. It had acquired a subtext. Like Handon, Ali was also feeling increasingly like life was short – you never knew how short, in this fallen world. And talking around the real topic was silly at best. At worst, it might prove tragic – put off too long, and forever regretted.

She stole another look at the side of Homer's face. She could see it written there.

"You've been thinking about your family, haven't you?" She said it gently. Not as an accusation.

He hardly hesitated before replying. "How not?"

Homer never knew how to talk about his wife and children with Ali. It was like two parallel universes, ones which could never intersect. As if, when he was in one, the other was totally unreal, notional, theoretical. As, he supposed ruefully, his old life and family now *were* unreal.

They were gone. Almost certainly.

But Ali seemed to understand all this, without him having to say anything. He said it anyway. He had to clear his throat first, and then spoke very quietly.

"I swore something to myself going into this mission…" But then he trailed off.

Ali put her finger to his lips, shushing him. She had felt this coming. It had always been coming. She knew that things were changing quickly. On this mission, which was of such unspeakable importance… well, for Homer, duty had always come first.

And it would still come first now.

But this mission would soon be drawing to a close. (*One way or the other*, Ali mentally amended.) They had the mission objective. All that remained was getting it out, and safely back to their command authority. There were still a huge number of question marks, and terrible risks still lay ahead. But they had already traversed half the length of Lake Michigan – halfway from Chicago to Beaver Island. Only half remained.

Ali was also aware of the biggest change: they were now on the other side of the Atlantic. And Homer was out on the ground. She could feel the pull his old home exerted on him, so much closer than it had ever been before. She could feel the growing weight and leverage of everything he'd left behind.

Of course everyone had left so much behind. And none of it was coming back. But once they got to extraction, and Homer's duty was fulfilled… maybe then he would be free? Ali didn't know. But she was afraid.

When she looked up again, there were three magpies now, clustered and hopping around the base of an ancient and bare cedar-hemlock at the edge of the clearing.

Homer spoke evenly, as if in a trance.

"Three for a wedding."

But to whom? Ali thought to herself, sadly.

She guessed she'd find out.

DARKNESS REVISITED

She still jumped at most noises, and thought every movement in the old tenement building had to be one of the dead. The bump of a closing door or the creaking of old floorboards set her nerves on edge every time, even though she told herself that it was just other people moving around. It was an instinct born of two years inside the darkness of the Channel Tunnel, always listening for signs of movement that shouldn't be there, or sounds that weren't being made by her fellow survivors. It would be a long time before she could put that aside and live normally – as normally as life in Fortress Britain allowed.

It had only been a couple of days, though, she kept telling herself.

The daylight was also painful, the light hurt her eyes, and that wasn't even the full glare of the sun; just stepping out into the daylight clouded her senses as though the sun itself were on fire and burned a hundred times brighter than it did for everyone else.

Amarie glanced down towards Josie, who lay breathing, and making little whistling noises, in the cot next to her. A few moments of peace as the child slept. This was nothing to be taken for granted, as Josie also suffered from the same problems. Bright light, odd sounds, all of these things were alien to the tiny girl, who had been born and developed for eighteen months in near complete darkness. If they went outside during the day she was apt to cry or twist around in her stroller trying to turn her face away from the sunlight.

They would both adjust in time, Amarie thought as she stroked her daughter's thin, soft hair. They would get used to daylight and the noises that people made, and they would find some place to be in this new world. That much she was very grateful for; all the time she had spent in the tunnel with her fellow refugees from France she had thought – had been convinced – that the world outside was finished, dead and gone, humanity wiped out on a global scale forever, and that they would have to spend their entire lives living underground, fighting off the zombies that always found them again. Now, outside of the tunnel, she had discovered that not only were people still surviving, but they were surviving in their millions; a whole nation on one island still fighting against the tide of the dead that crept ever closer.

And it was an island that had defended itself in the same way for centuries before – by being an island. Zombies could not get on boats and launch an invasion.

Amarie stared out of the window, trying to force her eyes to cope with even the dim light that shone through the net curtains that she had hung up, and she began to think, as she had done many times since their rescue, about what they would do next. London seemed the obvious choice, as it seemed the only choice to many, and she wondered when they would be allowed out of their quarantine. Two more days minimum, they had been told, and until then they were only allowed to walk in the tenement grounds.

London. She had dreamt of visiting the city all her life, and had nearly made the journey a couple of times. She had even hoped she might travel there with Wesley when he finished his security contract in Paris. That was what he had suggested a few weeks before… before that last time she had seen him.

"I've got a place there if you want to come with me," he had said, and she had smiled. Now she wasn't smiling. Back then she had been coy, and undecided. She hadn't wanted to seem too keen to follow him. She hadn't wanted to scare him away by being overpowering in her affections, even though she knew she would have followed the man anywhere, and career be damned. Now, she just wondered if he was alive – and if she would ever find him.

Find him and tell him that he had a child that he didn't even know existed.

It wasn't how she had wanted her first visit to London to be, but now it seemed she may get to visit the place after all. Though she wondered if it would still be the thriving, bustling hive of life that she had always imagined.

There was a small supply shop directly across the street; she could see it from her window on the fourth floor, and she watched as people came and went, carrying bags full of goods and walking off in whatever direction their homes lay. Every day a truck arrived outside, and two soldiers stood guard while two other men pushed overloaded carts through the doors and came back with empty ones. A couple of days more and she would be allowed to go there herself and not depend on the supply drop.

She watched two soldiers standing guard and talking to each other, wondering if they could give her any news of her homeland – for no one had been forthcoming about France. Everyone she asked merely frowned at her and tried to change the subject. They just didn't understand that all she wanted was a simple answer, in fact just a confirmation of what she already knew: that her homeland and everyone in it was dead.

She thought now of her parents in the south, the rolling slopes of the vineyard that she had played in as a child, and wondered if now the dead walked lumbering through those beautiful landscapes.

And that was when the sirens began to blare.

For a moment Amarie was confused. The noise was alien to her, but her head cleared and it all clicked into place as she watched the two soldiers force the delivery men to stay inside the shop, and jumped back into their truck. The door of the shop closed, and then the metal shutters lowered as the truck raced off up the road. Amarie looked down the street, and saw people coming out of their homes and looking up and down.

They had been told of the sirens, told about the drill if an imminent outbreak was happening. But they had also told them that it was very unlikely to ever be necessary. Amarie felt her heart beating in her chest, and tried to calm herself. This wasn't bad. This was nothing like what she had experienced every day in the tunnel. They said there had been no outbreaks near Canterbury for over a year. There was nothing to worry about. They would be in quarantine for a couple of days and then they would be shipped to London.

There would be no outbreak.

Then she heard the gunfire.

And then she heard the screams.

DALLIANCE

Sarah shifted slightly on the waterside log-bench she still shared with Handon. She paused a beat, then looked at him intently. "Were you ever married?"

Handon looked back across at her. He definitely wasn't used to answering personal questions – not in his past life and career, and definitely not lately. He answered anyway. "Once. But we divorced years ago."

"Is she..."

Monitoring the dirt and foliage at his feet again, Handon shook his head slowly. "I tried to contact her. Before the fall. During. A bit after."

Sarah's expression grew tender. "She was at Fort Bragg?"

This drew Handon up, and he looked at her, eyes slitted. "How'd you guess that?"

"Home of the Airborne," she said. "And Special Forces. Didn't take you for a mechanic."

Handon laughed. "Special Forces has mechanics. They're amazing."

"No doubt," said Sarah, and she meant it. For some reason, she felt like pushing her luck, intimacy-wise. "Kids?"

"No. We tried. But I probably did too much rescuing of nuclear materials casks or something."

Actually, the fertility problem had been with her. Or so the doctors had said. And it had been mainly

Handon who wanted a child. He had been looking forward to retirement from the military. And he'd been thinking about what might give his life meaning, after the fight was over for him.

Ha, he thought to himself. *Little did I know…*

But he pushed those thoughts away and changed the subject. Back to her.

"You're lucky to have your family around you. And they're obviously damned lucky to have you."

She gazed at the stream – seeming to Handon to be making a decision about her response, as well. "Of course I love my son very much…" *The hell with it*, she in turn thought. *Life is WAY too short to tell polite untruths.* "But they need so much management, reassurance, propping up, protecting… I'm sorry, I'm just very tired. It's been a long two years."

For a moment, Handon wasn't sure how to react to this. He spoke hesitantly. "Well, you must have them trained up pretty well now… and I'm sure Mark is very devoted to you." He braced himself, not knowing if he'd said the wrong thing.

She paused before answering. "Well, yes. On the upside, Mark has always been faithful. Then again, men are said to be exactly as faithful as their opportunities to stray are few."

Handon laughed. "And there are damned few opportunities these days."

"Oh, hell, who are we kidding? There were damn few for him back before all this."

The both laughed together now. They also both

rocked slightly – in sync with each other. Weight seemed to fall from Sarah as she plowed ahead. Basically, she hadn't had anyone to really talk to since she could remember. She spoke easily now.

"I fell out of love with Mark a long time ago." She exhaled through puffed cheeks. "I'd been waiting for the right moment, and the courage, to end the marriage. But then all this happened. Now, obviously, there's not much point – especially with the boy to look after. How could I get divorced, anyway? All the lawyers got eaten."

"One nice thing."

Her smile bloomed, then faded slowly, and she grew a little sad again. "Also, for all I knew, my husband and son were the last two living people I was ever going to set eyes on."

"And yet, here we are," Handon said. "Just goes to show, you never know."

"No, you don't." But Sarah didn't seem like she was done unburdening herself. As if she'd been burdened for an awfully long time. "Mark was never the most impressive or manly husband back in the world. He was an okay domestic partner when society took care of almost everything for us. But here in the Crunch… well, this has not been his moment to shine."

"May I ask why you got married?"

"Of course you can ask." The hours they had known each other were starting to seem like bigger units of time. And they were both starting to acknowledge that fact. Again, there was little point in dodging it – not when this hour might be their only one. "Mark happened to come along at a very bad point in my life –

when… well, something bad had happened. And he was there for me then. Afterward, I suppose we stayed together out of habit, or maybe my lingering gratitude toward him. It was pleasant enough for a while. And when the gloss of pleasantness wore off, it still seemed too much trouble, and too painful, to tear it all down – just for the sake of going out to try and find something better."

"And your son?"

"I think we had him because it seemed like the thing to do. To make the marriage make sense."

"But it didn't work. Or not well enough that you had another one."

"No. And God knows we're not going to now. I… I try to be maternal to the boy, but it doesn't seem to be my strongest trait. Also, when every little decision can tip your odds of survival, it's so much harder to take feelings into account, to forgive his mistakes, to be kind."

"You must have had him very young." He saw her raise her eyebrows at him. He went ahead and dug himself in deeper. "Being in your early thirties, I mean… very early thirties…"

She kept him in agony for a few seconds. "I'm thirty-eight, actually." She paused. "I just take care of myself. I suppose you have to these days, don't you?"

Handon nodded. "One nice thing about the apocalypse. No processed foods."

"Ha!" The green of her eyes warmed, right in front of his. "Yes. Vegetables from the garden, meat on the hoof. No pesticides. Though, to be honest, I've always been a bit of a health nut. Comes with the job, if you take it seriously."

Handon watched the ground as he said, "That also explains why you look like that."

"Like what?"

And Command Sergeant Major Handon experienced an emotion he had probably not felt since Basic: awkwardness. *Jesus – what the hell am I doing?* he asked himself. He had responsibilities. Danger was on all sides of them – and now, possibly, right here in front of him. In this… this thing that was happening.

Could he afford this kind of distraction, or weakness, or vulnerability? He'd seen what it did to operational efficiency, and seen it damned recently. He saw how a critical mission parameter, the one dictating that force protection be sacrificed to the mission objective, went out the window when Ali missed her drop and Homer followed her down onto the streets of Chicago. By rights, that should have resulted in his death on top of hers.

It was all very bad juju.

Handon simply couldn't allow himself to be… *dallying* like this. It wasn't like him. It was almost exactly *unlike* him, in fact. But the person who was having these feelings hardly felt like him at all. Certainly, Handon hadn't expected to feel this way. He hadn't expected his heart to lurch like this – probably ever again. And he was too self-aware not to recognize what was happening to him.

But I'd damned well better be strong enough to get it under control, he thought.

He also knew that in any conflict between personal feelings and his duty, personal feelings were going to go down hard. This was what made them so dangerous to indulge, or even to feel.

Because he still had a mission to complete. And he had a team to lead – six very important people he needed to get out of there alive. And they were all still deep in Zulu country, even if they felt momentarily safe. He simply couldn't allow himself to be lulled this way.

Or this badly distracted.

* * *

Mark appeared from outside, walking into the main room of the cabin. He carried an armload of firewood, his axe stacked up on top. He looked annoyed. Juice guessed maybe he'd heard the laughter from outside. Mark quickly saw his son with Juice's assault rifle, working the bolt and peering into the chamber.

"What are you doing with that?" he asked.

The boy looked up. "Juice is showing me how to use it."

"No," Mark said. "It's bad enough with all your mother's guns. Give it back. Now."

Juice gently took the weapon back from him.

Mark Cameron looked around the room – in particular to where Predator had his feet up. "Has anybody seen my wife?"

No one answered. Predator had to bite his tongue not to say, "I've seen the top of her head." Something about the emasculated patriarch of this clan brought out his inner bully.

Mark stalked across the room and let the firewood clatter down onto the stone beside the fireplace. He gathered himself before turning back to face the room. "Look," he said. "I don't know why you people are here. I'm not sure why Sarah brought you back. Maybe it's because she still hasn't given up on the world. She wants to know that there's something still out there. But there's not. There's only the three of us. All we've got is *us*."

No one had any response to this either.

"Look," Cameron finally said, "what is it you people want?"

"Honestly, dude?" Predator said, swiveling his huge head up to face the man in the fuzzy sweater. "Mainly I just want *this moment to end...*"

Juice stood up hastily. "Sir, we're just waiting for the radio to charge, then we're going to be on our way. Thank you for all you've done for us."

Mark looked to his son. "I want you to go out and find your mother. Now. Go."

Hair hanging in front of face, his body language broadcasting embarrassment and anger, the boy rose and stalked from the room. He paused long enough to grab the Mossberg shotgun from its place on the gun rack.

He slammed the door with an ugly report that shook the cabin.

* * *

In the silence that still lay unbroken between Sarah and Handon, she fought her own mini-battle with feelings that were very unfamiliar. And that were also not the least bit sensible, or salutary to any of their chances for survival.

There was something about the American soldier that was incredibly stirring. Obviously, he was manly and resolute, in every way that Mark was not. So if something had been missing for her, well, here it now sat. Also, as she turned these feelings over, trying to make sense of them… well, it seemed to her there was something about him that made her *want to live.* Through all of this. And to be more remarkable. To achieve more. To be her best self.

Though, of course, just surviving another day was a pretty damned remarkable accomplishment these days.

And these were also feelings she hadn't felt in a long time. And only now did she realize that maybe she hadn't been fully alive, also not for a long time. She had survived, sure. And she'd functioned at a high level, keeping her family alive, against the worst possible odds. But, still, some deep part of her that was the most authentic Sarah… well, she started to wonder if that part of her, out of sight, out of her consciousness, had been silently bleeding away. If maybe, without her noticing, she had already slid most of the way down the road to… well, to becoming no different from the dead that surrounded them.

If maybe she wasn't three parts dead already.

Was love the key to really being alive? And being more than just one of the walking dead herself?

But none of this meant she didn't recognize the danger. She changed the topic.

"Well, Sergeant Major, you told me where you've been. Why don't you tell me where you're planning on going. From here."

She thought he looked a little relieved at this.

"North," he said. "We need to get to Beaver Island."

"That is pretty northerly," she said. "And it explains the boat."

"It was sort of the other way around," Handon said. "The boat was our only way out of Chicago. And we were told there's an airfield on the island. So our big idea was to sail to it. But then we lost our wind. And the current took us up into… what is the name of that town?"

"It's called Glenbrook. Why Beaver Island?"

"There's an airport there. Someplace a plane can land and extract us."

Sarah looked impressed. "So there are still transatlantic flights, then."

"No," Handon said. "We have a ship, off the coast of Virginia."

Sarah looked confused. "What kind of ship can you land a…" But then she trailed off. The question obviously answered itself. Finally, she said, "Seriously?"

"Yes. The *John F. Kennedy*. Her crew's at half strength, less now, I gather. And most of her ops involve scavenging for supplies to keep going. But she floats."

Sarah nodded, eyes still slightly squinted. "I can believe that. With nuclear power, she'd be damned close to self-sufficient… closer than us, at any rate. Her captain certainly won't have to go around sucking on siphon hoses."

Handon laughed. And he thought he could almost see Sarah swell with hope – perhaps more than she had in a long time. He figured maybe she'd written off humanity. Now he had appeared with the news that it wasn't over yet. He gave her a few seconds with this, before getting back to immediate concerns.

"What's your recommendation for us on getting up to the top of the lake? Oh, did I mention that our boat sank?"

"Yes, I actually saw that." She looked sidelong at him, wondering if he knew how close she had come to leaving them to their fate. She guessed that maybe he did – and that he wouldn't hold it against her. He'd probably tell her to ditch the strangers next time. It was survival.

"Is there another suitable craft in town? Or can we try to go overland? Up the lake shore?"

"No – on both counts. If there were another boat in town, you wouldn't want to go back there for it. It's too dangerous now, maybe impossible, with the critters all riled up. I don't think they'll settle down for days, maybe weeks. And overland's too dangerous. Never mind that you'd have to get on the water eventually anyway, to get to the island."

"Good point. So what does that leave?"

"I know where we can get you another boat. Next

town up."

"Outstanding. Homer will be thrilled."

"That your swabbie?"

Handon smiled. "Yes."

"I don't mean to be flippant," Sarah said. "I think he's fascinating, actually. He looks a bit like an angel descended to earth. His soul just comes right out of his eyes." Handon arched an eyebrow at this. He didn't think she was wrong. But, once again, her perceptiveness took him by surprise. "What is his story?" she asked.

Handon wasn't sure that was for him to tell. "Well, he's a man of faith, I can tell you that."

"Christian?"

"Yes."

"Christians are often the loveliest people, aren't they?"

Handon nodded. He thought: *The fact that they're utterly deluded about the origin and nature of the universe hardly counts against them. Not in the scheme of being a good human being…*

Instead, he said, "I hadn't really thought about it. But of course you're right. It certainly seems to work for Homer."

"And where does all his sadness come from?"

Handon looked over at her again – amazed at how much she saw.

"He lost his family. And his duty to this job, to mankind really, prevented him from ever going to look for them. This has haunted him. I think it was bearable while he was an ocean away from them. Now that he's unexpectedly back here…"

Sarah nodded. "I hope he finds peace."

And for all of us, thought Handon. He paused, recalling their main topic. "I'm guessing we're looking at about a hundred miles of lake to Beaver Island from here?"

"One-ten or one-twenty, I'd think, depending on the course you chart. We can check the map. We also have to get you to th—"

A loud bang sounded, from the direction of the cabin. In fact, it merely sounded like a door slamming. But, as everyone who'd lived to this point had long ago learned to avoid loud noises, it signaled something amiss. Sarah hopped lightly to her feet.

"Come on. The radio should be good to go now."

Handon followed her back down the trail.

And, God save him, he did his best to avoid checking her out as she walked ahead of him…

RAVEN

For Ali and Homer out on the porch, three things happened almost at once.

First the front door banged open behind them, then slammed shut, as the boy came through it. He had a big shotgun cradled in his arms – and before Ali realized it, she had flipped the thumb break on her ballistic nylon holster, making her HK USP Tactical ready to draw. This was almost an autonomous reaction, and the kid was off the porch, out the gate, and running down the road before Ali even realized her hand was on the gun.

Second, Ali realized Homer was pointing toward the forest. Following his finger, she saw the three magpies scatter, taking off in different directions into the air. But it wasn't the sound of the door that spooked them. Rather, an enormous, hulking raven had come flapping in, and set down right where the other birds had been. It folded its immense wings, took a few steps, stalking around as if to consolidate the ground, and then looked balefully up at the humans on the porch.

"*Big bird,*" Ali half-breathed. And it was – thirty inches long at least.

And then, finally, Handon and Sarah emerged from the path in the woods, looking concerned. Ali saw Sarah just catch sight of her son as he disappeared down the dirt road – west, back toward town. She didn't go after him.

"What was that?" Handon asked, striding up with Sarah just behind him, still gazing off down the road.

"Dunno, Top," Ali said. "He just blasted out of the cabin and took off. He was armed."

With this, Sarah looked thoughtful – and more concerned. Handon stepped onto the porch and opened the front door. Inside, he found Juice standing, looking alert – but Predator and Henno still seated, lounging. Handon repeated his question, as Sarah followed him inside: "Hey, what the hell was that?"

"Dunno, Top," Juice said.

"Yeah, I got that story already. What the hell did you say to him?"

"Nought," Henno said. "We were just taking the piss a little. Anyway, it was his dad who run him off."

With that, Mark emerged from the bedroom. There was no way he hadn't heard this exchange. He flashed a distinctly unfriendly look at Juice, Henno, and Predator, then walked straight out the front door without a word.

"What did you say to *him*?" Handon asked, flicking his head at the open door. "No, it's my fault. I should know better than to leave the three of you in a room together, much less with normal people." But he was thinking: *While I was off dallying, everything was falling apart…*

Sarah stepped forward. "No, Handon, it's okay. It's the boy. He can be very sensitive. Temperamental." She paused fractionally. "Like his father."

"Of course the boy can be sensitive," a level voice added. It was Homer, stepping inside, with Ali behind him. "He's, what, fourteen years old?"

"Just turned fifteen."

Homer nodded. "His executive reasoning skills won't be developed yet. Everyone's sensitive and rebellious at that age. And he's going to want to prove himself."

"Is that what this is?" Handon said. It was an accusation, leveled at Pred, Juice, and Henno.

"Look," Sarah said. "Don't worry about it. He's run off before."

"Run off armed?"

"No. But he usually just needs to take some time to himself, in the woods nearby. He always comes back. I give him a couple of hours before I start to worry."

Handon didn't look convinced. "Two of my team can go out and look for him."

"Negative," Sarah said – suddenly sounding a lot more like a police officer. "He knows the area, you don't. And I don't want your people stumbling around in the woods looking for him. I don't think you'd catch him anyway. Let it go for now."

She crossed the room to the kitchen, and the big radio unit wedged onto a shelf. "And we need to make your call, anyway. It's ready to go."

* * *

"Charlie Whiskey Charlie, Mortem One receiving."

Handon used the call sign for the Composite Warfare Commander, which acts as the central command authority for the entire carrier battlegroup.

This person, or his designee, or *somebody*, should be on station in the carrier's Combat Information Center.

But no response came back. Only silence.

"Charlie Whiskey Charlie, this is Mortem One Actual, how copy?"

Handon's use of "Actual" indicated it was the commander of the unit himself transmitting, rather than a radio operator or subordinate. Handon rated this call sign ever since Captain Ainsley bought a farm for his family – and bought another day of life for Alpha.

Handon eyed the radio set. There was clearly a lot of juice running through it – it audibly hummed, and its face glowed with backlit controls. And he could see the copper wire snaking up the wall to the roof-mounted antenna. He brought the hand mic back up to his mou—

"Mortem One, this is Charlie Two Whiskey. We copy your last. Wait out for the XO. He's definitely gonna want to talk to you guys himself…"

Handon couldn't help but smile. They'd been a long time in the wilderness. He looked out of the kitchen to the main room. A lot of expectant eyes sat on him. The radio set spoke again.

"Mortem One, this is Drake. How you guys doing out there?"

Handon smiled a little bigger. "Still breathing air. Thanks to you finding us that ride."

"Where are you, what's your status?"

Handon glanced at his watch. "Stand by for grid reference. One Six Tango Echo Papa Six Six One Two

Zero Six Seven Eight One Niner. Readback."

"Mortem, we have 16TEP6612067819."

"That is a-ffirm."

"So about halfway up the lake, then."

"Affirmative. We're also a quarter of the way through the team. Ainsley and Pope are both Kilo India Alpha."

"Shit, Handon. I'm sorry about your guys."

"Copy that. We also lost the boat, but the Papa Charlie, and rest of mission objective, are still secure."

"Wait a second – PC? What PC?"

Precious Cargo was the usual spec-ops term for the human object of a hostage rescue.

"We found a living scientist, one of the staff at the biotech. We've not only got his research. We've got the guy. We've consolidated at this location, holed up with a small civilian group, and are refitting. It's their fixed radio set that's allowing us to transmit."

"That's a lot of living people. What's your intent? Can you get to Beaver Island?"

"Affirmative. Have you figured out how to extract us from there?"

There was a slight but distinct pause. *"That's also affirmative, Mortem. We're going to make it happen. You are advised to proceed as per that exfil plan. What's your ETA?"*

"Unknown at this time. We have a line on new transport, but won't know its capabilities until we're eyes on. Best estimate for now is probably twelve to sixteen hours, how copy?"

"That's all received, Mortem. Wait one." The line went

silent. Handon stood with his right elbow on the radio set, the mic held before him. *"Listen, Handon, we're seeing some… weird shit on the mainland. Zulu-wise."*

Handon blinked once and drew in the mic. "Copy on the weird shit, over."

Another pause. *"Basically, we're seeing something like extreme herding behavior. We see some territory that's totally clear of Zulus, or nearly so. But, elsewhere, we're eyes on with herds that are bigger than anything we've ever seen. Over."*

"Copy that. How big?"

"…Millions."

Handon shook his head just perceptibly. One more goddamn thing. "Interrogative: are you seeing any of those herds *near our position*? Over."

"Negative, Mortem. But we've got one headed our way right now. It's like a bad storm coming in. And we need to complete your exfil and RTB underneath it. So don't dawdle."

"Roger that."

"Mortem, you hail us and check in before you're Oscar Mike. And feel free to check in anytime before that, especially if you need anything."

"Roger that."

"And we'll keep you posted with any new intel when and as."

"That's received, with thanks. Mortem One out."

Handon placed the mic back on its mount, and turned toward the main room.

"You three frat boys. You're on me."

He nodded once to Sarah and walked out the door, not looking back.

* * *

Handon took them back to the glade by the stream, where he'd sat with Sarah. It was close, it was semi-private. He turned back to face them when he heard them follow him in. The three stood in a single parade rank.

Nobody sat down on the log love seat this time.

"Right," Handon said, humor notably absent from his voice, face, and body language. "I understand that we've all been out of the company of civilians for a long time."

Henno said, "Sorry, boss, we may have forgot our manners."

Handon gave him a look that would exfoliate skin at fifty yards. He didn't even have to say, *Did I fucking invite you to speak?* Henno got it, and piped down. Handon looked at Juice.

Juice hesitated long before speaking. "It was my fault. The father got upset that I let the boy handle my weapon."

"Why did you?"

Juice looked flummoxed. "Well, he's going to need to know this stuff."

Predator coughed. "His father sure didn't think so. Both of those two are well on track to ending up as Zulu food. They're not gonna be around long enough to have hurt feelings."

Handon's face twisted up at this. "Forget manners," he said tightly. "How about basic fucking human kindness? Just try to imagine what these people have been through in the last two years. And then this woman, a wife and mother, risked her home and family to rescue a bunch of gormless grunts from the shallow grave they'd dug themselves into. Think about how a bunch of heavily armed tough guys would seem to someone in her position. I invite you to imagine what another band of survivors might have done after being shown her cabin. Her supplies, her weapons, her fuel. Her body."

The others nodded. They didn't speak. They got it.

Handon wasn't done. His voice actually got quieter as he got worked up. "We're not merely their guests here. We're only alive at all on this woman's sufferance. And you three dipshits start screwing around, disregard the father's wishes, embarrass the boy so that he's run off God knows where – and now you say they're dead anyway, so it doesn't matter?"

The three men's heads were now hanging down around their waists.

Handon exhaled heavily. He looked like he'd expended most of his venom. He spoke more calmly and quietly now.

"Here's the main point." He paused and drew a deep breath, and looked each man in the eye. "*These are the people we're out here doing all this for.* Have you forgotten?" He let the question hang on the air.

"You're dismissed."

As they filed out, looking like giants in stature but schoolboys in demeanor, Handon turned back to the stream and let the sounds of its waters wash over him. He knew his guys wouldn't need to be told twice. But he was worried this incident would not prove to be isolated – but instead was indicative of something more worrisome, something deep under the hood.

Could they have forgotten how to regard living people as people? Had they been amongst the dead too long? All they had done for two years was battle, killing those that weren't even alive to start with. Had they lost the ability even to regard ordinary life when they saw it? Alpha had accomplished every mission it had been assigned.

But at what cost?

Handon didn't have to look far for the reason he was having these thoughts. The glimpse, the flash, the whirl of love that he had experienced… there was no use calling it anything else. And it had awakened him to a consciousness, a relationship with *life*, that he'd nearly forgotten about.

And he could see now that at least some of his men had forgotten as well.

He thought about how difficult, and dangerous, any kind of love or even tenderness were in the circumstances they were all trapped in. Were those things *even more* necessary, though? Did it matter most, when it was hardest?

Take the Camerons. Handon, the hard-eyed tactician, knew that Predator was right – these people were almost certainly doomed. That they'd survived this long was a miracle, and down to the meticulous planning and amazing abilities of Sarah Cameron. But with every day that passed, they cheated death and the odds a little more. And that bill would eventually come due.

They were doomed. As were the members of Alpha. Chicago had proven that.

But... and here Handon groped around, desperate to draw the right conclusion from this... but the fact that they were all living on borrowed time... maybe that made it *more* important for them to regard everyone's essential humanity.

Because if they lost the power to care, to love...

Then what was there for them even to fight their way back to?

* * *

Homer and Ali could hear the waterside dressing-down from where they sat. They'd taken up their previous position back on the porch – both to get out of the way of as many people as possible and because they liked it there. They found the giant raven almost where they left it, though it now perched heavily and menacingly on a bare branch of the tree the magpies had clustered around, before being driven off.

Ali didn't like it. Because she knew Homer was going to take it as an omen.

And there weren't a hell of a lot of ways to interpret a big black bird perching over your head.

Neither of them spoke at first. Then Homer surprised her by going literary, rather than theological. "'By the grave and stern decorum of the countenance it wore,'" he said. "'Ghastly grim and ancient raven wandering from the nightly shore.'"

"Is that Poe?" Ali asked in surprise.

"Yes."

"You can recite 'The Raven'?"

"Not really. A few lines. 'By that Heaven that bends above us – by that God we both adore -'"

Ali did know the poem, now that she thought about it. But could she recall it? One verse sprang to her mind. But it was not a very reassuring one. She wasn't so unkind as to recite it aloud. She just let it run in her head.

Nothing further then he uttered – not a feather then he fluttered -
Till I scarcely more than muttered 'Other friends have flown before -
On the morrow he will leave me, as my hopes have flown before.'

MOBILIZED

Lieutenant Jameson stared out of the back firing port of the Viking amphibious armored vehicle, breathing slowly and steadily, regulating himself and trying to ignore the chatter of the other Marines. He'd checked his assault rifle, his side arm, and his spare magazines at least twice so far and was resisting the urge to check them all again. Instead, he went over the last two hours in his head, trying to figure out how it could have happened.

First, how on Earth had Canterbury Patrol 15 decided that it was a good idea to take wounded men – wounded by Zulus – into a hospital? Everyone knew the rules. A shot to the back of the neck was the only fix for such, and they should have acted. But instead the two uninjured men in the patrol had driven three miles with half a dozen men who were all in varying degrees of injury from their encounter, three miles and straight into the emergency ward of the hospital. How could they be so stupid?

And how could the staff at Chaucer not restrict access? They also should have dealt with it differently. Two stupid mistakes that had now led to an outbreak right on the outskirts of a heavily populated town. Canterbury was a supply town, managing all of the farms for miles in the south, and London depended on it. Now it would be quarantined and purged, locked down for the duration, and nothing would come in or out of the place for how long? A month, at best?

Two stupid mistakes that Jameson was doing his best to focus on, but it was hard to ignore the basic fact that something – one of *them* – had gotten through the net that had been dropped around Folkestone. It had to be a fast one to have gotten away before they closed in, which meant trouble, a lot of trouble.

There was also the profoundly unsettling fact that Canterbury was scarcely sixty miles from London. Even on a tiny island like this, that was nothing. It certainly wasn't enough buffer between the planet-wide surging hordes of the dead and humanity's last stand. Hitler on his most ambitious day never dreamed of accomplishing such a thing.

But all that definitely didn't bear thinking about. And Jameson had to keep his mind focused on his immediate task.

The rolling fields of Kent flashed by the heavy all-terrain vehicle (ATV), the first in a line of over twenty vehicles, Vikings and WMIK Land Rovers, all rammed full of his Marines out of Risborough, reinforced by infantry from the Harbour barracks. The drivers were pushing these ungainly things to their limits.

Five minutes, he estimated. Just five minutes and they would be treading concrete on the streets of Canterbury, hunting down whatever was causing chaos there. It would be simple for the infantry from Harbour, they would be tasked with roadblocks and border checks, basically pulling perimeter security, and would soon be joined by at least two other regiments to put a stranglehold on the downtown area.

The Risborough Royal Marines – his men – would get the real job of hunting down the enemy. Under normal circumstances he might feel a rush of adrenaline at this thought, and might be psyched to the maximum by the time they got there, but the problem wasn't fighting Zulus.

No, it was fighting Zulus from his hometown that Jameson had a problem with.

BOY

Deep footprints in the dirt marked the way he walked down the road to town. The old track had been there for decades, but had been mostly unused, and somewhat overgrown, until the boy and his parents had arrived.

He hated living in the damn woods, he hated the isolation, and he usually hated his parents. Lately, it seemed, he pretty much hated everything. Two years had taken its toll, as had the utter lack of anything to look forward to.

All he could do was look back.

Just as he had started getting somewhere in school, just when he actually managed to make a few friends who didn't try to beat him down each day… also, there had been the girl, Andrea, whose attention he thought he had finally caught… And then everything had gone to complete shit. To make matters worse, he knew his mother, the über-capable police officer, looked at him with thinly-veiled disappointment. She seemed to know everything about survival.

But what did she know about her own son? Nothing.

And his father could be even worse, as everyone had seen just now. He hardly seemed aware of the situation they were living in – and he certainly didn't regard his son as a complete person who could help the family survive. All that was bad enough.

But that he'd humiliated him in front of Juice and the other commandos burned like acid.

He continued to trudge along the path, not particularly taking in his surroundings. He'd walked this way so many times, it was all familiar to him, and none of the dead came this way. Their place was so remote.

That was another thing that drove him crazy. Being so far away from the town, from anything else, from anyone his own age. At his stage of life, pretty much the last people on Earth he wanted to hang out with were his own parents.

Unfortunately, his parents might actually be the last people on Earth.

He knew why the remoteness was necessary. His mother never let him forget it for a second – with her chiding, and her reminders about avoiding noise and light. And about never going too far alone.

Especially not to town.

It wasn't until he could see the back of the first building through the trees that his nerves started to tingle. The dead were everywhere that people had been, and there would certainly be some of them down there now, hidden amongst the overgrown and crumbling ruins of the town.

I shouldn't be down here. I know I shouldn't be down here. But I just don't give a damn right now…

They didn't scare him, the dead. They were just lumps of lifeless meat wandering aimlessly. And if you kept your distance, and kept quiet, they usually didn't even notice you. Brainless, stupid, robotic. He knew how to handle them. And if one of them came near him now, it wouldn't matter. He had the shotgun clenched tightly in both hands, and felt a deep satisfaction at its touch. The cold metal somehow made him feel stronger.

Even with that, he knew that this was probably the worst idea he'd had in a long time. As much as his mother harped on at him to be careful, and as much as he hated how she did that, he knew deep down that she was right.

Of course, that was what infuriated him most of all.

She was always right.

But some part of him needed to do this. To prove to himself and, okay, to the soldiers, that he could handle himself. If he came back with the timing belt they needed, if he got out from underneath his mother and father, maybe they'd be impressed. Maybe they'd take notice – and not laugh at him, as so many of the other kids in school had. Come to think of it, he wasn't sure why he looked back so fondly on his old life; maybe it just looked good by comparison. He needed to look forward now. His parents would never see him as more than a child.

And, even though he knew it was a fantasy, he couldn't help fantasizing: if he completed this mission on his own, maybe the soldiers might take him with them, and he could get the hell out of this dead place.

That would be something.

* * *

The truck wasn't far or hard to find, parked out front on the main road, near the northern end. The dead were all on the other side of town, at the church; he'd figured out that much from the adults' conversation. Now was the perfect time. He would get in there, snag the belt, and get gone in just a few minutes.

A cold wind blew through the buildings as he approached the back of the nearest house. His stomach churned like it was full of bugs. Why? He'd been this way before, even at night, and there was still daylight now. So what if it had always been with his mother? He no longer needed her to watch over him, to tell him when he was doing something wrong.

The house at the end of the street was one of the newest in town. He'd seen it often enough. Now, two years in, with its broken windows, its overgrown back garden, the peeling white paint, it didn't look so new. He knew that the front door would sometimes swing in the wind and bang against the cracked frame, and he knew that the front porch, a thing that defied gravity by clinging on to just a few rusted nails, would creak and sway. One day he would walk down here and find it had collapsed, but not today. As he crept alongside the house and into the street, he saw that it was still hanging in there.

The end of the road was a cul-de-sac with four houses facing onto the small, round patch of cracked and weed-riddled tarmac, all of them in a state of disrepair and degradation that seemed to have progressed more rapidly here than elsewhere. His mother said they had been holiday homes, thrown up on the cheap and offered at extortionate prices. She and his father had carefully surveyed the town and its occupants, before buying the plot to build their cabin on.

The boy stood by the fence for a minute or so, waiting and watching, looking up the road toward the church. He couldn't see it from here – too many buildings in the way – but he knew the direction it lay in, and he squinted in the late-afternoon light, trying to see if there was any movement.

Nothing.

He moved across the road as quickly as he could, and started to make his way up the main street. With every footfall on the ground he told himself that he was one step nearer. He passed a dozen houses before the buildings began to close in. This section of the street was mainly shops, or had been shops. He remembered visiting them when he was younger: the bakery, the general store. Now every one of them had broken windows – gaping holes, dark even in the daytime, that set his nerves on fire. Any one of them could conceal a mass of the dead.

But he knew differently. There were some of them in the buildings, of course, but those still left were trapped in rooms, forever unable to escape – well, maybe not forever. They might break down a wall or a door eventually, but for now they were going nowhere. Some of the things were strong enough to break through wooden walls and windows, but not the pathetic ones trapped in these streets.

Finally, as he passed what used to be Andy's bar and grill ("The best baby back ribs on the lakefront"), he spotted the Ford pickup. It was parked as it had been for two years, half on and half off the pavement, both front doors wide open. The hood was already popped as well – this would not be the first replacement part they had scavenged from this vehicle.

Unfortunately, the original driver was also still in his seat. Whenever they passed this way, the boy always looked at that driver with his empty chest cavity, eaten through all the way to the back of his ribcage. His parents said that there would be hundreds of millions of them wandering North America now, but when he saw what was left of that man it always made him think they were wrong. Half their estimate, maybe, but the other half? He thought the other half had become food.

When he reached the vehicle he stood up straight and looked around, making one last check before he propped the Mossberg against the side of the truck. He kept glancing at it as he worked, missing its heavy, cold touch and constantly paranoid that he would turn back to see the gun was gone.

For God's sake. I'm as paranoid as my mom.

He pushed the thought away and went to work, leaning in under the hood and peering in at the engine, and his goal – the timing belt.

I knew it. Perfect condition. And she doubted me. As always.

He worked as quickly as he could, pushing aside the hoses in his way, and forcing the belt's heavy rubber away from each of the pulleys that it wound around. For one panicked moment he thought that it was trapped, and that it was too tight to remove, but then one of the pulleys clicked and moved; some sort of tension switch.

The belt went loose and he easily unwound it. Finally, after a few minutes longer than intended, he hauled the thing out and held it up in triumph.

And, somehow, the hood slammed closed.

Shit.

He scanned the gloom down and across the road. Sure enough, some of them had been roused by the noise. It looked like two or three were now perked up, and shambling his way. They were also starting to make noise – which the boy knew would bring others. This was scary, but it was okay. All he had to do was hightail it.

He knew he could outrun them.

He pocketed the belt, hefted the shotgun, and turned on his heel. But he'd only taken two steps when he heard other footfalls behind him – approaching fast.

Way too fast.

Steeling himself, he spun around while raising the shotgun and bringing it to his shoulder. Over his sights he saw one of them, closing terribly quickly. It moved with a speed and a fury that the boy had never seen, its torn clothing actually flapping behind in its slipstream. Yes, he had seen the fast ones, and even seen his mother kill a pair of them. They were pretty frightening, and may have been quick, but they were just as predictable in their movements as the slow-moving ones. But this one was different. The boy sensed this immediately.

I can't outrun this one.

He had half a second to consider all this before he

pulled the trigger. He had expected the creature to clamber around the truck to get to him, but it did something he hadn't anticipated; it leaped up onto the hood, scrambled over the top of it, and then dove, arms outstretched and reaching for him.

The shotgun went off with a shuddering boom and the hurtling corpse came apart in mid-air. The shot was low, and while the pelvis of the creature vanished in a spray of black gunk and lumps of flesh and bone, and the legs dropped off, the top half carried on, smashing into him and sending him backwards, shocked, to collide with a rusted-out newspaper box behind him.

He felt a sharp pain in his upper thigh and, as the nightmare creature flailed at him, he scrambled frantically away, pulling the shotgun behind him. The legless monstrosity began to drag itself across the sidewalk with its fingernails, and the boy lurched to his feet and lined up a second shot. *Boom!* The head disappeared, and with it the threat.

Feeling again the burning in his leg, he put his hand down and felt warmth and wetness. For a moment he stared dumbfounded at the dark red blood on his hand when he drew it away. He looked frantically at the sharp corners of the newspaper box, then back at the dead thing with its claws. For a moment his stomach lurched and he thought he would vomit, but a deep breath calmed him.

And he saw the slow-moving ones – still locked onto him, and much closer now than they had been.

The boy hefted the shotgun, turned around, and got himself moving again. Another sharp twinge of pain seared his leg as he put weight on it. Scanning the street over his shoulder, he saw that not only were the first few still coming toward him – but more were appearing behind them. The shotgun blasts had woken the town. Now every corpse there was focused on him.

I have to get out of here. Before more like that one turn up, and they're too fast to lose…

He limped frantically toward the head of the dirt road.

SHUT THE DAMN GATE

Amarie's daughter Josie woke up whimpering, the sound of the sirens startling her, but her mother was there so quickly the child barely had the chance to build up to a full-on wailing cry.

Amarie spoke to her softly, holding the little girl close as she opened the door of the tiny flat and carried her out into the hallway.

Already other doors were opening, and as Amarie stepped out into the hallway the one directly opposite opened, and Alderney, the aging shopkeeper who had been Amarie's self-appointed support throughout their time in the Channel Tunnel, rushed toward her.

"What is with the siren?" she asked, her eyes wide and her heart beating as she rocked Josie in her arms.

"It may just be a drill," said Alderney as he rushed past, heading for the stairwell.

Amarie followed, and soon there were a dozen of the tunnel survivors heading down the stairs to the ground floor. They were quickly joined by others, including Hackworth, the middle-aged Englishman who had been on holiday in France when the outbreak had started, and who had been the group's informal leader during the two years they had spent in the dark. By the time he opened the front door of the building, all the occupants – the entire surviving group from the tunnel

– were together on the ground floor. The group's survival instincts, it seemed, would never leave them.

The tenement building was old, one of the oldest structures not in the Canterbury town center. It was set twenty feet back from the main road, and had a yard at the front surrounded by a five-foot stone wall. The Folkestone military commander – Amarie had forgotten his name – had insisted that the entire group be housed together and in a place that was suitable as a soft quarantine. The tenement was the best they could find.

Colley, a dark-skinned Moroccan man of immense size, followed Hackworth out into the yard, and together they rushed to the main gate. The big man was already wielding a large wood axe, but this didn't surprise Amarie. They had been strictly forbidden any weapons inside the quarantine, but Colley was a very resourceful man – and the one most responsible for the plan to construct the barricades inside the tunnel that had kept them alive. He was Hackworth's right hand – and a heavy, massive hand it was.

"They said we shouldn't be opening the doors," came a voice from the back, and a few others mumbled quiet agreement. But another voice, that of Siobhan, Amarie's friend, shut them up.

"They didn't survive the tunnel," she said aloud. "I say we follow our own instincts."

Hackworth and Colley still stood at the double gates, with three others. They peered up and down the street, and spoke quietly to one another, while the rest of the group stood patiently awaiting their verdict.

Hackworth shook his head.

"No one else is coming out of any of the buildings," said Colley.

"I know," replied Hackworth, shrugging off the bigger man's obvious comment with a sniff of arrogance. "That doesn't mean it's the best thing to do. If those things are here then our best plan of action is to get as far away as possible."

They all startled at a sharp crackle of distant gunfire, far away up the street.

"What is that?" asked Colley, pointing at something that Amarie couldn't see from her position at the bottom of the steps. She craned her neck, trying to pinpoint what he was looking at, but the building next door to the tenement was in the way.

Hackworth stared up the street, and Amarie could almost hear the cogs ticking in the man's head.

"Is that…?" But Colley stopped speaking.

"Yes," said Hackworth. "That is them. They fucking got out. I knew it. Gods, I knew it. Pissing zombies."

Colley's big bright eyes flared, and he took a deep breath, gripping the axe even tighter.

"No," said Hackworth. "Look. There are a lot more of them behind those coming down the street."

"How long do we have?" asked Colley.

"Five minutes. Ten at most. And there are a lot."

Hackworth turned and walked back into the yard, leaving his giant friend at the gate.

"Okay, folks. We go back inside."

There were a few cries of surprise at this, and more

than one voice that asked *Why?*

"We can't run now. It's too late. They're already nearly on top of us."

Silence was the only reply. No one could argue with Hackworth when it came to survival tactics. They had even left all the rooms on the ground floor of the building empty on his orders, even though he hadn't said why. Now he made it clear.

"We've only got minutes to get ready. So everyone needs to go back inside now. Get up on the second floor or above. No one stays on the ground floor. Do not go back to your rooms. Start on the second floor and block all the windows. Then the next floor, then the next. Shut all the doors. Bar them if you can. Then everyone goes up to the top floor and all the lights stay off."

At this everyone started to move as one, including Amarie. As she followed the other survivors up the stairs, she could still hear the old shopkeeper firing out commands.

"Randall, you make sure that all the doors get locked, especially the ones at the back. Brown, get up that fire escape and pull that fucking ladder up and away from the ground. You can climb in the window on the third floor. Colley, get ready with that axe. You're going to smash the ground-floor stairs out. In fact, go and get started now, but leave enough intact for me to climb up."

"What about you?" asked Colley as he ran toward the main doors. "Surely, you're not staying out here?"

Hackworth laughed. He always managed to squeeze

a laugh into any situation, even the most dire.

"Don't be a fool. I'm just going to shut the damn gate."

WHAT REMAINS

Brains and spinal fluid exploded out the back of the very recently deceased doctor's head and splattered across the whitewashed walls, a stark contrast that looked strangely like some bizarre and twisted form of contemporary shock art. The body fell backward, hitting the metallic operating table with a loud clang and sending an instrument table and IV drip clattering to the floor.

Jameson grimaced at the sight on the table. The man there, the actual patient, had clearly been in the middle of a surgical procedure, and Jameson hoped he had been under sedation and out cold when they started to eat him. Poor guy probably went to sleep thinking he would wake up in a few hours with whatever had been wrong with him fixed.

Three other bodies lay sprawled on the ground nearby, all taken down in the last couple of seconds by the lieutenant and his men. When Jameson, leading his team along the main corridor of the Chaucer Hospital, had glanced into the room, all three white-clad surgeons had been covered in blood as they clawed at the body and crammed steaming flesh into their mouths. The fourth in the room was in desert combat dress, a soldier, and probably one of Patrol 15; one of the men who had caused the bloody outbreak.

Gunfire flashed up and down the corridor that was already slick with blood and littered with bodies, and

Jameson stepped backward to resume his position on the right flank. He raised his bullpup assault rifle and sighted in on the nearest door, stepping sideways into the opening, giving himself as much clearance as he could. Across the corridor his point man, Eli, did much the same.

There was no movement in Jameson's sights as he scanned left to right over a room with upturned furniture and a heap of sealed cardboard boxes, but behind him Eli's rifle erupted in short, sharp bursts. He heard another thud of a body hitting the ground, and then another.

"Room clear," said Jameson.

"Check, room clear," said Eli.

They moved forward, their boots pacing in time, keeping their formation less than a foot one from the other. Behind them, the second rank of Royal Marines called out, going through their room-clearing drills.

Always check everything twice.

That was Jameson's first rule. And the team followed it to the letter. Double-tap the dead. Double the eyes on the ground. Jameson had yet to lose a single man in combat since they arrived back in the UK after their escape across Europe from Germany. He'd lost men then, as they struggled across the deadlands that Europe had become, and sometimes it had been unavoidable. But mostly it had been because they just weren't careful enough. And they had learned.

The squad rolled along the corridor, with each rank of Marines stepping past the one in front, each checking a set of doors, moving forward to the next and then holding position. In rank after rank, the team sped through the hospital interior until they reached the final area.

Jameson was at the front once more, and he followed Eli into the room, moving swiftly to the nearest obstacle, a sofa, and making room for two more Marines to move in behind him. Eli took the left side and swept around the perimeter of the large canteen, checking the kitchen and then backing off.

"Room clear," said Jameson.

"Room cle—" but then Eli stopped and hissed, "Quiet."

Everyone stopped moving.

At first they couldn't hear it, but Eli had.

They listened, but still no sound.

Jameson frowned, and was about to speak. Eli was hearing things, surely.

But then there it was. Sobbing. Muffled sobbing coming from somewhere.

Eli moved around the room, looking increasingly frustrated as he tried to locate the noise, but it was everywhere and nowhere. He tried the kitchen.

"Where is it coming from?" asked Jameson, following him in.

"I don't know," said Eli. "It's everywhere."

They both looked up at the ceiling, and at the air vents above. There were four of them, one in each corner of the kitchen.

"Up there," said Eli, as he let his rifle fall onto its sling and hopped up onto the kitchen counter. He reached to his waist, pulled a multi-tool from its nylon pouch, and extended the sturdiest tool, a saw blade. He then shoved it hard into the grill of the vent, and yanked the cover free. Dust and plaster spewed outwards, but he ignored it, craning his head towards the dark opening to listen.

"Don't get too close," said Jameson, but then he smiled as Eli drew a flashlight with his other hand and switched it on. He didn't need to tell Eli to be careful. The man's combat instincts were one of the main reasons the three squads of Marines were alive.

Eli panned the beam of light across the darkness.

"I can't see anything," he said, and then coughed. "Hello? Where are you? Can you hear me?"

The sobbing continued, but more muffled now.

"Hello? You in the air vent. Can you hear me?"

The noise stopped.

"Hello?" came the reply, a quiet sound, almost inaudible.

"I can hear you. Where are you?"

"Hello?" came the voice again, now unmistakably that of a small child, a boy. "I'm in the cupboard."

"Okay. Stay where you are and we will find you," said Eli.

"Right," said Jameson, speaking loudly into his chin mic. "Pair up and go back over everything. Report back to me for every damn movement you make. Check cupboards and closets and under beds and any crevice that could hold a moppet. Be careful. There still may be dead we've missed. Find the boy and call in when you do. Let's make sure we rescue the only damned living person left in this fucked-up place."

"You know this is now out of containment, right?" asked Eli, after the other men had left and they were alone. "The back door is open and whatever was here has gone out there."

"Yes," replied Jameson. "I know. Canterbury is lost – unless we move fast, and hope that everyone else does as well."

HERD

Night fell.

Or, at the very least, was falling fast. Sarah and the team had been huddled around the little kitchen table over maps and rugged smart phones for an hour, putting together a plan to get Alpha on their way, out of Dodge, and moving toward home and safety.

Or at least toward the extraction point where the carrier crew would be looking for them.

"Basically," Sarah said, "you've got two transportation options for getting you to the next town, where this boat is docked. It's actually more of a recreational development than a real place. But, still, it had a year-round population, so it's now dangerous."

"What's this place called?" Predator asked.

"Lakeview."

"Sounds lovely."

"It probably was," Sarah said. "But back to your options. One, we can cram you all into the truck and I can drive you out to the edge of town. But not too close – the last thing we want is engine noise waking the place up just as you're going into it. Two is you can hike it. You're only looking at about eleven miles, and over reasonable terrain."

The team decided to hoof it.

They were now starting to pack up, while Handon and Sarah stepped out onto the porch.

"Listen," Handon said quietly. "We're not leaving until we get your son back."

Sarah shook her head, firmly and immediately. "Oh, yes you are. You've got a much bigger mission to complete. I'll take care of my family."

Handon clenched his jaw. He needed to figure out some way to argue with her logic. Because he couldn't forget that they were the reason the boy was missing. And he couldn't except himself from the lesson he had tried to impart to his team: *that these people were the reason they were doing all of this.*

Then again, he couldn't sacrifice the whole world for one lost boy. Could he?

"You must be out of your mind with worry," he said.

Sarah just looked at him knowingly. She clearly wasn't going to be drawn by that one.

"If you are, you don't show it," Handon said.

She shook her head no, equally firmly.

Handon remembered the line from the Michael Crichton story, the one with the Vikings: "Fear profits man nothing." Whether or not this woman was fearless, she certainly never let fear interfere with her operational effectiveness.

"Look," he finally said. "We don't want to head out until nightfall anyway. With our NVGs, we've got a compelling advantage in the dark."

"You don't all have NVGs," she said.

God, the woman misses nothing… "Nonetheless. Let me just send out two guys, while the others gear up."

She shook her head again – but then saw the seriousness of Handon's expression. He was starting to look pretty unyielding himself. She cocked her head slightly. "*If* we send people out, I'm one of them. I know the terrain."

Handon knew she had a point and he was considering it. While he was thinking, she softened a bit and said, "Oh, why the hell did he go out without a radio… foolish boy."

"I think half the point was that he be out of touch. Out on his own."

"Good point," Sarah said.

"And he's armed," Handon said. "That's good. He knows how to use the shotgun, right?"

Sarah opened her mouth. But before she spoke, something sounded, a sort of bump, very faint, and seemingly from very far in the distance, or through a lot of forest. Then a second one.

They looked at each other. Neither could say for sure whether it had been shotgun blasts.

But they definitely couldn't rule it out.

And there weren't a hell of a lot of other explanations to hand.

* * *

Shit, shit, shit…

The boy clomped up the road, willing his leg to keep holding his weight. They were back there somewhere – and it was all he could do not to look over his shoulder every two seconds, to make sure they weren't right behind him. He had to keep moving.

The light was seriously fading now, and the walls of the forest on either side of the dirt road seemed to collapse in upon him.

Why did it have to be my leg…? Shit. And how had that one moved so damned FAST?!

He couldn't hear any behind him. That was good. Because he had to get away clean. And, much more importantly, he had to avoid using the shotgun anymore. The weight of the weapon was no longer a comfort to him – it was now a heavy, awkward burden, as he faced the prospect of traversing six miles of uneven dirt road, almost all of it uphill. And he knew that, whatever else happened, however much he had screwed up so far, he couldn't fire the weapon again. To do so would risk bringing the whole town down on their cabin.

And that was too horrible to contemplate. He just couldn't screw up that badly.

He could no longer hear them back there. But he could still feel them, somehow, the great mass of the dead behind him, looming like the sea lapping in with the flood tide. And… and God save him if another one of the crazy fast ones turned up. Then he'd have no choice but to shoot – and that was if he got lucky enough again to make a shot like that.

Shit shit shit.

What he couldn't track, through his growing fatigue and delirium, was how much his pace was slowing.

He breathed heavily, the sweat beading on his forehead and starting to soak his shirt through. And he focused on keeping his legs moving. Stealing a look down, he could see his pants leg was totally wet with blood now. He couldn't stop to try and bandage it, even if he had anything to bandage it with… but would a blood trail also lead them back to the cabin?

He couldn't lead them back. He had to make it, he had to get away.

Though… there was one other possibility.

He didn't absolutely have to go back.

If it got too bad, if they got too close… he could give up, let them catch them. Or else lead them off in some other direction, away from the cabin.

And he still had the shotgun, with six shells in it.

If it came down to it… it would only take one.

* * *

"You're facing one other decision point," Handon said to Sarah.

She nodded. She already knew what he meant. "Whether we come with you."

"Yes."

"Don't think it hadn't occurred to me."

"We're headed for a U.S. Navy carrier strike group. And then back to Fortress Britain."

She smiled at this. "Is that what you're calling it these days?"

Handon looked serious. "It's all humanity's got left. And if we can get Dr. Park back there, maybe it can be a starting point. For rebuilding. For fighting back. In any case, it's without a doubt the safest place left on the planet. The English Channel's a hell of a lot harder to get across than your fence here. No offense."

Sarah looked into his eyes. "None taken. But there's a lot of open air between this cabin and Britain. A lot of danger. And we've got a pretty decent set-up here, all things considered."

Handon held her gaze. "You also heard what the XO said, on the radio. What they've seen, with the extreme herding behavior – *millions* of them. But moving across the continent. What happens when one of those storms blows through here?"

"Then we'll be dead." She looked up at him, reading his mind again. "But we're dead anyway. I know that's what you're thinking. And you're right. We can't last here forever. Not alone. It's only a matter of time."

Handon clenched his jaw. He hadn't wanted it out in the open like this.

"But listen, Handon," she said, taking his arm in her strong grip. "*It's only a matter of time for all of us*. We're all on a clock. Always have been."

He shook his head no, but she clasped his arm more tightly. More intently.

"But it's because our time is limited that life is so precious, so beautiful. And what matters is *what we do in the time we've got*. And you have got a job to do – what's probably the most important job in the world right now. And you don't need the three of us slowing you down."

This actually brought Handon back, and made him smile, albeit with a half a tear at the corner of his eye. "That's a good one. *You*, slow anybody down? I'm pretty sure you'd be ranging way out ahead of us. Certainly while we were on your turf."

She smiled in response. "Maybe so. But there are three of us. And my responsibility is to my family. First let's get your team, and your scientist, out of here safely. Then we can talk about your ships or planes coming back and picking us up. That radio's not going anywhere."

In the end, Handon knew she was right. Nothing was more important than getting the vaccine, or as much of it as they had, back to civilization. Ultimately, nothing else mattered much beside this, no matter how Handon felt in this moment.

And nothing he might say could change that.

As words reached their end, the two of them inched into the gap between them, met in the middle, and embraced. Heads on shoulders, they clutched each other fiercely.

For two seconds.

Then the front door opened. And Mark Cameron came through it.

He looked at the two of them wordlessly as they separated. He then pulled a cigarette from a pack and stepped off into the yard.

"I didn't know Mark smoked," Handon said, after the two of them ducked back inside and shut the door again. He couldn't think of anything else to say.

"He keeps claiming to have quit. But he continues to pick them up on the sly, when we're out scavenging." She looked balefully out the front window. "Normally he bothers to hide it. Not tonight, obviously."

With that, she pulled a long-reach butane lighter from a drawer and went around the room, lighting oil lamps.

Night had fallen for real.

* * *

The boy's strength was failing with the last light.

He wasn't able to work out that this was mostly due to the blood loss. He still couldn't take time to stop and deal with his wound. He was just plowing on blindly, desperately, toward home.

In addition to the bleeding, there was also the strain of two six-mile hikes, practically back to back. And, much worse than that, the acute stress of combat, of being in mortal danger – first in the town and, to a lesser extent, now on the trail.

No one who is not used to combat situations is ever ready for the strain it creates. Those who've been in contact say it's like the terrible moment of vividness just before a car crash – when you can see the mortal peril you're in, and can see the accident happening in slow motion... but it's too late to do anything about it. They say combat's like this split second – except stretched out *for hours and days.*

You can't endure it. Except that you have to.

On the upside, he was nearly home now. He recognized the details of the forest here, the way the road gradually flattened out. The bend before the cabin was only another fifty yards ahead. And the dead were still nowhere to be seen.

He had lost them. He *had* to have lost them.

And as he lurched forward, favoring his bad leg, and as the beads of sweat arced from his dappled forehead, and as he scanned ahead, desperate to see that bend in the road…

He heard it behind him. Close and coming fast – very, very fast.

The fear told him to just keep going, to run faster, to get home. To get to his mother.

But it was too near, and he had no choice but to turn.

With inhuman motions on a vaguely human shape, the thing juddered up the road at him, impossibly fast, locked on, its dead eyes fixed on the boy's defenseless, fleshy body, its withered arms half-pumping and half-outstretched to take him.

The boy brought the shotgun up to his shoulder.

And he tried to take aim.

EXTREMITY

Inside the cabin, the operators were in the final stages of kitting up – either to head out for Lakeview and their nautical ride north, or else to kick off a missing-person search. As usual, they were ready for anything. They'd go where they were told. And they'd get the job done.

Regardless of the cost.

Dr. Park sat at the kitchen table now. With power up, he had brought his laptop back online.

And he was getting his head back into his vaccine research.

Because he knew that everything the people around him were risking, and daring, and sacrificing, was all because of that – because of him. And he knew that his hardest and most indispensable work was probably still ahead of him. Surviving, getting out of undead North America, was just a starting point. After that, he had a whole world to save.

Right now, he needed to use the time to make sure he was up to speed.

Everyone in this group contributed.

No one shirked.

* * *

Mark smoked his cigarette down to the filter – and possibly a little past that. He ground the butt out on the fence before him, gazing balefully through the dark at the generator and bulbous fuel tank to his left.

Sarah and her goddamned fire safety…

It was starting to look like safety was a one-way street. At least as far as their marriage was concerned. He started to pocket the cigarette butt, but then remembered Sarah's obsession with policing the area around the cabin, her visceral hatred of littering – and he flicked it high over the fence, into the darkness, and out onto the dirt beyond.

Threading his fingers through the wire of the fence, he gazed again down the dirt road, seeing only to the point where it bent in the forest, thirty yards out, very dim and indistinct. He could see almost nothing now, with the light nearly completely gone.

And their son still wasn't back.

Mark frequently failed to understand his wife's tactical logic. He was nevertheless always obligated to comply with it. But what he *really* couldn't understand now was her willingness to leave their only child out in the wilderness, a wilderness filled with monsters, even as the sun went down. The leader of the soldiers had specifically offered to go out with his own men and search. As it had been their abysmal behavior that had caused the boy to run off, this seemed more than fair to Mark.

But it seemed like his feelings, long discounted around here, had dropped in importance down to nothing.

He began to reach for another cigarette, then thought: *Fuck it. And fuck HER.*

If Sarah wanted to hide out inside with her soldier

boys, while their son was missing and in danger, she could do so. But he didn't have to play along. He turned on his heel, stalked back to the woodpile, and unwedged the axe from the stump it was stuck in.

As he pulled it free and hoisted it up onto his shoulder, a sound behind him caused his head to snap around, and his eyes to drill into the gathering darkness.

A figure, lurching and hobbled, rounded the bend of the road.

For one second, Mark thought the walking dead had found them.

Then he looked closer.

It was his son.

* * *

Less than a minute earlier, when the boy had turned to find the Foxtrot hurtling down on him from up the road, his first reaction had been to bring the shotgun to bear, and try to make another seemingly impossible shot on the galloping nightmare.

But then his mother's voice somehow sounded in his head.

No gunfire near the cabin. NO MATTER WHAT.

Even in extremity, even in his mortal peril, she scolded and judged him.

And he complied.

With no time to spare, with the slavering abomination nearly upon him, he switched his grip, flipping the weapon around and hefting it instead by the barrel. And he drew the stock back behind his head, and then swung it at the creature's head like an incoming fastball.

Nearly miraculously, he hit it straight on, and with full power – splattering the already-rotten head like a sausage piñata, and sending it splashing in a broad arc across a wide area of dirt and foliage. Unfortunately, the body lost little of its momentum, and plowed straight into the reedy youth, sending him five feet up the road and over onto his back.

Spluttering and coughing, marshaling his last strength, he heaved and rolled the twice-dead and headless body off of him. He then levered himself to his feet, his wounded and fatigued leg howling in protest, leaned over to retrieve the shotgun – and then paused to feel in his front jeans pocket that the timing belt was still there.

It was, thank God.

He then took a couple of deep breaths and resumed his stagger up the road. It would only be another few dozen yards, and then he would be home. And safe.

But at this point he was so pummeled, and exhausted, and weak from unceasing terror and blood loss, that he was totally oblivious to the sounds that followed behind him up the road.

Had he heard them, he would have understood that his progress had been even slower than he knew. And that he'd more than once blacked out and slumped down to the dirt, only rising and carrying on after precious minutes had bled away.

Finally, if he'd worked out all of that, he might

have lamented the irony of his successful, and silent, swing for the fences on the head of the fast one that came for him.

Because if he'd fired his weapon instead, he would have alerted the others in the cabin.

They would have had precious seconds to react.

And everything might have played out differently than it did.

* * *

Inside the cabin, everyone heard a shout, and all eight of them startled. Handon surveyed the room. "Stand fast," he said, his voice not brooking any dissent. He nodded at Sarah, who moved to the door, lifted her rifle from the rack, and put her hand on the doorknob. Handon stepped up behind her, his HK416 now also held two-handed, by the pistol grip and the tactical foregrip on the front rail.

The two stepped outside together.

And they beheld a scene with terrible depth of field.

In the foreground was the back of Mark Cameron, up against the fence, one hand on his axe, and the other on the locking mechanism of the gate.

In the middle ground, on the other side of the fence, was their son, looking weak and terrified and on the verge of collapse. And he was, Sarah Cameron instantly clocked, her eagle eye zooming in on the blood and the limp, wounded in some indeterminate but very disturbing way.

And, finally, in the background there was a crowd scene. Dozens of the dead, lurching up the dark road and spilling out into the clearing. They were maybe five seconds behind the boy.

Sarah and Handon both pulled their rifles to their shoulders and sighted in.

Flicking at her safety with her right thumb, Sarah put her finger inside her trigger guard. But before she discharged her weapon, she shouted a single syllable:

"*MARK…!*"

Her voice was so emphatic, and so commanding, and he so well trained, that he stopped in place and twisted back around to face her.

"Do *not* open the gate!" she shouted, her eyes pleading. There wasn't time to explain more – that the dead were too close, that she and Handon had to clear away some breathing room first… and, most critically, and damningly, that the gate itself opened *outward.*

Mark only got the short-form message. And it validated for him everything he hated, and now thought he knew, about his wife. He didn't bother trying to answer her in words. He simply narrowed his eyes and gave her a single acid look that communicated itself perfectly even in the near-dark. It said:

What the hell is wrong with you?

He then turned, worked the latch, swung the gate out, and jogged out and forward, his axe held high and wide over his right shoulder.

* * *

Handon knew the game was up now. He surveyed and evaluated the situation, as was his job and native calling, nearly instantly. He gave Sarah one beat to call to her husband. But when he saw the man go out anyway, he went to work. He started putting chin points behind the bright-red dot of his EOTech holographic sight.

And he began blowing infected brainstems out the backs of heads.

The crisp chuffs of his suppressed shots faded under the unsuppressed ones of Sarah's Mini-14. Her rounds only came at about half the rate of Handon's.

But she was shooting around her family.

And they were both shooting to save them – to buy them the precious breathing room that might allow them to get back inside the wire. There was no time for anything else, only to shoot from where they stood. There was just too little slack in the system.

But for at least the next second, Mark reduced it even more – he was still moving away, toward the horde – and the boy was still moving away from it too slowly. Slower than the horde was coming in.

Five rounds triggered off, then ten, then twenty, alternately jarringly loud and whisper-smooth, the identical long, golden 5.56mm casings raining down around the porch, tinkling on the wood, bouncing dully into the dark around them. Sarah expertly held her barrel way out on its length, for more stability, rather than amateurishly in close by the magazine well; and Handon held his foregrip; and they both shifted their aims fractionally, panning from side to side, over and again, making shots and sometimes missing them, but developing a sense that they were at least thinning the mass of the dead.

But it was all happening too quickly and chaotically really to assess or analyze, even for Handon. And then, a second later, they saw Mark Cameron reach his son.

The boy collapsed into his arms. His father caught him with his left arm and shoulder – but instantly had to defend them both, bringing the axe heavily into a dead forehead directly in front and bearing down on them.

And with this, a single sob choked Sarah Cameron's throat – because she could not shoot through her husband or her boy, and had to simply watch as the man engaged the attackers to his the front. But she swallowed the hot sob down, pulled her rifle tighter in to her shoulder, and carried on making herself every bit as useful as she could possibly be.

She'd been trying to avoid this day for a very long time.

But now that it was here, she'd use every ounce of her skill and energy trying to save it.

And to save her family.

* * *

Mark Cameron held up the limp weight of his son, while he tried to unwedge the axe from the head he'd buried it in. Terrifyingly, the creature was still clawing at him – he simply hadn't penetrated far enough into the brain, coming in from the top down. An explosion sounded below him and to the side, and knocked them both back a step, and Mark realized the boy had fired the shotgun.

The animated corpse rocketed backward from the sheer muzzle energy of the buckshot round fired point-blank.

But the corpse also took Mark's axe with it.

And another dead man was on them instantly. The boy, running on adrenaline and terror now, elevated his barrel and lined up a point-blank head shot. The twelve-gauge boomed again, almost knocking the weakened boy to the ground, and he and his father both saw the head of their attacker disappear in a red and gray mist.

Tragically, once again, it was the wrong part of the head.

The doomed and hellish creature had simply stopped existing above the nostrils. But the brainstem abided – and the half-headed, sightless monstrosity still lurched at them, gnashing and grasping. Mark gave it a mighty kick in the chest with his boot, sending it over backward. He then shrugged his son up a bit higher, and pulled them both back toward the fence, stumbling like also-rans in a three-legged race.

The boy was audibly crying now. And Mark's own mind was screaming in protest as well, nearly whited out by terror and regret. It was all going wrong, and it didn't look like ending well, and he couldn't figure out how to fix it. Instead, he just lurched the two of them forward, his own muscles failing from the cold horror and exertion, toward the possibility of salvation.

Around them, bodies continued to hit the ground – their disanimation not obviously connected to the sounds of rapid chugs and barks from the porch. But Handon and Sarah were still mowing the grass. And though everything was still happening too quickly to track… it was also pretty clearly still falling apart.

The father and his son reached the fence.

They both banged into the outward-opening gate, slamming it fully closed.

As Mark pulled them both upright, and tried to back away to make room to open it…

Nightmare hands clamped down on their backs and shoulders.

SADDLE UP

Fifteen silhouettes stood in the failing light of sunset that fell across the Virginia air station, buffeted by the blasting wind that had arrived out of nowhere during the early evening. Most of them were staring at the massive metal monstrosity that had been towed out of the last warehouse to be searched. Among them were some of the most skilled surviving aircraft maintenance personnel and aeronautical engineers on the planet, who just happened to be part of the air wing crew of the USS *John F. Kennedy*.

Over by the plane, which sat at the end of one of the main runways, facing outwards, another dozen people were busying themselves. Four pilots had come over from the *JFK*; not one of them had flown anything remotely like *Chuckie* before, but all of them claimed that it would be “no problem.” The Flying Fortress might be ancient, and the dazzlingly gaudy silver and yellow might be difficult for a naval or Marine aviator to take seriously. But the B-17 Flying Fortress had been kept in immaculate condition up until the day it was left abandoned in the warehouse, and its engine was in perfect repair – though it hadn’t turned over in years.

But someone had loved this plane.

Chuckie. Wesley had to admit even the name made him smile. This plane had actually flown in World War II, and thanks to one of the engineers being a complete geek and history buff, they knew that it was one of only a dozen of its kind still working when civilization fell. *Chuckie* had spent most of its later service entertaining civilians at the air station's many air shows, or sitting on display in the museum in Virginia Beach. How it ended up hidden at the back of a dusty warehouse was a question that would probably never be answered.

Wesley took a deep breath and turned to Fick.

"Is it airworthy?" Wesley asked.

Fick shrugged. "They're still trying to unfuck themselves and figure that out. And Drake is stewing over us using it, but even he admitted that it may be the only option. Though they definitely can't land that big bastard on the flat-top. Its landing distance is too long, there's no tailhook – and if we mount one, they're pretty sure the whole goddamned airframe will tear apart when we try to stop it that fast."

"So how do they think they'll get everybody back if it can't land?"

"It's got to launch, fly out, make the extraction, and fly back in time to land here before the storm arrives."

"But that's just hours away."

"If they don't make it, we'll do it the old-fashioned way: everyone onboard can just jump out over the ocean with packed canopies. Then they'll ditch the plane in the sea and try to fish everyone out afterward. It's a goddamned shame, not to mention dangerous as hell. But that's life in the ZA."

Two of the engineers approached, both with uncertainty in their eyes. Fick looked upon them with an expressionless gaze. "So. Is it going?"

"Yes," said the taller of the two men. "It can go."

For the next half-hour Wesley stood by and watched organized chaos. He had a distinct feeling that he should be doing something helpful, but didn't really know where to put himself. He did manage to make himself useful for a few minutes, helping to load some ammunition crates. The Marines stood hunched over the monstrosity of a twin-barreled machine gun that was perched at the tail of the plane. He overheard them as he loaded boxes of ammo.

"Jesus Christ, dude," one said. "Are these really Ma Deuces?"

"Look for yourself," the other said. "The M2 hasn't changed since fucking World War I. Best heavy machine gun design ever. And we've got nothing but belted fifty-cal."

The first shook his head. "Hilarious. I manned one of these on a Humvee in the First Battle of Falujah."

"So then you know how to load one. Get to it."

The other complied, though muttering, "I only got the job 'cause the first two guys got hit…"

At this point, Wesley wandered off.

Chuckie was, with his limited opinion and knowledge of aircraft, one of the shiniest, gaudiest things he'd ever seen. When the dust had fallen away from the skin of the plane it had revealed a gleaming, reflective body with bright yellow, red, and blue markings, including a *W* stamped on the tail. *W* for Wesley, he thought, though he didn't share that with anyone. He didn't think they would see the humor in something so vain applied to such an ancient and storied flying machine.

The grounds of the base had become a beehive of activity. The pilots spent the time either pacing around the plane, pointing at things that Wesley couldn't see, nodding at one other, or huddling in the cockpit.

Then the time came, and they tried to start the engines. Somewhere, probably from his memory of war films, Wesley expected the thing to keep them waiting, for the engines to fail, or not start right away. It would look grim until the very last moment that it needed to take off, and then the old Flying Fortress would spring to life and save the day.

But the engines started the first time and roared to life.

The pilots boarded a last time, and Wesley wondered for a moment if he would see any of them again. An engineer was also going, and it seemed a four-man fire team of Fick's Marines as well.

Fick passed him, heading towards the open hatch, radio in hand.

"You're breaking up, sir, and I do not copy your last… Repeat all after 'Now listen to me you son of a bitch'…," and then he turned to Wesley and tossed the radio at him. Wesley caught it and looked at it for a moment, wondering why he could hear Drake's voice blazing at him when Fick had just said tha—

But then he saw Fick was also carrying all of his gear, backpack, assault rifle, and tactical vest, and as the stops were pulled out from under Chuckie's wheels, Fick jumped into the open door of the plane, turned, gave Wesley a sharp salute, and then pulled the door shut.

The plane began to rumble slowly down the runway, gradually gathering speed, and Wesley couldn't help but smile at the man's stubbornness. But at the same time he wasn't looking forward to speaking to Drake.

"Fick!" barked the radio. Drake did not sound amused. *"Fick, answer me, damn it. Don't you dare get on that plane."*

Wesley sighed and put the radio to his ear.

"Wesley here, over."

"Wesley. Where the fuck is Fick? Put him on right now."

"Ahh… I would sir, but the plane just took off and he was on it."

CHAOS REVISITED

Even with a bit of lingering daylight left, the streets of Canterbury seemed somehow full of darkness. In the distance, Jameson could already hear the crack of gunfire. He didn't need telling where it was coming from; he knew. The radio earpiece inside his helmet was buzzing with activity as contact reports were shouted out in a half-dozen places within minutes of one another. Just a few streets over, Sergeant Elson's squad was engaged in house-by-house clearing maneuvers as a newly turned nest burst from the doors and windows around them. And Jameson could hear every blow.

They moved quickly, Jameson at the front of the column and the rest of his men spread out in a *V* shape behind him. They only broke formation when a car or other obstacle blocked their path. He could see frightened faces looking out through windows as they passed, but couldn't afford the distraction of looking behind him, where those frightened expressions would turn to relief as the living were ushered out of their houses and hustled down the street behind them.

Neutralize. Secure. Evacuate.

They had done this many times in small towns before, but never in a place as big as Canterbury, and Jameson wondered where in hell they were going to put all these people. Even though the population was less than a quarter of pre-ZA numbers, it still meant over thirty thousand people had to be moved out of the area and given a place to stay. CentCom was prepared for this, apparently. When Jameson's platoon and supporting units had arrived, there were already quarantine-management crews arriving, and the A2 and A28 were crammed full of military and government vehicles heading toward the city center.

How they were going to deal with the possibly infected, but not yet turned, was happily somebody else's nightmare problem.

Jameson now saw movement in the distance, farther down the road. There were at least ten of them, some lumbering in the opposite direction, but half of them, the faster half, dashed up the street towards them. Jameson sighted in on the leading runner, or Romeo – for that was evidently what these were – and fired as soon as it came into effective range. Several shots from either side of him, and two more runners dropped. Then the third writhed, and tried to get up again. A wounding shot, he guessed, enough to cripple it but not accurate enough to destroy it.

Switching his radio to the command net, he said, "CentCom, we are in heavy contact with multiple Romeos." He knew the mention of that would send people higher up the chain of command into action. More calls would be made and more troops would be on their way in minutes.

He switched back to the squad net and said, "Tighten up." His voice was quiet, but clear enough over the channel for his squad to hear, and the *V* shape closed in.

Six shots and the other three Romeos dropped.

They hadn't even gotten within fifty yards, but the noise had now attracted more. A dozen, and then two dozen, and then more, burst onto the street from doors further down. Some of these were already covered in the blood of their victims.

Their lunch, Jameson guessed.

"Two ranks; engage the enemy; single, aimed shots," he said, and went down on one knee. The two Marines flanking him did the same, and he sensed, more than felt, the others standing behind him as they doubled up the *V* shape and began putting out enfilading fire.

The mass of zombies rushing down the street toward them was still growing as more of them homed in on the noise.

How the hell did there get to be so many so fast? Jameson thought in between shots. The alert had only been an hour ago, and the incident at Chaucer Hospital ten minutes before that.

But if the Royal Marines couldn't somehow gain control of this situation, then the next ten might be even worse...

GO BOOM

Sarah Cameron stared wide-eyed into the chaos of her own front yard – and, in so doing, she also stared down into the dizzying maw of the worst dilemma she had ever known. The two options she faced now were both so intolerable, so gut-wrenching, that they threatened to split her down the middle of her soul. On the one hand, she saw her only son, the blood of her flesh, hurt and bleeding, terrified and fleeing. And begging for succor, for rescue.

Begging for his mother to come to him.

On the other hand, she saw an insuperably large herd of ravening corpses about to overrun their perimeter, all of them chasing a boy who was already badly wounded – and most likely infected. And, inside the cabin, behind her, was what might be the vaccine that could save the human race. That mission couldn't fail, and its heroes couldn't fall. Not here, not today. No matter what.

For a moment, Sarah found it inconceivable to choose between them.

But she didn't falter, she didn't collapse, and she wasn't frozen. She kept shooting, and kept assessing. But she could see which way this was going.

And it might not resolve in a way that anyone, never mind any mother, could live with.

Another boom sounded from the point of struggle

at the gate.

* * *

Smoothly changing magazines, Handon could see through the near-darkness that the man and boy were trapped behind the gate in the fence. There was no way they could get it open. They couldn't push back the great mass of bodies that heaved up against them. All that dead weight sealed the gate.

And almost certainly sealed their doom. Nothing could humanly be done.

But, then again, Handon was actually in the superhero business, long had been, and impossible rescues were not outside of his capabilities. He left off shooting for a half-second to call for reinforcements – knocking twice on the heavy door behind him and shouting "Squad up on the line!"

As he sighted in again, a blur of motion registered over the top of the glass square of his sight. Instinctively, he tracked upward, then immediately down again. By the time he gained a sight picture, it was on top of him.

A flying Zulu. A Foxtrot.

Not these fucking guys again, Handon grumbled in his head. He let his rifle fall on its sling, instantly drew his 6-inch Mercworx Vorax combat knife from his chest rig, and as the Foxtrot landed and sprang up into him, he brought the wicked double-edged blade straight down into the top of its head. He then put his boot sole into its chest and launched the monster out into the yard. He dropped the knife point down into the wood of the porch, and brought his rifle back up in the same motion, firing immediately and unerringly.

Now that he was ready for them, he dropped the next two that ran up the backs of the mob and leaped clear over the fence, through the air, and into the yard. Flipping his selector switch to three-shot burst, he made head shots on both, dropping them to the dirt.

It was like shooting skeet. And not in a good way.

They kept coming. And the larger, slower mob still heaved against the fence.

Handon saw and heard the shotgun go off again, its muzzle flash like a sheet of lightning in the dark. The boy had the weapon pressed across his body, wrestling with the creature that was trying to eat him, and it had fired off to the side and behind him – pointed at the generator and its fuel tank. Handon saw sparks kick up in the dark as the buckshot pellets flecked off the curved metal.

Handon didn't panic – he knew that in real life, unlike in the movies, shooting at fuel tanks tended not to make them blow up.

A second shotgun blast went off now, impacting beside the first.

On the other hand, Handon thought, *if the tank did go up, it would do some hellacious damage.* Including taking out the fence that was currently the only thing between them and the surging horde of dead. Handon looked over to Sarah, who briefly looked back before resuming firing, her unsuppressed muzzle flashing brilliantly with each discharge. She looked steady at first. But then her eyes went wide, shining in the reflected light.

Handon could feel more than hear the door open behind him. His team, his back-up, were getting their guns the fight.

And then he looked forward again – and saw what Sarah saw. The fuel tank was still intact.

But the fence was coming down anyway.

The sheer weight of black bodies pressing against it in the dark was ripping the poles out of the ground. The whole edifice tilted precariously now, threatening to go over. It had never been designed to hold up a whole lynch mob of the dead, or that much weight. It would only be a few more seconds before it came down, and then the clearing and the cabin would be swarmed.

Simply, they were going to be overrun.

In seconds, the night was going to come alive around them, and try to devour them.

And, out there in the evil night, within sight but unreachable, trapped between the force of the dead surging forward and the buckling fence, were the Camerons, father and son. They were trapped between the millstones. They were now producing some noises that Handon could not quite resolve underneath the firing – wasn't sure he wanted to – and beneath the howling and moaning of the herd in full frenzy.

Handon didn't immediately see how he was going to get them out of there.

But he knew he had to try.

Because if his humanity failed him here, and he left them to die… then maybe nothing they did had any real meaning. They might as well just all go be zombies.

He flexed his powerful leg muscles to lever himself up and forward.

And as he did so he felt a tug at his right side…

* * *

Sarah watched the fence coming down. She also sensed Handon tensing beside him. In whatever weird, preternatural, seemingly mystical connection they shared, she instantly knew what he was planning. She knew what kind of man he was.

And she made her own decision.

She'd clocked the pair of egg-shaped high-explosive fragmentation grenades on Handon's rig earlier. She had practiced using them, briefly, with the Toronto ETF. And she had absolutely no doubt about what she was doing now, and no doubt that it was necessary. Her husband and son were already infected or dead, or would be in seconds, and there was simply no way they could be saved now.

But humanity still could be.

That her family might still be alive and human in that moment made her actions as impossible as they were necessary. But there'd be time for doubt, and for regret, later. There'd be years for that, if she lived.

She snatched the grenade off its nylon loop.

Handon stutter-stepped, as his forward leap turned into a turn at the waist.

"I need this," she said, her voice somehow audible, somehow intimate. And Handon saw something beyond steeliness in her eye. Something like the peace of the committed.

Handon opened his mouth to ask what she was doing – but he instantly knew. “Fire safety…” he whispered, under all the chaos. It was clear what needed to happen now for any of them to have a chance. And it was totally obvious that only Sarah could do it.

She pulled the pin, wound up, and gave the grenade a solid underhand pitch. It hit the dirt fifteen feet inside the buckling fence, bounced once, arced up and forward – and came to rest nestled up underneath the pot-bellied fuel tank.

Handon knew a couple of things now. One, he knew that grenades were a whole different deal than bullets – they actually *did* tend to make flammable things go boom. He also knew something that Sarah did not: that this grenade was a custom job with a two-second fuse.

He pivoted, wrapped his left arm around her waist and dove back inside the doorway, pulling her along. The door was fortunately open – but filling the doorway was the rest of Alpha team, tooled up and rifles to shoulders and heading out into the fray. The unyielding force of Handon’s dive more or less tumbled everyone back inside the cabin door, in a tooled-up domino chain.

As they sprawled out on the floor, Handon approvingly noted that down on the deck was an outstanding place for them right now. And, for the second time in as many days, he kicked closed a door with his assault boot fractions of a second ahead of a detonating grenade.

But the grenade was only a primer charge in this scenario.

A single sound like Judgment Day – the grenade and the tank went up too close together to differentiate – shook the very foundations of the cabin, knocking objects off shelves, and blowing in every single window on every wall of the structure, as well as blowing out the oil lamps. Dust and debris rushed in the empty windowpanes, filling the air around them, and reducing visibility in the dark down to nothing.

Just as, in the same instant, it reduced Sarah Cameron's family down to nothing.

Handon and Sarah looked at each other blindly from a few inches away, lying on the floor face to face, tangled up – other bodies and limbs and random objects draped across them. And they both thought the same thing in that moment: *She'd done what she had to do – and now she was somehow going to have to live with it.*

But Sarah only thought this for one quarter-second. After that, she was up and moving. Even in the wake of the resolve she'd had to show with her terrible decision of a few seconds ago, she was already acting again.

"Everybody up!" she shouted. "Move, move, move!"

Because she knew that she had only bought them a few seconds. And they had to use that time masterfully. Or they were all still dead – and the vaccine with them. She actually moved more quickly, and more decisively, than CSM Handon himself.

And in that second, Handon knew.

Her tragedy was not foremost for her right now. It was in the past – and it was very much in her future, if she lived to see it. There would be years to live through, and oceans to cross, and a thousand crushing moments of doubt and regret and longing to endure.

But for Handon, right now, this was not about her sacrifice. It was about her action. Her decisiveness. And, above all, her resolve. She had acted, doing the necessary, with *zero* hesitation.

Seeing all this in action, from inches away, and in fractions of seconds, was not a revelation for Handon. It was instead validation – of everything he had felt about her, up until this minute. He could see it had all been perfectly right – and that he could now trust himself and his feelings for this woman.

She had expressed her love, her human goodness, in action, not words.

And that was unfakeable.

JOYRIDE

Sarah rose up in the darkness and destruction inside the cabin, and she moved out into the utter desolation that lay outside, rifle to shoulder.

The others followed. And they quickly found that the desolation outside was *not quite utter enough.*

The crashing explosion had disintegrated or simply disappeared the fence, had tossed the generator into the treeline, and had wiped out the first dozen ranks of the dead that had been pressing against the fence – as they had struggled blindly to gain entry, desperate to devour life.

And to doom the very future of it.

Most of those near the epicenter of the explosion had been destroyed – if not completely, then effectively. Limbs, faces, random hunks of meat wiggled and thrashed, their life force, or death force, not extinguished by mere dismemberment. The virus still coursed in their putrid veins and black tissues, and with it there was animation. Anything that was still connected by nerve endings to a brainstem struggled to get up and resume the hunt.

It was a horrific, writhing mass of dead-guy goulash, corpse *a la carte*, and every body part still a menacing vector of attack, or of infection. Or both.

And, worse, farther back down the road, came the camp followers – the rest of the deceased population of

Glenville, drawn by the drama, drawn by the moaning, drawn by the prospect of living flesh to gnaw. Just as the first ones had been drawn by the boy, as he tried to stagger his way home, to safety, to his mother… but instead pulled them on behind him like the Pied Piper of the Damned, down on some level of Hell where even Dante never dared go.

And still they came.

* * *

Sarah spared one look through the darkness to the mass of meat that was her front yard. She knew her family was in there, was now some part of this horror. She didn't want to see, but spared one irresistible look anyway. Then she realized she could only make out the details because of some light source behind her. She turned – and found the whole front face of the cabin burning, from the spray of ignited gasoline in the tank.

Now she noticed small burning pools dotting the ground here and there.

She turned on her heel, and curled around the left side of the cabin.

Where the Ford Expedition still sat parked.

As she expected, its windshield was gone, blown out into a million diamonds of safety glass that glittered on the front seats. The radio antenna had been shorn off, the grill dented by shrapnel, the whole front of the vehicle blackened with soot and blast residue – and the truck itself knocked back five feet.

But it fucking started.

When Sarah got the drivers-side door open, swept the seat clear of glass, swung herself inside, and turned the key that was always in the ignition… it fired right up.

Now, if it would just roll.

She had gone straight for the truck because she knew they only had seconds to work with – the vehicle was their only way out, and the window for it was fast collapsing. The dirt road uphill, to the west and away from town, was still more or less clear.

But it wouldn't be for long.

The others did as Sarah expected: they followed her straight out. But they almost immediately began skirmishing in close combat, taking shots on those dead that were still walking, and now lurching up to the house. These ones were no more shaken by the blast and the carnage than they would have been by a breeze. They plodded right through the burning patches of ground. Nothing troubled them. If they still locomoted, they tried to feed.

It was that horribly simple.

And they weren't even the group's main cause for concern. The second wave was, and the wave after that – the ranks of which were slouching and lurching up the road and into the clearing. They had been untouched by the blast. And when they flooded in, Sarah and the commandos would be just as jammed up as they had been by the first group, before the resetting explosion.

The area around the house and truck, the whole clearing, was becoming a hellish, perilous, and seriously confusing melee.

Operators padded around cat-like in half-crouches, rifles to shoulders, backlit by the terrible flames, some with NVGs protruding from their faces like Mardi Gras masks, weapons chugging smoothly and mercilessly. They spun and pivoted, clearing through the space, and creating breathing room for the living.

One of the gunmen, Sarah couldn't tell who in the darkness and chaos, pushed ahead of him the only one not armed – and Sarah knew it must be the scientist.

"Here!" she shouted. "Into the truck!"

The pair turned toward her, while others pushed out to cover them. As the two piled into the back, Sarah could finally make out Homer.

Sarah twisted around to face him.

"We've got to go," she said. "If this truck doesn't get onto the road now, it's not going."

It caught her by surprise when she realized that Homer looked exactly as serene as when he'd been sitting on the porch earlier watching magpies. He nodded and slapped the back of her headrest. "Good to go," he said. "Hit it." Then he turned and stuck his rifle barrel out the rear left window and started shooting.

He also shouted out into the yard: "Ma-*rines! We are LEA-ving!*"

Answering shouts came from out of the darkness, a call and response. Sarah thought it sounded like Predator and Juice, both in mocked-up southern accents, and just audible over the moaning and gunfire and chaos, and the roar of the flames.

"Well, folks, it's time to call it a night!"

"But do what you feel, and keep both feet on the wheel!"

"You don't have to go home, but you can't stay here!"

Sarah shook her head in amazement and hit the headlights – thus illuminating a scene from well beyond the gates of hell. Dead center in the glare of the lights was Ali, her NVGs on, bringing her sword down in a double-handed overhand slash. Before her, a middle-aged dead man in a mottled terry-cloth bathrobe cleaved in half from the top of his head all the way to his sternum. Ali jerked slightly as the headlights came on; but finished her stroke, shuffled smoothly backward like a boxer slipping a punch, took one hand from her sword pommel, and flipped her NVGs up onto her head. Her eyes were slitted underneath.

Around and behind the whirling woman commando, a hundred other things were going on, many of them desperate mini-fights and engagements, but Sarah didn't have time to clock them.

Sarah considered killing the lights for the night-vision users. But she wasn't one of them, and she had to drive this truck – or they were all dead. She had to get them out of there.

She saw something fly at Ali's head now. It was practically airborne, and moving *much* more quickly than the others. Ali fell underneath it, sitting down in place and rolling up on her back, as her blade flashed upward and across. The flying zombie hit the ground in two pieces, both of them thrashing. The torso kept tumbling, and slid and rolled under the front bumper of the truck.

Sarah threw the vehicle into gear and rocked it forward over the torso – her only goals being, first and foremost, to get the hell out of there and onto open road; and, secondly, and of secondary importance, to avoid hitting any currently living humans – the battling operators.

She accomplished both tasks as the truck shuddered and rumbled over dead bodies in various states of disintegration and animation. The mud, rocks, and other debris also fought her, and she said a little prayer of thanks for four-wheel drive. The headlights continued to pan and illuminate little cones of absolute horror – lurching dead, wheeling operators, crawling half-bodies, things on fire, wood dust kicking up from tree bark as rounds penetrated rotting bodies and continued through to the forest around them…

But in a few seconds, albeit a few seconds that felt like many lifetimes, Sarah made it out onto the dirt road heading east, uphill, toward the bigger trunk road that led north up the lakeshore. She'd had to run down God knows how many people to make it happen; but so far as she could tell, all of them had been dead already.

Within seconds of seeing open dirt track ahead, she checked the rearview, pressing the brake pedal lightly to get some illumination back there. In the back, she could see the scientist still huddling down in the footwell, clutching his laptop bag; and Homer leaning over the seatback, his rifle now pointing out the empty rear window.

And out beyond that…

Figures moved after them in efficient, and thus recognizably human, movements – bounding and covering, some of them running, while others turned back and stemmed the tide with heavy but efficient fire. The sound of gunfire was still so pervasive that Sarah didn't realize she was still hearing it for a moment. She concentrated on holding her speed to a steady 10mph, as she juddered up the dirt road.

And then… in ones and, well, ones… the other Alpha team members began to open doors, including the back one, and sling themselves inside the truck. As each did, he or she also established a shooting position and posture, facing backward to cover the others.

And then, finally, Homer was slapping her headrest again.

"All aboard," he said. "Punch it."

But before she looked forward again, she saw the color drain from his face, even as he said the words.

Because they both knew that all were not aboard.

Only everyone who would be coming was.

She punched it anyway.

THE ROAD

"This is some *bull*shit," Predator said. "Every time we collect so much as two sticks to rub together, we immediately have to abandon it all again." He was sitting in the very back compartment of the truck, wedged in amongst boxes and duffel bags, his gimpy leg stuck out the destroyed back window.

Handon, sitting in the front passenger seat, couldn't really disagree. That was in fact most of their shit gone again. First the sailboat, with the resupply pallet, then the cabin.

"At least we were dressed this time," said Ali, riding outside the truck on the right running-board. She sounded blasé as usual. Maybe she'd seen too much of war, and too much of the dead.

Sarah no longer had to wrestle with the wheel since they hit blacktop – the narrow county route that meandered north to Lakeview. She looked over her right shoulder in the dark. She could see Homer and the scientist still in the back seat, with Henno slumped beside them, curled around his rifle. Predator was in the cargo compartment. And finally Ali and Juice, holding their rifles and riding out on the running-boards like stagecoach guards.

"Well, it is less gear to hump," Juice said from outside on the left, looking on the bright side as usual.

Predator: "Hump you."

Henno seemed to sum it up: "Shit happens in the Zulu Alpha."

Sarah tried to elevate the mood. "I've got a bug-out bag, and a couple of days of supplies, in the back." Weirdly, only now did she really work out that Handon had ended up with her in the front passenger compartment. She looked across at him, even as he looked at her – with a deeply compassionate, or even tortured, look in his eyes. He didn't hold her gaze long. He wanted her looking at the road.

He also wanted very much to tell her: "I'm sorry. I'm so sorry." But now wasn't the time.

Maybe there'd be time later.

* * *

They drove in silence for a few minutes. Wind flowed freely through the cabin, making its own restless murmuring. The road was well-paved and had a bit of shoulder. On the other hand, the night and the surrounding forest pressed in upon them. They also had to navigate around the variety of years-long abandoned vehicles that littered every road now.

Many of the infected had turned while they and their families tried to escape by car. This generally brought the vehicle to a screeching halt – and left a lot of skid marks. Also, frequently, it left scenes locked inside that you just did not want to see.

Finally, Predator broke the silence, slapping one of the body panels beside him. "Good old Ford trucks. Never stop running." With his big voice, he could be heard from the back over the wind noise. "Goddamn, I miss my F350."

Sarah smiled at this, happy to think of something else, even if only for a second. She raised her voice to ask him, "Where's your truck now?"

"My ex-wife has it."

"I'm sorry. I know a lot of military people end up divorced."

"I didn't. But she's not really my wife anymore." He snorted again, in mordant amusement, then paused in thought. "At least she won't be driving the truck."

Sarah stifled a laugh, then looked up into the rear-view mirror – not a hundred percent sure Predator wasn't screwing with her. A couple of the others laughed, but nobody else commented.

Handon made a mental note to brief her later. He'd been in the room while Predator was on the phone with his wife of fifteen years – after she was bitten, but before she turned.

He said to Sarah, "You said eleven miles?"

"On foot. By road, more like fifteen."

"So we're ETA about ten minutes."

Sarah nodded. "Yes. But we're not going all the way in. I recommend we do the last two miles on foot. Save the noise."

"Roger that," Handon said. He turned back toward the others. "I don't suppose anyone got a wind and tides report before we left?"

Homer got his drift. They'd be back to trying to get a very gunked-up boat engine running, which might be a day-long job. "I'll make it happen," he said. "And I'd be surprised if we don't have enough wind to get us out onto the lake. Then I'll have time to make the repairs."

"We were surprised by the utter lack of wind last time," Handon said.

"Good point."

"It's going to be okay," Sarah said. "I said there were boats at this pier. And there are. But there's one I know in particular. A little thirty-foot cabin cruiser. More of a runabout. The engine will start."

Handon looked at her in the light of the instrument panel. "How do you know?"

"Because I used to take it out myself. Sometimes did a bit of fishing, or a bit of scavenging. But mainly I used to range up and down the coast, looking for survivors."

"Why didn't you tell us earlier?"

Sarah swallowed once. "Because the others didn't know about it. I considered it too dangerous for them, so I'd go out alone, early or late. The last time was three or four months ago. It might not start right up. But it should turn over with a little coaxing."

Handon nodded and let it lie. He guessed Sarah had probably kept more than a couple of secrets from her family. And he knew how she felt.

Leadership was lonely.

* * *

She rolled the truck to a stop just beyond a "Lakeview – 2 miles" sign. In a well-practiced choreography, four of the team pulled security, two up and two back; while the others apportioned out the supplies in back amongst their rucks – mainly long-life food, bottled water, a few boxes of 5.56 rounds, and survival sundries.

"I'll take these," Predator said, palming two boxes of twelve-gauge shotgun shells. "Good ole double-aught buckshot."

Handon and Sarah both looked at him. He hefted the Mossberg tactical shotgun into view. "I found it in the yard. It looks okay." Handon, remembering how Pred had lost his rifle when Captain Ainsley took it off to make his last stand, now looked at Sarah with concern.

"It's okay," she said. "May it save a life, in capable hands."

Handon nodded. He remembered once again his cop friends from back in the world. The job of a police officer, they'd told him, was always "to preserve life." End of story.

When they were loaded up, Sarah took Handon by the arm. "You need to walk in from here. But I've got to drive the truck back to a spot a mile or two back."

"What?" Handon said, his brow lowering.

She dredged up a smile. "There's a chance we may need to come back, so I've got to cache the truck where I can get it. It's too valuable."

Handon wasn't sure that made sense. "So we drive back there, and all walk in."

"No," Sarah said. "Not with Predator's leg. Dr. Park's exhausted, too. You need to do it the easy way. I can catch you up." She started to pull away, and reached for the truck door.

Something tugged at Handon's BS detector. He said, "Okay. But I'm sending someone with you, for security." She looked back at him. "No discussion on that one," he said.

She could see that there wouldn't be. She looked over to Homer, who had perked up at this, and now stepped forward.

"I'll go," he said.

"Fine," Sarah said. She asked Handon, "Are you still on the same radio channel?"

"Yes. But come straight back."

"I will. Now go. You can't miss the pier from the main street. The boat's called the *Three Brothers*. It's in the southernmost berth. It's probably going to take a little doing to get it started. So go get started."

Handon nodded, and watched her for one last second. Then he hitched up his ruck, stood to the side, and waited for the members of his team to set off first. He suddenly had cause to wonder if he hadn't been failing to focus on his job sufficiently.

He'd fix that starting now.

Henno, Juice, and Predator set out in column formation, at a fast walking pace. Ali squeezed Dr. Park by the shoulder and got him moving. Then she looked over to Homer, and the two of them locked gazes in the dark.

There was nothing she could say, nothing at all.

Homer mouthed two words to her:

Stay alive.

* * *

Sarah drove the truck in silence, Homer also wordless in the passenger seat beside her – and still strangely at ease. Like he no longer had a care in the world. Or as if he had made a decision.

When they were two miles from where they'd dropped the others, she rolled the truck to a stop again, took it out of gear, and put the brake on. She turned in her seat and said, "I'm not going with them."

"It's okay," Homer said. "Neither am I."

This pulled Sarah up short. "What?"

He just looked warmly at her. He thought now about what he ought to tell her. But before he could formulate it, she pulled the hand mic from the radio under the dash. She powered it up, flipped through channels, and hailed Handon, all while looking at Homer. The antenna was gone, but it was only a couple of miles, and line of sight. In a few seconds, a response came back.

"Handon. Everything okay?"

"Everything's fine," Sarah said. "But listen to me. I'm not coming with you. Not right now."

"What?"

"I have to go back to the cabin. I might not love my husband anymore, but I can't leave him like… that. And my son… I'm the one who has to do it."

"Do what? They're gone, Sarah. The explosion…"

She swallowed heavily, before pressing the transmit

button again. "I don't think they died in the blast. And if they did, I can't know that they'll stay dead. Also, I saw… something… in the headlights as we were escaping. I've got to go back and make sure."

"Fine. We'll wait for you."

"The hell you will." Her voice went deadly serious now. "Don't make me remind you what you've got there, or what your mission is. We left when we did to ensure the success of your mission. And you're going to keep going now for the same reason. We're not risking that. Not for me, not for my peace of mind."

Handon didn't immediately respond. She clicked back on. "Get to your extraction point. I know where it is – the airport on Beaver Island. And I'll join you there – with a little luck, before your plane leaves. Maybe before you get there yourselves. Now go. I'll meet you there."

"It's too dangerous on your own. You'll never make it."

Sarah looked tired in the dark. "Look, if anyone can make it up the coast of Lake Michigan, it's me. Believe me, I'm prepared for this. I know the terrain. I know their behavior. I'm ready. Now – you have to go. This discussion is over." She let her hand and the mic drop toward her lap – but then brought it back up again. "Oh – I don't think your SEAL is going with you either." She let off the button and held the mic toward Homer.

He nodded his head no. "Tell him Ali can explain."

She nodded, keyed the mic, and said it.

There was a long pause on the other end. Sarah swore she could hear the sergeant major gritting his teeth, and cursing in his head, from two miles up the road. Finally he spoke. "*Sarah. Listen. COME BACK. You hear me? You make it to that extraction point. We need you.*"

What Handon didn't say, but what she could hear perfectly well, was: *I need you.*

"That's received," she said quietly. "Five-Five-Eight Tango Papa out."

* * *

She looked over at Homer in the dim instrument lights as she put the truck back in gear. Then, looking forward again, down the long dark road they faced, she got the vehicle rolling. And she asked Homer a question.

"So what's your new mission?"

Homer looked across at her in the dark, and felt the weight, the impossibility of what he was doing now. Duty to unit, to country, to humanity, had always come first – for very good reasons. They had to come first. That he was putting all that aside now and seeing to his family instead was wrong. He knew it was wrong. And he knew he'd be judged for it. He just no longer had the strength to resist. He was weak. And he was a sinner.

"My mission is the same as yours," he said. "I'm going back for my family."

"Small world," Sarah said.

Homer smiled. "Why don't you let me help you with yours, before you drop me off."

She nodded. "You can help me. But after that… wait, where's your family?"

"Virginia. Tidewater region."

Sara nodded again. "I hear it's nice there."

Homer looked across at her again.

STRONG woman, he thought…

TWO ZULUS WALK INTO A BAR

Handon shook his head in the cold, exhausted, dark march along the roadside.

He hadn't argued with Sarah on the radio because he knew there was no point – no point in trying to make her do anything. He had wanted desperately to stop her, but knew full well that he couldn't. He had clocked that about her immediately; it was the very first thing about her. The woman had *resolve*. She was never going to be made to do anything.

And it was precisely because he couldn't stop her that he needed her to stay so much – for that exact quality.

Though, the way she had head-faked him with driving back, and then radioing in her goodbyes, rankled a bit. But she almost certainly did it that way because she knew Handon would be equally obstinate. He also figured maybe this was karma, and he deserved to lose her. Some part of him felt like he had taken out his rival, namely her husband – not to mention the death of her son…

If it hadn't been intentional, or at least negligent, he had at any rate failed to save them.

It was all a terrible, sprawling emotional minefield. And Handon was out of his depth.

Not only did he need to be focusing on his job and

his team right now – his team *was* precisely his job – but getting back to that would probably be mentally healthy for him. The squad didn't need hand-holding; they were pros and would get the job done.

But they deserved proper leadership.

And Handon had just had his first desertion. Which couldn't be a good sign.

He closed the gap with Ali ahead of him, and touched her on the shoulder. Placing his mouth near her ear, he said, "Sitrep on Homer." Handon was pretty sure he already knew. But he needed to hear it. Ali exhaled, just audibly in the nearly silent night, then spoke in a thin whisper.

"He's gone back for his family."

Handon held his temper at this. "*His fu*— his family's in Virginia. Wouldn't it make more sense to get on a plane with us, than try to fight his way back overland?"

"I think he figured this might be his only chance to get away."

"He's a fucking SEAL, he can exfiltrate from anywhere."

"You're preaching to the preacher here, top. I didn't want him to go way more than you did."

Well, Handon had the story now. And, within seconds, tactical concerns demanded his attention, anyway. From the back of the column, he could now make out the squat shapes of the few buildings of Lakeview as Henno, on point, made a *disperse* hand signal and led them in. Handon slung his rifle and drew his short sword – and thought about how much he'd miss Homer's boarding axe.

But he still dared hope they might get back onto the water with a little less noise and chaos than they'd perpetrated getting off it…

* * *

Homer gently pushed the rifle's night optic away from Sarah's eye. He pressed his mouth to her ear and said, "Let me do it." She nodded rapidly a couple of times and slid to the side. Homer slid into her place behind his own weapon.

The two of them were belly-down on a rise in the forest, three hundred yards from the overrun and burnt-down cabin. A lot of trees interceded, but they could peer through them, and had a pretty decent view of the clearing.

It was now yet another piece of property squatted upon by the dead.

This was damned difficult, but Homer thanked God they were able to spot them from here – both the man and the boy. Horrifyingly, the two writhed on the ground beside each other, thrashing, grasping. But if they hadn't been visible from here, Sarah and Homer would have had to go back and scour the scene from close up.

Homer hadn't really expected to find them at all, not still moving. But they must have been protected from the worst of the blast by the great mass of dead that had pressed around them. And Sarah knew what she had seen. Homer also figured they had already been in the process of turning. Handon would probably lacerate himself about the way this had played out, for years, if not forever. But there had never been any saving these two.

Sometimes the only possible salvation is God's.

So Homer sent them off to Him, first one, then the other, with single shots at range.

They were too far for the sound of the suppressed rounds to carry to the clearing. Homer slid the rifle back off the rise along with his body, then rose and took Sarah's hand. He led her through the forest back to the high section of road where the truck was parked up. He thought he had to lead her – it was pitch black, and only Homer had NVGs. He had ardently wanted not to take one of the team's dwindling supply of night-vision gear.

But he would have had to explain why he was leaving them.

That had been the moment when his irreconcilable duties had finally come into fatal conflict. And for the first time, his duty to the uniform, and the team, and the world, had come in second. There was no point in wallowing in guilt about it. If he had acted wrongly, one day he would be judged.

Though that day might at least be a little further off, with the help of the NVGs…

* * *

Lakeview was a tiny place, and its dead slept. But several of them stood slumbering between Alpha team and their ride. Handon moved up to point. He'd rather take the risk himself. Plus Henno's cricket bat, while no doubt very satisfying to swing, wasn't the quietest melee weapon the team possessed.

Ahead of him in the dark, on the main and only street, two figures stood a few meters apart, their heads and bodies at those very uncomfortable-looking angles the dead favored. Handon padded forward silently like a big cat, slid his blade through the first head from behind, lowered the weight of the body with the sword, withdrew it, and did the next one, all in two seconds.

The others followed him out from the cover of the buildings. Ahead of them was the small wooden slat marina – more a single main pier with a few branches off it, and perhaps a dozen moorings. Sure enough, in the leftmost berth, a squat little cabin cruiser bobbed lightly in the swell. In ten seconds the team had scampered aboard, unslung their rucks, and taken up defensive positions – mainly facing back toward the town, but not solely there.

Because they'd been attacked from the water once already, and nearly to their great cost.

Handon laid his pack down then moved across the little cockpit to the controls, as Ali cast off the mooring lines. Sure enough, the engine cranked on the first press. And as the backlighting on the instrumentation came up, Handon also saw with a smile that it had a completely full tank.

Good old Sarah. Always prepared. And a little preparation goes a lo—

The sound of throat-rattling moans approached

fast from behind, followed by suppressed gunfire. The engine had woken the town.

"Now would be good, Sarge," Henno said, head down to his sight.

Handon spared a look behind him. Eight or ten palsied figures were running at them, across the street, and then down the pier. *Romeos*, Handon thought. *Hmm, haven't seen them in a while.* They fell in ones and twos from the accurate fire from the boat, and as Handon pushed the throttle forward, he thought how harmless the runners looked after the new ones.

But as he thought it, and as the boat pushed away, two crazy-ass sprinters broke through the ranks of the others, making that screaming noise, and *launched* themselves through the air toward the rear deck of the boat. Henno and Juice, belly-down on the deck, fell over each other scrambling away, toward the front of the cockpit.

But the Foxtrots fell short and splashed in.

Already sitting down, Predator stuck his hand up and gave them the bird, high and proud.

"Sce-reewww you, Lakeview!"

The town, and the shore, receded rapidly behind them into the blackness.

* * *

Homer and Sarah sat in silence in the dark of the truck for a few seconds.

"Thank you," she said finally. "I thought I could do that. I thought I *had* to."

"You could have done it. But you shouldn't have had to."

She nodded and squared her shoulders. "So tell me how you plan to get to Virginia."

Homer shrugged. "Pick up a vehicle. Make my way overland."

"I've got a vehicle," Sarah said, wryly. Homer inched away from her on the seat, not liking where this was going. "I've also got supplies," she said.

"Last I checked, your cabin was burnt down and overrun. And the team cleaned out your truck."

"You don't think those were our only supplies, do you? I've got a cache in the woods a mile from here." Homer looked skeptical. "We had to be ready to go on a second's notice if we lost the cabin. It's even bear-proof."

Homer smiled, but shook his head. "It's incredibly kind of you. You've already done so much for us. And I'm sure I'll never forget your kindness. But you need to get to safety, to the carrier. You don't need to be messing around with me on highways and in population centers."

"But your carrier's sitting off the coast of Virginia, right?"

"Yes."

"So if we can make our way to the Virginia coast, we can certainly get to the carrier."

"Those are big *ifs*. Including fighting our way across a third of North America. No, this is for me to do. Alone."

Sarah knew she was making an impulsive decision. But she was feeling her sudden freedom, and this decision felt like the right one. The only thing that could mean anything, now or anytime, was our love for the people in our lives – however strangely they had come into them.

"Handon told me about your family," she said. "About how you'd had to leave them, to try and forget about them, all this time. Well, you came with me for mine. You didn't leave me alone with that. And I'm not going to leave you alone to search for yours. Also, maybe… maybe yours can still be saved. But I'm not letting you go alone."

Homer looked across at this radiant woman in the dark. Simply, he was trying to figure out if she was an angel. He remembered someone saying: *There might not be angels, but there are people who might as well be angels.*

"Okay," he said, exhaling fully. "It's a road trip, then."

They both laughed at the silliness of this. If it was a road trip, it wouldn't be like any they, or anyone, had ever taken before.

Both of them looked ahead into the darkness now. Sarah started the engine, released the brake, put it in gear… and then she and Homer went forward into the night.

* * *

The boat and the team zipped now over the glassy black surface of the enormous inland sea of Lake Michigan, the sky above them slowly clearing and starting to leak starlight, though the moon was still missing in action. The air rushing by and around them was cold and flecked with spray, but clean and rejuvenating. It felt good.

It was all starting to feel something like… hope.

Once Handon had the boat four miles out into the lake, he swung it north, put them on a heading for Beaver Island, and set the marine autopilot. Then he called a team meeting. The last time he had called any of his people aside, it had been to give them a dressing-down. He had been right to do it, but he needed to make sure they knew they were forgiven, and that they were welcomed back into the fold.

Now the remaining four of them, plus the silent scientist, gathered around.

Handon looked each one in the eye, just giving it a minute.

He didn't come out and say what he needed to say. He just started showing it. "How's everyone?" he asked. And he meant it. "Predator. How's the leg?"

"Won't slow me down," Predator said. "I'll get it set on the flat-top."

Handon nodded. "Ali? Your arm?"

She smiled. She hated to admit how nice it felt to be asked after. "Sore as shit, honestly. And probably not healing right, but oh well. It's not the first time."

"You get down to ship's hospital when we get back." She nodded in the darkness. Handon scanned the group again. "We'll do a hot wash after we RTB. But any tactical concerns or input at this point?"

Various heads shook.

"Nought," said Henno.

"All squared away here, boss," said Juice.

They got Handon's message, which was all subtext, but no less clear for that: *I know I let myself get distracted. And things got very weird for a while. But my mind's still on my job, and on my people – on you.*

"Okay," Handon said, finally. "We're still a team, and we've still got a job to finish." Both his expression and his tone softened now. "But, you know what, I think just maybe we're going to make it. And complete not just the most important mission in our operational history. But the most important op ever run by anybody – ever. Not to mention a damned-near-impossible one. So we should feel good."

Ali seemed to be giving him a troubled look.

Handon stared back at her. "*Feel good*, I said."

"No, not that." She was actually looking over his shoulder, where she pointed now. There was something in the water, coming up on them quickly. Handon turned and throttled the boat all the way down. It immediately slowed and splashed in the black, glinting water.

The shape loomed out of the darkness, still drifting toward them, or rather them toward it, fast enough to make the operators bring their weapons to bear.

"Is that…?" Juice said, his question drifting off into nothing. It didn't need to be said. They could all now see what was coming toward them, even though the shape was obscured by the mist that now rolled across the lake surface.

Slow ripples of water lapped against the side of the cabin cruiser as a tiny rowboat passed by, heading in the opposite direction, and within ten meters of them. It was only in view for a few seconds. Sitting facing each other, motionless and staring soullessly into each other's eyes, were two human figures. They turned their heads and looked at the bigger boat, and its passengers, but otherwise just sat without moving, oblivious to the world around them. It was a man and a woman, both caked in bloodstains, clothing rotting and flesh falling away.

And just as quickly, the boat was gone, slipping silently into the darkness.

Juice shook his head and said, "What a goddamned crazy-ass place this is."

"What I can't for the life of me figure out," said Henno, "is how that *happened…*"

Ali said, "Newlyweds?"

Everyone busted out with laughter. Predator cupped his hands and shouted after the rowboat, "Don't worry, dudes! Hang in there! We're gonna fix it!" He clapped his hand on Dr. Park's shoulder, nearly causing him to collapse.

The whole group roared with laughter.

Handon shook his head, but he smiled deeply as well. He thought, *Well, I suppose you do have to look on the lighter side of things… including the goddamned ZA.*

He dug around in his pocket for that cigar stub,

which he had half-smoked on the last boat. To his delight, it had both dried out and held together. He even found a waterproof match and got it lit. He drew deeply and exhaled, scenting the cold and clean lake air.

Thinking about it, he realized they were in pretty good shape. They still had the mission objective safely in hand, the scientist and his work. They'd only lost one more guy – and might still get him back. It was now a straight shot up the lake to their extraction point, barely a hundred miles of open sailing, and they weren't dependent on the wind this time. They had more than enough fuel for the trip, and Drake had promised them a ride when they got there.

What could possibly go wrong?

He pushed the throttle all the way into the panel, and the engine roared back to life.

And the boat, and all of them, surged powerfully forward into the black night.

Alpha team returns in…

ARISEN, BOOK FOUR - MAXIMUM VIOLENCE

ABOUT THE AUTHORS

GLYNN JAMES, born in Wellingborough, England in 1972, is an author of dark sci-fi novels. In addition to co-authoring the bestselling ARISEN books he is the author of the bestselling DIARY OF THE DISPLACED series. More info on his writing and projects can be found at www.glynnjames.co.uk.

MICHAEL STEPHEN FUCHS, in addition to co-authoring the bestselling ARISEN series, wrote the bestselling prequel ARISEN : GENESIS. He is also author of the D-BOYS series of high-concept, high-tech special-operations military adventure novels, which include D-BOYS, COUNTER-ASSAULT, and CLOSE QUARTERS BATTLE (coming later in 2014); as well as the acclaimed existential cyberthrillers THE MANUSCRIPT and PANDORA'S SISTERS, both published worldwide by Macmillan in hardback, paperback and all e-book formats (and in translation).
He lives in London and at
www.michaelstephenfuchs.com, and blogs at
www.michaelfuchs.org/razorsedge.

Printed in Great Britain
by Amazon

76072552R00381